ESCAPE FROM ICE MOUNTAIN

CASSIE MILES

CAVANAUGH JUSTICE: UP CLOSE AND DEADLY

MARIE FERRARELLA

MILLS & BOON

First Published in Great Britain 2022
by Mills & Boon, an imprint of HarperCollins*Publishers* Ltd
1 London Bridge Street, London, SE1 9GF

www.harpercollins.co.uk

HarperCollins*Publishers*
1st Floor, Watermarque Building,
Ringsend Road, Dublin 4, Ireland

Escape from Ice Mountain © 2022 Kay Bergstrom
Cavanaugh Justice: Up Close and Deadly © 2022 Marie Rydzynski-Ferrarella

ISBN: 978-0-263-30360-5

0922

This book is produced from independently certified FSC™ paper to ensure responsible forest management.

For more information visit: www.harpercollins.co.uk/green

Printed and Bound in Spain using 100% Renewable electricity at CPI Black Print, Barcelona

ESCAPE FROM ICE MOUNTAIN

CASSIE MILES

To my Salem family, Marya Hunsinger and
Dave McConnell, a mystery-solving
maven and a skier extraordinaire.
And, as always, for Rick.

Chapter One

Timing was everything. In the next fifty-five minutes, Jordan Reese-Waltham would be on her way to freedom with her twin sons. Her countdown began when she was in the kitchen of the stucco, tile and flagstone mansion in the forested hills outside Flagstaff, Arizona. For almost five years, she'd shared this palatial home with her ex-husband, Hugh Waltham, and she'd learned everything about the property—details that were vital to the success of her mission.

At 7:34 p.m., Jordan stepped away from the chopping block, wiped her eight-inch stainless steel knife and slipped the razor-edged blade into a leather sheath. On the opposite side of her belt, she carried another holstered weapon: an expandable, titanium baton that opened to twenty-six inches and could be lethal when used properly in martial arts, which was one of her most well-practiced skills. Also, she was a decent chef—good enough to pose as a caterer.

Exiting the kitchen, she carried a platter of savory hors d'oeuvres into the ballroom. Her uniform—white shirt and black slacks—included a puffy chef toque over her curly brown hair, a gray pin-striped apron and the black surgical mask required for the catering staff. A decent disguise. Not that she'd be recognized at this posh event. The guests in attendance seldom paid attention to the help.

It was 7:36 p.m., which meant she had ten minutes to scan the ballroom, entryway and staircases to assess potential threats. She set her platter on a linen-covered buffet table, adjusted her thick woven leather bracelets and began fussing with other bits of food. As far as she could tell, nothing had changed in the lavish decor. All of it—the crystal chandeliers, gold-filigreed sconces and marble floors—still made her uncomfortable with its over-the-top display of wealth.

Tonight's event was a fundraiser to kick off Hugh's campaign for the US Senate. The ostentatious setting was appropriate for men in tailored suits carrying cash-heavy wallets and bejeweled women draped in designer gowns. Once, she'd been one of them.

Jordan positioned herself to see the entry foyer where Hugh stood beside his fiancée, Helena. His security chief, Ray Gruber, observed those who were entering. Gorilla Gruber had long arms, heavy shoulders and a sloping forehead like a Neanderthal. He looked relatively civilized in his three-piece suit, but she knew he was a monster. Three months and six days ago, he'd nearly killed her. His assault was called a suicide attempt and landed her in a mental health institute under lock and key. Someday, she'd get even with Gruber. But not tonight.

For the sake of her children, she needed to stay on schedule. It was 7:39 p.m. As she expected, the gracious, curving staircase to the left of the doorway was guarded and cordoned off with a velvet rope. More security guards were stationed throughout the ballroom.

At the end of a serving table, three stunning, classy ladies had gathered. Their smiles were uncomfortable. Their glances, furtive. Jordan suspected they were talking about her. After adjusting her mask, she edged closer to eavesdrop on her former associates—political wives.

The tallest was a former, one-named supermodel, Sierra, who would never admit to being over thirty. She flipped her long, auburn hair and said, "I guess none of us have heard from Jordan. She's been in the Gateway Institute for over three months. Does that sound about right?"

"I just don't understand why a woman who seems to have everything—a handsome husband, beautiful house, tons of money and healthy twin boys—would attempt suicide."

"I never thought she was suicidal. My friend was brave and strong," Abigail said, quick to defend Jordan. "When she was working full-time before the kids were born, she was a respected journalist, embedded with the troops in combat zones in the Middle East. She covered politics in the US House of Representatives."

"Which was where she met Hugh," Sierra added.

"But he's not a congressman," said the trophy wife. "Not like my hubby."

"Wake up, sweetie." The model sneered. "Hugh is a consultant for several of our husbands. He gets our boys elected, and he's more powerful and connected than any of them."

"Is that why he dumped Jordan? Trading her in for a newer model?"

"She did the dumping," Abigail said. "Jordan moved out over a year ago with the kids. I always thought she should have married a guy she got close to a long time ago when she reported on the troops. A far better man than Hugh Waltham. A marine with chiseled abs and the sweetest dimples."

Standing by a basket of fresh-baked breads, Jordan stiffened. *Stop talking, Abigail.* She didn't want her friend to mention Blake Delaney. He was essential to her escape plans, and she needed to downplay the connection between them.

Abigail continued, "I only met him once and never forgot the way he looked at her. If he knew Jordan was in the hospital, he'd be here at her side."

Nervous, she fidgeted. *Am I going to have to shove a baguette down Abigail's throat to make her be quiet?*

Sierra interrupted. "I never cared for Jordan's hard news. I liked it better when she did those cute undercover assignments, like when she pretended to be a chef or a stuntwoman or a fashion designer."

"Fluff pieces." Abigail scoffed. "Not worthy of her talent."

Jordan appreciated the compliment. Though they came from different generations, Abigail counted as one of her best friends.

"She's been in the Institute for months," said the trophy wife. "What's really wrong with her?"

"I heard she had other mental problems," said Sierra.

Jordan looked away from the conversation. Absently, she twisted her bracelets. Hugh was a master manipulator. He'd turned everything to his advantage, building a platform for his candidacy as a mental health advocate and using Jordan as an example of how the current system had failed.

His buddy, Dr. Stephen Merchant, ran the Institute where she'd been incarcerated, drugged and misdiagnosed. As soon as she got her kids safely away from Hugh, she'd find a way to expose Hugh, Dr. Merchant and all their cronies.

After one last scan of the ballroom, she returned to the kitchen and glanced down at the wristwatch above her bracelet. Her time was 7:46 p.m., right on schedule for the next phase of her plan. Since the front staircase was cordoned off and guarded, she needed a different access to the second-floor bedroom shared by her twins. The back stairway from the kitchen was locked. Picking it would arouse suspicion, but Jordan knew another route.

With a wave to the guy who had hired her to work for him as a caterer, she signaled that she was slipping out for a smoke. Once outside, she removed the mask. The October temperature was in the low fifties with a crisp, piñon pine–scented breeze. During the years she'd lived here, she'd explored every inch of the mansion and surrounding grounds. The place held no secrets from her, and she doubted that her ex-husband had changed anything. Why should he? This was *his* house. Everything suited him.

She circled the glass-enclosed turquoise swimming pool and ran to a gardener's shed hidden in the trees at the edge of the forest where she peeled off her caterer's outfit that was too white and bright for stealth. Underneath, she wore black leggings and a fitted, black, nylon hoodie. She stuffed the apron, toque and shirt into a backpack that she'd take with her so her friend in the catering business wouldn't get in trouble. Wearing a second backpack she'd stashed here earlier, she put on black gloves and darted through the night like a fleeting shadow.

At the far end of the house, she climbed a rose trellis as she'd done many times before. Several feet off the ground, she reached toward the window to the bathroom that adjoined the twins' bedroom and prayed that security hadn't noticed the window lock that had never fastened properly. She was in luck. The lock twisted and the window opened. After getting her balance on the ledge, she lowered herself inside.

Her watch read 7:58 p.m. *Perfect timing.* Whenever she and Hugh entertained, they made a point of coming to the twins' bedroom at exactly eight o'clock to tuck them in. Even though she wasn't here to remind him, he'd probably follow that routine.

Silently, she opened the bathroom door a crack so she could hear what was happening in the bedroom. The boys were talking about superheroes. The last time she'd seen them—when their father brought them to the Institute to show them that it was a lovely place with marble sculptures and a garden—Jordan had been drugged into a near stupor. It was all she could do to keep from collapsing.

Now, she was a different person, alert and revitalized. The sweet sound of her children's voices echoed in her ears with perfect harmony, even though they were arguing.

"It's way better to be super strong," said Alex. "If anybody gets in your way, you can punch them in the nose."

"I'd rather turn invisible," said Cooper, who had been a Harry Potter fan since birth. "And cast magic spells."

"You're a butthead."

"If I had a magic wand, I'd make you into a frog."

"Frogman," Alex said. "I'd swim faster than a shark."

Jordan's chest swelled with pride. Her sons were not only smart, but they were funny. She could hardly wait to wrap her arms around them. Their bedroom door opened with a click, and she stiffened, preparing herself to hear Hugh's voice.

Instead, the sound was high-pitched and feminine. "How are my two favorite guys?"

"I'm fine, Helena." Alex was only five years old but managed to sound gruff. "You're wearing my mom's necklace."

"Gosh, I don't think so." Hugh's fiancée gave a twittering laugh. "Does it look good with my dress?"

"How should I know?" Alex muttered.

"Will you help me?" Cooper sounded friendlier. "Will you deliver a letter? In person."

"Sure thing, cutie-pie."

"This is important," Cooper said. "It's for Mom. I've sent her about a million letters, and she never answers. I don't think she's getting her mail."

Jordan hadn't seen a single note from either of the twins, and it was safe to assume that the letters she'd sent to them hadn't been delivered. No doubt, Dr. Merchant had cut off that possible communication. She had had no visitors, no telephone privileges and no access to a computer. They had wanted to keep her isolated. But she'd figured out how to get around the restrictions and tap into the Institute's internet system, where she connected to the underground network used in her reporting.

"I'll give her the letter," said Helena. "Did you boys take your pills?"

"Why doesn't Mommy write back?" Jordan heard the pain in her son's voice. He continued, "Did she forget about us?"

"Your mother," said Helena, "is very sick. Don't think about her, okay?"

"Where's Dad?" Alex demanded.

"He's very busy, but he sends a hug and a kiss. Get into bed."

"I want a story," Cooper said. "Read to us."

"Sorry, boys. I've got to go."

Another voice joined the conversation. "I'd be happy to read something."

Abigail! What on earth was she doing here? Jordan held her breath. She hadn't planned for this interruption. There wasn't time. The clock was ticking, and she had to be out of the house with the boys before half past eight when the security team would make their hourly sweep of the grounds. At 8:09 p.m., there were only twenty-one minutes left.

"Thanks, Abigail," Helena snapped. "But I don't need your help."

"I'm not here for you." When she tried, she could put the authority of age into her voice. Helena didn't stand a chance against her. Abigail said, "Come here, boys."

Jordan heard her sons jumping out of bed and rushing to Abigail. There were happy sounds of laughter, babbling and snuggles. Desperately, Jordan wanted to be in that room, wanted to hug them, kiss them and rub her cheek against their soft brown hair.

"That's enough," Helena said. "I need to get back to the fundraiser."

"Sorry if I disturbed you," Abigail said. "I remembered that Hugh and Jordan always came upstairs at eight o'clock to tuck the boys in, and I wanted to see them."

"Now you have. Let's go."

"Sure thing. But first I need to go to the bathroom."

Jordan heard Abigail's voice coming closer and ducked behind the shower curtain before her friend stepped inside, flicked on the light and closed the door. "Jordan, are you in here?"

She pulled aside the curtain. "How did you know?"

"Did you really think I couldn't see through your disguise?"

She pulled Abigail into a hug. "No time to talk."

"Tell me what I can do to help."

"I don't want you involved," Jordan said firmly. "Hugh and Gruber are dangerous. The best thing you can do is walk away."

Abigail ran water in the sink and flushed the toilet. "I've been in touch with Blake. He's back from the Middle East."

Stunned, Jordan couldn't believe what she'd heard. "Why?"

"When you were eavesdropping, you must have heard what I said about Blake. He was worried when he couldn't get ahold of you. Finally, he contacted me."

"Go. Read to the boys. I'll join you in a minute."

When Abigail closed the bathroom door, Jordan sank onto the closed toilet seat. *Blake was worried about her.* Over the years, she'd thought of him so many times. If she had believed in soul mates, he would be hers. But their relationship hadn't worked seven years ago. They'd both been too dedicated to their careers.

Listening to the voices from the bedroom, she heard Helena leaving as Abigail settled down to read *The Hobbit*. The time was 8:13 p.m. Jordan had to go now, right now. But she hesitated.

Blake was back in the States. His unexpected arrival could ruin everything. Her plan had been to take the twins to Blake's cabin in Colorado where she'd once spent five amazing days with him. Since he was supposed to be stationed overseas, his house ought to be vacant. No one would think to look for her there. But now…

Fear surged through her veins. For the first time tonight, she doubted her ability to pull off this escape. So many things could go wrong. An orderly at the Institute could notice she was gone from her bedroom. The car she'd hidden at the edge of the property might be found and towed. Hugh's security staff, led by Gorilla Gruber, could catch them.

But she couldn't leave her boys here. Couldn't stop now.

She slipped through the door from the bathroom into the dimly lit bedroom where both of her sons were in their beds. Jordan placed a finger across her lips, signaling silence as Abigail stopped reading. Keeping her voice low and calm, Jordan said, "You have to be very quiet. Nobody can know what we're doing."

Kneeling, she held out her arms. Alex threw off his covers and bounded toward her. His skinny arms clamped around her with surprising strength. Cooper was less aggressive. He nestled close and whispered, "I knew you didn't forget us. I knew you'd come back."

After a handful of kisses, she issued orders to the boys. "Don't bother changing clothes. Put on your shoes and jackets. Throw some jeans and T-shirts in your backpacks. Do it fast."

Like little energy balls, they burst into action.

She turned to Abigail. "Are there guards posted outside the bedroom?"

"Only one. I'll distract him."

"And then, you'll forget you ever saw me. I mean it. I don't want you to get hurt."

"How are you getting out?"

"I'll take the boys across the landing to the back stairway."

"If I wasn't here, what would you have done?"

"I'm armed." Jordan patted her expandable, martial arts baton. "But I'd rather not use violence in front of the kids."

Abigail slipped out the bedroom door and went directly to the security guard. Though Jordan couldn't hear her conversation, she could tell that her friend was apparently claiming that she felt sick and needed help. The guard escorted her down the hallway to the staircase.

The time was 8:21 p.m. Nine minutes until the security sweep at the half hour. She drew the boys close to her. "We're going downstairs into the basement, then outside. Are you okay?"

"Tired," Cooper said, rubbing his eyes.

"Did you take the pills Helena gave you?"

Cooper nodded while Alex said, "No way. I don't like being sleepy."

"Try to keep up, boys. Be quiet, like ninjas."

After crossing the landing, they reached the stairway that descended to the kitchen level and then below it. In the basement, a single bulb lit the corridor. Years ago, she'd explored down here and remembered the layout. The wine cellar was in a room to the right.

Jordan went left through darkened rooms used for storage. Though tired, Cooper gamely followed, stumbling with every other step. Alex was bright-eyed and energetic, darting beside her like a small, nocturnal creature.

When she pushed open the door leading to the backyard, she used moonlight to check her wristwatch. It was 8:27 p.m. In three minutes, it would be too late.

She lifted Cooper into her arms. "Stick with me, Alex."

Together, they ran to the gardener's shed. When they ducked inside, the lights in the backyard burst into full illumination displaying the well-tended landscaping. Had they made it?

From the corner of her eye, she saw a man leaving the forest, coming out of nowhere. A tall, handsome marine wearing his dress blues. *Blake Delaney.*

He joined her in the shed and shut the door. Darkness surrounded them. For the first time in three months, she felt safe.

Chapter Two

Blake didn't ask why she was hiding in the garden shed with her twin sons. He didn't inquire about plans she'd made or weapons she was carrying. Instead, he closed the door to the shed behind himself and took charge of the situation. The apparent objective was to avoid being discovered by the security guards who were fanning out in the grounds behind the mansion. Before entering the shed, he'd counted five of them, which wasn't enough for a thorough sweep. No doubt if they found something suspicious, they could summon backup in seconds.

Inside the shed, the round October moon shone through a high window and gave enough light for him to see the two children and Jordan, who was even more striking than he remembered—beautiful, sexy and fierce as a mama grizzly. She pushed back her black hoodie, releasing an explosion of rich, chocolate-brown curls. Her enormous blue eyes stared up at him. Her full lips stretched in a grin as she extended her index finger and pointed to the gold-plated button in the center of his chest.

"You're a little bit overdressed," she said.

"Abigail's idea," he explained. "I didn't have an invite to this party, but a ranking marine in dress blues can get into almost any political gathering."

"I like the uniform." The moonlight made her look mysterious and seductive. "But there's no time for talk. We've got to—"

"I know." He interrupted and shushed her at the same time. "I got this."

He herded the little group to a far corner of the shed behind a riding mower and arranged lawn furniture to provide sufficient cover. When they ducked down, they couldn't be seen from the window or the door. In an almost silent voice, he said, "Stay here. Be quiet."

The boy Jordan had been carrying looked at Blake with wide eyes. "It's too dark."

Blake took out his key chain and detached a tiny LED flashlight. "Hold the light so nobody can see it from outside."

The other twin asked, "Are you a soldier?"

"Not exactly." He lifted his chin. "I'm a marine."

"You smell funny."

"My cigar."

Smoking the hand-rolled Havana, with its sweet, earthy aroma, had provided a good excuse for him to wander the grounds. As soon as he'd arrived at Waltham's place, his instincts had activated. This palatial home sure as hell didn't look like a fortified enemy stronghold, but the sense of danger was palpable. His suspicions had been confirmed moments ago when he got a text from Abigail. It said: Situation dire. Watch for J in backyard.

The spunky twin confronted him. "You shouldn't smoke."

Someday, the kid might understand the difference between a ceremonial cigar at the start of a mission and a bad habit. A discussion for another time. "No matter what you see or hear, remain hidden. Take care of your mom and brother."

"Okay."

Blake snapped a salute. "Give me a 'yessir.' Quietly."

"Yes, sir," the boy whispered.

Before he left them, Blake glided the back of his hand down Jordan's soft, pale cheek and patted her shoulder. In her blue eyes, he saw strength, courage and…hope? He could tell that she truly believed she could pull off this impossible scheme to save her kids. Strange but, God help him, he'd do his best to make that happen.

Behind the riding mower and the lawn furniture, they were well hidden, but he needed to create further distraction by drawing attention to himself. Straightening his gleaming white hat with the gold Marine Corps insignia, he slipped through the door and left the shed. He stayed in the shadows until he reached the rocky ledge where he'd abandoned his half-smoked cigar.

Though he wasn't carrying his M18 pistol or ceremonial sword, he was prepared for conflict. A few weeks ago, when he heard that Jordan was an inpatient at the Gateway Mental Health Institute, he'd been worried. Though he'd lost touch with Jordan, who was, after all, married to another man, he'd never stopped thinking about her, dreaming about what might have been if they both hadn't been so attached to their careers. *Not anymore, not for him.* Blake teetered at the edge of retirement, which was another reason he'd wanted to meet with Jordan. He had to find out if there was a chance for them, a possibility of a future together.

He'd tried calling, to no avail. Then he'd come to Flagstaff and had been stonewalled at every turn until he contacted her friend, Abigail, who told him that Jordan was being held at the Institute, not allowed to communicate with anyone. Abigail suggested meeting at this fundraiser, where he might be able to talk to Hugh Waltham, the ex-husband, and get a pass to see Jordan.

He fired up his Zippo and lit the fragrant Havana. About fifteen feet away from the door to the garden shed, he stepped onto the winding flagstone path that circled the enclosed swimming pool and led to a gazebo. It only took a few minutes for two of the security guards to approach.

Both were muscular, dressed in suits with white shirts and conservative neckties. Both wore earpieces with attached wires for communication. They strode confidently toward him. He guessed that the taller guard—almost equal to Blake's six feet four inches—was former military from his buzz cut and obvious respect for the uniform. The other guy had a broad chest, wide shoulders and long arms like an ape. His attitude of authority was unmistakable. The gorilla was the boss. He spoke first.

"What the hell are you doing out here?"

"Good evening, gentlemen." Blake tugged on his brim. Worn low on his forehead, his hat provided cover. "I'm enjoying a smoke. Wish I could offer you a cigar, but this bad boy is my last hand-rolled Havana."

The beanpole asked, "Were you stationed in Cuba, Captain?"

Definitely military—he'd recognized Blake's rank from the stripes on his sleeve and the two silver bars on his jacket. "I've been in and around the Middle East for the past decade or so."

"In combat?"

"Oorah."

That word cemented his credentials as a leatherneck marine, not a man to be treated with disrespect. Still, the Ape-Man squared off in a confrontational pose that he probably thought made him look bigger and tougher. Blake saw him as a larger target.

Gruffly, Ape-Man said, "Put out the cigar and go inside. The yard is off-limits."

Blake had to wonder why. Had there been threats? Had anyone gotten wind of Jordan's plan? He inhaled deeply and blew out a cloud of smoke as he turned toward the beanpole. "Where were you stationed?"

"On a carrier in the Pacific. The navy was a long time ago. Sometimes I miss it."

"I can tell you do." Blake turned to Ape-Man. "How about you?"

"Not that it's any of your damn business, but I never enlisted. I learned my skills on the street. I was a cop in Chicago."

"That can be a dangerous assignment." *If you're dumb enough to get into fights.*

"Damn right."

Ape-Man stuck out his square jaw. His squinty eyes fired a challenge. He was a boss and a bully…and a fool to think he could take a marine in hand-to-hand combat. Blake was seriously tempted to jab his knuckles into Ape-Man's face, ram a knee into his groin and tie his long arms into a square knot. But tonight wasn't about him. He needed to tone down his natural impulses, to think of Jordan and the twins. "Mind if I walk with you for a few paces?"

"No problem," said the beanpole. "Things have changed in the Middle East. What can you tell us?"

"I'm not a politician," Blake said. "I follow orders and try not to get into trouble. All I figured out is that the people are smart, generous and funny. And the food is great, especially shawarma and hummus."

As they continued talking, they walked past the garden shed without giving it a second glance. This distraction had been more successful than Blake thought possible. They were approaching the path that led to the gazebo when Ape-Man had a second thought. He snapped off an order to the beanpole. "Go back to that shed and take a look inside."

"Okay, I'm on it."

With surreptitious glances, Blake watched the tall, skinny security guard trot to the garden shed, pull open the door and stick his head inside. The obstacle course Blake had set up should be a deterrent to exploring, but he wouldn't relax until the guard called out an all clear. The greater threat came from Ape-Man. If that guy got his paws on Jordan and the kids, he'd do serious damage.

Blowing another puff of smoke, Blake spoke to the boss. "How many guards do you use for an event like this one?"

"More than a dozen."

"Why so many? Have there been threats?"

"You wouldn't understand," said the Ape-Man. "As you already noted, you aren't a politician. These men have a lot of enemies."

"Have you worked for Hugh Waltham before?"

"I've been on the payroll for years." His squinty eyes turned dark and angry. "You ask a lot of questions."

"Just curious." Blake watched as the beanpole closed the door to the shed and came back toward them. He hadn't spotted Jordan and the kids. They were safe.

Ape-Man said, "If you're smart, you'll mind your own business."

With a sigh of relief, Blake stubbed out his cigar and turned away from the Ape-Man. "Have a good night, gentlemen. I'll see you inside."

As he strolled toward the front of the house, he wondered what had happened that made Hugh Waltham think he needed a full-time security staff. Had he made enemies? Or was he just paranoid?

At the end of the path, he ducked into the trees and foliage at the edge of the manicured lawn and returned to the garden shed. Crouched behind a rock, he watched the security patrol complete their rounds and return to the party. The last man to enter was the boss, who scowled as he scanned the entire yard and then nodded with satisfaction. Didn't suspect a thing.

The guy was blinded by overconfidence and not all that bright. He hadn't frisked Blake, hadn't noticed the bulge from his ankle holster, hadn't even asked for his name to check against the guest list. Not a genius. But still dangerous.

He slipped into the garden shed and went to the corner where Jordan and the kids were hiding. Both boys were awake. He gave them a two-fisted thumbs-up and whispered, "We're cool. The security guys are gone."

Jordan hugged her twins and released them with obvious reluctance. "We should go."

He agreed. As soon as the twins' disappearance was discovered, the security force would be more intense in their search and pursuit. "Where to?"

"I have a car hidden on the other side of the golf course," she said. "Follow me."

Blake eyed both twins. Cooper seemed to have recovered his strength—a side benefit of fear and adrenaline. Alex was okay for running on his own. If they needed help, Blake could carry either or both kids and their backpacks. He unbuttoned his jacket and stuck his hat inside, which would probably ruin it, but he couldn't be secretive while wearing a bright white hat.

Jordan stepped outside, followed by the twins, and Blake brought up the rear. Holding Cooper's hand, Jordan moved swiftly through the forested area beyond the house, dodging through stands of ponderosa pine, golden aspen and flat boulders that mimicked the plateaus and mesas of the high desert. This part of Arizona reminded him of Colorado, where he had a log cabin in the wilderness.

Jordan paused in the rough at the edge of a golf course with a green fairway that contrasted with the autumn foliage. Obviously, she and the boys had walked this way before. Quick and sure-footed, they covered a lot of ground in a minimum amount of time.

Her car, a Prius, awaited on a residential street beyond the golf course. With every step he took, Blake came up with another question. How had she escaped from the Institute? Where did she get the cash to finance this escape? Whose car was this?

While she helped the twins get belted into their booster seats in the back, he got behind the steering wheel and adjusted the seat for his long legs. Finished with the boys, she stood outside the driver's side window with her fists on her hips. "You're not driving, Blake."

"But I am," he said. "Our first stop has to be my motel so I can change clothes. I love my dress blues, but they're too obvious to blend in with the crowd."

"Why do you think you're coming with us?"

"You need me."

She didn't deny it. Instead, she circled the car and got into the passenger seat. "You have ten minutes to grab your stuff. After that, I'm driving, which only makes sense because I know where we're going."

When the little Prius pulled away from the curb, the surge of acceleration surprised him, but he missed the vroom-vroom sound of a regular engine. "Exactly where the hell are we going?"

Jordan didn't want to answer him. Having Blake as a partner gave her a boost of confidence, not to mention the obvious fact that she truly enjoyed looking at him, memorizing his high cheekbones and stubborn jaw. When he touched her, she catapulted back in time to when she was a giddy, young reporter, swept off her feet by a studly marine. However, having him show up wasn't all lollipops and rainbows.

First question: Could she trust him? He might feel compelled to turn her in to the authorities. No matter how justified, kidnapping her children violated federal law, especially since she intended to take them across state lines. Blake wasn't a lawbreaker.

Not like her ex-husband, who would be justified in calling in the FBI. She doubted he'd take that step. Hugh had been playing fast and loose with the law for many years and couldn't afford to have her tell all she knew. At least, she hoped he wouldn't call the feds. If the FBI got involved, there was a good chance she'd be caught. But she might be able to outsmart Hugh's private security team.

She tilted her head and looked up at Blake. "I guess I owe you an explanation."

"I guess so."

"It's complicated."

Her first objective in taking the twins was, of course, to rescue them from a life with Hugh and Helena that already included drugs at bedtime, tight controls and ultimately being shipped off to boarding school. In his way, Hugh loved the kids, mostly because they made photogenic props for campaign photos. But he'd never enjoyed playing with them or listening to them. From the moment she gave birth, Jordan had been the primary caregiver.

The boys were the most important thing in her life. In second place was her ongoing work as an investigative reporter. While on the run from Hugh, she intended to solidify her case against him, which was her primary reason for going on the run. Her ex was a crook, possibly a murderer, and she couldn't let him get away with any of his wrongdoing. After he assaulted her and had her locked away in the Institute, her investigation into his crimes had taken on more urgency.

Aware that she still hadn't responded to Blake's question, she twisted around and looked into the back seat. "How are you boys doing?"

"Good," Cooper said.

"You didn't answer Mr. Marine," the other twin said. "Where the hell are we going?"

"Language, Alex."

"Sorry, Mom."

"We're going on an adventure."

Blake cleared his throat. "I'm going to need more details."

"Don't worry. I planned strategically for this trip. Nothing has been left to chance."

"Every mission I've undertaken has taught me to expect the unexpected. For example, you didn't plan for me to join you."

"Definitely an issue, and I'll need to make adjustments," she said. "I knew it would be difficult to travel anonymously with adorable twin boys. Now I've got Thor driving the Prius."

He shot her a look that was probably supposed to be glowering. Instead, the laser gleam from his intense blue eyes set fire to a passion she hadn't felt in years. His deep voice rumbled. "You still haven't given me our destination."

Might as well get this over with. "When I first planned this trip, I wanted to go somewhere isolated, which made me think of your cabin in Colorado. I figured that you'd be stationed abroad and would never know that we moved in for a couple of weeks."

"You remembered our time at Ice Mountain."

"I think about it frequently."

"Smart choice, Jordan. My cabin comes equipped with the latest in security protection and has superinsulation for when it snows, which could happen soon."

"You don't mind?" she asked, with a slight hesitation.

"I'm honored."

"So, after you get your clothes from the motel, we'll go west on I-40."

He shrugged. "It's faster to go north on US-191 and hook up with I-70."

"But I don't want to make a beeline from Flagstaff to your place. We could be traced, tracked or followed. Our first stop needs to be a diversion."

"I agree with the logic but don't get too complicated. Where is this diversion?"

"Vegas."

Chapter Three

"Las Vegas is the opposite direction from our real destination," Jordan explained. "That's why we're going there."

"Tell me more," Blake said.

"We're setting a false trail, and Vegas would be the perfect place to establish that we're headed toward the coast. It's the sixth most heavily surveilled city in the country."

"What they say is *not* true." He grinned. "What happens in Vegas doesn't necessarily stay there."

With her head swiveled around like an owl, Jordan peered through the back window of the car to make sure they hadn't been followed into the parking lot of the Silver Stirrup Motel. The coast was clear. She watched as Blake glided the Prius into a space outside room twelve at the far end of the one-story rectangular building. Not an upscale place but she approved of the anonymity. At 9:24 p.m., she saw few cars in the lot, and the sidewalks outside the rooms were vacant. Nobody around. *Good news.* She didn't want to be noticed.

Before Blake got out of the car, she said, "You've got exactly ten minutes. We'll be timing you."

"Seriously?"

"I have a plan." According to her calculations, it would take almost four hours to reach Las Vegas. When they arrived, it would be around 1:30 a.m., and she had a lot to do between arrival time and departure. "I have a meeting scheduled at 3 a.m., and I can't be late."

After he snapped a quick salute, looking every inch a marine, he strode toward his motel room. She hadn't intended to have him with them on the trip but was glad things turned out this way. Blake provided much-needed protection from thugs like Gorilla Gruber and whatever else Hugh would throw at her.

She got out of the car, circled around to the driver's side and adjusted the seat, scooting forward for what seemed like a mile so her feet could reach the pedals. Then she turned her body so she could see into the back where the twins watched from their car seats. A glow from the motel lights reached into the car and showed confusion shining in their sweet blue eyes. They must have had questions but said nothing. Though proud of them for not freaking out, she felt a twinge of regret shudder through her. Once again, she'd introduced chaos into their lives. Her darling boys deserved an explanation for why their mommy had crept into their bedroom and carried them off into the night.

She passed her analog wristwatch with the extra-large numbers to Cooper, who was more diligent with his lessons and knew how to tell time. Actually, he enjoyed timing things. "Ten minutes," she said. "Tell me when it's up."

"You got it, Mom."

"Do you guys remember what happened about a year ago?" She kept her voice low and calm in spite of the anxiety that constricted her throat. "It was a night like this, with a million stars in the sky."

"An adventure," Cooper said. "Daddy was in Washington, and you took us to live in the little blue house with the tire swing."

"I liked it there," Alex said.

She agreed with him. In the family-oriented neighborhood, the twins had plenty of friends. Their lives without

Hugh were blessedly normal. She reached between the seats and patted his knee. "We're going to live somewhere else for a while."

"Can we go back to school?" Cooper asked. "I miss the teachers."

She hadn't known they weren't enrolled in school. "What are you doing now?"

"A tutor," Alex said. "He's a dorkface."

"I promise to get you back into school as quickly as possible."

"Will Daddy be at our new home?" Alex asked.

"No." The pain of ripping their little family apart twisted in her gut. She hadn't wanted to be a single mother, but she'd brought this on herself when she'd been foolish enough to fall in love with Hugh Waltham and then to marry him. No excuses. And she wouldn't lie to her kids about getting back together with their father.

Alex had another question. "Are you divorced?"

"Yes."

She'd talked to the twins about divorce before the separation and had taken them for sessions with a child psychologist to help them deal with this complicated topic. "Your dad and I will never live together again, but that doesn't change how he feels about you. Your dad cares about you, and you'll be able to see him when you want to."

Alex blurted, "I don't like Helena. She wants me to call her 'mommy,' but I told her to go jump off a bridge."

Good for you. Though cheering inside, she knew better than to encourage hostility. "She's your dad's fiancée, so you should try to get along with her."

"Six minutes left," Cooper said. "What are you going to do if Blake doesn't make it in time?"

"What do you think I should do?"

"Spank him," Alex said. "Punch him in the nose."

"Again with the violence?" Blake would probably love

to be spanked, but she definitely wasn't going to go there, not with the kids watching. "Have you been playing those psycho-killer video games again?"

"Dad said I could."

"Your father and I don't agree on that policy. Actually, there are a lot of things we think differently about." She gestured with her hands held wide. "The door is open. You can talk to me about absolutely anything."

Questions poured forth. Cooper wanted to change their bedtime to an hour later. Alex claimed they should be paid an allowance. Really? Wasn't five-almost-six too young? They both stated a need for cell phones. Before she could come up with detailed answers and rationales, Cooper had another announcement.

"Blake has one minute left," he said loudly.

"Do a countdown," Alex said. "Mommy won't let him get away with this. If he's not here, Mr. Marine is going to be in deep doo-doo."

She loved the way the boys considered her rules to be law but didn't know how she could effectively discipline Blake. While the twins initiated their countdown, the door to Blake's room whipped open, and he stalked out, wearing cargo pants, a black T-shirt under a denim jacket and black sneakers. The uniform was gone, but he still looked like a strong, tough, impressive marine. He carried a duffel and a garment bag to the rear of the car. She popped open the trunk and he shoved his belongings inside.

"…three…two…one," the twins chanted as Blake slipped into the Prius and adjusted the passenger seat all the way back.

"Made it," he said.

"Lucky for you," Cooper said.

"Yeah," Alex jeered. "Mom was going to smack your bottom."

Blake raised an eyebrow. "Is that right?"

"Rules are rules," she said as she retrieved her watch from Cooper and fastened it to her wrist above her woven bracelet.

The time was 9:37 p.m., which was slightly more than two hours from the time she'd started her plan into motion. The twins had been missing from their bedroom for one hour and twenty-four minutes. If old patterns held true, the nanny would check on them at eleven—an hour and a half from now. Jordan needed to put significant distance between the Prius and Flagstaff before then. At 11:30 p.m., she'd call Abigail's cell phone using a super-encrypted phone of her own. She'd get an update from her friend and another chance to warn her not to tell anyone about seeing her or Blake. Abigail shouldn't be involved in this dangerous escape.

In just a few minutes, she maneuvered her little car out of town and onto I-40, where she set her cruise speed at no more than five miles over the limit, which was seventy-five. The little Prius was flying. Though she tuned the radio to a low-key jazz station in the hope of lulling the twins to sleep, they'd caught the spirit of adventure and babbled energetically. Cooper wanted to know where they could go trick-or-treating at the end of the month and said he'd wear a Harry Potter costume, again. Alex repeated his need for an allowance and hinted that a hundred bucks a week would be cool.

While concentrating on the road, Jordan listened to the chatter with half an ear. Were they never going to be quiet and get some sleep? She glanced toward Blake and mouthed the words, *Help me.*

He gave her a grin and poked his head into the space between the seats so he could talk to the twins. "I know you guys are too grown-up for fairy tales," he said, "but I've got a war story you might appreciate. By the way, I've got intel on this very road we're driving on: Interstate 40.

The nickname for this stretch through Arizona is Purple Heart Trail. Do you know what a Purple Heart is?"

"Some kind of medal," Alex said.

"You got it, kid. Warriors wounded in battle receive the Purple Heart. This highway celebrates those heroes."

Jordan spotted a road sign with the emblem for the Purple Heart and pointed it out. The kids craned to see.

"Have you got a Purple Heart?" Alex asked.

"Sure do." Blake spoke casually as though the medal wasn't an important honor. She knew better. He had two Purple Hearts and a Medal of Honor. Captain Blake Delaney pretty much defined heroic. He had another question for the twins. "Do you know what a squad is?"

Alex launched into an answer that had something to do with football and didn't make a lot of sense. Cooper called him on his far-fetched explanation. "You don't know."

"Do too."

"Do not."

"Blake can tell us."

"The kind of squad I'm talking about," Blake said, "is part of a military platoon, which is usually about fifty people. Squads can have special assignments, like reconnaissance or providing medical aid or handling search and rescue operations. I've got a war story about the Tiger Squad."

"A true story?"

"You decide."

Blake had captured their attention. As he continued to talk in his low, soothing voice, the twins settled down to listen. With any luck they'd be asleep in minutes, and Jordan was anxious for that to happen. She needed time to talk to Blake without the kids listening. Thus far, he'd been an amazingly good sport, but she couldn't expect him to continue this journey without knowing what he was getting into.

He continued his story. "The main thing you've got to know about Tiger is that he's fierce. A striped, orange tomcat with a torn ear and a bent tail, he used to live with me in Colorado."

"A kitty?" Alex scoffed.

"Have you ever fought with a cat? Tiger could back down a grizzly bear. A ferocious cat who was afraid of nothing, Tiger led his squad to glory. Once he and his team rescued a five-year-old boy—same age as you guys—who discovered a treasure chest full of gold bars that had been hidden by outlaws in a mountain cave."

"I want to hear that story," Cooper said.

"First, let me tell you about the Rocky Mountains." Blake's voice dropped into a compelling rhythm. "Towering peaks with snow on top, crystal clear lakes and rushing rivers with white-water rapids. The red rocks form incredible shapes like sculptures. Granite boulders are the size of station wagons. You can ski, snowboard, hike and climb. Or sit in the sun under a clear blue sky and read a book."

His tone had a calming effect. Nothing bad could happen while Blake told his story. He was good with kids, which shouldn't have surprised her. Blake made a positive impression on practically everybody he met. But five-year-old boys could be especially difficult—rambunctious, headstrong and prone to getting into trouble. Not that her handsome twins would ever be described as brats.

She checked the time on her watch: 10:56 p.m. In just a few minutes, the nanny at Hugh's mansion would discover the twins were gone. And then…what? They'd made good progress, had already left the hill country surrounding Flagstaff and were driving fast on the two-lane, divided highway headed west through high desert.

Blake's voice went quiet, and she glanced toward him. "Are they asleep?"

"Couldn't keep their eyes open."

"Thanks for handling them."

"My pleasure," he said. "One of my favorite jobs was teaching at a reconstructed school in Qatar. Being around the kids reminded me why we were there. They're the future, especially the little girls."

She liked this side of his personality. Sure, Blake could be a badass marine, but he was also gentle and happy to help others. "While the boys are sleeping, I want to explain a few things and tell you how I was driven to kidnap my own children."

"I'm listening."

"Long story short, I discovered that Hugh was involved in bribery, extortion, money laundering and possibly worse crimes." They had argued but were never able to reach an understanding. He'd refused to step back and blow the whistle on the criminals he associated with. He'd told her he was in too deep. He'd be ruined. "We went back and forth, and he convinced me he was cleaning up his act. It was the opposite. His crimes got more serious. About a year ago, I packed up the twins and bought a cozy, little house in town."

"Question," Blake said. "How did you afford the move?"

"I always maintained separate savings, investments and checking accounts. Money that Hugh couldn't get his grubby hands on. I continued to work freelance after the twins were born and banked all my earnings. Also, after years of working full-time as a reporter and correspondent, I had built up a decent portfolio."

"I always knew you were a survivor."

"You bet I am," she said. "Back to my story… It's not as satisfying as your account of the Tiger Squad."

"But it really happened. That counts for a lot."

"About three months ago, Hugh made an appointment to see me and sign the final draft of a divorce agreement his lawyers drew up. I arranged for the twins to have a playdate, so I was alone in the house. When he arrived at my doorstep, I was immediately suspicious."

"Why?"

"He was accompanied by his chief of security, Ray Gruber. Why would he bring the muscle unless he was expecting trouble?" The memory of that afternoon caused her to tense. Her fingers tightened on the steering wheel. "We'd already discussed the terms for the divorce, but Hugh tried to sneak in one more clause, stating that he'd have sole custody of the twins."

"You refused to sign," Blake said.

"Damn right, I refused." She'd exploded, stormed through the house, yelling and cursing. "I told him and his bodyguard to get the hell away from me. I had my phone in hand and hit the call button for 911. I didn't have time to do anything more than scream hysterically at the emergency operator. My address—that was all I could get out. Gruber came toward me, zapped me with a stun gun and injected me with some kind of fast-acting sedative. I crumpled to the floor. As good as dead."

The aftermath was, in some ways, worse than death. She should have been smarter, should have been prepared for violence when she made the appointment with Hugh. She knew he'd do anything to get his way.

"When I regained consciousness for a moment, I was being loaded onto a gurney. There was blood everywhere. My wrists had been slashed."

"The bracelets," he said. "I wondered why you were wearing them."

"Hugh explained to the paramedics that I had attempted suicide. Hours later, I woke up in Gateway Mental Health Institute. I had restraints at my wrists and ankles."

"Do you think Hugh meant to kill you?"

"I'm guessing that was the plan, but my call to 911 provoked the emergency response."

He reached toward her. With his large hand, he massaged the tight muscles at the base of her neck. "About this Gruber person, is he square-shaped with heavy shoulders and long arms? Built like an ape?"

"I call him Gorilla Gruber."

"Ape-Man," Blake said. "I met him outside the garden shed. If I'd known what he did to you, I would have taken a measure of revenge."

A measure of revenge? His phrase sounded civilized, but she knew his justified assault on the Gorilla would be ferocious. "You talked to him? Does he know who you are?"

"Ape-Man never asked for my name. He's not the brightest primate on the tree. And I never actually went inside the house and shook hands with your ex."

If Hugh initiated a search into her friends and associates, Blake's name might come up. "If Hugh and his minions have identified you, I might have to rethink my plan to go use your cabin as a hideout."

"The property isn't in my name. I bought it with a friend who was killed in battle. His name is on the deed."

She glanced away from the straight ribbon of road illuminated by her brights and focused on him. "Is it a secret hideout? Do you think of the cabin as your Fortress of Solitude?"

"It's a place I can go when I need to be alone and lick my wounds. But I do have friends who live nearby and keep an eye on my belongings."

He had friends everywhere. Many were former marines he had served with and with whom he'd formed unbreakable bonds. Oddly enough, she had a similar network. In her work as an investigative reporter, she had developed friendships with smart people who could help her dig for the truth. One of those friends—a former showgirl who now ran a helicopter service—was waiting for her and the twins in Las Vegas.

"Did anybody else know you were in Flagstaff?"

"I paid a visit to the Gateway Institute, so a couple of the nurses might remember me. And, of course, I called Abigail."

"Speaking of my wonderful friend," she said. "It's 11:22. I'll give her a call and let her know we're all right."

"Do you have further plans with her?"

"Absolutely not. Too dangerous. I don't want her to get mixed up in this."

After they decided not to use the speakerphone because it might wake the kids, Blake punched in the number and held the cell so she could talk. Abigail answered immediately.

"I've only got a minute," she said. "If I didn't know you grabbed the boys, I wouldn't have guessed. Hugh is keeping the situation quiet. Not notifying the police or the FBI or anybody else."

Jordan expected this to happen. Though Gruber was a fool, her ex-husband was a mastermind who always thought several steps ahead. Hugh knew that she had damning information she could use against him and didn't want her talking to the authorities. "What is he telling people?"

"Something about the twins going on a vacation." Abigail paused. "He's sent Gruber to find you."

"How on earth did you figure this out?"

"When you get to be my advanced age, it's easy to fade into the woodwork, which means I'm great at eavesdropping."

Jordan had never intended to put her friend in this situation. Betraying Hugh was a dangerous game. She knew from personal experience that the stakes were high. "Be careful. Don't underestimate Hugh and his friends."

"I'll keep my distance from him. But Helena is my new best friend and can't wait to tell me everything."

After thanking Abigail, Jordan turned her attention back to the road. Nervous, she glanced toward Blake. "What do you think?"

"It's all good," he said. "If the feds had put out an alert for you and the twins, there's no way you could hide from them. You'd be arrested, charged with kidnapping and sent to prison. Ape-Man will be easier to fool."

That wasn't the biggest difference between legitimate law enforcement and Hugh's private security force. "If Gruber finds me, I won't be going to jail. He'll kill me."

Chapter Four

"I understand why you kidnapped the boys," Blake said, forcing himself to set aside his outrage at the way she'd been abused. "You can't work with your ex and can't talk to him. He's unreasonable, untrustworthy. And he is one hell of a dangerous individual."

She glanced toward the back seat. "Keep your voice down. I don't want the boys to hear about—"

"About how dear old Dad tried to kill you?"

"I try not to bad-mouth him to his sons. Whether I like it or not, they deserve a chance to have a relationship with their father."

Though he agreed with her in principle, she might need to release the fantasy that her ex would turn into a decent human being. Hugh Waltham, the successful political consultant, gave new meaning to the concept of sleazy self-interest. Apparently, Blake wasn't the only person who thought so. In his brief conversation with the ape who he now knew as Gruber, he'd learned that her ex had hired a team of bodyguards, which meant he had enemies.

He wondered if the threat to Waltham connected with the reasons Jordan had for separating from him and taking the kids and moving to a house in Flagstaff. In the glow from the dashboard, he studied the stubborn jut of her chin and her unswerving gaze on the road ahead. Seven years ago—when she'd been an embedded reporter, he had admired her bravery and her grit. No challenge had been too great. No threat too daunting. She'd thrown herself into every project, including those bivouacked nights when they made love in the open air.

Before he'd heard the details of her ex's assault on her, Blake had hoped to convince her to reconsider the kidnapping. She'd broken the law and the outcome of that desperate act could destroy her life. Aiding and abetting her on this mission didn't bode well for him, either. But he wasn't concerned about the consequences for himself. From the moment he saw her and the kids, he knew in the raw depths of his soul that he had to protect them.

He trusted her. His value system included firm belief in the rule of law, and he also believed in justice. Sometimes, the legal system failed. Separating the twins from their mother was flat-out wrong. Leaving them with her ex-husband? Worse.

"You haven't told me everything," he said.

She shrugged. "What do you want to know?"

When he first got to Flagstaff, he'd gone to the Gateway Institute where he'd heard she was a patient. The sprawling complex with several two-and three-story buildings covered several acres on the outskirts of town. The grounds featured immaculate grooming, colorful gardens and a pleasant array of paths for strolling. A valet had taken his car at the front entry, which made him expect cooperation, but he hadn't made it much farther than the reception counter, which was staffed by people in beige suits. The atmosphere reminded him more of an exclusive hotel than a facility for treating patients.

"The Gateway Institute," he said. "From what I saw, it's a classy place."

"Most of the inmates would agree. There are attractive common areas, a spa, a gym and dining areas with gourmet chefs. The level of care ranges from minimal assisted living to inpatient hospital care. If I had actually needed medical or psychiatric treatment, I might have chosen the Institute. But I wasn't sick."

"How did they keep you there?"

"Hugh's hotshot lawyers drew up the paperwork to have me committed, stating that I was a danger to myself and others. According to them, I couldn't be trusted with my twins."

"And that fooled the people at the Institute?"

"The legal petition was granted because the man in charge at Gateway, Dr. Stephen Merchant, is one of Hugh's cohorts. Once under his thumb, I was helpless. When I regained consciousness, I was drugged out of my mind."

"Why didn't you contact a lawyer or someone to help you leave?"

"Not possible. All my communications were cut." The corner of her mouth twisted in a bitter scowl. "Whenever I demanded my rights or showed signs of disobedience, I was locked in a windowless, padded room, sometimes in a straitjacket."

Blake had witnessed horrific mistreatment in military prisons and hostage situations, but he didn't expect to find similar tortures at a fancy spa tucked away in the mountains of Arizona. "How did you escape?"

"Lucky for me, I knew someone on the inside. I did an article on the Institute and their research on Alzheimer's. The woman who was my primary source recognized me and helped me out. She gave me access to a computer, and I plugged into my network of researchers. It took a while, but I worked out the details of paying cash and using a fake identity for the registration on this Prius—an excellent getaway car that's silent and seldom runs out of gas. I was able to contact a chef who helped me find work as a caterer at Blake's campaign party. A nurse at Gateway—

who hates Dr. Merchant almost as much as I do—arranged for me to sneak away from the Institute."

Though her voice remained level and calm, he knew her three-month ordeal had been brutal. He didn't want to push too hard for details. "When you linked up with your contacts, why didn't you use them to get released? You have grounds to charge your ex-husband."

"Reality check—I don't dare challenge Hugh. He's a powerful man with high-powered attorneys. As for me? I'm easily dismissed as a divorced wife who was so depressed that I tried to commit suicide." Her mouth stretched into a straight, hard line. "I couldn't take the chance that I'd lose."

He didn't want to believe that the court system could be so easily corrupted, but he understood why she felt powerless. "When you're in the clear, I hope you write a tell-all book about your experience."

"Don't worry, I'll get my revenge when my ex-husband is in prison."

"Ex-husband, right? Did you sign the divorce papers?"

"I didn't have a choice. It was the only way he'd let me see the kids."

She spoke with an edgy determination that made him glad he wasn't the target of her rage. "What's our next step?"

"After we're settled at your cabin and I've got internet, I'll reopen my investigation. There's an important witness I'm tracking down. When my case is airtight, I'll present it to federal and state prosecutors who will charge Hugh and his criminal buddies."

"And you're sure this is solid evidence?"

"Explosive," she said with grim satisfaction. "In the meantime, I'll lay down my false trail in Las Vegas. There are tons of surveillance cameras to record my presence, and I met the owner of the Magic Lamp Casino, Caspar

Khaled, when I visited last year. Caspar is kind of a gossip, and he'll be sure to report my visit to Hugh."

Blake didn't like the way this plan was shaping up. "Let me make sure I understand. You plan to contact this Khaled at the Magic Lamp."

"Me and the twins," she confirmed with some hesitation. "It's probably best if you don't accompany us. Can you find another way to meet us in Utah tomorrow morning?"

"There's a guy in Henderson who owes me a favor and could loan me a vehicle," he said. "I suppose you've already made travel arrangements for you and the twins."

"Do you remember the James Bond movie with the sexy female pilot?"

He paused to catch his breath. She'd tossed out a lot to consider—Caspar Khaled, the Magic Lamp and 007. Still, he remembered with a smile. "You're referring to the lady pilot, Pussy Galore."

"I know a real-life version. Her name is Emily Finnegan. She used to be a showgirl, but her real talent is poker. She won a helicopter and built her own fleet. I did a couple of articles on her business and the resulting publicity gave her a boost."

"Rags-to-riches story," he said.

"More like G-strings to g-force, if a chopper went that fast." She flashed a grin. "So? What do you think?"

"I'm not great at plotting like a criminal," he said, hoping to dash cold water on her enthusiasm for the adrenaline rush of dancing outside the law. "But I see flaws."

"Such as?"

"While you're in the Magic Lamp, Khaled has home-field advantage."

She nodded. "I'll move fast. And I'm counting on the element of surprise."

She wasn't being realistic about the danger of confronting a casino owner. Las Vegas might not be run by the mob anymore, but that didn't mean the city was totally family-friendly. "If you run into trouble at the casino, how will you keep the twins safe?"

"I've been worrying about that. We'll have to run. The kids are pretty darn speedy."

"Are they fast enough to outrun grown men who know their way around Vegas?"

Her brow furrowed. "This plan isn't going to work, is it? But I don't have much choice. I can't very well leave the kids in the car."

"Things change," he pointed out. "You have me riding shotgun."

"True."

"I'm your backup."

"True, again."

He took his cell phone from his pocket and scrolled through his encyclopedic inventory of contacts until he found the listing for his buddy. "I'll call Harvey in Henderson. When we get to Las Vegas, you can head for the Magic Lamp, and I'll keep the twins out of harm's way."

She concentrated on the road when merging onto US 93, a highway that led to Lake Mead, Hoover Dam and Las Vegas. The increase in traffic was noticeable, even in the middle of the night. "We're more than halfway there," she said, "only an hour and forty-five minutes to go. We'll arrive between 1:30 and 2:00 a.m. My rendezvous with Emily is scheduled for 3:00 a.m."

"Call her and let her know I'm taking your place. Me and the twins will go to the airfield and meet up with Ms. Pussy Galore."

"A word of advice. Don't call her that to her face. She'll knock your block off."

"Thanks for the warning." He shrugged. "Are you okay with this change in plans?"

"I'm relieved. It's better not to put the kids in danger."

"Do you want me to come with you into the casino?"

Her jaw clenched. "I can handle myself."

IN AN ALLEY behind Fremont Street in the heart of old Las Vegas, which had been revamped with street performers, light shows, neon artwork and zip lines, Jordan tensed her grip on the car door handle and squeezed her eyes closed, mentally preparing herself before entering Caspar Khaled's casino. She blinked and checked her watch—2:13 a.m.

Their little troop had made two stops. Once in Henderson, where Harvey joined them with his SUV, and they formed a two-vehicle caravan for the balance of the drive. Their second stop was at a gas station where they shifted seating. The twins in their booster seats went into the SUV with Blake while Jordan rode in the passenger seat of the Prius with Harvey behind the wheel.

"Are you okay?" he asked.

"I think so." She had changed into a black outfit and a satin, neon green bomber jacket, which was designed to attract attention and then be easily discarded so she was wearing only black. In her jeans' pocket, she carried a switchblade that she hoped never to use. Her titanium baton that extended to twenty-six inches was holstered on her belt.

"Captain Delaney seems better," Harvey said. "I was worried about him."

She stared at Harvey's craggy profile, dominated by a nose that had obviously been broken more than once. Though his hair hung almost to his shoulders and his chin sported thick salt-and-pepper stubble, he carried himself like a marine. "Why were you worried about Blake?"

"His injuries after the IED explosion would have killed most men. Not the captain. When the docs told him he'd never walk again, he started training for a goddamned marathon."

Jordan knew nothing about his injuries. Every bit of her focus and energy had been directed at herself and her children with no room for anybody else. She and Blake had been riding in the Prius together for hours. He certainly could have said something. But she hadn't asked and felt deeply ashamed for not being more concerned. "He's recovered now, right?"

"How come you don't know?"

"I've been…out of touch…for the past three months."

"I get it." Even in the alley, reflected flashes from many colors of neon splashed across his face. "The captain don't like to talk about himself. Never whines, never complains. But that don't mean he ain't hurting. The top brass asked him to step back from field operations and take a more supervisory role. No way. Am I right? Captain Delaney ain't riding no desk."

Had he mentioned something about retirement? "Please tell me he's okay."

"Depends on your definition," Harvey said. "I will say this. You're good for him and so are the twins. I've never seen him so smiley."

As soon as she and Blake were together again, she'd get to the bottom of this explosion and possible retirement. For now, she needed to concentrate her energy on her mission. She inhaled, closed her eyes and visualized her goals: *Show my face to the cameras in the casino. Lay out a false trail for Khaled to pass on to Hugh.* Her eyelids lifted. It was 2:17 a.m. She opened the car door.

"Wait," Harvey said. "Where should I pick you up afterwards?"

"No need. I'll catch a cab."

"Just in case, I'm going to stick around. I'll be cruising on Fourth Street."

"Thanks, Harvey."

She blew him a kiss, closed the door and strolled down the alley to Fremont. On a Saturday night in October, the temperature hovered at a pleasant sixty-five degrees, and the streets hosted a mob of revelers, singing and dancing and having a good time. If she'd brought the twins, they would have been captivated by the churning overhead lights and blasting music from top rock stars. Alex would say they were trapped inside a video game while Cooper would, no doubt, find a wizarding comparison. The neon created an unnatural, mesmerizing atmosphere. Her contacts in Las Vegas had told her that she'd be picked up by surveillance cameras immediately, but she had trouble figuring out how anybody could find her in such a crowd.

When she slipped into the Magic Lamp Casino, Jordan took care to avoid metal detectors at the entrance. She meandered through slot machines toward the gaming tables. After being sequestered at the Institute for three months, she was overwhelmed by the casino's dazzling sensory overload. The Arabian Nights theme played out with cocktail waitresses in see-through harem pants and bejeweled bra tops wandering among the gamblers with free drinks. Belly dancers undulated on four circular stages. Shirtless young men, oiled and glistening, performed intricate sword dances that reminded her of kendo and the Filipino martial arts techniques she'd learned using her baton.

Amid the exotic background, the clanking of coins from machines paying out and mechanical voices beckoning gamblers to play combined in discordant harmony. She needed to get this unscheduled meeting with Khaled done so she could fly away with her boys.

She approached a well-dressed man in a shiny black suit and purple shirt with an open collar. His position at the center of several blackjack and poker tables made her think that he was the supervisor, the pit boss.

Tilting her head upward so she'd be readily visible on camera, she said, "Excuse me, I need to leave a message for Caspar Khaled."

Unsmiling, he replied, "Check at the front desk, miss."

The way she figured, her chances for escape were better on the casino floor where some of the gamblers crowded around looking for their next lucky break and others played with single-minded concentration, only occasionally glancing up at the jiggling belly dancers. Fixing her gaze on the pit boss, she spoke loudly. "It's okay to call him. I know him very well. Actually, my husband—" no need to mention that Hugh was an ex "—he's an associate of Mr. Khaled."

"I can't help you."

"My husband, Hugh Waltham, has political connections at the highest level. And he has business interests he shares with your boss." Though she didn't have enough evidence to make an accusation that would stick, she suspected Khaled's involvement with Hugh was all about money laundering. She gave the pit boss an exaggerated wink. "Business interests. You know what I mean?"

"A politician, huh?"

"I just want to leave a message." She fluttered her eyelashes in the direction she thought a surveillance camera might be recording. It would have been useful to have Blake with her. He could have pointed out the cameras. "Tell Caspar that Jordan Reese-Waltham is in town. I'm staying at the Flamingo. In a few days, I'll be at The Ritz-Carlton in San Francisco."

"What's this about?"

"A joint project." She shot him a huge, beaming smile. "Maybe you ought to write some of this down."

"What's your name again?"

"Jordan. Reese. Waltham."

He repeated it, then touched his ear, most likely listening to somebody through an earbud, and then grabbed her left arm above the elbow. Grabbed tight. His fingers dug into her flesh. "You need to stay with me."

His response surprised her. She'd expected to be mostly ignored, which was exactly how a pit boss usually acted. Best-case scenario: have her message passed on to Khaled, who would then contact Hugh and tell him she was headed to San Francisco. Worst outcome: Khaled wouldn't get the message, and she would have wasted her time.

She tried to twist away from him. "Let me go."

"Turns out that Mr. Khaled wants to see you."

Never had she thought the casino owner would be in his office at two in the morning, paying attention to camera feeds. She needed to get away from this thug and hustle out to the airfield.

As the pit boss dragged her through the crowd, she reached across her body with her right arm and unfastened her innocent-looking holster. About the size of her hand, the black case on her belt matched her outfit under the neon green jacket. She pulled out her baton. With a downward flick of her wrist, the titanium rod extended to twenty-six inches.

Her technique with the baton borrowed heavily from Japanese kendo and fencing, but the basics came from the Filipino martial arts that used rattan sticks. A calm came over her, boosting her confidence. *I can do this.* Twisting her body away from him, she whipped the baton against his elbow joint. With a gasp of pain, the pit boss released her. And she ran.

Weaving through the Saturday-night crowd, she sprinted toward the main exit, encountered another guy in a shiny suit and two of the bare-chested dancers with fierce expressions twisting their mouths, making them look like they wanted to munch on her arm for a post-midnight snack. *Retreat!* Jordan backpedaled and flew in the opposite direction.

Darting through the casino, bobbing and weaving, dodging around cocktail waitresses with trays of drinks, she found another way out. Three wide, carpeted stairsteps led to the street. At the top stood a huge man with a shaved head and heavy black eyebrows. He spread his arms, blocking her way. It was Caspar Khaled.

Chapter Five

When Jordan first met Khaled a couple of years ago, she'd recognized a glimmer of interest in his dark brown eyes, even though Hugh was standing right there. Neither she nor Khaled overtly flirted, but he'd kissed her hand instead of shaking it, opened doors for her and held her chair at a fabulous gourmet dinner in the Sultan's Cave. When speaking to her, his voice took on a husky tone that was suggestive in spite of his massive size. More than once, he'd asked her to try on a belly dancer's costume.

Not anymore. Like a soccer goalie, he was positioned on a landing at the top of three long stairsteps in front of the side-by-side, glass doors that opened onto Fremont Street. His dark brown guayabera shirt with strips of white embroidery down both sides stretched tightly over his chest. The short sleeves displayed muscular biceps and forearms. In spite of the modern clothes, he reminded her of an ogre—not a friendly cartoon monster but a ferocious creature known to devour babies. Going head-to-head with him would be foolish. She needed to distract, evade and escape.

"Happy to see you," she said as she tore off her neon green jacket and wrapped it loosely around her left hand, leaving the right arm free to use the baton. "Hugh sends his regards."

"How would you know? Your husband divorced you."

"Let's get this straight. I divorced him." Maybe her ex was closer to Khaled than she'd thought. With the volume of cash that flowed in and out of his casino, there was a great opportunity for money laundering if the restrictions could be circumvented with the type of larceny that was Hugh's special talent.

He took a step toward her. "I just spoke to him on the phone."

Bad news for her. Had Hugh mentioned the kidnapping? He must have. That might be the reason Khaled and his men hadn't already knocked her unconscious. They needed her alert to take them to the twins.

From the corner of her eye, she saw the two bare-chested guys approaching with their patterned harem pants flapping around muscular thighs. Her expertise in the martial arts might not be enough to defeat three large men, but no one had ever accused her of lacking self-confidence. She wouldn't panic. She had to concentrate, needed to believe she could handle any obstacle. *I can get past them. I have to. For my sons.*

She surveyed her surroundings. To her amazement, the gamblers at the slots were too intent on their machines to notice the life-and-death struggle taking place. That indifference had to change. She counted on the crowd reaction to help her as she faced off with Tweedledum and Tweedledee. Jordan put on a show. Whirling and waving her neon jacket, she launched into a series of high kicks, some of which connected. She accompanied her action with loud shouts. "Hai. Hah. Ho."

Her gambit worked. The gamblers were watching. Some actually turned away from their slot machines. A couple of women shrieked and grabbed their purses.

Jordan dashed toward Khaled, saw that he was braced and ready for her attack and evaded his grasp while delivering a swift rap on his outstretched fingers with her baton. Instinctively, he pulled back.

The gamblers contributed shouts of their own. "Hai. Ho. Ho."

A pit boss stepped between her and the shirtless attackers. He made an announcement. "Nothing to worry about, folks. It's all part of the entertainment at the Magic Lamp."

She played along with his scenario with a couple of leg sweeps and more kicks accompanied by fierce poses with her baton. Like a star performer, she scampered back and forth across the stairs, then she took a bow. Finally, she twirled in front of Khaled and flung her jacket into his face. After a pivot, she dashed out the door onto Fremont Street.

The glittering chaos of neon lights and rock music suited her mood as she holstered her baton and dashed toward the hotels on the corner. From there, she could catch a taxi. Sensing the presence of cameras, she pulled up the hood on her fitted, nylon sweatshirt. Clad from head to toe in black, she felt as intangible as a shadow, darting swiftly through the crowd, which had thinned out a bit. Unfortunately, she wasn't invisible. Glancing over her shoulder, she glimpsed the pit bosses and shirtless men in pursuit.

At a western-themed hotel, she plunged into the underpass and spotted the line of taxis at the curb. Stopping to get inside one of these vehicles seemed like a sure way to get caught, and so she kept moving. Her thinking was disorganized. She hadn't planned for this turn of events, hadn't expected Khaled to react so aggressively. She still couldn't believe he'd immediately called Hugh. *Disaster!* Or maybe not. If nothing else, she had succeeded in establishing a false trail that would lead to San Francisco.

She ripped through the hotel's doors into the lobby, which featured an incongruous decor combining glittering chandeliers and ranch-style fences. Instead of harem girls and belly dancers, the cocktail waitresses dressed like cowgirls with red boots, vests and hats. The male employees looked like they were part of a rodeo, and all of them wore guns on their hips…toy guns, she hoped. To her left was the registration desk for the hotel, and beyond that she saw a long wooden bar like one in an old-time saloon. An arched entrance to the casino was to the right. She spun around and dashed up a staircase to the mezzanine. Hiding behind a huge pot holding a tall saguaro cactus, she could look down at the entrance. The gang from the Magic Lamp charged through the doors, conferred for a moment and then split up, probably to search for her.

If she'd had more time, Jordan would have ducked into a more secure hiding place and stayed there until the coast was clear. But her departure on Emily's chopper was scheduled for 3:00 a.m., and she didn't want to be late. Already, the time was 2:42.

When the Magic Lamp guys had dispersed, she scampered down the staircase and out the door into the night. Turning on the speed, she headed for Fourth Street. Harvey said he'd cruise that area, and she hoped to find him. For a change, luck was with her. The Prius had just pulled up at a stoplight. Jordan threw herself into the passenger seat. "Go."

The former marine gunned the engine—a less than dramatic gesture in a hybrid. He cranked the steering wheel and swerved in an illegal right turn. Through the windshield, she spotted the shirtless thugs in harem pants. The Prius left them in the dust.

"I think we made it," she said.

"Just in case," he drawled, "I'm fixing to use evasive driving techniques." He accelerated and dodged through the late-night traffic like a Vegas native. "We damn sure don't want anybody hanging on our tail."

"Or following us to the airfield."

"Copy that." He left the main drag and zipped into a residential area, slowing his speed to match the few other cars on the road. "I don't mean to pry, but were those guys who looked like Aladdin's genies coming after you?"

"That's right." She could hardly believe she'd pulled off that escape.

"How did you kick genie ass?"

She showed him her baton and then collapsed it to fit back into the holster. "I have my ways."

"Damn, Jordan. You ain't playing around."

"Not when it comes to my kids."

Harvey drove with the assurance of a man who knew what he was doing. Nobody could follow this Prius. It helped that they weren't going to Harry Reid International Airport on Wayne Newton Boulevard but to a private airfield where Emily kept her fleet. Also, Jordan had mentioned to the pit boss that she was staying at the Flamingo, which should send them in the wrong direction. This phase of her escape was over. At least, she hoped it was.

After Harvey dropped her off, he would change the license plates on the Prius and hand the vehicle off to someone else who would take possession of the little car while Harvey drove home to Henderson in his SUV. Minutes clicked by on her wristwatch. Running late, but it shouldn't be a problem. Her friend in Utah would wait for her.

At 3:23 a.m., Harvey turned left onto a long, straight road that led to the airfield on the outskirts of town where several private companies and helicopter services housed their aircraft. In the distance, beneath the floodlights, she spotted a blue-and-gold helicopter outside a hangar. More importantly, she saw Blake, standing nearly as tall as the chopper blades with the night wind riffling through his short blond hair. His wide, muscular shoulders looked strong enough to carry whatever she loaded upon him.

Again, she felt a stab of guilt. What gave her the right to burden him with her emotional baggage?

She hadn't bothered to find out what was going on in his life. Harvey had said something about an IED explosion and serious injuries. *I should back off.* It was wrong to ask him to step into danger again.

WHEN BLAKE SPOTTED the Prius, he checked his watch. At 3:27 a.m., she was nearly a half hour late. Jordan had put him through twenty-seven minutes of raging anxiety. According to her damned plan, she was supposed to leave a message for Caspar Khaled at the Magic Lamp Casino and scamper out the door. *Yeah, right.* In what universe could she poke the bear and not expect a counterattack? She could have been shot or beaten or taken into custody.

No way should he have accepted her scheme. Blake knew what it meant to go into hostile situations. He was battle-trained. Not that his experience had helped in the most recent incident. When he got stuck in an IED explosion, he'd messed up. Big-time. And now, he doubted himself.

When she exited the Prius and strode across the tarmac toward him, he noticed a subtle difference in Jordan. Her curly brown hair had the same bounce. Her shoulders-back, athletic gait showed excellent physical conditioning. Her lips still curved in a confident grin, but her stormy blue eyes had taken on a new seriousness, and her fingers curled into fists. Whatever happened at the Magic Lamp had caused a shift in her attitude. He hoped this change would encourage her to consider the outcome of her actions before she—again—leaped with both feet into a churning sea of trouble.

When she was only a few feet away from him, he asked, "How did it go?"

She went up on tiptoe, wrapped her arms around his

neck and molded her slender body to his. Her heart fluttered against his chest as she exhaled a long sigh. In a ragged whisper, she said, "I shouldn't have taken that chance. I almost blew the whole escape and got myself caught."

"You're not injured, are you?"

"No."

"And Khaled didn't follow you here?"

"No. Harvey's a great evasive driver."

"You bet I am." His buddy sauntered toward them. "She's right about that."

"In a way, my plan worked," she said. "Khaled already contacted Hugh and will undoubtedly tell him that I'm going to San Francisco. That's the false trail I want him to follow. But it could so easily have gone wrong. I didn't take the level of danger into account."

This was as much his fault as hers. He should have stopped her. *As if I could...* "You can't let your guard down now. Nor can I. We need to assume that Khaled is hot on our trail."

"And we have to get out of here pronto."

Keeping his arm slung around her shoulders, he leaned close and caught a whiff of her sweet jasmine and coconut shampoo. "In future, you might consider ways to adjust your style."

"You're right. I need to be more careful."

Ever since he'd known her, she'd been a risk-taker—a reporter who chose to be embedded with combat troops, an investigative journalist who tracked down a serial killer by posing as a prostitute, and now she was a single mother who had kidnapped her children and gone on the run. "Don't change too much, Jordan. I like you the way you are."

"But I ought to change…somewhat. And I intend to." She stared into his face, confronting him. "There's something else we have to talk about. But not in front of the kids."

As if on cue, the twins burst from the hangar, laughing and shouting as they ran toward her. She crouched and held out her arms to corral the rambunctious five-year-old boys. She held them close and kissed them a dozen times.

"You changed clothes," she said. More kisses.

"Didn't wanna run around in my jammies," Alex said.

"You're my big boys." More hugs and kisses.

"Cut it out, Mom." Alex pulled away. "Emily showed us the choppers. Awesome. I wanna be a pilot when I grow up."

"Me, too." Cooper snuggled in her arms as he pointed at the blue-and-gold helicopter. "That's an ECO-Star, made by Airbus. Oh, and the tail rotor is called a Fenestron which means fan-in-fin. Do you see it?"

Before she could reply, Alex interrupted. "It goes fast. That's all I want to know."

Blake hurried them along. "Are you boys ready for take-off?"

The kids bounced up and down as they shouted a wildly enthusiastic assent. The time they'd spent sleeping in the car had apparently recharged their batteries. When Emily Finnegan—a stunning, six-foot-tall redhead—strode toward them, Harvey stepped closer to Blake and nudged his elbow. "I got to meet that woman."

The tone of his voice told Blake that his buddy wanted more than a handshake from the glamorous female pilot. Both were single. They shared a love of mechanics and speed. The minute he introduced them, sparks started to volley back and forth. Harvey moved fast, pulling a business card from the pocket of his weathered denim jacket. Emily responded in kind. This could be the start of a beautiful friendship.

Blake finished loading their duffel bags and the car seats into the cargo hold. He was impatient. Emily said the flight from Las Vegas to Fillmore, Utah, was about 250 air miles and, travelling at a speed of 125 to 150 miles per hour, would take roughly two hours. In Fillmore, they'd meet a former associate of Jordan's who had retired from a big-time career as a television news anchor to run a small weekly paper and spend all his free time on the nearby ski slopes. *Nice lifestyle.* Skiing and keeping track of local events might be something Blake would consider for his retirement.

During his tours of duty, he'd spent a lot of time in helicopters of all sizes and shapes. When it came to class and comfort, none compared with Emily's sleek, beautiful ECO-Star. Wraparound windows offered panoramic views. The leather seats were arranged with four, including the pilot's seat, in the front and four on a raised platform behind them. Though the boys wanted to sit in front, preferably on Emily's lap, she'd set up special elevated kid seats with safety harnesses in the rear where they still had outstanding views.

While Emily took her position in the pilot's seat and went through a series of preflight checks, Jordan climbed into the back with the boys and showed them how to wear the headsets. "These are voice activated," she said. "When Emily turns them on, we can hear every word you say, so don't be screaming into the microphone."

"Roger that," Alex said. "Emily said 'roger' means okay. And if it's not okay, you're supposed to say 'negative.'"

"And a helicopter is like a ship," Cooper said, not to be outdone when it came to new information. "That means we don't say left and right. It's 'port' and 'starboard.'"

"Starbucks," Alex said.

"Starboard. It means right."

While Jordan ran through the standard mom questions about potty breaks and drinking water and food, Blake turned to Emily. "Anything I can do to help?"

"Promise me that you won't let anything bad happen

to Jordan and the boys." She dropped her voice so only he could hear. "The twins are precious cargo, and she's a good person."

Though he'd never spoken that promise, he'd already given his allegiance to this mission and to Jordan. From the moment he saw her and the twins in that garden shed, he had dedicated himself to bodyguard duty. Not that he was doing a great job as a protector. Why the hell hadn't he gone with her to the Magic Lamp? "I'll take care of them."

"Not an easy task. Jordan can be unrelenting and a little bit scary. Still, I'd do anything for her. And the twins? Oh my God, they're so smart and so active." Under her breath, she added, "I don't know how she keeps up with those little energy balls."

"Ditto."

She glanced toward the rear. "You guys get ready. I'm starting the engine."

Jordan made sure the twins were okay before she moved to the front and settled into the seat between Blake and Emily. He had instinctively taken the outer seat, which was where he sat during most of his airborne military maneuvers when he needed to be the first out, directing his squad. Though he had braced himself for takeoff, the rumble of the rotors awakened unwanted memories of other flights, other missions. From the rear, the boys were screaming.

Blake clenched his jaw, fighting off a flashback. He hated the panicked, out-of-control feelings that came when he plunged into sensory recall. His nose twitched at the remembered stink of gunpowder. His ears rang with echoes of past explosions and the cries of the dying. He closed his eyes, blocking his visions of gunfire flashes, torn flesh and so damn much blood. His gut churned, and he tasted vomit in the back of his mouth. *Get a grip.* He told himself that they were taking off from Las Vegas in a chopper flown by a beautiful red-haired pilot. Forcing his eyelids open, he looked down and saw the shimmer of neon lights instead of jungle or desert.

Over the headset, Emily told them that she was turning off all the interior lights so they could have a better view. Though it was cool in the ECO-Star cabin, Blake felt sweat beading his hairline. The boys had ceased their screeching and babbled to each other about what they saw on the ground. They had no fear, none at all. Their voices on the headset were remarkably clear.

Emily informed them, "We're at an altitude of one thousand feet. I'll take a swing over the city, and then we're on our way to Utah."

Below lay Vegas. Glitter Gulch. On the strip, he saw a replica of the Eiffel Tower, the skyline of Manhattan and a pyramid. Nothing to be scared of, and yet the thwap-thwap-thwap of the rotor and the vibration of the cabin stirred his visceral panic. His pulse thumped hard and fast. His chest was tight, and he couldn't breathe. For a moment, he felt the cabin closing in, suffocating him. *Can't pass out. Need to stay alert. Got to be strong.* And then, he felt Jordan's caress on his closed fist.

His fingers opened, and she gently cradled his hand. When he looked down at her, relief flowed through his veins. Her nearness soothed his tension and loosened the stranglehold of his flashback. Being here with her felt right. *We'll be okay.* He would protect her and the boys... or die trying.

Chapter Six

An hour and a half later, Blake studied Jordan's profile, trying to decide how she'd changed from when they'd first met. Her thick brown hair had been cut and styled since the days she'd been embedded with the troops and tamed her curls in a long braid. A slight evidence of aging showed in the laugh lines at the corners of her big blue eyes—those remarkable eyes. He saw an indefinable maturity in her expressions: she was slower to laugh and less likely to cry. He wished he could see more clearly. The only illumination inside the cabin came from the pilot's control panel, but he could see by the light of a full October moon—a hunter's moon.

Below the chopper, a vast western terrain unfolded. Though Zion and Bryce Canyon lacked the visual punch of Las Vegas neon, he preferred natural beauty. Early snow outlined the jagged peaks in the distance, reminding him of their final destination in the Colorado Rockies. These wonders would have impressed the two kids in the back, but they'd both nodded off to sleep.

Beside him, Jordan leaned toward Emily and asked, "Can you turn off the headsets for the boys so they can't hear us talking?"

"Sure thing. And I'll switch my headset to another channel so you and Blake can have a few minutes of privacy."

"Thanks." She turned toward him, and her eyes got even wider. "I never meant for things to turn out this way."

"Could be worse." He ran his fingers through his hair and inhaled the oily mechanical odor of the ECO-Star.

"I need to apologize for being so self-centered. During the whole time we've been on the run, I never asked about your life. I focused on my problems. I made it all about me."

He had a bad feeling about this conversation and hoped to head it off before she got started. "Apology accepted."

"Harvey told me you almost died."

Some veterans enjoyed sharing war stories. He wasn't one of them. Not clever or eloquent, Blake didn't have words to describe the pain, terror and grief he'd experienced. "Seriously, Jordan. Drop it."

"I can be a good listener," she said. "My skills as a reporter are kind of rusty, but they'll come back. You remember, don't you? Seven years ago, when we first met, do you remember how we talked?"

"You were interviewing me, wanted to write an article about the life of an average marine…as if there was such a thing. All marines are above-average." He gazed through the window at the panorama of canyons and mesas. Seven years ago. They'd been so young. So much had changed. "Things are different now."

"Tell me how you were injured."

"Don't know." He shrugged. "The incident is a blank."

"When did it happen?"

"Four months ago."

"Where were you?"

He recognized her tactic of poking inside his memories until she found something he recalled, like the color of his socks or what he had for breakfast. "You're not going to give up, are you?"

"I never do." The ECO-Star jostled, and her shiny brown hair bounced. "Now, let's start again. Where were you?"

"On a rutted, dirt road in a Land Rover with the top down. Should have taken an armored Humvee, but we expected this to be a quick trip."

He paused, allowing the memory to form. And he realized that the ride in the Rover to pick up beer and vodka for a party bore a horrible similarity to her jaunt into Las Vegas to pass a message to Khaled. The initial objective appeared to be clear and simple, but neither of them had considered the many things that could go wrong. In her case, the potential for disaster had been avoided. In his, catastrophe hit full force.

"The weather," she said. "What was the weather like?"

"The sky was clear, and the high desert sun glared down on us. I sat in the passenger seat, and there were three other guys. Two of them insisted that we leave right away so we could meet our contact person. I wanted to wait until one of the Humvees was free, but I relented. And I damn well paid the price."

"You can't blame yourself," she said.

"The hell I can't. I'm a captain. I was in charge. Taking care of those marines was my responsibility, and I let them down. When our Rover rolled over the IED, the device detonated. We had no warning, no time to prepare. One second, the road was all clear. The next, we were in the middle of a fiery explosion, tossed in the air like a kid's toys. Nobody died, but Lance Corporal Hodges lost his left leg above the knee. We were all injured, seriously injured."

Somehow, the touch of her hand conveyed empathy, and he believed her compassion was sincere. Jordan had been in combat and had experienced her own tragedies. Softly, she said, "What happened next?"

"I honestly don't remember." He winced. "They tell me that I put through a call for backup on my sat phone, which is kind of amazing because I can't believe the phone was still working. I pulled the other men clear. And I fired—left-handed because my right wrist was messed up—at an invisible enemy with my M16 and my handgun."

"And you don't remember any of this."

"Not a bit. The next thing I can recall was lying on an operating table with a bunch of medics in masks hanging over me, cutting off my clothes and waving scalpels. Stat-stat-stat. They kept saying it. I tried to talk, to ask about the other marines, but I couldn't make a peep. I looked down at my body and saw blood and guts—deep lacerations, contusions and abrasions. Hell, I was a mess."

She stroked his cheek, then gently turned his face toward her. Her steady gaze reassured him and made him feel that everything was going to be all right, even though he knew nothing would ever be the same. She asked, "Did you have broken bones?"

"A couple of ribs and my right wrist." He pulled down his sleeve to hide the scars. "I'll probably never regain full range of motion. I'm learning how to shoot with my left hand."

"Any other permanent injuries?"

"I lost a piece of my right lung and one of my kidneys. I have muscle and nerve damage in both legs. Physical therapy is helping, but I might never return to peak condition."

And that was the problem. According to the doctors, he wasn't fit for full-time duty in a combat zone. Blake wished he could object to their opinion, but he knew they were correct. His marksmanship had been compromised, he couldn't run at top speed and his stamina was shot to hell. His formerly excellent skills in martial arts were no longer swift and sure. Jordan could probably kick his ass in kendo and karate. *How pathetic is that!* He'd been her first teacher—her first sensei.

She asked, "What comes next for you?"

Though he could continue his career, Blake would probably be assigned to desk work, maybe at the Pentagon or training recruits at Parris Island. That vision of the future felt as bleak and empty as the night sky that wrapped around the chopper. After he'd gotten out of the hospital and done the basic rehab, he had taken this time off to map his future. "I might retire."

She gasped, and he considered it a testament to the high quality of the ECO-Star headset that he could hear that sharp intake of breath. He had surprised her. Ever since they'd known each other and fallen in love, their careers had gotten in the way of their relationship. When they met, she was destined for great things as a journalist, and she wouldn't give up her ambitions to become a military wife. Likewise, he loved his work and lived for every day on active duty as a marine.

She leaned against him. The steady thump of the rotors provided a harsh background sound. "I know how much your work means to you," she said. "What are you going to do?"

"I'm not sure about tomorrow, but right now I'm going to make sure you and the twins are safe. That's my mission."

"I like that." After caressing the line of his jaw, she pulled him toward her and kissed his cheek. "I like it a lot."

"Don't be so sure," he said. No way would he have a repeat of this evening's mad dash into Vegas. "If I'm going to be responsible for you, I've got to be in charge. That means you either follow my instructions or come up with a damn good reason why you can't."

Her eyebrows pulled into a scowl. "I'm not good at taking orders."

But she'd already admitted her mistake—facing off with Khaled had been dangerous. "Let me remind you that your initial plan in Vegas included taking the twins into the casino with you. I convinced you that putting the kids in jeopardy wasn't a good idea."

"But I wasn't hard to convince." She stood up for herself, which was what he'd expected her to do. Jordan wasn't the type of woman who gave up control. "I won't be docile and utterly obedient, but I'm always willing to listen to reason."

"We share the same goal," he said. "Staying safe, which means minimal risk."

"The secondary goal is uncovering enough evidence to get Hugh charged with bribery, extortion, wire fraud, embezzlement and maybe even murder."

Murder? She hadn't mentioned homicide before. "When we get to the cabin, we'll organize our objectives and decide how to proceed. Until then, no more impulsive actions."

"Agreed." She shook his hand.

"What's this about murder?"

"A long story." She turned her head and peered through the windshield at the endless depth of darkness beyond the stars and the moon.

He reached across her body, held her chin and turned her head toward him. Earlier she'd given him a peck on the cheek, a small intimacy that left him wanting more. He answered with a firm kiss on her full, pliant lips. She tasted as sweet as cherries, and her fragrance eclipsed the mechanical smell of the helicopter. She transported him.

He leaned back in the leather seat and closed his eyes.

AFTER JORDAN GAVE Emily the signal that she and Blake had finished their private conversation and the communication channel in the headset could be opened, she turned her head to stare at the man sleeping beside her. His kiss still tingled. She glided her tongue across her lips and felt the unquenchable spark of passion they'd shared seven years ago. If she hadn't gotten pregnant with the twins, she wouldn't have married Hugh and would surely have returned to Blake. Or maybe not. Jordan had been an ambitious young woman who wanted to make her mark in the world.

Blake's chest rose and fell as his breathing deepened. *Impossible!* After that kiss, she couldn't believe he was falling asleep while her hormones performed a wild, sensual *lambada*, the forbidden dance.

She spoke into the headset. "So, Emily, how much longer?"

"About forty-five minutes." The redheaded pilot gave her a friendly grin. "I have some good news."

"Let me have it. I could use something cheerful."

"I just talked to my partner at the airfield hangar, and he told me that nobody has been asking around about late-night flights. Nobody's been looking for me." She gave a nod. "I think you're safe, at least for the moment. You managed to sneak away from Las Vegas without anybody knowing where you're headed."

Jordan exhaled audibly, letting some of her tension ease. "Very good news, indeed. Khaled has had time to figure out that I'm not registered at the Flamingo. He's probably reported to Hugh."

"Just in case," Emily said, "I plan to leave Utah as soon as I drop you off and hurry home. Nobody knows I was out tonight except my partner, and I trust him."

"I can't thank you enough for helping us."

"Stop it," Emily said. "Without you and your articles, I never would have established my own business. The only thanks I want is an invite to your wedding."

"Whoa there, lady. I'm not looking to get married. I tried it once, and I'm not very good at it."

"Don't let one loser dictate your whole life. You and Blake are sheer perfection." She paused. "With emphasis on the sheer. That happens to be the title of the last show I appeared in."

"And I'll bet you brought the perfection."

"Whatever." She shrugged. "In the meantime, you ought to follow Blake's example and take a nap. You've got a long day of driving tomorrow, going from Fillmore to wherever you're headed in Colorado."

Jordan had purposely avoided mentioning their final destination. The fewer people who knew, the better. "You're right. I need sleep."

She closed her eyes, trying to clear her mind and slide into slumber. Immediately, she ran into obstacles. There were a dozen things to do, starting with a call to Abigail to make sure she was safe. In Fillmore, her old friend and mentor, Michael Hornsby, would provide them with a vehicle, and she had another task for him.

Her mind wouldn't settle. Details swirled in dizzying array. Through the headset, she heard the twins mumble in their sleep and twisted around to see them. They appeared to be fine, doing well. But how long would their complacent mood last? She needed to have a long talk with each of them about leaving their father and starting a new life. How would she explain her investigation? Though she was compiling evidence against Hugh, the children couldn't be expected to understand. If she'd been given a choice, she might have preferred to step back and let her ex-husband get away with his criminal schemes. *No way. Not a chance.* Her last confrontation with Hugh showed her that he was capable of terrible retribution. His hired thug had nearly killed her.

She fidgeted in the leather seat, shifted her weight from one side to the other and tangled her fingers in a knot. "Can't sleep."

"Nervous?" Emily asked.

"A little bit." If she were totally honest, her tension ran

deeper than a case of nerves. Jordan was scared to death of what she was attempting and what might be lurking around the corner. Her fear of impending events kept slapping her awake. "I can't settle down. Tell me about your business. Maybe I can do another article about you and your choppers."

Emily talked, and Jordan listened, making mental notes for later when she could put together a story about her friend's success. Jordan had worried that she'd lost her journalistic skills, but the ability to focus and ask the right questions was deeply ingrained. And she needed the distraction. Thinking of somebody else's story allowed her to forget her own woes.

Beyond the windows, the night began to thin. Sunrise would bring a new set of challenges. Fresh adventures. More danger. Hugh would never let her get away with this. Her ruse in Las Vegas wouldn't fool him for long. The threat of his vengeance stalked through the dark caverns of her mind, coming ever closer, inescapable.

Without opening his eyes, Blake took her hand. Though she didn't want to admit it, she needed his protection.

Chapter Seven

The city of Fillmore in Millard County, Utah, honored the thirteenth US President, Millard Fillmore, who happened to be in office during the early 1850s when the county was founded by the territorial legislature. For a brief time, Fillmore had been the capitol of Utah Territory. As far as Jordan could tell, the city never regained its past glory and had become a pleasant, little place with a decent municipal airport.

At 6:55 a.m. Utah time, the ECO-Star landed outside a hangar at the far edge of the runways, and the rotors stopped twirling. Jordan took off her headset, and for a moment, reveled in the echoes of silence. She looked over her shoulder into the rear row of seats. "Are you kids okay?"

They pulled off the headsets, wriggled against their safety harnesses and started chattering. They both needed to go to the bathroom, and they were hungry, really hungry.

"So am I," she said.

"Breakfast sounds good." Blake reached into the back to release the twins from the seat belts. "I'm thinking of waffles."

"I want a pumpkin latte," Alex said.

"Coffee?" Jordan questioned.

"Dad said it was okay."

"Yeah," Cooper chimed in. "Dad lets us have coffee all the time."

She tamped down her irritation. Feeding caffeine to five-year-old kids was wrong for so many reasons, but now wasn't the time to complain about her ex-husband's lousy parenting skills. She climbed out of the cabin and helped the kids down to the tarmac. "Your choices are water, juice, milk or cocoa."

Peering through the dawn, she spotted Michael Hornsby leaning against the prefab wall of the hangar beside the huge, open doors. A tall, lean man with thick silver hair combed straight back from his tanned forehead, Hornsby had been her mentor from the time she snagged her first paying job as a journalist until she took an extended leave after giving birth. She trusted him implicitly and didn't like the way he was scowling. His deep-set eyes, his brows and even his long nose seemed to express disapproval. Something was wrong.

She approached him cautiously. Her hands rested on her kids' shoulders, and she brought them to a halt in front of the retired news anchor. "Alex and Cooper, you've met this gentleman before, but you were babies and too young to remember. This is Mr. Hornsby, the man who taught me almost everything I know."

As they'd been trained, the twins shook hands with her mentor and politely said, "Pleased to meet you, sir."

Hornsby's scowl evaporated like dew on a sunny morning. The adorable boys with their tousled brown hair and big, blue eyes had that effect on people. Hornsby dug into the pockets of his khaki trousers and pulled out a handful of change, which he distributed between the kids. "Inside the hangar," he said, "there's a vending machine with snacks. If it's okay with your mom, go for it."

"No chocolate." She tried to rein in the temptations. "Only one snack."

As they took off toward the machine, Blake stepped forward and introduced himself. "Jordan has told me a lot about you."

"She met you when she was embedded with the troops, correct?"

"Yes, sir."

"I was a newspaper editor back then. What did you think about the way she portrayed you in her article?"

"I speak for every marine in my platoon when I say that she did an excellent job. She understood us in a way that few civilians could."

While they discussed combat news coverage, she could tell that Blake and Hornsby liked and respected each other—a mutual appreciation that pleased her. Happiness bubbled up inside. These two men ranked high among the most important people in her life.

"I'm glad you're with her," Hornsby said to Blake, "because she's going to need all the help she can get. I had a call on my private cell phone about an hour ago from her ex-husband. He told me that Jordan suffered a nervous breakdown, and he had to find her before she injured herself or anyone else."

Her moment of joy popped like a bouquet of balloons. "You didn't believe him, did you?"

"Hell, no."

"He must have gotten your phone number from an old address book or my computer contacts."

"He has your computer?" Hornsby questioned.

She nodded. When Hugh and Gorilla Gruber attacked her and sent her off to the Institute, he stole her laptop. Though her files were encrypted, she suspected that he'd gained access and knew about some of her research into his criminal activities. Fortunately, she'd been smart enough to bury the more sensitive details in a tiny laptop that she tucked away in a safe-deposit box. "I'm sorry to drag you into this mess."

"Not a problem for me, but for you. He's trying to track you down." Hornsby glanced toward Blake. "If he has her contacts, he's probably trying to reach you as well."

Jordan asked, "What did you say to him?"

"Hey, I'm an old reporter. I know how to say 'no comment' in ways that won't arouse suspicion. And I might have played the old geezer card."

"What's that?" Blake asked.

"Pretended to be an old grouch which, of course, I'm not. I grumbled in a semi-coherent manner, causing that smug son of a gun to think I'm too ancient to know what's happening, certainly not sharp enough to aid Jordan in her escape. His call came through at a little after four in the morning. So the 'old geezer' persona was a fairly accurate portrayal of how I was feeling."

She wrapped her arms around him and squeezed. "I knew you'd have my back."

"And I got you a nifty Chevy SUV that I'll need to have returned in a few weeks." He hugged her back. "Now, I want to talk to the twins and to meet your beautiful red-headed pilot."

"We can't stop for long," she said.

"You've got to eat," he said. "And I know a diner where the waffles are fluffy and the coffee is hot."

"No coffee for the kids," she said.

"Who'd do a damn fool thing like giving them caffeine? Seems to me those boys are plenty wide awake without artificial stimulation."

She linked her arm through his. "There's something else I need to talk to you about."

"I know that tone," Hornsby said. "You have a piece you're working on."

"That's it," she said. "A project."

And this project represented the most important work she'd ever done as an investigative reporter. The stakes couldn't be higher. Her survival and the future of her children depended on the evidence she compiled. If there had been more time, she wouldn't have asked Hornsby to help. The potential for danger was very real.

She glanced over her shoulder and saw Blake. He looked up from the screen on his phone and made eye contact. It occurred to her that she ought to talk over her plan with him before charging forward. Hadn't she just promised to let him take the lead? But discussion seemed unnatural. Jordan didn't usually work with a partner. Her reporting had always been solo. Clearly, that had to change. Before confiding in Hornsby, she'd talk to Blake.

When the twins rejoined them, showing off their choices for one-snack-each, Jordan took advantage of the interruption. "I'm sure Mr. Hornsby would like to hear about your experiences on the helicopter."

"I always enjoy a good story," her mentor said, showing the same attention and encouragement to her sons that he'd given to her when she was a bright-eyed cub reporter. "Did that pretty lady pilot let you fly it?"

"She should have," Alex said with unshakable confidence.

"You're such a dope." Cooper got in a dig.

"Why? Because I want to fly choppers instead of wizard brooms?"

Cooper looked up at Hornsby. "Do you believe in wizards?"

"Some of my best friends are magical. Like your mother."

Cooper took his hand and pulled him toward a picnic table outside the hangar while Alex tore open the wrapper on his granola bar. Fondly, she watched them, wondering if Cooper—who loved to make up stories—would grow up to be a reporter. Or maybe Alex. He certainly had the curiosity and bravado. She rubbed at her eyes, wishing she'd managed to take a nap on the chopper. An hour and a half of shut-eye would have made a difference.

Blake stepped up beside her. "That project you wanted to talk to Hornsby about—does it have to do with your investigation into your ex?"

"Yes, and it's not exactly risk-free."

"Tell me more."

Sharing information with him felt right. She reached into her pocket and took out a key chain with two keys and a small, rotund plastic penguin. "His name is Tux, and he's a flash drive."

"Wow," he said with a straight face. "You're just like the CIA."

"All the evidence I've gathered on Hugh is recorded here."

"Not on the computer he swiped?"

"I hid the sensitive files, including names of possible witnesses, on a tiny computer that I kept in a safe-deposit box. That info is triple-encrypted. As soon as I gained access to a computer while I was in the Institute, I contacted a computer genius who remotely retrieved my data."

"Smart." His compliment rang true.

As an investigative reporter, she'd developed great resources in the computer world. Hackers, programmers and cyberspies were among her best buddies. "And I have a copy of Tux hidden with my stuff."

"Another penguin?"

"A fat flamingo," she said with a grin.

"How do these strange birds connect to Hornsby?"

Though it went against her natural instincts, she'd agreed to share her plans with him and intended to fulfill her part of the bargain. "I want to give Tux to Hornsby for safekeeping in case anything happens to me. Also, I'll find a way to communicate more details to him as I collect them."

Blake nodded. "He's your backup, somebody you trust to go after Hugh if, for some reason, you can't."

"Exactly." When he framed her plan in those terms, it seemed even more dangerous.

"Does he know what to do with the information?"

A fair question. If this had been a matter of writing an exposé, she'd trust Hornsby to have the best resources. But her case was geared toward providing federal prosecutors with the data they needed to put Hugh out of the crime business and land him in prison. "I included the names of my contacts in Tux. Here's my problem: I don't want to put Hornsby in jeopardy. Is it fair to ask him to do this?"

"He's a perceptive guy," Blake said. "Hornsby knows how much risk he can handle. Explain what you need, including the part about suspecting Hugh of complicity in a murder, and leave the final decision up to him."

"Is that an order, Captain?"

"More like a suggestion." The corner of his mouth lifted in a half grin. "Thanks for telling me your plan."

She gave a satisfied nod. She still wasn't thrilled about the need for backup, but her arrangement with Blake seemed to be working. "Do we have time for breakfast?"

"I'd like to get on the road as soon as possible." He held up his cell phone. "While you drive, I have some text messages to return."

"You shouldn't use your phone," she said. "The location can be traced, can't it?"

"I disabled tracking before we left Arizona." He glared at the phone in his hand. "I still don't completely trust this thing. You have other untraceable burner phones, right?"

"Only four are left, not including this one, which is my superphone, prepped and programmed by my computer genius." She took it from her pocket. "This innocent-looking device is encrypted and bounces the signal through hundreds of locations. You want to talk CIA? This is the real deal. Give me your phone, and I'll transfer your contacts onto this one."

He handed the cell phone over. "You like this spy stuff."

"I'm glad I can use it," she said, as she quickly made the transfer and gave his phone back. "I hate that spy stuff is necessary."

"Good answer." He dropped his cell phone to the smooth concrete floor in the hangar and ground the heel of his boot into the screen. "Now it's just plastic."

"A little violent but effective." She tapped the edges of her encrypted, untraceable cell phone. "You can use this one after I finish my call to Abigail."

"What are you going to tell her?"

"As little as possible. If she has information for me, that's great. But I'm going to encourage her to step away. She thinks this is a game—doesn't realize how dangerous Hugh and Gruber can be."

While Blake went toward the picnic table to join Hornsby and the twins, she put through her call. At 7:33 a.m. in Utah, it was an hour earlier in Flagstaff, not too early. Abigail, a fitness nut, was usually up at dawn's first light, jogging on the mountainous trails near her house.

The cell phone rang six times, seven times… Was she still asleep? Three more rings. Jordan glanced at the specially encrypted phone. Her name wouldn't show on caller ID because the phone was untraceable, but she'd called twice before, and her friend had answered without hesitation. *Come on, Abigail, pick up.*

The voice that answered was a stranger. "This is Abigail Preston's phone."

"May I speak to her?"

"Who is this?"

That authoritative tone didn't belong to an assistant or

someone who worked in Abigail's house. Jordan feared that something had happened, something terrible. "What's going on? Let me talk to Abigail. Who is this?"

"Officer Rita McNally, Flagstaff PD."

Jordan turned away so the kids, Blake and Hornsby couldn't see her horrified expression. Her pulse stopped. She felt the blood drain from her face. *No, this can't be happening.* She choked out the words. "I don't understand."

"I need your name, ma'am."

Jordan gasped and shook herself. Now was not the time to freeze up. "Was Abigail hurt?"

"There was an accident. Her car went off the road."

"Is she all right? Which hospital has she been taken to?"

"I'm sorry, there's nothing more I can say."

"I need to know," she said hoarsely. "Please, tell me."

"You'll have to call her husband."

Like hell she would. Stanley Preston worked with her ex-husband and idolized him. It might be possible that Stanley played a part in Abigail's supposed accident. Surely not. They appeared to be one of the happiest couples Jordan knew. But appearances could be deceptive. At one time, she'd thought herself in love with Hugh.

"Ma'am," the officer said. "Tell me your name."

Jordan disconnected the call. Her reporter's instincts told her that Abigail was dead. Otherwise, the officer would have given her a hospital. But she wasn't certain. She needed verification. Her computer genius, Spike Mauritius, could tap into the internal documents and communications of the Flagstaff PD. No matter how much she dreaded the truth, Jordan had to find out, had to dig deeper.

There were only two things she knew for sure. Whatever had happened to Abigail wasn't an accident. And she—Jordan Reese-Waltham—was to blame.

Chapter Eight

On the road again, Blake sprawled in the passenger seat of the Chevy Suburban, enjoying the extra legroom. Both the Prius and the helo had been okay, but the seating in this wide SUV gave him the room to spread out—pure luxury. He kept a watchful eye on Jordan as she drove north on the highway. She hadn't slept at all last night, but exhaustion took second place to the grief, horror and guilt that consumed her. The muscles in her jaw were tensed. Her lips stretched in a taut, straight line. As sunlight slanted across the horizon, she turned off the headlights and slipped on a pair of sunglasses that didn't cover the dark smudges below her eyes.

After she'd told him in a few terse sentences about Abigail's "accident," she'd put on a determinedly upbeat expression that he recognized as her mom mask. No matter what else was happening, even if the sky was falling, she wouldn't allow her emotions to show because she had to protect the kids, didn't want to scare them.

Though he wasn't buying her stoic attitude for one hot minute and knew she was hurting, he admired her ability to compartmentalize her feelings, a skill he often practiced when planning a mission or facing the negative results of failure. After the incident with the IED when the docs told him that he might never walk again, he'd gritted his teeth and tripled his time in physical therapy. Instead of raging at the fates or breaking down in tears, he'd concentrated on what was possible. More exercise would improve his odds of recovery. He didn't allow himself to dwell on the likelihood of being assigned to a desk job. Instead, he spent his time considering different future possibilities…maybe a life that included Jordan. He always tried to present a strong front to the rest of the world.

The shrink had told him that compartmentalizing led to increased stress and PTSD. He'd advised Blake to face his traumas rather than avoiding them, because they wouldn't go away. How long could he ignore the pain? Lock away the anger about muscles and nerves that didn't work? Yeah, the shrink might be right. Someday, Blake might unlatch the compartment and allow misery to pour over him. But not today.

Chatter from the twins in the back seat alerted him to the probability that they sensed something was wrong. Like him, the boys didn't buy their mother's fierce calm. Blake needed to deal with them. If the kiddos didn't settle down, this six-to-eight-hour cross-country leg of their journey would feel like an eternity.

In a low voice, he spoke to Mama Bear. "The cubs need feeding. We can grab breakfast at a drive-through."

Though he hadn't seemed to be paying attention, Alex picked up on what Blake said. "Yeah, Mom. We're starving."

"I want a muffin," Cooper said. "Two muffins and bacon."

"No eating in the car," Jordan said automatically. "You know the rules."

"And no junk food," Cooper said.

"No fair." Alex pouted. "We gotta eat something."

"When we get to Salina, we'll stop for breakfast," she

said. "Keep watching the road signs. You can count down the miles."

"Salina is still in Utah," Blake said, "but that's where we hook into eastbound I-70. After that, our route couldn't be simpler."

He'd driven this way many times before, sticking to I-70 past Grand Junction and through the Rockies to his cabin at Ice Mountain. If the worst happened and Hugh got wind of their destination, Blake knew how to elude anyone who tried to follow.

Behind him, he heard the inevitable questions from the twins.

"Are we there yet?" Alex asked. "How much longer?"

"How many miles?" Cooper piled on.

Blake made approximate calculations from the last mileage sign for Salina. "We've got thirty-three minutes to go."

There was a chorus of groans and complaints and statements about how they'd pass out from starvation before they got to Salina. Blake figured that the twins weren't much different from newbie recruits. The best way to get them to cooperate was to distract them. With recruits, he could wave a shiny beer can in front of their eyes. And with the five-year-old boys… Blake turned on the screens for the rear-seat entertainment centers and handed the kids the attached headphones.

"Cartoons," Cooper cheered.

"Awesome," his brother joined in.

The sound accompanying the screen images went silent when the headphones were activated. So did the twins. Blake glanced at Jordan and said, "I'm sure you'd rather not have them glued to the cartoon channel, but I need a break."

"Not a problem," she said. "Do you think they can hear us talking?"

He glanced into the rear and saw matching rapt expressions on the boys' faces as they stared at a cartoon Dalmatian in a firefighter's helmet. He tested their ability to hear by saying in a normal voice, "Did I ever tell you about how I can fly? My favorite food is raw squid."

No reaction from the peanut gallery. He turned to Jordan and said, "They won't overhear a word we say."

"About Abigail." In spite of his reassurance, her tone was soft. Her voice trembled with worry. "Her house is high in the Peaks outside Flagstaff, and those roads are relatively narrow with some hairpin turns. It's conceivable that she had an accident after the fundraiser."

"Conceivable," he echoed.

"But she drove that route every single day."

He wanted real information, facts. "When will you hear back from your computer genius?"

"He didn't give me a specific time."

"Are you ever going to tell me his name?"

"He uses several different handles," she said. "The guy is a legendary hacker with contacts at the highest and the lowest levels. He practically lives on the dark web, and he doesn't like for people to know him. I call him Spike."

No surprise that she'd buddied up to a scary cybergenius. Sweet, little Jordan with her shining brown curls and innocent blue eyes had a talent for attracting and taming complex people. "We should wait for Spike to get back to us with the facts from the Flagstaff PD. In the meantime, I think it's smart to assume the worst and plan from there."

"So we assume that…" Her voice caught in her throat and dropped to a whisper. "We've got to assume she's dead."

"Murdered by your ex-husband and his security chief," Blake said. "Let's also assume they questioned her. Before her so-called accident, how much did she tell them? How much did she know?"

A tear leaked from the corner of Jordan's eye, but she kept her attention on the road. "Every time I talked to her, I told her we weren't playing a game. Damn it, I warned her to be careful. Since I didn't want her to be forced to lie, I never mentioned the route I planned to take or that our destination was Ice Mountain."

"Before last night, did you talk to her about the time we spent together in Colorado?"

"I don't think so. The only time we talked about you was when you came to visit and meet the boys who were two-year-old terrorists in diapers."

That long weekend in Flagstaff nearly broke his heart. Jordan glowed with happiness, and the kids looked just like her. Her husband had been out of town, and Blake had desperately wanted to step into that role. "It's when I met Abigail, and she insisted on giving me her phone number."

"You talked to her yesterday," she said, "when you were looking for me. Did you say anything incriminating?"

"I didn't know squat. Until I met you in the garden shed, I had no idea we'd be going on the run. When I talked on the phone to Abigail, I didn't have a damn thing to tell her." He shrugged. "I might have whined a little bit."

She gave a snort and wiped away her tear. "You're cute when you whine."

"No man ever needs to hear that they're cute."

"Well, you are. With your dimples and crinkled forehead."

"Please. Stop."

She exhaled in a gush, and her mouth relaxed into something resembling a smile as she glanced over her shoulder into the rear seats. "I'm glad they're quiet, but I'm not going to let them watch cartoons all day."

He stayed focused on the current problem. "Assume she was questioned. You didn't tell her anything. And I didn't, either. Earlier last night, I bumped into Gruber on the grounds behind the mansion but didn't tell him anything. I don't think we have a problem."

"She was murdered. I call that a big problem." Her brief smile was gone, and her mood darkened. "It's my fault."

From his years in combat, Blake knew that blaming yourself for the loss of someone else, especially in combat, didn't make logical sense. The only person responsible was the one who pulled the trigger. But he understood how Jordan felt. Losing a friend was never easy.

He reached across the center console and stroked her arm while the Suburban rushed along the two-lane, divided highway leading to Salina. The dawn light spread across the high plains where the foothills had turned a dusty autumn brown and the Valley Mountains were iced with new snow. Weather predictions for the West indicated an early winter, and he hoped the heavy snow would hold off until Jordan finished her investigation into her ex-husband.

After giving her arm a final squeeze, he said, "I should use this quiet time to return messages from two people Hugh contacted to get information about me."

"How would he know these people?"

"Wouldn't take much to track them down. I noticed the messages before I destroyed my phone."

"Make your calls." She gave a knowing nod. "It's always wise to take care of business while the kids are absorbed by something else."

Using her super-encrypted phone, he texted his commanding officer and the clinical supervisor at Walter Reed to let them know he'd gotten their messages and his phone was out of order. Without mentioning his location, he indicated that he'd be on vacation and would stay in touch before he was expected to return to duty next month. He had one more call to return. It came from the man himself: Hugh Waltham.

When they reached Salina, Jordan drove into the parking lot for a diner beside a corner lot with a couple of scrubby pine trees and a small playground. As soon as they were out of the car, the twins launched themselves onto the monkey bars. In contrast, Jordan moved slowly, as though her sneakers were made of concrete. She took a seat on the bench beside a picnic table to watch the kids while Blake went inside and ordered breakfast to go, including a giant coffee for himself and a decaf for Jordan. Like it or not, the woman needed to sleep.

He brought the take-out bags of muffins, egg-and-sausage sandwiches, Tater Tots and orange juice to the playground and set them on the picnic table that Jordan had swept clean of fallen leaves. Though the air held a chill, the morning sunlight beamed down on the playground, warming their little group. While the twins tore into their food like starving critters, Jordan lifted her sunglasses and gazed across the picnic table at him. Though she hadn't recovered her equilibrium after the tragedy of losing her friend, her eyes reflected openness and trust as she shared her grief. Being a part of this little family felt special. He'd do anything to protect them.

And that included making a phone call to Hugh. Taking her super-encrypted phone, he left the table. "I'll be back. I need to put through one more call."

He strolled down the sidewalk in the small town, passing unlit storefronts. It was still too early for most places to open. The gas station on the corner showed signs of activity, and the lights were on in the pharmacy. But the only other signs of life centered on the diner.

Blake stared at the screen on the phone. Before he punched in Hugh's number, he reminded himself of the need for control. This callback was supposed to be a simple courtesy, but his real goals were twofold. First, he hoped to distance himself from Jordan so Hugh wouldn't follow clues that pointed toward him. Second, he wanted to learn how much Hugh had figured out about Jordan's escape.

Though he'd never met Jordan's ex-husband, Blake recognized his voice from Hugh's appearances on news shows. He introduced himself. "This is Captain Blake Delaney. I'm returning your call."

"You're the marine," Hugh said.

"Yes."

"What took you so long to call back?"

"My phone is broken."

"You and I seem to be missing connections," Hugh said. "My security chief, Ray Gruber, met you on the grounds outside my house last night, but I didn't see you inside."

"I changed my mind about attending a party."

"Any particular reason?"

"I'm not accustomed to galas. String quartets, canapés and ball gowns scare me more than fire fights." *Not entirely a lie.* "I walked for a while, called a car service and went back to my motel."

Blake felt like he was talking too much. He ran his thumb across his lips in a reminder to himself to let Hugh speak and spill the beans.

"You know my ex-wife," Hugh said. "Did you come to the fundraiser to see her?"

"I hoped to."

"I see." His tone held a combination of disgust and disbelief. "Did you find her?"

"No."

A complicated lie about trying to visit Jordan at the Institute occurred to him, but he said nothing. From the television news shows, he recalled an image of Hugh. Not just another talking head, the political consultant from Arizona was younger and better-looking than most, with blond hair, tanned cheeks and swampy green eyes. His features balanced in near-perfect symmetry, and his extremely white teeth glistened like a shark's.

Hugh cleared his throat and asked, "Did you know Abigail Preston?"

His use of the past tense was chilling. "I met her a few years ago."

"And you spoke to her recently."

"She told me about the fundraiser and suggested that Jordan would be there to show her support for your campaign. I wanted to see her."

"Hah! Abigail wouldn't tell you that." This time, Hugh didn't bother to camouflage his disdain. "My ex-wife doesn't support me. She holds me back, drags me down."

Blake gritted his rear molars so hard that his jaw hurt. At this point in their conversation, he should probably make some comment to show he was on Hugh's side and considered Jordan a difficult woman. But he couldn't do it, not even in jest. "Why did you call me?"

"I know you were in love with her. Having you turn up on my doorstep on the same night that she staged an escape from the Institute was too great a coincidence to ignore."

He hadn't mentioned the kidnapping—an odd omission. "Escaped? You make it sound like she was being held prisoner."

"Part of her delusion," Hugh said, smoothly covering the real story. "She's deranged, a very sick woman."

His practiced politician's voice was supposed to convey deep concern. An accomplished liar, he hit all the right notes to communicate sincerity and truth...and self-control. Hugh Waltham wasn't the kind of guy who spilled the beans. He danced like a classical sword fighter, agile with a rapier, darting close for a touché and pulling back.

Not my style. Blake charged forward with a broadsword, hacking and thwacking. He wanted to demand information about Abigail's so-called accident and Jordan's incarceration at the Institute. This slick, cowardly political creep had watched while Jordan's wrists were slashed. Hugh Waltham deserved to be smeared with the cold, hard knowledge of his crimes, but Blake knew his satisfaction would be short-lived.

"I can't help you," he said. *Even if I could, I wouldn't.*

"Don't underestimate yourself," Hugh said. "Come over to the house. We'll talk."

"I've already left town. I'm on my way to visit a friend in Texas."

"I intend to stay in touch with you, Captain. What's your friend's name?"

"Telling you—or anybody else—wouldn't be right. This is a lady friend."

Hugh chuckled. "She's a married woman, isn't she? Well, well, Captain Delaney, you're not as innocent as you pretend to be. I'm not surprised. To paraphrase Eleanor Roosevelt: 'Marines have the cleanest bodies, the filthiest minds, the highest morale and the lowest morals of any group of animals I've ever seen.'"

"She finished that quote with one more sentence. 'Thank God for the US Marine Corps.'" *And don't you forget it.*

"We have more in common than both of us falling in love with Jordan. Trust me about this, Captain. She'll hurt you just like she hurt me. You'd be wise to stay in touch."

He'd rather cuddle up with a nest of rattlesnakes. Blake straightened his shoulders and retraced his steps to the diner. "Don't count on it."

"Why not? Are you already committed to play for Team Jordan?"

"I'm on Team USA," Blake said, "dedicated to fighting for democracy, decency and human rights. Seems to me that you and I don't have one damn thing in common."

He ended the call with a sincere hope that he'd never hear Hugh Waltham's smooth, conniving voice again.

Chapter Nine

"Mom, wake up!"

"Come on, Mom, open your eyes!"

Jordan went from deep slumber to instant alert—a survival mechanism of all mothers who sensed their offspring needed them. From being curled up in the passenger seat with a parka tucked around her shoulders, she jolted awake. Her fingers drew into fists, ready for battle. Her posture straightened, and her feet planted on the floorboards. The car was parked at the side of a road with the headlights cutting through a thick wall of ponderosa pine and boulders.

She blinked. The skies above the horizon were streaked with magenta and coral. *Almost nightfall. When did that happen? I must have been asleep for hours.* The last thing she remembered was a lunch break at a taco shack in Fruita near Grand Junction.

The interior light in the Suburban went on. She saw Blake behind the steering wheel, then she peered into the back seat where her five-year-old twins were rolling their eyes like teenagers and giving her a hard time about being a lazybones. She cleared her throat. "Where are we?"

"Colorado," the boys shouted in unison. "In a forest. On a mountain."

"Ice Mountain," Cooper said, ever vigilant in reporting the details.

Squinting at Blake, she asked, "Why are we stopped?"

"We're less than a mile away from the cabin."

A chorus of cheers erupted from the back seat. Cooper said, "You've got to see this place. Blake's built it himself."

"Is that so?" She knew he hadn't.

"Yeah," Alex said. "A man's home is his castle."

"Did Blake teach you that?"

Before the boys could answer, he interrupted. "I called ahead to my buddy, Chester, who lives across the lake. Do you remember him?"

"Of course, I do." A friend of the family who'd known Blake since childhood, Chester had encouraged him to join the US Marine Corps and to purchase this cabin with another friend. She thought of Chester as a father figure for Blake, replacing his biological father who left before he was five.

Absent fathers seemed to be a recurring theme in her life, and she experienced a stab of guilt for causing her twins the same pain she'd felt. Her own dad had died when she was eleven. She shook her shoulders, not needing to think about death in the family…or among dear friends. "Why did you call Chester?"

"To get the cabin ready for us. I didn't want to walk into any surprises."

Her brain clicked into gear, and she realized that he was talking about a possible ambush. They'd already discussed his connection to this hideaway. Eleven years ago— just after his first deployment—Blake bought the cabin in partnership with a guy who put his name on the deed. His partner had been killed earlier this year. He left his share of the cabin to Blake who kept the taxes paid and managed the upkeep with help from his neighbor Chester but had never gotten around to legally changing the deed, which meant there was no official record of his ownership. No one, other than very close friends, knew about Blake's connection to this property on Ice Mountain. "And what did Chester tell you?"

"He opened up the cabin, and everything is A-OK. The toilet flushes. The heat is turned on. And he stocked the fridge with some basic groceries."

When she looked into the back seat, a genuine smile lifted the corners of her mouth. "What do you say, boys? Should we check out the cabin?"

While the kids shouted agreement, Blake eased the Suburban forward on the narrow, curving road through the forest. Excitement from the twins infected her as well. They were almost home safe. She'd pulled off the first part of her escape from Hugh and his minions, and that wasn't the only reason she was glad to be back to the cabin on Ice Mountain. It was here, seven years ago, that she'd spent an idyllic five days with Blake. They'd made love every night, talked about their dreams, laughed and hiked through the pine-scented forest until they were exhausted. She had seriously considered marrying him.

When the Suburban rounded a final curve, the shadows parted to reveal a two-story log cabin with a gently slanted, gabled roof of faded red shingles. The porch light cast a golden glow onto a covered porch that stretched across the first floor. Red hummingbird feeders dangled above the porch railings, and the tinkling sounds of wind chimes serenaded them.

He parked in the gravel drive to the right of the porch. The twins unfastened their seat belts but stayed in the boosters.

"Mom, Mom, Mom, can we get out?"

"Can we go, can we go?"

"Wait for us outside the front door," she said, "but yeah, you can go."

The back doors flung open, and they dashed through the trees.

"Why did you tell them to wait?" Blake asked.

"I seem to recall several security measures at this cabin, and I wanted to be sure the front door wouldn't explode when it was touched by unauthorized little fingers."

"Good point."

"There's a lot of other stuff I remember. Good stuff."

"Me, too." He gave her a grin. "During the five days and four nights we stayed here, I proposed marriage three times. Why did you turn me down, Jordan?"

"As you know, men and women are different."

"Agreed."

"When men fall in love, they're more romantic and less realistic than women. Most of the stories of unrequited love are about men who are pining away for the first woman they ever kissed or a great beauty seen from afar. On the other hand, women are down-to-earth and practical. They like to see bank statements and evidence of steady employment."

"You've given this a lot of thought," he said. "Did you write an article on the topic?"

She bobbed her head. "An interview with two sex therapists—a man and a woman. I agreed with the woman."

"Not surprised."

"Like her, I'm pragmatic. I looked at our relationship and evaluated. The sex was amazing. The same was true for the camaraderie. It was great to be with someone who could always make me laugh. However, we were both defined by our careers. I couldn't ask you to give up being a marine. And vice versa for me and journalism."

He pushed open his car door. "Things are different now."

What does that mean? Unfortunately, now wasn't the time for a deep discussion. On the porch, the boys were bouncing back and forth between the railing and the side of the log cabin. "We'd better let those two jumping beans go inside before they break the door down."

"FYI, there are no weird locking devices, but it'll take a minute for them to figure out the keypad system. If they get it wrong, we get blasted with an earsplitting alarm."

She fell into step behind him. "Did the kids drive you up a wall while I was sleeping?"

"We were cool. I gave them a history lesson about Indigenous people and pioneers coming west. Cooper had a couple of stories I've never heard. Mostly from educational television."

He unlocked the front door and disabled the alarm using the keypad, which he promptly reactivated when they were inside. When she was here before, she had questioned him about the need for security, and he explained that since the cabin was vacant for long periods of time, he needed the alarm to scare off burglars. Any break-in also sent a phone notification to Chester, who could be at his front door in ten minutes. If she'd come here without him, the alarm would have been a problem, but now the precautions reassured her. Every extra ounce of protection was welcome.

Blake strode through the front room with the moss rock fireplace, a sofa, comfy chairs for reading and a long walnut dinner table with eight chairs. He directed the boys. "The kitchen is back there. My office is tucked away on the other side of the staircase, and the bathroom and washing machine are there, too. Upstairs, there are two bedrooms."

The floor plan took a moment to register in her mind. Two bedrooms meant one for the twins and a master for her and Blake. One bedroom, and she remembered one very comfortable king-size bed. When she'd first initiated this escape plan, he hadn't been part of the picture. Now, Blake stood front and center.

They hadn't talked about sleeping arrangements, and she didn't know what to say or how to react. Was it too soon for them to dive into the sack together? Was she expecting too much, pushing their relationship forward too fast? On the other hand, if they didn't sleep together very soon, she'd be overwhelmed by some very uncharacteristic leanings toward romantic love. *Hah! That's what I get for claiming I'm immune and don't get carried away.* She'd been so glib about her cool, pragmatic nature. In truth, the idea of lying beside him on the great, big bed sparked a fire in her belly. If she didn't get herself under control, she'd melt into a sloppy little puddle of unrequited lust.

BLAKE BELONGED HERE in his cabin on Ice Mountain. This was home.

He loved his mom and two half sisters, but their contact was minimal, and he hadn't lived with his family since he went to college on a football scholarship. With the twins walking on either side, he showed off the kitchen and returned to the staircase near the front door where their mother stood, frozen in thought. Her stillness worried him, and he was glad when she drifted toward the kitchen.

To the boys, he said, "Your bedroom is upstairs."

"Can we see it?"

"Sure, knock yourself out."

"I love this place," Alex announced as he clambered up the stairs.

"Me, too." Though he hadn't built the cabin, despite what Cooper thought, he'd added a two-car garage and done a ton of work on the septic system and the well. Running water and a flush toilet were two of the major reasons Chester had advised him to buy this three-acre property when it came on the market. Way back then, Blake hadn't understood the importance of water rights in Colorado and a well that could provide a steady flow. He'd grown up in Illinois, in cities where water was a given. Proudly, he continued the grand tour as the kids rejoined him and they went to the bathroom/laundry room.

"How come there's no bathtub?" Cooper asked.

"Real men like showers," Alex said.

From the front room, Jordan spoke up. "I like showers, too."

Instead of debating the question of which method got you cleaner, Blake launched into a lecture on water conservation that included not using too much water when you brushed your teeth, not washing clothes until you've got a full load and not taking a shower every day. "Not unless you're really dirty."

"Got it. Really dirty." Alex nodded. "I'm going to like living here."

Jordan appeared in the doorway. "It's a fantastic bathroom, but I like the kitchen better. Chester left us a selection of ham and cheese for sandwiches. And chips."

The boys ran toward the kitchen, and he joined Jordan in the narrow hallway. "Does the cabin live up to your memories?"

She gave him a quick hug and stepped back, putting distance between them. "I thought you were going to take down the wall between the kitchen and dining room to make a counter."

"A pending project." There was always something. "I'll unpack the car and put it away in the garage while you feed the kids."

"And then, we have something important to talk about."

He guessed she wanted to discuss plans for the investigation into her ex-husband's affairs. "You're going to start making lists, aren't you?"

"I always do. I need lists and schedules to stay on target."

"What's the number one item?"

"After dinner and getting settled, there's only one task

for tonight." She turned her face away from him and studied a watercolor painting of a mountain lake that hung on the wall between the bathroom and the study. "We can talk about it later."

Obviously, she was hedging, and her unwillingness to bring up a troublesome issue bothered him. "Tell me now."

"Sleeping arrangements." She refused to look him in the eye. "There's only one king-size bed in the master bedroom, right?"

"Correct." He couldn't believe this was a big deal. Did she think he was going to jump her? Force her to have sex as payment for using his cabin? He shoved open the door to his study and pointed to the full-size, foldout sleeper sofa against the wall. "I'll bunk there."

Relief splashed across her face. Apparently, the idea of sleeping with him freaked her out. "That doesn't seem fair. I should take the sleeper. It's not long enough for your legs."

"I'll manage."

Her phone dinged, and she took it from her pocket. "A text from Spike."

The computer genius had taken his time getting back to her. For a moment, Blake dared to hope the message would be good news about Abigail's accident.

As Jordan stared at the screen on the cell phone, her face crumpled and a tear leaked from her eye. "She's dead."

Don't cry. Damn it, don't. Other tears spilled down her cheeks, breaking through barriers he wasn't aware he'd built and making him feel helpless. He hated to see her— or anybody else—weep. When he heard the twins yelling from the kitchen about sandwiches, he was grateful for the distraction. They'd found a bag of corn chips and bottles of a strawberry-flavored drink. He took a step in their direction. "Should I make sandwiches?"

"Stay with me." She passed him the phone. "My eyes won't focus. Read the rest of the text for me."

The tiny print covered most of the screen and dribbled onto another. Spike's precise details about contusions, concussions and internal brain bleed sounded like a medical examiner's report and made him wonder how an outside computer guy managed to access those records.

He skipped the painful details of her physical condition and summarized from the police report. "Her BMW broke through a guardrail and flew off the mountain road. Not wearing her seat belt, she was thrown from the car. Her injuries were fatal. She smelled like booze."

Jordan hiccupped a sob.

He continued, "The state highway patrol and the Flagstaff PD will investigate. As of now, they're calling her death an accident, possibly a DUI."

"What?" She swabbed at her eyes. "Abigail wasn't a heavy drinker. How could they make that kind of mistake?"

Blake suspected the police had been influenced by Waltham and his many contacts. In his mind, he could almost hear the smooth politico talking about the tragedy and bemoaning Abigail's heavy alcohol consumption. "Spike has two more bits of unrelated information. I'm not sure how he taps into this stuff, but he's incredible."

"What does he say?"

"Number one: Hugh's security team, led by Gorilla Gruber, is working with Khaled. They're looking for the Prius in Las Vegas but haven't found the car."

"Nothing about Harvey? Or Emily and the chopper?"

"Not a peep."

"That's good. They haven't figured out how we left town." She dabbed at her eyes again. The tears were gone. "Do they mention San Francisco?"

"Spike says no."

"You said there were two bits."

"I don't know what this means." He held up the phone and read verbatim. "Retired squirrel makes nest in Aspen—a multi-million-dollar house is pricey for Rockwell from Flagstaff."

"I'll explain later," she said.

Before his eyes, her expression transformed. No more crying, her gaze hardened. She was a fierce huntress who had sighted prey. He almost felt sorry for Rockwell from Flagstaff…whoever that was.

Chapter Ten

After being separated from her kids for three months, Jordan enjoyed the relative normalcy of making a dinner of sandwiches and corn chips, unpacking the few items in their duffels and supervising while the boys took showers and brushed their teeth. She noticed tiny differences in their height and weight, scrutinized every new scrape or bruise and wondered if Alex had cut his own hair. Cooper showed signs of not sleeping well, with dark circles under his eyes, and he seemed to be squinting as if he needed glasses. Alex had perfected the embarrassed eye roll and developed a new habit of stubbornly sticking out his chin. Though she hadn't expected Hugh or Helena to directly abuse the kids, her ex-husband had never been a loving, nurturing father. The psychological injuries he inflicted would be more difficult to detect, but she knew the boys were hurt when their father dismissed them or ignored them or sternly demanded that they always, always, always be the best, the winner, first place.

In their second-floor bedroom of the cabin, Jordan tucked the twins under the heavy quilts, turned on nightlights and settled into a rocking chair under a lamp to read a bedtime excerpt from *The Hobbit*, which was the one item Cooper had chosen to bring with him. The small, well-worn volume trembled in her hands as she remembered. Before they fled from the mansion, Abigail had been reading this book to the twins, using different voices with dreadful British accents for each of the characters. She'd been a good, loyal friend. If only she'd listened to Jordan's warnings, things would have turned out differently.

"Page sixty-three," Cooper said. "That's where Abigail stopped."

Of course, he kept track. Tolkien wasn't his favorite but a close second to Harry Potter.

"Mom," Alex said, "is there really such a thing as dwarves? Do they live in caves? Some of them might be around here."

"We'll look."

When she started reading, Jordan didn't attempt to mimic Abigail's high-spirited performance. Instead, she dedicated every word to her friend's memory. *Oh, Abigail, with your bright brown eyes and pixie haircut, you'll be often mourned and deeply missed.*

In minutes, the twins succumbed to slumber. Jordan doused the lamp but kept the night-lights lit. If the boys needed to go to the bathroom in the middle of the night, they'd find the path leading down the staircase.

Mentally, she prepared herself for a confrontation with Blake. He'd been insulted by her attitude about sleeping together, and she was certain that he'd gallantly insist on taking the sleeper bed in the study even though his long legs would be cramped. She peeked into the master bedroom, where he'd collapsed across the king-size bed with his arms flung wide. *Out cold.* He'd already kicked off his boots and discarded his parka.

She crept onto the bed and gazed down at him. Stubble outlined his jaw. His short, golden-blond hair looked messier than she'd ever seen it. Breathing heavily, his lips parted, and she was tempted to lean down and kiss him until he was awake. *And then...what?* He'd kiss her back, and they'd be off to the races, even though the kids were sleeping right across the hall.

Instead, she scooted off the bed, pulled the denim-colored comforter over him and turned off the light. On her way out, she grabbed her duffel bag and carried it down the staircase into the study. After she showered, changed into flannel pajamas and converted the sofa into a sleeper, she stretched out on the bed—which left plenty of extra room for her tootsies—and told herself to relax. If she'd been a praying woman, she would have expressed a combination of gratitude and sorrow. Thanks for the successful escape from Flagstaff. And sadness about Abigail.

Her eyelids refused to close. She rolled onto her side and consciously tried to wish the tension away from her muscles, but she couldn't let go. Her fingertips danced on the pillowcase, writing an invisible list, and her toes twitched with a desire to run. *Settle down! You need your rest.* But her brain whirred and pinged in high gear. If she didn't get these details out of her head, she'd never fall asleep. *So much to do. So little time to do it.*

Bolting from the sleeper sofa, she slipped into cozy socks and her puffer jacket before she sat in the swivel chair behind Blake's desk. Still a bit chilly, she pulled up the hood on her deep purple coat and rubbed her cheek against the fake fur lining. Fingers spread on the desktop, she looked down at the flat, blank space before her. *Where to start?* Blake had a laptop she could use, and she had her flamingo flash drive, which she took from her duffel and centered on the desk. She flashed on a memory of handing over the penguin flash drive to Hornsby. She was lucky to have so many good friends.

Should she start by reviewing data? Not yet. Too complicated.

"Lists," she said aloud. "I need to set my agenda."

In the middle-right desk drawer, she found a yellow

legal pad. In a clear mason jar that sat on the desk beside a stapler and a brass lamp, she saw an assortment of pens in different colors. *Perfect!* Color-coding her schedule made it easier to follow. For the easy tasks, she wrote with calming turquoise ink. First, she needed to go shopping to pick up winter clothes and other items for the kids. Then she'd take a trip to the grocery store for supplies and food. The page quickly filled. Even these everyday errands would be difficult since she didn't know the location of the nearest market and shops. Luckily, money was no object. When she first moved out of Hugh's mansion, she'd established a new identity complete with a driver's license, library card, bank account and credit cards to access her cash from savings.

She flipped to the next page in the legal pad and picked up the red pen, symbolizing urgency. Across the top, in capital letters, she wrote: "Accountant from Flagstaff."

Tim Rockwell, aka Rocky the Flying Squirrel, had been off the grid for the past several months. According to Spike, he was now in Aspen. She needed to meet with him, to convince him to testify against Hugh or, at least, to provide her with documentation to back up her accusations of fraud and money laundering.

She'd left the door to the study ajar in case the kids needed to find her, but Blake knocked anyway before opening it wider. "Jordan?"

"Come in," she said softly.

His gaze went from her hooded, purple jacket to her flannel jammies decorated with leaping reindeer to her fuzzy pink socks. "Are you trying to turn me on?"

She stuck a woolly foot into the air. "You like?"

"At least you're warm. Maybe even hot?"

"Want to find out?"

"I'll take a chance on getting burned." He licked his lips. "Where should I touch? What needs to be kissed?"

This was the closest they'd come to privacy since they'd met on the grounds behind the mansion. The twins were still nearby, tucked into their beds upstairs, but if Blake closed and locked the door to the study, they'd be mostly alone. She grinned. "Have you been stifling your lusty passion all this time?"

"Just trying to be appropriate." He took the legal pad from the desk and flipped to the first page. "How do you plan to do all this shopping?"

"Drive to a market?"

"I'm serious." He flopped onto the bed, which was—as she'd suspected—much too short for his six-foot-four-inch body. "We need to use precautions. The first rule should be to keep the twins secret. Anybody who sees those two little monkeys will remember them. Might as well send out an alert to Hugh and his minions: Pretty Mom and Twin Boys Shopping Near Aspen."

She knew he was right. Disguising herself wouldn't be all that hard. During the years she'd spent doing undercover research, she'd learned to alter her appearance with a change in hairstyle and makeup. She could easily pass for a mountain mama, but her adorable boys attracted too much attention. She suspected Blake, who was as muscular and handsome as a superhero, had a similar problem with being memorable, even though the ski bums and mountain men were a good-looking bunch. Blake had the additional problem of people in the area knowing him. If they went out together, he couldn't introduce her.

"I can manage a trip to the store on my own," she said.

"How about if we split the list? I'll do half in the morning. You finish in the afternoon."

"Fair enough." Several other projects fell under the category of urgent. Getting online and onto the dark web required expert instruction from Spike. Plus she needed to mine her old contacts and develop new ones. This inves-

tigation covered a lot more territory than her usual journalistic articles. She needed to provide the appropriate
district attorney with enough evidence to convene a grand
jury and charge Hugh.

"Rockwell from Aspen," Blake said, reading the second page of her list. "Is this the squirrel Spike was talking about?"

Immediately, she hushed him. "Keep your voice down.
The less the twins know, the better."

"Agreed, but I'm not a kid, and I want a briefing on
your current plan."

Not accustomed to working with a partner, she hated
to share her information. "Maybe tomorrow we'll find
time to talk."

Lying on his side, he propped his head on his fist. His
gaze narrowed as he studied her expression. "You don't
trust me."

"Good guess."

"Not guessing," he said. "I know you better than you
realize, Jordan. You can't hide your feelings from me."

"Is that so?" Nobody else could read her like Blake
could. "What makes you think I'm holding back?"

"When you lie, the right corner of your mouth twitches.
If you're hiding something, your eyelids lower a fraction
of an inch."

"You sound like an interrogator. Or a profiler."

"I've learned some self-preservation techniques. I need
guideposts to understand what's going on with you, and it's
smart to analyze your microexpressions." His lips spread
wide in a grin, and the dimples appeared to distract her.
"Here's what happens after you change your mind about
holding back: your eyes pop wide open in a flash. I like
that look. It happens right before you unbutton your blouse
and wriggle your jeans down your hips. Or your pajamas."

Not something she intended to do at the moment. "We should both go to sleep…in our separate bedrooms."

"Not until you tell me what's going on."

"I can't," she whispered. "It's too complicated. Hugh has committed scores of crimes ranging from larceny to money laundering to fraud, and maybe to murder. He has dozens of accomplices scattered across three or more western states. I don't even know where to start."

"At the beginning." Apparently, he had no intention of dropping this subject until he had answers.

"Let it go, Blake. It'll be easier for you to understand the big picture when I have the computer programs up and running."

He unfolded himself from the sleeper sofa, crossed the office and stood on the opposite side of the desk. "Here's the deal, Jordan—you're an amazing reporter. One of your best skills is breaking complex issues into logical bites. I want to know what we're up against. Talk to me."

"Not here." She clenched her jaw, determined to hold back. But resistance was futile. He was wearing her down. "I know the boys look like they're sound asleep, but they've got super-hearing, like bats. Even from upstairs, they can listen."

"And you don't want them to overhear and think you're bad-mouthing their pop."

"That's correct." If Hugh was guilty of half the crimes she suspected, that knowledge would be difficult for his sons to accept. She wanted to shield them from their father's evil.

Blake came around the desk and turned the swivel chair so she was facing him. He took her hand. "Come with me. We'll go outside to talk."

"And leave the kids here? Unguarded?"

"If anybody attempts to break in, an earsplitting alarm will sound."

"And if they open the door?"

"Same thing. Loud whooping alarm. I'm guessing your boys will love it." He tugged gently at her hand. "Come on, you're already wearing your parka."

She jammed her feet into sneakers, noticing that he'd already donned his boots. He grabbed his parka and slipped it on. "You're ready to go. Did you plan all along to take me outside?"

"The thought entered my mind."

At the front door, he disarmed the alarm system and set it to reengage in one minute, after they stepped onto the porch. In the stillness of the surrounding forest, the glow from the round, full hunter's moon lit the skies above the tall spires of trees and jagged granite rock formations. She saw no other lights. No neighbors in sight. No cars on the narrow dirt road at the base of the steep hill below the cabin.

She inhaled and exhaled with a sigh. The crisp breeze carried the scent of pine resin. A pleasant chill pushed inside her jacket, and she zipped up.

On the right side of the cabin, he found a winding path that led uphill to a clearing—a route she remembered fondly from their visit so many years ago. They'd made love in this small mountain glen, and life had seemed nearly perfect. At that time, she'd thought her experiences working for big-city newspapers and magazines combined with real-life moments in war zones had made her worldly, intelligent and capable of handling anything. *What a joke!* Though not helpless, she'd been naive.

Becoming the mother of twins had taught her more about life than any armed conflict or newsroom deadline barked by ferocious editors. Her deep, transformative love for the boys was unlike anything she'd felt before. She'd grown emotionally. The current threat from her ex-husband

and the danger she now faced had forced her to mature in a different, more painful way.

She paced to the edge of the tree line where leaves on the low shrubs had turned yellow and crimson. Pivoting, she faced Blake—a muscular silhouette with moonlight tangled in his hair. "I'm a different woman now than I was seven years ago. It's not the same as when we were lovers."

"I know." When he walked slowly toward her, she noticed a hitch in his step. He continued, "I've spent a lot of my adult life in war zones, but I somehow believed that I was going to live forever. Confined in the hospital after we hit the IED, I shook hands with death. And it changed me."

She looked past him down the slope to the outline of the cabin where faint streaks of light glimmered through curtained windows. The idea of moving any farther away from the twins made her nervous. This was far enough. A circular firepit made of stones occupied the center of the clearing. A long wooden bench and a couple of tree stumps provided seating. Sitting, she faced the cabin. "It's peaceful here."

"We can't let ourselves get too comfortable." He prowled across a carpet of pine needles and twigs, pausing to peer into the darkness. "We may have eluded Hugh for the moment with the trip through Las Vegas and the unexpected drive to Colorado, but we can't underestimate him. He's dangerous."

"I know."

She didn't want to be reminded, but Blake was one hundred percent correct. Though momentarily comfy, she needed to plot her next escape route and to find somewhere safe for the twins. Though she hated to imagine a scenario where Hugh would hurt the children, she had to consider the possibility. If the choice came down to eliminating them or saving his own skin, she knew which option he'd pick.

A shiver trickled down her spine. Coming up with a future escape plan climbed to the very top of her list of priorities. She'd need a new color of ink for her legal pad. And she'd also need Blake's advice. He knew this land around his cabin intimately.

He sat on the bench beside her and lightly caressed her cheek. "I wish I could stay here with you all night, kissing those soft lips and getting to know the woman you've become. But I don't think we should be away from the boys."

"Thanks for understanding."

"Yeah, I'm a peach." He patted her cheek and pulled his hand away. "You've got fifteen minutes to tell me about your ex-husband's crimes and your investigation. I need to know, Jordan. We need to change this escape effort into a pursuit."

"Exactly." She liked the way that sounded.

"We'll put together enough evidence to make sure Hugh will never be able to come after you or the boys again."

"I'll be stalking him." The thought gave her a buzz of satisfaction.

"There's that look," Blake said. "You've made up your mind."

Not the first time she'd tracked down a story and stitched the pieces into a coherent whole. She knew the techniques of interview and research. She had the energy, drive and a whole lot of motivation.

Looking toward him, she opened her mind and started talking. "I'll start at the beginning. The first incident I uncovered was border fraud. Hugh used his political influence to open the border and allow weapons and contraband to flow across."

There it was: the tip of the iceberg. There was more, so much more, to come.

Chapter Eleven

Sitting on the wood bench at the edge of the forest, Blake tried not to be distracted by the glow of moonlight that played across Jordan's cheekbones and stubborn little jaw. It was hard for him to concentrate when she gazed at him with her enormous blue eyes, ringed by thick dark lashes. How could he think about anything other than how truly beautiful she was? *Get it together, dude. You're a marine, not a lovesick puppy dog.* He had to ignore his natural urges and pay attention.

"Are you listening?" she asked.

"Sure. Why wouldn't I be?"

"I want you to understand what we're up against, and I'm going to talk fast so we can go back inside and get some sleep. Agreed?"

"I'm ready for bed." *Not a lie.* In his opinion, going to bed was an excellent idea that didn't necessarily include sleep.

"Here goes."

She spewed a torrent of data—including names, dates and amounts of cash payments—showing how Waltham had arranged with state police and ICE officials to open a corridor for a Mexican cartel. Though Blake didn't know much about how drugs were packaged and shipped, he had a high level of expertise when it came to weaponry. If

Jordan's figures were correct, these semiautomatic guns, grenades and rocket launchers were enough to supply a small army.

"Wait." He held up his palm, halting this gush of information. "You've got plenty of evidence. Did you inform a prosecutor?"

"There are a couple of problems."

He assumed super-organized Jordan had efficiently labeled the obstacles. "Such as."

"I don't have clear chains of evidence to present in a court of law." She held up her index finger symbolizing number one. "That's because Hugh distances himself from the paperwork. Too much is hearsay. I've never actually seen the contraband weapons."

She popped up another finger. "Number two. My witnesses aren't about to come forward and talk to the feds."

He nodded. Betraying the cartel would be signing a death warrant. "What else?"

"Here's the biggie." She scowled. "I wanted to approach the attorney general's office in Arizona, but too many people on his staff were in Hugh's pocket. My ex knows everybody, and most of them owe him favors. The cops are no better. I can't very well hand him over to law enforcement when he's regularly making payoffs to many of them."

"Are you telling me that the entire legal system and all the police are corrupt?"

"Of course not. In spite of the rumors spread by Hugh and the guys in white coats at the Institute, I'm not completely paranoid. However…" She paused. "It's really hard to tell the good guys from the baddies. I didn't want to provoke all-out warfare between them."

As the pieces to this puzzle snapped into place, his brain finally got into gear. Blake understood betrayal and had encountered many such obstacles in combat zones. In addition to traitors in the military and among outside contractors, he faced tribal warlords who could be unpredictable and disloyal. "It's the same everywhere."

"They're all out for themselves."

"And whoever has the biggest war chest gets to call the shots. What about contacting the FBI or DEA?"

"Too much of a risk. If I got unlucky and reported Hugh to one of his sleazebag cronies, I'd be in deep trouble."

"When did you first become aware of the border fraud?"

"About a year and a half ago." She rose from the bench and took a step away from him. "Earlier than that, I had suspicions but not solid evidence. Turning in my husband was an extreme measure. I hesitated. I didn't want to destroy my family."

"What changed your mind?"

"Hugh beefed up his security force." She paced across the front of the clearing and looked down at the cabin. "Having so many armed guards around the house scared me."

"Hugh must have thought somebody else was after him."

"For a while I thought Abigail's husband, Stanley Preston, was on Hugh's enemy list because he was involved in border issues and protested the unfair treatment of immigrants. He and Hugh are both dynamic men. I could see them facing off with each other. But I read the situation wrong. Stanley, a defense attorney, was part of a team that represented a high-ranking member of the cartel."

"He and Hugh were working together."

"I think so." She took a step toward him, then pivoted in a graceful pirouette and stepped back toward the cabin. Her movements were part of a complicated dance, balancing her desire to find the truth with her love for her children.

He asked, "When you started digging, what did you find out?"

"After wasting a lot of time reading Hugh's bank statements and monitoring his computer records, I was on the verge of giving up. Don't get me wrong. I found a ton of wrongdoing, including the Las Vegas connection where Hugh was laundering cash payoffs through the casinos, but all my investigating seemed futile. Even if I produced enough evidence to have Hugh convicted of fraud, extortion and embezzlement, his sentence wouldn't amount to much more than a fine and less than five years in a white-collar prison."

"He'd lose his influence as a political consultant."

"And he couldn't run for the US Senate." She threw up her hands. "Not a big deal for him, especially if he'd stashed away a small fortune in offshore accounts. Anyway, I almost dropped the whole thing."

"What stopped you?"

"His crimes went from bad to worse. He transformed from being a greedy, money-grubbing sleaze to becoming nearly demonic. I swear there were times when I could almost see his horns and tail. I had to find a way to stop him. For myself…my kids…and others."

Her gestures became more vigorous as she built to a climax. Gently, he asked, "Are you all right?"

"If I'd acted more quickly… If I'd been braver…" She stopped moving and stood completely still. "I'll never know if he actually wielded the knife, but Hugh was responsible for the bloody murder of a young woman. Her name was Bianca Hernandez. She was sixteen and pregnant with twins."

Jordan's legs collapsed. Shuddering, she sank onto the bench beside him. Her head drooped forward on her chest. Her arms wrapped around her middle. When she'd been outlining Hugh's participation in fraud, embezzlement and money laundering, she'd been disgusted and outraged. The murder of a young woman was a heavier emotional burden. Blake wanted to comfort her, to touch her and tell her that everything was okay. But when he reached toward her, she flinched.

She spoke so quietly that the rustling of wind through the pines nearly swallowed her words. "I have to stop him before he kills again."

"How did you learn about what happened to Bianca?"

"Investigating the border fraud. I started hearing rumors about women being funneled into a service that provides cheap labor, maids and nannies. These women, mostly un-documented, are promised employment when they cross the border. They aren't told that the wages are substandard or, in some cases, nonexistent. Basically, they're recruited to become domestic slaves."

"That sounds like the type of article you used to really get into." He recalled her zeal and youthful enthusiasm. "You used to love tracking down sources, interviewing victims and making a difference for people who have no one else to speak for them."

He'd been proud of her investigative journalism. Sure, Jordan did fluff pieces on purebred dog shows and celebrity spats. But she had a conscience and a solid focus on right and wrong. When she sank her teeth into a story, she held on like a pit bull.

"Needless to say, Hugh wasn't thrilled when I told him that I intended to write about Bianca's death. He knew me well enough to avoid making an outright demand for me to drop my investigation. Instead, he manipulated me by putting me in touch with the medical examiner and his handpicked sheriff, who headed up the team of detectives." Ruefully, she shook her head. "I had to beg the ME for the autopsy photos. And he still managed to leave things out. He and the sheriff were hiding evidence and leading me down the wrong path. Also, they made it clear to everyone involved that I was a bored politician's wife looking for a cheap thrill as a journalist."

"A cupcake," he said.

She grinned. "That's what the guys in your platoon used to call me—cupcake, sweetie pie, Jordy the jelly bean."

"Until you confronted and disarmed a teenage punk armed with a Kalashnikov."

"Good times," she said sweetly. "And I understand why I'm not taken seriously. I show up with a recorder, a smile and a pocketful of questions. Then I go home to my safe, warm life. It doesn't look like I've got skin in the game. Reporting on a crime isn't the same as being victimized."

Her recent experiences—the life-threatening attack by Gruber and incarceration at the Institute—must have given her a different perspective. Now, she was the victim. Desperate enough to dodge outside the boundaries of the law.

"Was anyone arrested for Bianca's murder?"

"Unsolved." She shivered as though the cool, crisp night had turned ice-cold. "I met her sister, who had also been trafficked, and told her that I'd get justice for Bianca and her unborn twins. I never make promises like that, but I couldn't let go. I identified with this young woman who was five months into her pregnancy. I remembered the miraculous joy I'd felt. To have that power snuffed out is just so damn wrong."

When he met her gaze, he saw strength and determination. At the same time, she'd begun to fidget as she stared at the cabin. "You want to get back to the boys, don't you?"

"I do, but there's more to tell."

"It'll wait," he said. "Our basic plan for tomorrow includes gathering supplies and establishing our emergency escape routes through the forest."

"Yes."

Without further comment, she approached him, grabbed the front of his parka and went up on tiptoe to kiss him full on the mouth. The pressure of her lips against his was demanding. She wanted more. And yet, she shoved him away. Blake was a little bit stunned and a whole lot confused…in a good way.

AFTER BLAKE FED the twins breakfast and listened to the many reasons why—including a magic recipe—their mom's pancakes were better than his, he decided it was time to establish their emergency escape routes in case they were tracked down and surprised by Gruber. The boys needed to be educated about security. In the front room, he went to a window and placed the flat of his hand against the pane.

"Do you see how gentle I'm being?"

"So what?" Alex demanded.

"If I press harder, I set off the alarm."

Cooper frowned. "Is there some kind of force field or something?"

"Cool," Alex said. "Can you make the window explode?"

"I'm trying to show you something about the alarm system," he said, stating the obvious. "If somebody or something breaks the glass or pushes too hard against the interior or exterior, it sets off a loud alarm."

"Can I do it?" Alex marched toward the window with both hands sticking straight out. "How hard do I hit the window?"

"Stop right there," Blake said. "Your mom is still sleeping. Do you really want to wake her with a screeching blast from a security alarm?"

The boys gave identical nods and grins. "Yeah, let's do it."

"Bad idea." They weren't listening to him. He was losing control. "Get over here by the door. I'll show you how to lock and unlock without engaging the alarm."

"Then can we set it off?"

"Why would you want to do that?"

"A joke on mom," Cooper said. "She's really goofy before she has coffee."

"Have you got coffee in the kitchen?" Alex asked.

Blake recalled the conversation from yesterday. "No caffeine for you guys. But yes, there's a fresh pot made."

They exchanged a sneaky glance that turned all wide-eyed and innocent when they looked up at him and asked him to please explain the alarms. The five-year-old boy who lived in Blake's memory warned him not to trust these two. He really wanted to believe that his adult self was in charge.

He illustrated the use of the keypad that was just reachable for their three-foot-ten-inch height, which Jordan said was tall for their age. "Within sixty seconds of opening or closing the door, you tap these numbers into the pad. If you fail to do so, an alarm sounds from here, and an emergency call is placed to my buddy, Chester, who can be here in ten minutes."

"How come?" Alex asked. "Why would your buddy rush over here?"

"To protect the house or to help me deal with intruders."

"Do you get many burglars?" Cooper asked.

"Few. This cabin is remote." He grabbed the opportunity for a teachable moment. "It's better to be overprepared instead of not being ready for a break-in or an attack."

"Why would you get attacked?" Alex demanded.

"You know," Cooper said. "That's why Dad has all those dumb security guards. He's got enemies. Do you, Blake? Are there bad guys after you?"

Rather than attempting to explain that the bad guys worked for their father, he sidestepped the question. "Let's go over the procedure for the alarm again."

They tried it once and then again. He sent the boys out

to the porch to open the door and disarm the alarm. The twins caught on to the procedure more quickly than some of the newbie recruits he'd worked with. "I think you've got it."

"One more time," Alex said. "I want to be sure."

"I'm okay," Cooper said as he went toward the kitchen.

In spite of a nagging sense that he was being played, Blake took a step back from the front door. "Go for it."

Alex opened the door and took his position in front of the keypad. He shifted his weight from one foot to the other. "Um, how long before the alarm goes off?"

"Sixty seconds," Cooper yelled from the kitchen.

Alex bobbed his head up and down, then gave an elaborate shrug. "Uh-oh, I think I forgot the code."

"Ten seconds to go," Cooper said as he returned to the front room. "That's eight…seven…six…"

Alex spread his arms like a soccer goalie, keeping Blake away from the keypad. Their plan to "accidentally" activate the alarm siren became apparent. *Fine, let the little monsters have their fun.*

The alarm screamed with shrill, piercing notes that reminded him of a barn owl and a howler monkey in a blender. Alex covered his ears and chortled. After a moment, Cooper joined in. Blake turned off the alarm and braced himself. Disaster struck.

The beast had been awakened. Wearing her colorful reindeer jammies, Jordan leaped into the front room and landed in a karate pose that resembled the cat leg stance. Her curly hair stood up in tangles on her head. She kicked in all four directions, shouting a fierce accompaniment to each movement. "Hai. Hai-hai-hai."

Blinking repeatedly, she glowered from Blake to the boys and back again. The twins reacted. Alex and Cooper stood on either side of her and pointed her toward a padded walnut chair that matched the long table. As soon as she was seated, Cooper placed a ceramic coffee mug on the table in front of her.

"Sorry, Mom." Alex patted her shoulder. "Blake made us do it. He thought it'd be funny to wake you up."

Just like that, the kid threw him under the bus. Not a smart move. Blake knew his way around Ice Mountain and had a few tricks of his own.

This incident represented a lesson learned. Never get into a squabble with twins. They were twice as hard to defeat. When they were five years old, they were twice as cute.

Chapter Twelve

Jordan hated pranks. She didn't know whether to applaud Blake's ability to bond with her children or to treat him like another kid. Before she could sort out her reaction, he stepped forward.

"Earlier, the boys learned about the keypad alarm system," he said in the mature voice that befitted a big, handsome marine. "I have more plans for this morning."

"Tell me."

"We'll explore the terrain surrounding the cabin before we check out nearby caves and hideouts."

"Looking for dwarves," Alex explained.

"I'm in," she said. Her head was still fuzzy from the rude awakening, but she needed to be a part of this effort. She took a gulp from her mug. The strong, fragrant coffee warmed her throat. "Give me a minute." She sipped again. *Come on, caffeine, do your stuff.* "If you boys pay attention and do as you're told, I might be inclined to believe that the wailing banshee alarm was an accident. I just might forgive you."

"Okay," Cooper said, "we're ready to go."

"Don't push me." The three of them took a backward step, giving her space and enough time to guzzle her coffee and get ready. Still not caught up on sleep, she'd come back to the cabin last night and set up Blake's computer.

Without using internet or Wi-Fi, she plugged in her fat flamingo flash drive and read over the notes, witness statements and documents she'd already compiled. Her review
had been worth the exhaustion. She was on the trail to
solving Bianca's murder.

She took another slug of coffee, keeping Bianca at the
forefront of her thoughts. Jordan didn't dare call or text
the murdered woman's sister for follow-up. Not after what
had happened to Abigail. She didn't want to cause another
murder.

It occurred to her to approach the Flagstaff PD, but they
hadn't helped when Hugh had her locked up at the Institute. Not one single officer would listen to her.

She needed Blake's clear thinking on this problem. With
a clumsy gesture, she waved him toward her. "Please come
with me."

The twins chuckled and hooted about how he was in big
trouble. Their giggles ceased when she shot them a glare.
"Don't go outside. Don't get in trouble."

"Okay, Mom."

"I mean it. Don't go outside." She glanced toward the
kitchen. "I see a mess on the counter. Clean up the dishes.
Now."

While they rushed to obey her order, she pulled Blake
into the study. She pointed to the chair behind the desk,
indicating he should sit, and she closed the door. "I don't
want to leave the kids unsupervised for long, so listen up."

"Yes, ma'am."

BLAKE COVERED HIS mouth with his hand, hiding a grin.
Clearly, Jordan wasn't in the mood for more goofing
around. He considered himself lucky that she hadn't
whipped out her titanium baton and pummeled him from
top to toe for the stunt he'd allowed the twins to pull.

"I need to show you something." She took another swig

of her coffee. "It's a vital piece of evidence about Bianca's murder, but I don't know how to use it to best effect."

"Are you sure you can't go to the police?"

"Positive."

She turned on the laptop. Without a connection to the internet, the small device was basically a word processor and storage space for the information she'd gathered and stored on her fat flamingo flash drive. Blake was glad she'd saved this data. Maybe her story would have a happy ending after all.

She clicked on an icon labeled ME. "This is information from the Flagstaff medical examiner's office about Bianca's autopsy."

"Can you trust the ME?"

"You'd think so." But she scoffed. "Hugh instructed him to work with me on my so-called story assignment, and he complied...to an extent. Here's an example of his cooperation: he did DNA testing on the unborn twins and told me that there were no matches."

"Which you don't believe."

"No way. The paternity issue could be a motivation for Bianca's killing. I'm not sure Hugh's DNA is on file, but I could certainly provide a toothbrush or hair samples."

He nodded. "If Hugh was the father, he'd want Bianca out of the way."

"Or it could have been any of his cohorts. Hugh would have been doing them a favor by eliminating this inconvenient young woman." She sipped more coffee and shrugged. "I've found my best contacts in law enforcement are the tribal police at the Navajo reservation. Unfortunately, they didn't have tribal jurisdiction for Bianca's murder, not to mention that those officers are massively overworked. They don't have the time or resources to mess around with a cold case that's over two years old."

From outside the study, he heard the twins dashing

across the hardwood floors and arguing loudly while telling each other to keep quiet. "Should I go check on them?"

"Yes." She took a final sip and held out her mug. "And bring me more caffeine."

When he stepped into the front room, he saw the two curly-haired kids studying the keypad alarm. The last thing their mom had told them was not to go outside. In a gravelly voice, he reinforced that order. "Don't even think about it. Don't go outdoors. Got it?"

Unimpressed with his growl, they bounced up to him. "Is Mom done yet?"

For a moment, he was tempted to use the roar he'd perfected after years of giving orders to newbie recruits. Then he remembered that these were five-year-old puppies, not devil dog marines. "As soon as she's done, I'll tell you."

He took her mug into the kitchen and filled it. When he returned to the combination living room/dining area, he pulled open a drawer in the lower section of a breakfront and took out several rolled and folded papers. "These are maps," he said as he placed them on the long, walnut table. "Be careful with them. Don't tear them up or write on them. I want you to study them and figure out which ones apply to our current location."

With the kids momentarily occupied, he returned to the study where Jordan had seated herself in his swivel chair. She stared intently at the computer screen. Without turning her head, she said, "It took me a long time and a lot of luck to put this evidence together. I hope it makes a difference."

"How about the FBI? We could contact them." He placed the fresh mug of coffee on the desktop beside the mouse. "Didn't you tell me that Bianca was victimized by traffickers? That's the feds' jurisdiction. Maybe her murder can be used to dismantle the forced labor enterprise."

"It's a possibility, but we've got to be careful about who

we tell. According to my research, this isn't a sloppy operation. The name used by the traffickers has changed a couple of times, and the paperwork is almost nonexistent, making it nearly impossible to uncover the identities of men like Hugh who skim a percentage off the top."

"How does their operation work?"

"Back in Flagstaff, while I pretended to be a good little politician's wife, I heard about this 'employment service' from another of the wives, the ex-model Sierra, who has a full staff of household help and two nannies for her three kids. She described an extortionist's dream where you first pay a lump sum, a portion of which is supposedly passed on to your newly hired employee. If you're still happy after six months, you pay again. All cash, no questions."

"What's the name they're currently using?"

She looked up and gave him a sad smile. "I can't remember. Let me think. It'll come to me."

"Chester has a couple of contacts in the FBI, former marines. Men we can trust." He hoped she would agree to calling in outside investigators and stepping out of the direct line of fire. If not for her own safety, she needed to think of the kids. "Show me your new evidence."

She turned the computer screen so he could see. "These are autopsy photos of Bianca from the ME's office. I asked if I could take photos of my own, but he refused. To get these copies, I had to beg and plead."

Though battle-hardened, Blake felt a queasy tremor in the pit of his gut. Bianca was so young, only sixteen, and so vulnerable. Before the autopsy surgeon made the V-incision on her chest, he photographed the lacerations on her body. A slash across her breasts. Another on her abdomen. There was an X at the base of her throat, like a signature. "You said he used a machete. Is that right?"

"A weird choice for somebody living in Flagstaff."

"Not if he came from a cartel in a jungle area."

"The marking at her throat looks too delicate to be a machete," she said. "And take a look at this."

She zoomed in on the photographs taken of wounds inflicted at the victim's wrists. Horizontal slicing criss-crossed the veins and arteries. Blake squinted at the photo. "Not an efficient murder method. The carotid or femoral would bleed out more quickly. These wrist lacerations could take up to fifteen minutes before death was assured."

"Does it look like a machete wound?" she asked.

"I'm not an expert, but the width of the blade appears to be finer than a heavy-duty hacking tool. And then, there's this." He pointed to the screen. "At the end of the smooth slice, there appears to be a jagged nick. You might get that pattern using a hunting knife with a serrated edge below the tip."

He watched as she braced her elbow on the desktop and carefully removed the colorful, braided bracelet that cir-cled a wide portion of her wrist. Her bared skin revealed a scar that was identical to the one on Bianca's arm. The scar beneath the second bracelet on the other arm matched the first. Those lacerations were given to her by Ray Gru-ber after he knocked her out with the stun gun.

Blake wanted to believe the scars indicated proof posi-tive, but he said, "It's not an unusual style of blade—could belong to someone else."

Her gaze locked with his. She unfastened the top but-tons on her jammies to reveal Gruber's signature X below her clavicle. "What are the odds?"

"This looks like solid evidence," he said. "And it's an-other reason for Hugh and Gruber to come after you."

The more evidence they uncovered, the more motivation the bad guys had for eliminating Jordan. They needed to think seriously about finding a safer place for the kids to hide out. He wanted to believe he and Jordan could protect them, but the odds weren't in their favor.

IN THE BATHROOM, Jordan washed her face, dragged a brush through her hair and checked her reflection in the mirror above the sink. In spite of the ever-present danger, she didn't look too bad. Her eyes weren't bloodshot, and she had a bit of color in her cheeks. She scowled at herself, trying to remember. *What was the phony employment service called?* She remembered Bianca's sister telling her, but the name wouldn't come clear.

She retreated to the study to get dressed. Today, she'd text information about the trafficking operation to Spike. Maybe he could figure it out. He was supposed to be in touch with an update on Rockwell in Aspen. Finding that evil squirrel and his stash of nuts was top priority. The name came to her in a flash: B and W Employ. She'd thought of the initials standing for "Bad" and "Worse," and she needed to track down connections to that supposed business.

When she emerged, she wore sneakers, jeans and a coral turtleneck under a lightweight khaki jacket—totally appropriate for hiking this morning and shopping this afternoon. She found the three guys sitting at the dining room table. Blake had spread a topographical map of the area that showed towns, landmarks and highways.

Alex motioned for her to join them. "Mom, take a look. It's old-fashioned."

For once, Cooper agreed with him. "Why would anybody use this instead of GPS?"

"Harry Potter has maps," she said defensively. "And the hobbits."

"But that's not real life," Alex said as if he knew.

"Maps are a good way to get an overview," Blake said. "Remember when I told you about the Tiger Squad? One time they parachuted out of a Cessna 208 Caravan into enemy territory and had to find their way to safety. Suppose you boys went skydiving into the forest at the edge of this mountain." He pointed to the map. "How would you find your way to this cabin?"

"I'd use my cell phone," Alex said. "If Mom would get one for me."

"The cabin isn't listed under regular addresses in your GPS. All you've got is this map." Blake leaned back in his chair. "See if you can figure out where this cabin is located, based on the highways, towns and geographical features."

"That's a great exercise." Jordan leaned over the table and quickly realized that she was as lost as the twins. "You're going to have to give us more clues."

"When we drove here, we turned south off the interstate at Glenwood, then west, then south again."

She rotated the map until she had the directional marker pointing toward north at the top of the paper.

"This way," Alex said. With his finger, he traced the thick line for I-70.

"You got it," she said. "After going south on route 82, we turned west."

"Just before this town that starts with a *C*," Alex said. "Here's a curvy road. If this was on a computer, we could zoom in and get details."

"You catch on quick." Though Alex had always been good with spatial relationships, she was wowed by his swift, easy comprehension of mapping. "Have you done anything like this before? Maybe on the internet?"

He shrugged his skinny shoulders, but Cooper stepped up to fill in the blanks. "Alex plays that dumb computer game all the time. It's about carts and graphs."

"Cartography," Alex corrected.

"Impressed," Jordan said. "This is useful knowledge."

Cooper nudged against her and pointed to the elaborate directional marker above the legend of the map. "What's this?"

She explained how the marker, called a compass rose,

showed the four directions and gradations in between. "You can design one for yourself."

Now Cooper was enthralled. "How do I know which way is north?"

"I thought you might ask," Blake said as he dug into his jeans pocket and pulled out two circular metal cases in army green. "These are military lensatic compasses. Flip open the lid. The needle always points north."

Jordan was glad he'd found two compasses and pleased to see the boys asking so many questions. Learning about these "old-fashioned" navigational instruments felt more real and solid than accessing directions on the computer. When she needed the internet, she loved it. Other times— like now—she enjoyed being off the grid.

Eventually, they solved the puzzle of finding the cabin by triangulating the turnoff from the highway and following a squiggly line that was Chipmunk Creek. She checked her watch. It was 8:45 a.m. Blake had planned to leave at 10:30 to do shopping for a couple of hours. Her turn to shop was from 2:00 until 4:00 p.m. The schedule made her feel grounded, and she'd learned something valuable while studying the map.

The location of the cabin was closer to Aspen than she'd thought. Though shopping at the acclaimed ski resort would undoubtedly be more costly, the proximity to Rockwell enticed her. Maybe she'd go there first, to get an idea of where he lived and what kind of security he used. Discovering the connection with the scars encouraged her to move forward with her investigation. The solution felt closer than ever before.

Chapter Thirteen

When they left the cabin, the boys showed Jordan how to use the keypad, proving to her that the earlier "accidental" alarm had been very much on purpose. Though she could have scolded, she didn't want to ruin the happy mood of hiking together and being outdoors. Blake led the way up the slope to the clearing where they'd gone last night. The twins dashed around the edges of the clearing and circled the firepit.

"Can we build a fire?"

"And cook weenies?"

Ignoring a plethora of demands and questions, Blake said, "Okay, I want you to use your compasses to find a path that goes northeast."

After a couple of false starts, they scampered down a trail, passed a grove of gold-leafed aspen and went deeper into the woods. She strolled beside Blake. The earthy scents of the forest comforted her. After being sequestered in the Institute, she felt lighthearted and free. Sunlight warmed her cheeks. The beautiful, blue-sky autumn day almost made her forget the peril hanging over them.

"I like the way you're handling this," she said, looking up at Blake. "You're teaching them an escape route without being scary."

"We'll follow these paths every morning until the directions are stuck in their memories. They're good kids. Smart."

"In terms of more aggressive protection," she said, "are you prepared?"

"If that's a roundabout way to ask if I have weapons, the answer is… Oh. Hell. Yes."

"Not surprised."

"Four hunting rifles and two handguns, all of which are locked in my gun safe except for my Glock, which I slept with under my pillow last night."

Her feelings about guns seesawed back and forth. As a young woman growing up with a single mother in Boston, she wasn't much interested in weapons. When she started in journalism, guns equated in her mind with street violence, and she favored gun control. That attitude changed. While embedded with the military in combat zones, she understood the vital function of weaponry in self-preservation. She learned to shoot with handguns and rifles but frankly preferred her titanium baton and karate moves. Her latest stance was the result of being the mother of energetic twins. Her brain fixated on the statistics for accidental shootings and gun deaths for kids under eighteen in 2021. It was over 5,200 in the United States. In many situations, guns were necessary, but she didn't like them.

"I'd prefer to keep the guns away from the boys," she said.

He nodded. "I hadn't planned on target practice."

"They get into everything." Ahead of them on the path, the twins had come to a fork. They checked their compasses before deciding to go right and head uphill. "I can't turn my back on them for a second."

"I know what you mean."

She also knew that he had an awareness of safety and how guns should be used. Still, she couldn't stop herself from asking, "What if the boys stumbled across your Glock when you weren't looking?"

"I'm always looking."

"Really? I mean, do you know where your gun is right now?"

"In a concealed holster fastened to my belt at the small of my back." He brushed back his untucked flannel shirt to show her. "If Gruber attacks on this trail, my fire power isn't much good if it's locked in a safe. FYI, I'm also carrying a hunting knife and a switchblade."

She sighed. "I keep forgetting that you're no stranger to violence."

"I am now and always will be a battle-ready marine."

"Exactly what I need." She dropped her voice to a soft, intimate level. "More than that, you're exactly what I want."

Up ahead on the path, the boys were waving and shouting. "We'd better catch up to them," Blake said, "before they tear the mountain apart."

On a ridge above the trail, they'd located the entrance to a mine that was closed off by rough, weathered boards. Though not readily visible from the path, Jordan had the feeling that this was the destination Blake had intended for them to find. Her impression deepened when he unzipped the pack slung across his shoulders and took out four LED headlamps with elastic straps.

He passed a headlamp to her. "You're going to need this."

Not thrilled, she dangled the headgear between her thumb and forefinger. "Do you remember how I feel about dark, enclosed spaces?"

"Claustrophobia," he said. "Sorry, Jordan, but you've only got two choices. Either you get over it or you explain to the kids."

He joined the twins outside the mine, handed them the

headlamps and showed them how to put them on and adjust the straps.

"Where did you get this stuff?" Alex asked.

"Some are gifts from Chester who likes to go caving, which is also called spelunking."

Cooper laughed. "Spelunking? That's a funny word."

"The headlamps are handy to see where you're going at night when you want to keep your hands free, like when you're hunting or fishing after dark."

Very little about caving or nighttime hunting appealed to her, but her sons were observing Blake with something akin to hero worship. He had headlamps and compasses, not to mention the holstered Glock and switchblade, which he hadn't shown them. She didn't want to be the sissy who was scared to go into the mine, but she couldn't ignore the involuntary flush of apprehension that raised her core temperature. Under her light jacket, she'd begun to sweat.

Blake pointed to the thick boards blocking the gaping entrance. "If you ever see another boarded-up mine, do not enter. You got that? It's not safe. This place is special. Chester and I checked it out, reinforced the supports and made it secure. It's a tricky route, meant to slip into and come out of."

"What about dwarves?" Cooper asked. "They work in mines. Is this a gold mine?"

"I'm not sure. All the ore that was there has been removed."

"So…no dwarves?"

"Not that I know of."

He went to the side of the entrance and pushed aside a clump of sage and juniper to reveal the edge of a long board. He pulled and twisted until there was a space just large enough for a regular-sized person to slip through. Jordan guessed it would be a tight squeeze for extra-large Blake.

Cooper echoed her thought. "Blake's too big. He's not going to fit."

She gave a nervous laugh. "You might be right about that."

"No problem. I'll go first and check it out." Blake turned on his headlamp, dropped into a squat, ducked under the boards and disappeared into the darkness. From inside, he called out, "Who's next?"

Jordan dragged her feet. She was content to wait outside and cheer for them when they emerged. For her, the spelunking wasn't going to happen. She hugged both of her brave boys. Her job was to protect them, not the other way around. "You go ahead. I'll see you on the other side."

After the kids darted inside, she adjusted the shrubs so the opening into the mine shaft wouldn't be obvious. From inside the cave, she heard the echo of Blake's deep voice. "This way. Keep to the right."

Stepping away from the mine entrance, she found a comfortable seat on a granite rock and tilted her head back. Sunshine poured over her like a soothing balm, and all her senses came alive. The breeze tickled. She heard the sounds of the forest. The temperature had begun to cool. She tasted the approach of winter and snow.

This time, claustrophobia won. What was that quote? "Discretion is the better part of valor." She didn't need to take unnecessary risks.

JUST BEFORE LUNCHTIME, Blake returned from the market with groceries, miscellaneous supplies and a rotisserie fried chicken. After they ate, Jordan left the twins with him and took the car for her turn at a general merchandise store to purchase clothes and office supplies. With the skies clouded over and the cool weather sliding toward cold, she needed to make sure the twins were prepared—with boots, mittens, hats and jackets—for the impending snowfall. During the brief time she'd spent in Colorado, she'd experienced sudden weather changes, and Blake assured her that October wasn't too early for a blizzard. While he'd been shopping, she and the twins took advantage of the still-temperate day to hike along Chipmunk Creek, a twisty little stream, too shallow for fishing, that led through the forest to Paddington Lake, named for one of the first settlers in the area.

The twins had spotted the short dock at the water's edge where a couple of rowboats were moored. If they'd had more time and less urgency, she would have immediately agreed to take them out on the lake. But the threat of danger crept closer with every passing minute. She couldn't let her guard down.

Earlier, she'd received a text message from Spike indicating activity from Khaled. The casino owner blamed Hugh for her investigation and decided to pursue his own search for her. Dissent among the bad guys seemed like good news for her. If they bickered with each other, they'd be less likely to worry about evidence she might be gathering. One of them might even decide to turn on the other, giving evidence of wrongdoing in exchange for a lighter sentence. As she drove toward the turnoff near Carbondale, she worried that Khaled might stumble across information about Emily. Would it be smart to toss a bit of misdirection into his path?

She pulled the Suburban over onto the shoulder and texted that question to Spike. The response from him was lightning quick. He had two more tidbits of information. First of all, Khaled and some of his men had flown on a private jet out of Harry Reid International Airport at dawn. Their destination was unknown. Jordan breathed a sigh of relief. If the gang from the Magic Lamp wasn't searching in Vegas, Emily the chopper pilot wasn't on their radar. Secondly, Spike texted the address for Tim Rockwell in Aspen.

When she hadn't known the precise location, the idea of tracking down Rocky had been too vague. Now, she knew where the squirrel was holed up. If she finished her shopping fast, she might have time to check out his house before she rushed back to the cabin.

Merging into the minimal traffic, she remembered the topographical map on Blake's dining room table. Up ahead was a fork in the road. A left turn, heading north, took her toward Glenwood Springs. To the right was Aspen, only about thirty miles away. *Tempting.*

She did the math in her head. A detour into Rocky's neighborhood would add about an hour and a half to the time she'd allotted for shopping. Too long to be away from the boys. And she wanted Blake to be with her for backup.

But if she took a chance and met face-to-face with Rocky, she might bring a swift and positive end to her investigation. As Hugh's accountant, Tim Rockwell had access to all the financial paperwork that could prove extortion and fraud. Before he abruptly quit six months ago, she'd found him in Hugh's home office at the mansion, a place he seldom went to work. She'd slipped into the large room on the first floor. After checking to make sure none of the security guards were around, she had closed the door and greeted Rocky. "Good afternoon, I'm surprised to see you here."

"There are a few records I needed to access for tax purposes." He'd stood behind the massive piece of carved, antique furniture that suited Hugh's large frame very well. In contrast, Rocky seemed dwarfed by the monstrous desk. "I'll be done in a minute."

"Take all the time you want," she'd said as she sauntered across the large, well-lit room with a wall of arched, multi-paned windows. "It's nice to see somebody who isn't carrying a gun or pushing a political agenda. I've always thought we had a lot in common, you and I."

She hadn't been lying. With her penchant for making agendas and plans, Jordan had accepted that she was kind of a perfectionist who liked having everything organized.

"I think so, too." When Rocky smiled, he revealed two prominent buckteeth that reinforced his nickname. His dark eyes—magnified by round glasses—made him look even more like a squirrel. "I can tell that you like details. So do I. And you're very careful with your money, aren't you?"

She and Rocky had had this discussion before. For years, he'd wanted to combine her private savings, investments and accounts with the Waltham estate. Thank goodness, she hadn't listened to his advice. "I won't change my mind, not until I have unfettered access to everything Hugh owns. We both know that's not going to happen."

"Afraid not."

"I like doing my own accounting. It's a grown-up activity, and I sometimes need a break from the kids." She lowered herself into a chair on the opposite side of the desk and gestured for him to sit. With a welcoming smile, she hoped to get him talking. "You handle all the payments for the house staff and nannies, right?"

"I do."

"Did we ever have a young woman named Bianca working here?"

"Oh my, no." His nose twitched, and he blinked nervously. "Are you talking about the Bianca who was murdered?"

She didn't try to hide her interest. Rocky would see through a ruse. "I want to write an article about her death. You know I'm a journalist. Can you help me?"

"I knew her. A beautiful girl with long black hair. She was so young. A tragic murder."

Jordan bit her lip to keep from debating the idea that the death of a pretty girl was more important than the demise of one who wasn't so lovely. She strongly believed all murder was heinous but didn't need the distraction. Reading Rocky's sad eyes told her that he'd known Bianca and mourned her. Maybe he knew who killed her. "Did you ever talk to her?"

"I heard her singing a lullaby in Spanish. I speak the language fluently, you know. Bianca confided in me, told me she was pregnant. Couldn't believe it, I just couldn't. She was so very young."

"So young." She leaned forward, resting her forearms on the desktop. "Did she speak of the father?"

"The father of her child? Why, yes. Yes, she did. She had fallen in love with him. He was older, a powerful man."

"You didn't approve," she said, encouraging him to keep talking.

"Of course not. He had obviously taken advantage of that sweet, young lady."

The name, tell me his name. She had been on the verge of an important discovery. Before she could push her advantage, the door to the office swung open and Ray Gruber stalked inside.

He snapped at her. "You don't belong here, Jordan."

"Well, maybe I don't live here anymore but it's still my house, Gruber. I can go anywhere I want."

"Don't play dumb. Move it."

She stood opposite Rocky at the desk and grinned at him. "I enjoyed our chat. I hope we can talk again soon."

They never had a chance. Less than a week later, Rocky had quit, causing her to wonder if their conversation had played a part in his disappearance.

She stared through the windshield and made a U-turn back toward the cabin. If she could talk to Rocky again—in person—he might tell her who was the father of Bianca's babies and who had murdered her. But she wouldn't take that risk until Blake could return with her. For once, she would exercise caution.

Chapter Fourteen

Blake had chosen his position carefully. Halfway up a craggy slope, he sat on an outcropping of red stone with his legs dangling. From there, he could see the kids at the lake and the driveway that led to the garage behind his cabin. Jordan was running late, only ten minutes, not enough for him to be seriously worried, but he couldn't help the stabbing anxiety that got worse as the seconds ticked slowly. The same foreboding had infected him at the airfield in Las Vegas. Jordan tended to get into trouble when she took off on her own. No matter how much she wanted to talk to Rocky, he needed for her to be careful, to curb her impulses and think ahead. More than anything, he wanted to pull her out of this risky investigation and establish a new normal for her and the twins—a normalcy that included him.

When he turned his head to the right, he had a view of Paddington Lake where the boys, wearing orange life jackets, zoomed across the glassy surface of the water in a motorboat owned by Chester Prynne. Blake had wanted to teach them how to handle a rowboat, in keeping with his old-fashioned-but-still-cool way of doing things, but when Chester glided up to the dock with the little red motorboat, the twins went wild. They loved going fast, and Blake didn't blame them. He often felt the need for speed.

Rotating his perspective, he looked back at the cabin. *Where the hell was she?* Earlier, when they talked about her shopping trip, he'd pointed out the advantages of going to the closest stores. There was nothing to be gained by driving to Aspen. Shopping would cost more, parking was a drag and she was more likely to run into wealthy people she knew from Arizona in the resort town.

Yelling from the twins drew his attention to the lake where Chester had allowed Alex to take over the steering. The small boy behind the wheel let out a squeal—so loud that he could be heard over the boat's motor—as he swooped from left to right. As far as Blake could tell, there was nobody else on the lake. The temperature had dropped to a chill that made it uncomfortable to drop a fishing line into the water and sit, waiting for a bite—somewhat like his current predicament. He couldn't force Jordan to be cautious. Nothing to do but wait patiently.

When Cooper took his turn and proved to be no less reckless than his brother, Blake silently cheered him on. *Attaboy!* Cooper tended to be more thoughtful and analytical, like his mom. It was good to see him acting like a kid.

When Blake spotted the Suburban, he stood on his outcropping and waved to Jordan with both arms, attracting her attention. She passed the turn onto the driveway, drove up the road below where he was standing, pulled over to the shoulder and parked. As he climbed down from the rock, she ran to meet him. "What's wrong? Where are the kids?"

"It's all good," he said. "Did you get your shopping taken care of?"

The roar of the motorboat on the lake drew her attention. She turned and stared. Her breath caught in her throat. "Is that my son driving the boat?"

"I think it's Cooper."

"Oh my God." She charged toward the dock. "How could you let them do that?"

"Stop." He caught her arm. "Chester is in the boat with them. They're wearing life jackets. And they're fine."

"How cold is that water? It looks freezing, and I want them out of there." She pulled away from him. "This is not your call, Blake."

Her attitude surprised him. Jordan never hesitated to take a risk with her own safety. She didn't needlessly put her twins in harm's way, but she'd literally stolen the boys away in the middle of the night and dragged them across the country. "I never thought you were one of those helicopter moms."

"What?"

"Isn't that what you call it when a parent hovers over their children, watching every move and being overprotective?"

"It is," she said. "And I'm not. At least, I never thought I was."

"Don't stop your kids from having fun."

At that moment, Chester took control of the boat and circled toward the dock. Both boys waved. She weakly lifted her hand and forced a smile. "I don't want to hover, but I worry about them, especially now. I keep thinking I've made a terrible mistake, and they're going to get hurt."

He slung an arm around her shoulder and gave her a hug. Though not a parent, he understood the delicate balance between protecting your loved ones and giving them enough freedom to make their own choices. Moments ago, he'd been worried that she intended to rush into Aspen on her own and confront her witness. But here she was. And everything was fine. At least, he hoped so.

In a carefully nonjudgmental voice, he asked, "Where did you shop?"

"Are you asking me if I drove to Aspen and tracked down Rocky the Flying Squirrel?"

"I was trying not to ask," he said.

"I thought about it," she admitted. "Earlier this year, before he disappeared, I had a talk with him. He knew about Bianca's pregnancy and might be able to name the father. If I could get a couple of minutes alone with him, I'm sure he'd tell me."

Bad idea. He wasn't in favor. "Approaching him would be a risk. You'd give away your location. You can't trust Rocky to be on your side."

"Frustrating." Gazing down at the dock, she leaned her back against his chest. The jasmine scent of her shampoo tickled his nose. "I'm running in place, not making headway."

He wrapped her in his embrace. "Did I mention that Chester is here?"

Blake tried not to make it sound like his old friend and mentor had flown across the lake to rescue the twins from boredom like a superhero with his cape flapping in the wind, but he couldn't help feeling that Chester had the all the answers, including the solution to her stuck investigation. Over the years, he'd made a lot of friends, ranging from the President of the United States to the guy with the waist-length beard who was responsible for running the snowplow on the roads in their area. Chester firmly believed that if you asked the right person, you could accomplish anything.

When Blake had given him an outline of Jordan's suspicions, he came up with the name of a high-ranking official in the FBI, someone trustworthy to take over the official investigation and hand it off to a federal prosecutor who would like nothing more than to take down a sleazy political consultant who was using his position for corruption. They'd relieve Jordan of all responsibility and take her out of danger.

Chester hiked up the slope behind the boys, who had already moored the motorboat and stowed their life jackets. Without even trying, the seventy-plus former marine looked wise, determined and honorable. His weathered features under his thick crest of white hair were chiseled by time and experience. His athletic gait matched his ramrod straight posture. *Semper Fi.* He embodied the finest traits of the Corps. Surely, Jordan would listen to him.

Cooper reached her first and flung his arms around her middle while he looked up at her, reading the nuance of her expression. "Did you see me, Mom? I drove the boat. All by myself."

"Were you scared?" she asked.

"A little bit."

Her lips pinched together, then relaxed as she swallowed her reprimand. Instead, she focused on the positive. "Good for you, Coop. You overcame your fear but were still careful. And had fun."

"So much fun."

"I wasn't scared at all," Alex said as he grabbed her opposite side. "I think maybe I'll be a ship's captain instead of a helicopter pilot."

"Or you could be both," she said.

Now that they had their mother's approval, the kids turned to Blake, telling him how it felt to go really fast with the wind blowing and the water splashing and the fish jumping. "Better than any old rowboat," Alex said.

"Don't be so sure," Chester said. "Did you ever hear of being up the creek without a paddle? I'm telling you, kids, motorboats can run out of gas. Then you're stranded."

When he greeted Jordan, she gave him a hug and a kiss on the cheek, then said, "Thanks for watching over these little monkeys."

"Great kids." He beamed. "Any time you want to leave me in charge, I'm up for that duty."

She reflected his grin. "I fully intend to cash in on that offer."

"That's the idea," he said. "From what Blake told me, you've got enough on your plate."

AFTER THEY RETURNED to the cabin and had dinner, Jordan sent the boys upstairs to put away their new winter clothes, play with a sketching and tracing notebook and check out their brand-new snowshoes, which left tracks like monsters. After they rushed up the staircase, she refilled the coffee mugs and set out a plate of macadamia nut cookies Blake had picked up that morning from a bakery in Glenwood.

"How much did Blake tell you?" she asked Chester.

"I'll break it into three parts," he said. "First, he told me how your ex-husband—a real bastard—assaulted you and incarcerated you in an institution. The proof is your direct testimony."

"And the reason I won't be believed is counter-testimony from Hugh and from Dr. Merchant at the Institute who claims that I'm a danger to myself and others."

"Second," Chester said, "you've compiled a stack of evidence—paperwork and witness testimony—accusing your ex-husband of fraud, extortion, smuggling and money laundering. All this makes me wonder why you haven't contacted law enforcement."

"Hugh is a powerful man with far-reaching influence. Every time I put out feelers with district attorneys and police, my investigation was shut down. I want to be sure— one hundred percent sure—that Hugh will be tried and convicted."

"You've done remarkable work for a person who doesn't have the authority to compel cooperation from witnesses."

"She's good at convincing people to help her," Blake put in.

She had to agree. "My best witness is Tim Rockwell, my ex-husband's former accountant, who now lives in Aspen. I don't know if he'll talk to the authorities or not."

"If he's offered a deal, he'll talk," Chester said. "Blake can verify this truth. When the bad guys get in trouble, they all talk."

"I hope you're right." If Chester Prynne could lift this responsibility from her shoulders, she'd be happy. Of course, she liked doing her own research and investigating, but these issues had grown exponentially too large for her to handle.

"Moving on to the third issue: the murder of Bianca Hernandez. You believe the ME withheld important evidence about the murder weapon and the DNA of her unborn twins. Additionally, the Flagstaff PD did a poor job of investigating this case."

"Correct." She appreciated his succinct analysis. "What do you think, Chester? Can you help me?"

"I'm retired." He reached for another cookie. This elderly gentleman had one of those metabolisms that allowed him to eat whatever he wanted and stay as lean as a whippet. Blake had the same ability. Maybe it was a military thing.

He continued. "I was never actually in law enforcement, but I worked with a number of federal officers when I was a marine."

"A full bird colonel," Blake said. "You can't get much higher."

She leaned back in her chair and sipped her coffee. "Chester, are you talking about the FBI? DEA? ICE? Any other acronym?"

"All of the above," he said. "I suggest we coordinate the

investigation through a supervisory special agent for the FBI based in Denver, SSA Ferris Taggart."

"Taggart has an excellent reputation." Though impressed that Chester knew this guy, she didn't quite believe that such a high-ranking, important fed would be interested in her complicated issue. "Why would he get involved?"

"Why wouldn't he?" Chester sat up straight, took a bite of cookie and chewed. "According to your evidence, your ex-husband has broken dozens of laws, including murder. It's the duty of the FBI to check him out. Not only will Taggart organize the gathering of further information and scare the pants off those idiots in Flagstaff who concealed evidence, he can install you and the twins in a safe house."

Relief washed over her like a gentle, warm wave, soothing her tense muscles and relaxing her choke hold on self-restraint. The stress had been extreme, nearly unbearable. She'd hardly dared to admit how frightened she'd been for the kids. If her actions had inadvertently put them in danger, she'd never forgive herself. A safe house sounded like a decent solution.

For the twins…but not for her.

Jordan wasn't ready to give up. Months of her life had been invested in sifting through investment documents in her ex-husband's office, snapping photos of dangerous people who came though their mansion with payoffs for Hugh and tracking down the household workers, like Bianca and her sister, who had been forced into unpaid labor. Working with Spike, she reviewed reams of computer records from the casinos—including the Magic Lamp—that had performed money-laundering operations.

"When can I meet with SSA Taggart?" she asked.

Chester took his cell phone from the pocket of his fishing vest and held it aloft like the Statue of Liberty's beacon. "I'll call him now."

"It's not too late?"

"Only seven o'clock. He'll be awake."

With a heartfelt smile, she said, "Thank you."

While Chester left the table and sauntered into Blake's office, she drained her coffee mug and looked over at the man who sat beside her. Though she had dozens of valuable contacts, including Hornsby, a former news anchor, and Spike, the computer genius who helped her pursue her investigation, Blake's friend held the key to concluding her ex-husband's crime spree.

She leaned close and whispered in his ear. "And thank you, too. I couldn't have done this without you."

"You would have found a way," he said. "Like I said before, when you're on the trail of an investigation, you're a pit bull."

"Those dogs are fierce." She stroked his cheek, feeling the stubble that had grown over the past few days. The more she relaxed, the more she was able to express the attraction she felt. "Pit bulls also have the reputation of being extremely loyal and affectionate."

"Like you." He caught hold of her hand, held it to his lips and ran a trail of kisses down her index finger to her thumb. "Fierce but loyal."

"If you were a dog…"

"Let's not go there," he said. "I'm not interested in being another species."

Nor was she. Being this close to him awakened the womanly urges she hadn't allowed herself to feel for years. "Great Dane. Because you have a smooth coat. You're big and strong and very handsome."

"Tell me more," he murmured.

"Let's not start something we can't finish." She glanced toward the closed door to the office. "Chester is going to rejoin us at any moment."

"We've been apart for too long. I've missed you."

She felt the same. She missed the sound of his voice,

the look in his eyes, his taste, his scent. So often, she'd thought of the little kisses, hugs and touches that led, more often than not, to passion. More than that, she savored their companionship. He always seemed to know what she was thinking. Not that their relationship had been all about lust. He supported her needs and desires. He could always make her laugh.

Through the years, even after she married Hugh, her abiding fondness for Blake had comforted her. In moments of great joy, she had longed to share her heart with him… like the day when the twins were born. She'd been in the delivery room alone because Congress was in session and Hugh—even though he wasn't an elected senator—didn't want to miss anything. At least, that was what he'd told her. And she'd been so wrapped up in the impending birth that she didn't have the time or inclination to figure out if he was lying. When she held her tiny baby boys, she didn't think of Hugh. Instead, she saw Blake's dimpled smile and heard his voice telling her that she'd done a good job. She'd imagined his kiss on her forehead. With a sigh, she returned to the present. "I'm glad we're finally together."

Before she could show him how much closer she wanted to be, Chester returned to the table. He sat and gave a quick nod. "Taggart wants to see you as soon as possible."

"Yes!" She raised both fists in victory.

"I have a helicopter pad at my ranch on the other side of the lake," Chester said. "SSA Taggart and a couple of his top agents will be here tomorrow, if we don't get hit by a major snowstorm."

Tomorrow? That meant she still had tonight to make a difference. "Chester, can you stay with the kids for a couple of hours?"

"Sure," he said. "What do you have in mind?"

She glanced toward Blake. "I want to take one last run at Rocky in Aspen. Will you come with me?"

"Oh, hell yes. You're not going alone." He rose to his feet, towering over the table like Thor. In that one move, he asserted his physical dominance. "I'll drive."

She didn't need to ask who he thought was in charge. In his mind, he would—for the most part—direct the mission. She decided not to interrupt his fantasy.

Chapter Fifteen

Buckled into the passenger seat of the Suburban, Jordan didn't tease herself into thinking that her current plan had much chance of success. The possibility of Rocky agreeing to talk to her was minimal, and she promised Blake that she wouldn't force the issue.

"Here's what I want to do," she said. "We'll park outside his multi-million-dollar mountain chalet, and I'll make a phone call to him on Spike's encrypted phone. Rocky won't know where I am, and I'll be careful not to give away my location."

"Don't expect a chalet," he warned her. "Millions in Aspen doesn't guarantee a mansion. I don't know the exact location of this address, but the area is known for simple houses on multi-acre lots. Your squirrel is paying for privacy."

"Makes sense." Tim Rockwell wasn't the type of person to hire a bunch of security guys to protect him. "We should assume he has sophisticated camera surveillance."

Blake nodded. "Why is it necessary for us to drive to his house if all you're going to do is make a phone call?"

"He might invite me to come inside."

"Doubtful."

"And if he runs, we can follow him."

"I'm not loving this strategy, but I guess it can't hurt."

Even if he was merely humoring her, she appreciated

his presence. Gazing through the windshield at the night sky where ragged wisps of clouds obscured the waning moon, she snuggled into the heated bucket seat and exhaled a sigh. "What do you love, Blake?"

"What?"

"You said you don't love my plan. So, tell me, what do you love?"

He took a long pause before answering, and she studied his strong profile, which was outlined by the dashboard lights. Sometimes, she forgot how handsome he was with his high forehead perfectly balanced with a rugged jaw. His deep-set eyes, which were a brilliant blue in the sunlight, stared straight ahead. She knew he was thinking, choosing his words with care.

"This," he said.

Jordan had hoped for more. "Could you be a teensy-tiny bit more specific?"

"Right now, in this moment, I'm almost perfectly happy. We're on a mission. Together. I love the sense of purpose, even though your plan isn't great."

Oddly, she knew what he meant. They'd never been a couple who were content to sit quietly in front of a crackling fireplace with nothing to do. "What else?"

"I love being in Colorado, cruising along a mountain road with the night shadows playing hide-and-seek across the faces of hills and depths of valleys. The crisp taste of snow in the air pleases me. Also, I love knowing the boys are safe at home with Chester watching over them."

So far, his words reflected a near match for her own feelings, except in one particular arena. He'd mentioned how he liked her as a companion, a teammate working toward a goal. But he hadn't spoken about his feelings for her as a woman, hadn't mentioned an attraction to her or complimented the way she looked. Though it seemed silly to worry about such superficial things, she wanted to know. They'd been together 24/7 since Saturday night, and it was Monday evening. They'd shared a few kisses, hugs and touches but nothing approaching intimacy. She wanted to know…if he wanted her…as much as she wanted him.

In a quiet, humble voice—not her style at all—she asked, "How do you feel about me?"

"Are you asking if I love you?"

"Of course not." She scoffed. "I'd never put you on the spot like that."

"Good, because there's no way I'd risk an answer to that question. Too dangerous."

"Don't tell me that a big, strong marine is scared of falling in love."

He pantomimed zipping his lips and throwing away the key before he said, "The forecasters are predicting heavy snowfall tomorrow."

"What are you talking about?"

"When in doubt, talk about the weather. Or sports. How about those Broncos?"

Her question wasn't really answered, but his admitted nervousness gave her reassurance. When he thought of her in that special way, he lapsed into tongue-tied panic. *Good.* "Actually, I wouldn't mind hearing how the Broncos are doing."

"Three wins, two losses. They play Kansas City on Sunday."

"Really." Her eyes narrowed. "I haven't seen you reading a newspaper or noticed you listening to sports radio, and we don't have easy access to internet. How do you know the team standings?"

"True sports fans have chips implanted in their brains that constantly spew out stats and details about their favorite teams." He glanced toward her and raised his eyebrows. "Speaking of chips, didn't you tell me that Spike was going to hook us up with some kind of mysterious, black-market computer connection that couldn't be traced?"

She dug into her beat-up, leather messenger bag and pulled out a tablet with a ten-inch screen that she generally used for reading mystery novels. "I'm hoping he can do that tonight."

"What are you going to do with the tablet?"

"Rocky has always been kind of a computer geek. I'll bet he has surveillance cameras and maybe even hidden microphones around his house. Spike might be able to hack into his system, giving us a view of what's happening inside his modest multi-million-dollar home."

"I like it. Good way to gather data without putting ourselves in danger."

Barely consulting the GPS, Blake confidently made all the turns until he was driving along Highway 82, which followed the flow of the Roaring Fork River. Clearly, he'd taken this route before. Suspicious, she asked, "How do you know where you're going?"

"I come up here to ski. I tried snowboarding a couple of times but didn't like it as much. Nothing beats swooping downhill, flying over moguls. Maybe you can come with me on my next run."

If she stayed in Colorado, she'd like nothing better than to ski with him. But there was no point in making future plans. She might be on the run again, might be sequestered in an FBI safe house or locked away in prison, charged with kidnapping. Shaking her head, she tried to shove those dire, depressing possibilities from her mind.

As a woman who liked to have things organized, she hated not having a clue about what her future would be. How could she consider a relationship with Blake when tomorrow might bring unforeseen complications? She had to rely on other skills—abilities she'd developed as an investigative reporter. She'd dig for all the information she could find while keeping an open mind. Most of all, she'd stop worrying about things she couldn't control.

"The twins," she said in a clear voice that didn't betray her tension, "they should learn how to ski."

"Kids catch on fast. When they fall in the snow, they don't have far to go before they hit the ground. Your boys will be racing down the slopes in no time."

"You didn't grow up in Colorado." She remembered a long-ago conversation about their early lives. "It was somewhere in Illinois."

"Peoria," he said. "I went to college at Texas A&M on a football scholarship. Go Aggies. That was when I started scheduling my vacations for Colorado, and I met Chester. Whenever possible, I'd stay with him."

"And ski."

"He was my surrogate dad, newly retired with plenty of time to take me on as a project, especially after I tore my ACL and couldn't play football."

He was lucky to have found a strong male role model to replace the father who had abandoned his family. "If you hadn't met Chester, what do you think you'd be doing?"

"Maybe I would have become a teacher." He glanced toward her. "And you? Did you ever consider a career other than journalism?"

"Not that I remember, but I didn't do a lot of heavy thinking. Like Alex, I thought I'd take on all kinds of different occupations. Then I realized that, as a journalist, I could pretend to be all those things and more." She shrugged. "One thing I never imagined was being a mother."

Reminiscing and just talking with him felt comfortable and pleasant. She leaned back in her seat and stared out at the night landscape as they rolled along the highway toward Aspen, coming closer to her witness, the squirrel who might bring a satisfying conclusion to her investigation. If only she could get him to talk to the FBI, Rocky would provide reams of evidence about her ex-husband's fraud, larceny and money laundering.

Blake exited the highway and drove into an area known as Cougar Gulch. He quickly assured her that the cougars weren't all sexy, wealthy, older women who preyed on handsome, young ski bums. "The area is named for real mountain lions."

"I'm sure you didn't come down this twisty road to go skiing," she said. "Are we headed in the right direction?"

"I dated a woman who lived around here."

"Your own private cougar?"

"Not that it's any of your business, but we were the same age. She flew jets in the navy."

Jordan was immediately interested. "Is she one of those pilots who take off from aircraft carriers? I'd love to talk to her. Can you set up a meeting?"

"A meeting with two of my former girlfriends? Hmm, let me think about it." He shook his head and mumbled something that sounded like a negative. Then he switched topics. "Hey, I heard the temperature would drop twenty degrees in two hours tomorrow afternoon."

When in doubt, talk about the weather... At a stop sign, she craned her neck to read a street sign. As he'd suggested, the houses were smaller than mansion-sized and set far apart on large, wooded lots. "We're getting closer."

"It's just over the next hill," he said, checking the GPS. "I'm going to drive past. We can check the place out and then find a vantage point to observe Rocky's nest."

As they cruised down the street, she peered through her window at a long, paved driveway leading to a two-story home with an impressive entry facade of chiseled granite blocks. Cedar planks alternated with several picture windows to form the other walls and a large deck. On one side a granite rock formation echoed the entryway architecture.

A grove of aspen separated the house from its neighbors to the north. Though there was a three-car garage, two vehicles parked at the front door—a black SUV and a dark sedan—both had tinted windows.

"Looks like he has guests." She checked her wristwatch. "It's 9:47 p.m."

"A dinner party?"

"Not Rocky. He's not a guy who does a lot of socializing."

"Aspen might have changed him. Does he have a girlfriend?"

"I don't know." She'd never bothered to ask, which was a lapse in judgment on her part. When researching a subject, she usually gathered as much info as possible, starting with the most important people in their lives.

Blake circled through the streets of Cougar Gulch, passing wide-spaced houses and artistically placed trees and shrubs until he found an overlook above Rocky's granite-and-cedar house where he parked at the curb. From her window, Jordan peered through a thicket of pine trees. She could see the driveway and the front door. The place looked innocent with light glowing from the picture windows. She narrowed her gaze. *Who was visiting Rocky?*

"In the glove box," Blake said, "there's a pair of night-vision binoculars."

"You're brilliant." She popped the latch and took out the lenses, which were easily adjusted and clarified the view. "There's nothing going on. You'd think with all those windows, few of which have curtains, that I could see somebody walking around."

He reached into the back seat and grabbed the handle on a gym bag. "I brought other supplies. Flashlights, a burner phone, granola bars, bottled water and anything else we might need for a stakeout."

Being on a stakeout conjured up visions of dark, dirty

streets and seedy neighborhoods. Instead they were parked in a lavishly landscaped area with incredibly expensive homes, a clear reminder that wealthy people—like her ex-husband—also committed crimes.

"Do you have your Glock?" she asked, still staring through the binoculars.

"Yes."

"Did you bring a weapon for me?"

"There's no need," he said resolutely. "You aren't going to be confronting anybody."

Though she didn't like the restriction, she knew he was correct. She didn't worry about her own safety, but if she revealed her presence to the wrong people, the twins would be in danger. "I'll be careful," she promised, "but I want to get out of the car and find a better spot for watching."

"Wait." He reached up and disabled the light that came on when the car door opened.

"Smart. We don't need to attract attention."

"Go. I'm right behind you," he said. "If I tap your shoulder, stop."

"Why?"

"We need to avoid sight lines from Rocky's house that might pick up our movements. Trust me on this. I know how to evade enemy detection on an approach."

She darted between the trees and carefully moved to a different angle. Fallen needles and pine cones crunched underfoot, not too loudly, but enough to scare away the critters. A chilly breeze spun through the tree trunks and brushed her cheeks. She pulled up the hood on her purple puffer jacket and dug into the pocket for knitted gloves. Following close behind her, Blake might have been nearly invisible—in his black parka and black watch cap with a smudged "N" for *navy*—if he hadn't been such a large man.

After poking around in the landscaped forest, she found

a hiding place behind a thicket and a boulder where they had a clear view of Rocky's house. She still hadn't spotted anyone moving around inside. She leaned against the large, warm body beside her.

"If something happens, what should we do?" she whispered.

"We can't arrest them. We're not cops. And we don't have backup." His low, stakeout-level voice caressed her. "Maybe record it on your cell phone."

She'd almost forgotten her super-encrypted phone. Now would be a great time for Spike to hack into Rocky's surveillance system. She pulled off her gloves to text him. Before the screen flared into light, Blake opened his parka and made her a warm tent where she could hide the cell phone. As she sent her text, she realized that it wouldn't be necessary for them to do a physical stakeout if Spike could access cameras inside the house.

She had just received a return text from Spike, telling her that he could manage the hack but it would take a while, when Blake whispered.

"Something's happening," he said.

With her cell phone dark, she emerged and raised her night-vision binoculars to her eyes. The front door had opened. A heavyset man came onto the porch. Twice as big as Rocky, who scampered beside him, the giant threw both arms wide to embrace the night and turned his big, round face up to the skies. There was no mistaking his identity.

It was Caspar Khaled.

Jordan covered her mouth to hide her gasp of surprise. Two other men with parkas emerged from the house, and she recognized casino bosses who had chased her down Fremont Street in Las Vegas. Spike had told her that Khaled took off in a private jet. Apparently, this was his destination.

A simple explanation for his visit might be that Rocky

worked for him. Possibly, Khaled's connection with the accountant had nothing to do with her ex-husband's many crimes. But she doubted the casino owner's innocence. Her visit must have alerted him to potential issues with the money-laundering scheme, and he came here to make sure Rocky didn't implicate him.

Another man stepped outside. He covered his shaved head with a furry Russian hat. His sleek jacket was tailored leather, and he strutted as he descended the two stairs from the porch and went to the dark sedan. The sight of him fired her rage. Blood boiling, she glared daggers.

"Dr. Stephen Merchant."

His cruel diagnosis had kept her imprisoned in the Gateway Institute. At his direction, she'd been drugged and restrained. She'd suffered solitary confinement, electroconvulsive shock treatment and hours in a straitjacket. Merchant was worse than Gruber because, as a doctor, he ought to know better.

His presence at Rocky's house represented definitive evidence that Hugh was involved in this late-night meeting. In a sharp but quiet voice, she said, "I want to go down there."

"Let the FBI arrest them."

"They're too rich," she said. "They'll get away with their crimes."

"Not this time."

Together, she and Blake would take their vengeance. For Bianca. And for Abigail. And for all the people Hugh and his associates had hurt and swindled. When these monsters were locked away, she and her children would finally be safe.

Chapter Sixteen

"Don't worry," SSA Ferris Taggart said. "Jordan Reese-Waltham will not be charged with kidnapping. You have my word."

Though relieved, Blake had to ask, "Why not?"

"The story her ex-husband has been telling is that she's taken the twins for a short vacation, and I'm choosing to believe she has his permission. My guess is that he wanted to avoid contact with the FBI or other law enforcement."

"Good guess."

Taggart and three other FBI agents had landed at the helipad on Chester's property less than an hour ago and commandeered the use of Chester's rugged Land Rover for their stay, leaving him with the Silverado. Their initial plan was to question Tim Rockwell, aka Rocky the Flying Squirrel, at his home in Aspen. Weather-wise, they'd been lucky. No snow, not yet, but the blue skies had already begun to fade as the storm over Ice Mountain came closer.

While Jordan and the kids stayed at his cabin, Blake had driven the Suburban to Chester's property for the meeting. The two old warriors, Chester and Taggart, had greeted each other with an exchange of salutes and hugs. Both tall and lean, they resembled each other in other ways as well. They both had white hair, neatly trimmed, and no facial hair. Taggart's most prominent feature was his thick, gray eyebrows, which pulled into a scowl when they got down to business.

Jordan had sent the fat flamingo flash drive with the evidence she'd gathered to use against Hugh along with a packet of photos and witness interviews. Her explanation of the data might have been clearer than Blake's would be, but she preferred to have Blake make the first contact. Some of her research involved somewhat illegal methods, especially when using Spike's cybertalents.

Before Blake left the cabin, she made him promise not to reveal Spike's unauthorized hack of the surveillance cameras at Rocky's house. Using her tablet, she could see the front and back doors to his house as well as the interior entry and his office, where they'd watched him open a wall safe hidden behind a painting of Mount Sopris.

"I'm looking forward to meeting her," Taggart said.

Blake shot him a suspicious look. "But not to arrest her, right?"

"The opposite," Taggart said. "I want to recruit her. She'd make an outstanding agent. Did you see the video posted on YouTube by a tourist at the Magic Lamp?"

"No, I haven't." A headache thrummed against his forehead. When she'd ventured into Las Vegas, he hadn't been thrilled about the plan. Now that they'd seen Khaled at Rocky's, he disliked it even more.

Taggart summoned one of the other agents and asked for his phone. After thumbing through the memory, he held up the video for Blake to see. "Check it out. Using her titanium baton, she takes down three guys, including Khaled, who's a giant."

On the screen, he saw Jordan evading shirtless men in harem pants with kendo moves and Filipino martial arts. She was fast, graceful and dangerous. While Blake still didn't approve of the risk she'd taken, he couldn't help being proud of her.

"Amazing," Taggart said. "Where did she learn how to do that?"

"I taught her."

"And I'd try to recruit you if Chester hadn't already told me that you're a marine to your core." He stalked toward the Land Rover. "Let's head out. I want to beat the snow."

Before he left, Blake spoke to Chester and asked him to return to the cabin with the Suburban. "I don't expect trouble, but I'd feel better if you were there with Jordan and the kids."

"Don't worry." Chester echoed the advice from Taggart. "This is going to turn out okay."

Blake wished he could be that certain.

JORDAN COULDN'T AVOID having this conversation any longer. The twins had cooperated in every way that was truly important. With little encouragement, they'd accepted her directions, ranging from boarding a helicopter to not drinking coffee. She owed them explanations for why she'd torn them away from their bedroom in the middle of the night, why they hadn't been able to say goodbye to their father and why they had to keep running.

After they lit a fire on the hearth in the front room of the cabin, she seated them on the plaid sofa. Alex sat on her left, and Cooper on the right. She wrapped her arms around them. As best she could, Jordan vowed to tell them the truth. Snuggling them close, she dropped kisses on the tops of their heads. "Everything I've done, every decision I've made comes from love."

"What are you talking about?" Cooper asked. "What decisions?"

"I had good reasons for taking you away from your dad." No way could she explain the complicated crimes Hugh had committed. Nor would she mention the terrible murder of Bianca. Not wanting to irreparably poison their relationship with their father, she wouldn't talk about the violence he'd done to her. "The important thing is this. Your dad still loves you. And I love you. None of this is your fault."

"Okay," Alex said. "Can we go outside? I want to put on my snowshoes."

"But there's no snow. Not yet."

Cooper said, "We ought to go down to the lake and check on Chester's boat. He left it here."

"I want you to know," she said, "that things might get dangerous."

Alex rose up on his knees, put his arms around her neck and kissed her cheek. "It's okay, Mom. We'll take care of you."

"You told us this stuff before," Cooper said. "When we moved into the little blue house with the tire swing. I liked that place."

That talk had taken place over a year ago when they were four, and it surprised her that Cooper remembered. He was so much older and wiser than his chronological age. "Here's what's different about this time. Chester and Blake talked to a friend of theirs. His name is Ferris Taggart. He's an FBI agent, and he's going to help us."

"FBI?" Alex's eyes opened as wide as saucers. "An FBI agent. Cool."

"The thing to remember is that he's a good guy." She looked from one twin to the other. "He might want you to stay at a safe house. Do you know what that is?"

Cooper guessed. "A house built out of steel that nobody can break into?"

"Or iron," Alex said. "Iron is stronger."

"It looks like a regular house, but a safe house is a supersecure location with surveillance and security. There will be other FBI agents to guard you and keep you protected. I know that sounds scary, but it might be necessary."

If Hugh or Gruber or even Dr. Merchant came after her, she didn't want the boys to be hurt by accident. Though she hoped that Hugh wouldn't endanger his sons, she couldn't be sure about him or the others. She continued, "If you have questions, ask me. I'll tell you the truth."

"I've got one." Cooper raised his hand as if he were in school. "Is Blake your boyfriend?"

In spite of herself, she grinned. "And what does that have to do with safe houses?"

"You promised to tell us the truth," Alex said. "Is he your lovey-dovey?"

"I like Blake."

"Are you going to marry him?" Cooper asked.

She gestured helplessly. "He hasn't asked me."

There was a knock at the front door. Chester called out, "Hey, you guys, let me in."

The boys dashed to answer. While Cooper punched in the code in the keypad, Alex waited for the lock to disengage and pulled the door open. He hugged Chester and said, "You're friends with an FBI guy."

"You betcha. He's a supervisory special agent."

"How come he's so special?"

Chester shrugged. "All the agents call themselves special. I don't know why."

Though Jordan felt like she'd lost control of her conversation with the twins, she hoped they'd gained some level of understanding. On the plus side, they didn't seem frightened at all.

She grinned at Chester. "Did you get all those special agents pointed in the right direction?"

"I did, and Blake went with them to Rocky's house."

She excused herself and went into the office to check on the computer feed Spike had arranged. Since Rocky's surveillance camera didn't have audio, she could only guess at what the tall, lean agent was holding up, probably a wallet with a badge. No doubt, he was saying something like, "Open up, we have a warrant."

Faced with three FBI agents and Blake, Rocky trembled. Behind his round glasses, his eyes blinked several times as though he could erase the sight of them. For him, the arrival of the feds meant the end of his life in crime. No more multi-million-dollar properties. No more hiding out in one of the most beautiful resorts in the world. No more freedom. The flying squirrel was losing his wings.

THOUGH ROCKY'S HOUSE wasn't as big as a mansion, Blake could tell that no money had been spared with the furnishings. Original paintings hung from the walls, and unique sculptures lurked in every corner. The real treasure couldn't be purchased at any price—the picture windows framed panoramic views of forests, rock formations and snow-covered mountains that were partially obscured by gray-blue storm clouds. A family of elk, including a buck with a full rack of antlers, drank from a creek and darted into the pine forest. A golden eagle soared overhead.

Though the two agents accompanying Taggart set out to search the house, Rocky tried to treat the appearance of the FBI as a social event. He went to the kitchen, made a fresh pot of coffee and put together a plate of sausage, crackers and cheeses, which he placed on the dining room table along with square appetizer plates.

"It's not quite lunchtime," Rocky said, "but you gentlemen must be hungry. Please help yourselves."

Apparently, Taggart decided to play along. He took the seat at the end of the table and gestured for Rocky to sit to his right. He put a slice of cheese onto a wheat cracker. "You're a busy man, Mr. Rockwell. You had guests last night."

"Caspar Khaled and some of his men stopped by." He

grinned, showing off his prominent buckteeth and trying to look friendly. "I used to work for him."

"At the Magic Lamp in Las Vegas."

"A lovely casino on Fremont. Since I was based in Flagstaff, I didn't get to visit him often. Most of our business was online."

"You were his accountant."

"One of many."

"Did Hugh Waltham introduce you?"

"I believe so. My work with Khaled mostly involved advice on investment and taxes."

Unprompted, he launched into a discussion on how profit and loss had to balance each other out, and the unique issues faced by casinos. The more he talked, the calmer he became. His words worked like a pressure valve, alleviating the tension he had to be feeling.

Taggart interrupted the monologue. "You said you were Khaled's former accountant. How did your relationship end?"

"We're still friends. That's obvious. That's why he felt comfortable visiting me." He jumped to his feet. "I retired. That's why I don't work for him anymore."

"I'll need to see your records for the Magic Lamp," Taggart said. "Just to review the paperwork."

"Fine." Rocky spat the word. "Look all you want. You won't find anything wrong."

His attitude told Blake that Rocky either had a double set of books that wouldn't show the discrepancies of money laundering or the squirrel had great confidence in his abilities.

Taggart gave an easygoing smile and rubbed his clean-shaven chin as if remembering a beard. His thick eyebrows arched as he nodded. "You're correct, Mr. Rockwell."

"About what?"

"I won't find anything wrong when I look over your

books. I'm not a numbers guy. But the forensic accountants at the FBI are among the best in the world at sighting discrepancies. If your digits don't line up exactly right, they'll figure it out."

The color faded from Rocky's face, and he sank into his chair.

Blake wished Jordan could be here. She was familiar with Rocky and all his ploys. Her knowledge might prove invaluable. Unfortunately, the hacked video feed from Rocky's surveillance cameras didn't include the dining area, which meant she wouldn't be able to see what they were doing.

He had an idea. Excusing himself from the conversation between Taggart and Rocky, he went to the office where the other two agents searched through file drawers. Blake waved to the camera, hoping that Jordan was watching. He borrowed a cell phone from one of the agents, held it up toward the camera and used it to call her super-encrypted number.

She answered, "What are you doing?"

"I'm putting you on mute but leaving this phone on. When I go into the other rooms, you'll be able to hear what we're talking about. So far, Rocky hasn't said anything we don't know, but he's nervous as hell."

"Thanks," she whispered. "Be careful."

He dropped the cell phone into a pocket in his fleece vest and returned to the dining table where Rocky sat, shoulders slumped. The squirrel looked like he was about to vomit.

Taggart continued, "Your other guest last night was Dr. Stephen Merchant. Did you do accounting work for him?"

"He's my doctor."

"Dr. Merchant is a psychiatrist."

"A while ago, I had a breakdown. Hugh arranged for me to be treated at Dr. Merchant's institute."

"When was that?" Blake asked.

Since he'd been mostly quiet, his question was unexpected. Taggart repeated it.

"About a year and a half ago," Rocky said.

Which was right around the time that Jordan had become aware of her ex-husband's crimes and started poking around. And when Hugh beefed up his security team.

Rocky pulled off his round glasses and swabbed away tears before they streaked down his cheeks. "Dr. Merchant saved my life. I'd do anything for him."

"What set off your breakdown?" Blake asked.

Glasses back on his nose, Rocky glared at him. "You're the boyfriend, aren't you? The guy Jordan used to be in love with."

"We're talking about you," Blake said. "What caused your breakdown?"

"No, no," Rocky said, "we're talking about you. You live nearby. On Ice Mountain. Near Chester Prynne. Is that where Jordan is hiding? Did she take her kids there?"

He could almost feel the cell phone in his pocket buzzing and imagined Jordan yelling at Rocky, telling him it was none of his business where she'd gone or who she'd been with.

"You don't get to ask questions," Taggart said. "It's your job to give me answers."

"Let's drop this charade," Rocky said as he straightened his spine and drew himself up to his full height, which couldn't have been more than five-six. "I have nothing more to say. It's time for me to call my lawyer."

"You'll need a criminal lawyer, somebody who knows how to work a jury."

"Oh, please. I might have fudged the numbers, but any crimes I may or may not have committed are minor, punishable by a fine. No big deal."

"Think again, Mr. Rockwell." Taggart glared while Rocky fidgeted. "I expect to charge you with murder."

A harsh sob pushed through the small man's lips. Then he whispered her name.

"Bianca."

Chapter Seventeen

At the cabin, Jordan listened, mesmerized, as Tim Rockwell reported that he had not seen the killers inflict those fatal injuries, stabbing and slashing. But he admitted that he witnessed the aftermath. Rocky had found the body.

In a park in Flagstaff not far from his home, he'd gone for an evening jog and noticed her, broken and bleeding, at the side of the asphalt path. In a ragged voice, he told them how he recognized her, remembered her beauty and her gentle smile. "I knew right away that she was dead. So much blood, so much. Her eyes were wide open, staring up at Heaven."

He'd made an anonymous call to the police, not wanting to get involved, and then he went back to his house and pulled down the shades.

His cowardice disgusted Jordan. Too frightened to sit with the body, he'd left Bianca alone and unattended in the night. A final insult.

Taggart pressured him for more details. "What time was it? Did you see anyone else? Why would Bianca be in that neighborhood? Who killed her?"

"I don't know." She imagined Rocky wringing his small hands. "I didn't really know her, didn't know anything about her, except…"

"Tell me," Taggart insisted.

"She had a beautiful singing voice. Sweet as an angel."

"Where did you hear her singing?"

"Sometimes, she worked at the Flagstaff house as a kitchen helper. She wasn't on the regular payroll but filled in when necessary. Waltham throws a lot of dinner parties and needs extra staff to help out."

Taggart instructed him to repeat his testimony again and again. Each time, Rocky recalled more detail. He spoke of the scratchy chirp of crickets in the night and the strangely metallic smell of blood when he neared the body. On the fourth repetition, his description had expanded from a few sentences to a long, complicated story. Still, he swore that he hadn't seen the murderer.

Finding an actual witness to Bianca's killing represented a big leap forward in Jordan's investigation. She wished Rocky had taken pictures with his cell phone, especially when he described the body being blood-soaked and lying in the green, green grasses. Had Bianca been killed somewhere else and moved to the park? The police description of the crime scene had been too vague to draw meaningful conclusions, but the police couldn't ignore the similarity between the scars on her wrist and the medical examiner's photos of Bianca's wounds. She had new evidence. With the addition of Rocky's testimony, she could force the Flagstaff police to reopen the cold case.

Right now, she had something more urgent to worry about. Rocky had recognized Blake and knew about this cabin. If he knew, she suspected the others were aware of her supposedly safe hideaway. They needed to move. The time had come to tuck the kids away in a safe house.

After punching in the code to deactivate the alarm at the front door, she went outside and headed down to where Chester had taken the boys, to the edge of Paddington Lake. She saw them at the end of the dock, throwing pebbles at the water and watching the ripples spread.

Still holding the cell phone, she listened to Taggart and Blake questioning Rocky about his other clients. His employers, including B and W Employ as well as two smaller casinos, formed a web of connections with Hugh sitting at the center like a poisonous spider.

She waved to the kids and signaled for them to climb the hill. As soon as they got here, she'd herd them into the Suburban and drive to Chester's house. A prudent solution.

Over the cell phone, she heard a door slam. Someone else joined the group at Rocky's house. The voice of her ex-husband came through the cell phone and echoed through her memories like a nightmare.

"YOU MUST BE Captain Blake Delaney," Hugh Waltham said. "Finally, we meet."

Blake sized him up. When he saw Hugh on TV, he thought the guy was good-looking. In person, he wasn't as polished. Hugh wore appropriate clothes for the mountains: boots, jeans and flannel shirt under a fishing vest with multiple pockets. Jordan's ex-husband appeared to be a confident, successful gentleman, but Blake saw a monster who had ordered an attack on Jordan and had locked her away at the Institute. Hugh's velvety, politician's voice oozed with treachery, ready to lie at the slightest provocation. Though he wore expensive aftershave, a rank smell emanated from him. Their handshake reminded Blake of the scaly appendage of a lizard.

Blake turned his back and distanced himself.

Taggart presented himself in a more civil manner. "What brings you to Colorado?"

"I'm here to visit my old pal, Rocky."

Blake saw terror in the small man's eyes. Though Rocky tried to smile, his mouth trembled. All his self-control focused on a simple question. "Would you like coffee?"

"You bet." Hugh sat at the table and leaned back in his chair. "Well, gentlemen, what are we talking about?"

"Murder," Blake said.

Hugh bobbed his head, and his carefully barbered blond hair skimmed across his tanned forehead. Everything about him showed a careful, camera-ready polish, from his buffed fingernails to his perfect teeth. His eyes were a swampy green instead of bright blue like Jordan and the twins. He gave a condescending chuckle. "Murder, eh? That's a big issue. You like to jump right in, don't you?"

"I don't waste time," Blake said.

"And so, Captain Delaney, who do you think Rocky killed?"

"Not funny." The small man darted back into the room with a fresh mug of coffee for his former employer. Wielding a glass carafe, he refilled for the others. "Please help yourselves to cheese and sausage."

"Charcuterie," Hugh said. "One of my favorite snacks."

"I know," Rocky said.

Blake wondered if he'd been expecting Hugh to drop by or if he kept stocked up on sausage and cheese just in case. The tension around the table was enough to give anybody indigestion, but Hugh and Taggart continued to fill their square appetizer plates with cheese, crackers and sausage, as if to show they weren't disturbed.

"The victim's name," Taggart said, "was Bianca Hernandez."

"Oh, yeah, I remember." Hugh stacked Swiss cheese on top of something that looked like pepperoni but was probably ten times more expensive. "It was a while ago. Did she work for me, Rocky?"

"I believe she did. In the kitchen."

Blake much preferred Rocky's earlier angst and nervousness. The more casual attitude offended him. Bianca deserved better. "She was sixteen years old and pregnant with twins."

"Tragic," Hugh said. "But I don't know what this has to do with Rocky. Or me."

"The killer was never arrested. The murder became another cold case, tucked away in the depths of the police archives," Taggart explained, with a bitterness that made Blake think he'd been in this position before. "The initial police investigation was sloppy, with questionable handling of DNA. And—surprise, surprise—we have new evidence."

"Good for you," Hugh said as he reached for a fat, red, smoked chorizo sausage. "I'm surprised the FBI has time to check on local police matters. What am I missing? Is a serial killer involved or another murder?"

"One brutal death is enough," Taggart said.

"I didn't mean to imply otherwise." Hugh placed the sausage on his appetizer plate beside a sliver of Gouda cheese. "I seem to recall that the young woman worked for Stanley and Abigail Preston. A shame about her accident."

The bodies had begun to pile up, and Hugh had cleverly implicated his coworker and friend, Stanley. As if to refute this bit of misdirection, Blake fastened a hard-edged stare at Hugh Waltham—the man responsible for this death and mayhem. Somewhere under that mask of cruelty, there must be a glimmer of decency and kindness that had drawn Jordan toward him and convinced her to marry the monster.

Blake watched as Hugh reached into a pocket in his fishing vest and took out a pocketknife with a buffalo horn handle. While talking about the unfortunate rise of violent crime in the city, he pulled out the long blade, probably four inches. Damascus steel, with a serrated edge near the hilt. Hugh sliced into his chorizo and lifted his gaze to return Blake's glare.

Brandishing the knife, a weapon that matched the scars on Jordan's wrists, was a direct challenge. The bastard thought he was bulletproof, and nobody could catch him.

Blake intended to prove him wrong. "Your ex-wife tried to investigate the murder of Bianca Hernandez," he said. "She mentioned that you helped her gather evidence."

"Another one of her causes," Hugh said as he cut another slice of sausage. "Jordan always gravitated toward the underdog. Have you spoken to her recently?"

Blake kept his expression calm. "Have you?"

"She took the boys on vacation, but we didn't really speak."

"Do you know where she went?" Blake stretched out his long arm and took a slice of chorizo from Hugh's appetizer plate.

"Not really."

"I have a pretty good idea." Taggart leaned forward and held out the phone with the video of Jordan at the Magic Lamp. "That's her in Las Vegas with your pal, Caspar Khaled. She's kicking his butt."

Hugh looked away from the screen. "Jordan has a strange sense of humor."

"Doesn't look like a joke to me," Taggart said. "Last night, Khaled paid a visit to Rocky. And now you're here. Can you explain that coincidence?"

"Whatever my ex-wife does isn't my problem." He pointed the tip of his knife at Blake. "Maybe you should ask *him* where she is."

"Captain Delaney couldn't possibly have had anything to do with the death of Bianca Hernandez. He's been overseas."

"In the Middle East?" Hugh asked.

"I could tell you, but then I'd have to kill you." Blake hoped that his slow grin indicated how much he'd like to inflict grievous bodily harm on this scumbag. "Many of my missions were classified."

"Mine, too."

"In Congress, which is where you hope to work after the election, that's called a cover-up."

"What's it called for a marine?"

"My covert activity was done in the service of my country," Blake said. "I'm guessing that your secrets are to advance yourself and your bank account."

"What a shame." Hugh put away his blade. "I heard that you'll be retiring soon. You're no longer fit for battle."

I could take you with my eyes blindfolded and one hand tied behind my back. He wasn't surprised that Hugh knew the extent of his injuries. "I might be stationed in the Pentagon where I can keep an eye on people like you."

"If you're lucky, you might be standing guard outside the Oval Office."

"Another place you aspire to work," Blake said. So many elected officials set their sights on the highest office in the land. "You keep your eyes on the ultimate prize, and you don't allow anybody to get in the way."

Instead of backing down, Hugh leaned toward him. Blake stared back, but this was more than an old-fashioned contest to see who'd be the first to blink. Hugh was issuing a threat.

"I always win." Over his shoulder, he spoke to Rocky. "Isn't that right?"

The small man responded quickly. "Yes, sir."

"Any person—male or female—who tries to stop me will be sorry," he said. "He or she will lose everything, maybe even their life."

Blake clenched his fists to keep from strangling the man who sat with him at the table. Message received. Blake understood. Hugh would kill to reach his goal. Bianca's

murder was only the start. Abigail had also been eliminated. Jordan was next.

"Excuse me," Blake said as he rose to his feet. "Special
Agent Taggart, I need to speak with you."

Taggart followed him out of the dining area and into
the hallway. After a stop at the office where Taggart sent
one of the other agents to keep an eye on Rocky and Hugh,
Blake took SSA Taggart into the lavish bathroom with gold
fixtures and a marble tub. Even after turning on multiple
jets in the luxurious shower to cover the sound of their
conversation, he kept his volume on extra low. Anybody
could be listening with long-range devices or the whole
house could be bugged.

"You heard him," Blake said. "Hugh admitted that he's
going after Jordan. It's time for her and the kids to go to
a safe house."

"Agreed," Taggart said. "I'll talk to Chester."

Blake took the cell phone from his pocket and spoke
into it. "Jordan, are you there?"

"We're leaving your cabin and going to Chester's place."
She adjusted her cell phone, so the screen showed her face.
Her smile twitched nervously. "The boys just realized that
it's almost Halloween. They couldn't care less about cos-
tumes, but they want the candy."

"How much of my conversation with Hugh did you
hear?"

"Most of it. I wish I could have seen what was going
on."

He thought of Hugh gesturing with the knife that had
probably been used to slash her wrists and possibly to
kill Bianca. He shuddered, glad that she hadn't witnessed
Hugh's oversize ego in action. Jordan didn't need to be
confronted with any other sick images. "Your ex-husband
is an ass, but we have to take him seriously. He's danger-

ous. If he doesn't come after you, Khaled will. Or Gruber. It's time for you and the boys to go to a safe house."

"We're on the same page." Her head bobbed, setting her dark curls into motion. "Chester and I already talked about the safe house. He'll stay with the twins, so they'll have someone familiar. Put Taggart on the line so he can make arrangements with Chester."

"Wait," Blake said. "What about you?"

"I can't put the final pieces of my investigation together if I run away and hide. I'm so close, Blake."

Though he understood her feelings of ownership when it came to the evidence it had taken years for her to compile, he wanted her to step aside. "Please, Jordan. Go with the boys. Let the FBI handle this."

"I can't quit now."

His protective instincts surged. He doubted she would change her mind but made one more try. "Nobody is taking you off the case. You'll be informed every step of the way."

"I know how investigations work." She spoke with the authority of a reporter who had been embedded with the troops because she needed to see and experience the battles for herself. A secondary source wasn't good enough. "I'll be careful."

The best he could do was to stay by her side and keep her as safe as possible. Before he handed the cell phone to Taggart, he said, "Wait for me, Jordan."

The doctors who treated his recent injuries might not think he was fit for duty, but Blake had to find the strength and skill for this mission. He had to guard this woman and defend her against the many people who wished to do her harm.

Chapter Eighteen

Seated at a Formica-topped table in the kitchenette of a nondescript motel suite in a small mountain town, Jordan stared into the plain white mug and wished she had something stronger than instant coffee to drink. When Chester and the twins took off in the FBI helicopter, leaving her behind in the shadow of gathering snow clouds, she'd kept grinning as she waved goodbye. Inside, she was sobbing hysterically. She wanted to scream. *Don't go. Stay with me.* But her children needed to be in a safe house, surrounded by high-level protection.

And she needed to stay.

The danger belonged to her alone. Her choice. She claimed it. After the FBI drove her to the motel, one of the agents offered to stay with her until Blake arrived, but she didn't need a babysitter. It was a point of pride—Jordan could take care of herself.

She pushed away from the small table, paced to the second-floor window and peeked out at the chilly scene outside from behind the edge of the closed curtains. Before he left, the agent had warned her about being too visible, and she agreed, mostly because she'd promised Blake that she'd be careful. As soon as she entered the room, she checked out the security. There were two exits. The door on this side of the room opened onto a concrete walkway.

On the other side, she could step into a carpeted interior hallway. She'd added portable door locks to the standard-issue systems already in place. Not that her attempt to turn a motel suite into a fortress would be effective. The thugs who were after her could crash through a window or shoot off a lock.

If they wanted to get to her, they could. But why? Capturing her wouldn't make any difference in the FBI review of the evidence she'd already turned over. The best proof—hopefully the final proof—had to come from Rockwell's accounting records.

After all her digging, she had to ask herself if the investigation was worth the effort. A dream team of attorneys could help Hugh dodge those white-collar crimes and get off with a slap on the wrist. But the murder charge was a different matter, which was why she would see this investigation through to the end.

It was also why her ex-husband would do everything he could to get her out of his way.

The approaching danger cast a spotlight on the great dilemma of her life. *Who am I?* Oh damn, where to start? When she was younger, her dedication to her career took center stage. She chose her tiny, sparsely furnished apartment in New York because it was close to the newspapers and magazines that bought her articles. Decisions on her travel plans were dictated by headlines and breaking news. Her friends and associates came mostly from among the journalists, editors and investigators who she met on the job.

Even her relationship with Blake happened because she was working on an article. Her lover—former lover—represented the second phase in her life. She tapped her fingernail against the window. Where was he? Outside, she heard the slam of a car door and angled her neck so she could see who emerged from the unfamiliar Chevy sedan that slipped into a slot at the outer edge of the parking lot.

Watching and waiting, she felt like she was engaged in a weird version of Russian roulette. The man who got out of the car could be Gruber or one of his security guards. It might be an employee from the Magic Lamp. If she was lucky, she'd find herself looking down at Blake. It was him!

She recognized his knit watch cap with the US Navy logo, his wide shoulders, his towering height and his long strides as he mounted the staircase to the second floor. Blake carried a pizza box, which thrilled her almost as much as seeing him.

She unfastened the locks. One second after his bare knuckle rapped on her door, she whipped it open and pulled him inside. She kicked the door shut with a loud slam.

"About time," she said as she yanked the pizza box from his hands, dropped it on the desk near the door and tried to plaster herself against him. Something was in her way. "Ow, what's that?"

"My six-pack." He unzipped his parka, took out his six-pack and set it on the desk. "Got to have beer for pizza."

She gave him a long, hard kiss that literally took her breath away. Gasping, she stayed in his embrace, snuggled in the crook of his neck. A sense of belonging and longing enveloped her. This was exactly how things should be. She tilted her head back to peer into his eyes. "You changed my life, Blake. I've been thinking, and it's true. Before I met you, I was laser-focused on my journalism."

He tucked a curl behind her ear. "Before we talk, we need to lock the door."

"And then eat the pizza. What's on it?"

"Everything but anchovies."

Happiness bubbled through her like fizzy champagne. In this moment, she felt no fear from the menacing threat, no sadness at being separated from her boys and no anger at the injustice of crime. Only joy. The rest of the world faded away, and she lost herself in the pleasure of being held by a strong, good-looking man. Unable to hold herself back, she kissed him again.

As she watched him fasten the door locks, his every move seemed excellent and perfect. Whether driving a car or shooting a Glock, he'd always been skillful—the sort of man who could take care of whatever needed to be done. Her giddy observations went way over the top, but she couldn't stop herself. *Sweep me off my feet, Blake.* When he looked back at her and smiled, she desperately wanted to caress his jaw and kiss those endearing dimples.

In his gentle baritone, he asked, "How are the kids?"

"I wish you hadn't asked."

"Why not?"

She didn't want to return to reality, didn't want her fantasies to disappear. Not yet. She wanted to cling to the dream of being with him, covered in fairy dust and rainbows. *What's wrong with me?* How could she forget about Alex and Cooper? The twins were the most important people in her life, and she'd allowed them to drop off her radar. *I'm a fool.* This must stop. She swiveled away from him, paced a few steps and sank onto the edge of the bed.

"I'm not supposed to call them." Her voice fell flat, devoid of tone or rhythm. "The FBI didn't think I was being traced or monitored, but they didn't want to take chances."

"What's wrong?" He sat beside her. His large hand rested at the base of her neck and he lightly massaged. "You look like somebody popped your bubble."

"Like I said, I was thinking about my life. First, I was a journalist. Then I met you and had a taste of romance that left me wanting more."

"I did that?" His chest swelled. Proud of himself.

"*We* did that," she corrected. "It takes two. I don't know

if it was a matter of timing or hormones or fate, but my world changed from harsh black-and-white to gentle pastels."

This kiss was different. He took his time, and the pressure of his lips against hers reminded her of the past and, at the same time, gave a glimpse of what might happen in the future. The veils of fear and anger swirled in a capricious wind as her mood lightened. Still, she pushed away from him.

"Again," he said, "tell me what's wrong."

"My life changed again when our romance ended. I became a mom. My life had a new purpose. Those first couple of years when the twins were babies, I was overworked, exhausted, confused and terrified that I was doing everything wrong. I had never been happier."

He continued to stroke her back. "And who are you now, Jordan?"

"Trying to balance my journalistic instincts with being a full-time mother. And now, there's you. I'm juggling all these balls in the air, and I can't let any of them hit the floor." She turned her head and looked at him. "Am I being overdramatic?"

"A little bit." He held his thumb and index finger about an inch apart to indicate the small amount of drama. As she watched, he stretched the space wider and wider. "Maybe you're a diva reporter, like Brenda Starr or Lois Lane, but I like your grit."

"You advised me to walk away from the investigation and go to the safe house."

"I might have spoken too soon."

"You? Make a mistake?"

"It happens." He shrugged. "Seems to me that you can be all three. You can't stop being a mom. Why ignore your talent and training? You're good at digging for news stories like a rabid ferret. And that leaves romance. I think you can make time for me."

"I like that you made a list." She inhaled deeply, drawing in good vibes. "My obsessive habits are rubbing off on you."

"I'm beginning to understand how life works in Jordan's world. And I'm happy to volunteer for romance duty." He stood, took her hand and pulled her to her feet. "But first, we eat pizza."

"And drink beer."

While they chowed down, he told her about Taggart's progress on the investigation. The FBI supervisory special agent had reprimanded the police officials in Flagstaff and demanded the cold case be reopened. "He ran through a whole series of crime scene details that needed to be sent to him and ordered the medical examiner to find a DNA match for Bianca's twin babies."

She washed down a savory bite of pizza with cold beer. "It's nice to have that kind of authority on an investigation. What's going to happen with Khaled?"

"His fate depends on Rocky. The squirrel is still denying any part in criminal activity, especially money laundering, but he's on the verge of taking a deal in exchange for testifying against his former employers."

She nibbled at the crust, her favorite part of the pizza. With the details of her investigation falling into place, she had second thoughts about not joining the twins at the safe house. "I have an emergency number for Taggart."

"So do I." Blake took a long swig of his beer. "There's something else I want to talk about. You and me and the romance we started seven years ago. You aren't the only one who thinks about those days. When I saw you hiking in the forest outside my cabin with the wind tangling in your hair and bringing out the roses in your cheeks, I went back in time. I was a healthy young man with my whole life ahead of me."

"You still are."

"I want to be the guy I was back then," he said, "in my prime. You deserve the best."

She wasn't sure she understood. "Have you looked in a mirror lately? You're not exactly a washed-up old hulk."

Instead of speaking, he stood, took off his belt holster and placed his Glock on the bedside table within easy reach. He unfastened the buttons on his flannel shirt.

She cleared her throat. "What are you doing?"

He slipped off his shirt. Only the thin layer of a short-sleeved camouflage T-shirt covered his chest. "Ready?"

For what? She played along. "Yes."

He peeled off his T-shirt. His bare chest, lightly sprinkled with dark hair, displayed firm pecs and abs. And she saw his scars. Some were deep and puckered, ridges that tore across the muscles. Others faintly marked his skin and might, in time, fade to almost nothing. Hearing that he'd been badly injured had worried her but seeing the evidence made the explosion more real. She could almost feel his suffering. His buddy, Harvey from Henderson, had told her that the doctors didn't think he'd ever walk again. But Blake had recovered.

"I'm so proud of you," she said.

"Why?"

"Survival requires more strength and more courage than charging into battle."

She rose from her chair and came toward him. Her fingers traced the thickest scar that traversed his upper chest, where something had probably stabbed between his ribs and pierced his lung. Heat radiated from him. His flesh trembled under her touch, and his breathing became ragged. This response to her nearness delighted her and reflected her own pleasure. She saw his scars as medals of honor, evidence of his heroism and service.

When she pushed him down on the bed and started to climb on top of him, he caught hold of her arm. "Not like this," he said. "Take off your blouse."

Like him, the first item she removed was her physical protection in the form of the titanium baton fastened to her belt. The other layers—sweatshirt, blouse, T-shirt and bra—that kept her warm didn't make for a sexy striptease and took a while to remove. Finally, naked from the waist up, she straddled him, arched her back and flung her arms wide.

"I've changed, too," she said. "Giving birth and nursing twins can take a toll on a woman's body."

"You look good. Real good."

His gravel-voiced compliment teased her like a rough caress. When she slowly leaned down and joined with him, pressing her breasts against his chest, she felt fulfillment. The warmth from his large body was strong enough to keep an entire house cozy. The scars added an extra dimension. "I missed you."

He moved his hand along her spine, tapping her vertebrae like a xylophone. "I dreamed about you all the time, thought about you. Especially in the shower."

They had taken many fantastic showers together. "Why didn't you call?"

"You were busy, having another man's babies. And getting married to him."

"The wedding didn't happen until after the twins were born." She'd put off that final commitment for as long as possible. After the babies arrived, she wanted them to be part of their father's life. Worst mistake she'd ever made. "I'm lying in bed with you, Blake. The last thing I want to think about or talk about is my ex-husband."

This time, when their lips met, she tasted the pleasant

tang of beer and pizza. His tongue penetrated her mouth and swirled, setting off a whirlwind of sensation. Her skin tingled. Her ears rang with the sound of his breathing.

He rolled her onto her back, and she put up zero resistance. But when he reached for the switch to turn off the lamp, she stopped him.

"I want to see what's going on," she said.

"It's too bright."

He was correct. The direct light wasn't conducive to the mood. "I'll fix it."

She darkened the room, except for the desk lamp. Then she tuned the radio to a smoky jazz station because a wailing saxophone and hot drumbeat were the best accompaniment for hot, hot sex. When she returned to the bed, she saw he'd made changes of his own. Obviously naked, he stretched out between the sheets.

In a few hasty seconds, she matched him by kicking off her sneakers and wriggling out of her jeans. As she snuggled beside him, his long legs tangled with hers. His muscular grasp overwhelmed her, and her brief struggle for control faded in utter capitulation. The best way to win this battle was by surrendering to his clever hands fondling her breasts. His fingers stroked the delicate flesh between her thighs. His lips kissed, and his teeth nipped.

He teased and teased. No man had ever aroused her the way Blake did. When he entered her, she was so very ready. Though she knew she'd felt this way before, seven years ago when they'd had sex for the first time, her climax felt brand-new.

With tremors racing through her body, she closed her eyes and accepted the incredible sensations that washed over her in wave after wave, predictable as the tide and equally miraculous. In the back of her mind, a tiny voice whispered. *Who am I?*

"I'm yours." Though unfeminist to think so, it was

true. Blake owned a part of her that no one else would ever know.

"Did you say something?" he asked.

"Don't want to repeat it." She watched as he left the bed and went to the window. For a moment, she admired his back, scarred though it was along his spine. It was weird to stare at his bottom, but she couldn't look away. "What are you doing over there?"

He whipped the drapes open to reveal a thick, heavy snowfall against the black of night.

This storm brought more than high wind and heavy moisture. A blizzard. This would be a final test of their survival on Ice Mountain. Winter had arrived.

Chapter Nineteen

"I've changed my mind," Jordan said. "There's nothing more I can do for this investigation. It's time for me to give up and go to the FBI safe house."

Mindful of security, Blake closed the curtains and stalked across the motel room to the bed where she sat with pillows behind her back and the sheet tucked around her hips. Being naked with her had always been one of his favorite things. Jordan wasn't the least bit coy. In spite of what she'd said about the way her body looked after childbirth—which was, in his opinion, outstanding—she wasn't ashamed of her curves or the size of her perfect, round breasts. Her confidence enhanced her natural beauty.

He slid between the crisp, white sheets. This motel wasn't a five-star lodging, but the room suited their needs and didn't seem like the sort of place where Hugh would search for his ex-wife. Blake locked his gaze on her lovely face.

They had a lot more to talk about. "I'm sorry," he said.

"About what?"

"You can't go to the FBI house. Until Hugh is taken into custody, the boys are more secure if you aren't near them."

She cocked her head to one side and stared at him. "I don't understand."

And he didn't want to explain. Instead, he'd rather dive

under the covers and make love to her again and again until they were both too exhausted to move. He glided his hand along the smooth curve of her waist. "Maybe we should wait. We can talk in the morning."

"Now, we talk now." She slapped his hand away. "There's something you aren't telling me. Why can't I see my kids?"

"When you listened to my conversation at Rocky's dining room table with Hugh and Taggart, you didn't have the full picture. You couldn't see what was happening."

Clueless, she nodded. "Did Hugh pull a gun on you? Did he throw poison darts? What?"

Her ex-husband had given the appearance of civility. As a politician, he'd learned to mask all sorts of wrong behavior with the right moves and the right words. "We were eating cheese and sausage."

"I know. Hugh complimented Rocky on the charcuterie, an extra-fancy word for a common snack. Like referring to broccoli and carrots as crudités."

"He likes being extra fancy."

"Because he has no real taste." Her eyebrows pulled into a scowl. "He wouldn't mind if I dressed in garbage bags as long as they had designer labels. Tell me what happened."

"Hugh reached into a pocket on his fishing vest. And he took out a knife. It was a long blade, over four inches. Damascus steel, serrated at the hilt." He held her small hand in both of his. His thumb stroked the scar on her wrist. "The murder weapon."

Her eyelids fluttered as though trying to erase the picture he'd painted, but she couldn't escape the facts. The knife that killed Bianca belonged to Hugh. He was the murderer…which also meant he was the one who attacked her. As Blake watched her expression, he saw that realization dawning. She hadn't suspected him before now.

Three months ago, when she was abducted and taken to

the Institute, she'd remembered Gruber zapping her with a stun gun and giving her an injection that knocked her unconscious. She'd assumed that her ex-husband's hench-man slashed her wrists and nearly caused her to bleed to death. She hadn't seen the attack, but Hugh's knife had left the unusual scar.

"Unbelievable." Her voice faded to a sad whisper. "How could he? We were married. I'm the mother of his children."

Not a damned thing he said would ease her bone-deep disappointment and pain. Her ex-husband was evil, un-redeemable. With a groan, she collapsed against Blake's chest. Her slender shoulders trembled, and her breathing came in ragged gasps. On some level, she must still have cherished memories of birthdays and Christmases when she and Hugh and the twins were a family. A good mother like Jordan couldn't help clinging to the hope that Alex and Cooper could have a decent relationship with their father.

He held her, trying to absorb some of her pain and wait-ing for the shock to subside. When she finally looked up at him, her enormous blue eyes were dry. No more tears for Hugh. Good. "He can't allow you to meet up with law enforcement," Blake said. "Three months ago, he turned you into the best evidence against him. You're the proof."

"The scars on my wrists match Bianca's wounds. Both were made by the same weapon. A knife that belongs to my ex-husband." A shudder went through her. "What if he throws it away? Or gives it to Gruber?"

"Taggart and I both saw the serrated blade. I'm guess-ing there are other witnesses. And photos from hunting or fishing trips."

"Still, Taggart should have seized the knife as mate-rial evidence."

"He didn't want to tip Hugh off."

"I don't like this strategy," she said. "Hugh's good at playing cat-and-mouse games."

"My money is on Taggart." This was a classic case of allowing an egomaniac enough rope to hang himself. "No way in hell is Hugh going to get away with this."

She left the bed, still naked, and went to the desk where her battered messenger bag rested on the floor beside the drawers. She took out a legal-size pad and a marker pen. "We need a plan."

Exactly what he expected her to say. He knew that Jordan would hold her rage, frustration and denial in check as long as she had a project to hold her focus. She wanted to get to work, to complete her investigation in spite of Hugh's minions, the casino thugs from the Magic Lamp and a snowstorm that promised to dump several inches overnight. "You make me proud," he said.

She thrust her arms into his plaid flannel shirt which was large enough to wrap around her small, slender body three or four times. Jordan had gone into planning mode and would ignore distractions. "First, we figure out the end goal."

Fortunately, he'd been paying attention when he was with Taggart. He leaned back against the pillows and folded his arms behind his head. "The FBI investigators, led by SSA Taggart, have been in touch with the federal prosecutors in Denver who have been reviewing the evidence."

"Any problem using illegally obtained evidence in their prosecution?"

"Some, but most of those federal legal eagles think you're brilliant."

Her lips stretched in a sly grin. "Because I am."

"They're putting together airtight cases against Hugh and some of his coconspirators. They're waiting for you. You're the final evidence. After you give a deposition, the whole gang will be charged and held pending indictment by a grand jury."

"But they'll still be eligible for bail," she said. "We won't be safe if Hugh makes bond and is released. The kids and I might be stuck in safe houses for a very long time."

"True enough." Blake wasn't a legal expert, but Taggart had answered this question for him. "On the charges of fraud, extortion and money laundering, they'll be able to get bail. But the brutal murder of a young, pregnant minor is different. Especially when it's compounded by the assault on you."

"And Abigail's supposed accident," she added.

Hugh's crimes almost qualified him for status as a serial killer. "A decent judge won't turn him loose after he reviews the evidence. No matter whether he's best friends with the President or not."

"How about Dr. Merchant?" she asked. "Will that quack be going to prison?"

"Taggart thought so." The psychiatrist had already returned to Flagstaff, but Khaled and his men were still in the Aspen area. "They're all going to pay."

"Just so you know, this isn't about revenge." She curled against the pillows beside him. "Well, maybe it's a little bit about revenge, but mostly I'm after justice. These men have done terrible things and need to be stopped."

He kissed the top of her head and inhaled the jasmine fragrance of her shampoo. "Tomorrow, we'll drive down to Denver and meet the prosecutor."

"Tomorrow?" She slapped her legal pad down on the bed. "Why wait?"

"I could tell you that it's because Hugh and Gruber are still combing the roadways, looking for us. Not to mention Khaled and his guys. There are a lot of people with vested interests in finding you and keeping you away from the federal prosecutor."

"Are you saying you're not up for a car chase over Independence Pass?"

"Not in Chester's Chevy Malibu. I mean, it's a great little car but not for high-speed pursuit."

"How did you end up with the Malibu?"

"Taggart and his men took Chester's Land Rover and Silverado. The zippy little car was all that was left."

"What about the Suburban?"

"It's at my cabin." He climbed off the bed, slipped into his jeans and returned to the window. This time, when he opened the curtain, the snow was blowing nearly horizontal. "That's a blizzard."

She stepped up beside him. "I didn't come this far to be defeated by weather."

"The reports I've heard predict six to twelve inches of snow and winds of more than thirty miles per hour. But the blizzard isn't supposed to last too long. Before noon tomorrow, it should slow down."

She turned away from the window. "I guess we're stuck here until morning."

"Sorry it throws a wrench in your plan." He tugged the curtain closed, took her hand and led her back toward the bed. "But it gives us a chance to finish the pizza and beer."

"Don't kid yourself, Blake. I have plenty more planning to do."

"Of course." He resigned himself.

"We need to map out a driving route," she said. "If all these bad guys are looking for us, we have to find an alternate way to get away from Ice Mountain."

He groaned, remembering their circuitous escape from Flagstaff. "Many of the roads aren't marked, and most of them feed into highways and central routes. Lucky for us, I've spent a lot of time up here in all sorts of weather."

"You know your way around."

"I do, but I've got to warn you. The back roads won't be plowed or cleared. It's going to be slow going."

"Where do we start?" Her marker pen poised above the legal pad.

"Back to my cabin."

"The opposite direction from Denver."

This twisted logic only made sense if he looked at the big picture and visualized an old-fashioned map in his head. "There's a one-lane gravel road that zigzags over Ice Mountain Pass. It's not a great drive in any weather. Nobody will follow us there."

"And then?"

"Once I know we're safe, we contact Taggart. The FBI will give us a ride into Denver."

"Sensible."

"Really?"

She popped the lid back onto her marker and dropped it. "Let's make the feds our first option."

He was surprised that she was willing to give up so easily. "Is it strange for you to let somebody else take the lead?"

"Not a bit." She allowed the flannel shirt to slide off her shoulder, exposing her creamy skin. "I don't think of myself as a superheroine."

"You don't?" He bared her other shoulder.

"I need all the help I can get. There was a nurse at the Institute and an accountant who made sure I had the funds for my escape. Not to mention Emily Finnegan and her helicopter crew. And Spike. And dear Abigail." She exhaled a sigh. "And, of course, there's you."

"I like where this is headed."

Before they contacted Taggart in the morning, he had an excellent idea about how their time should be spent. When she gave him a wink and a slow, sensuous kiss, he suspected she was on the same page.

THE NEXT MORNING when Jordan stepped from her motel room into the grayish light of early morning, she might have been walking into a snow globe. Frigid winds tossed the fat, white flakes into swirling patterns. Heavy silence blanketed the parking lot. A plow had scraped off a layer and deposited the snow in a growing mountain beside the dumpster. The boughs of pine trees at the edge of the parking area were heavy with snow and bent low, almost touching the twelve inches that had fallen during the fierce overnight blizzard.

Gripping the handrail, she made her way to the concrete staircase at the far end. Though she wore gloves and a black knit cap with a pom-pom, she hadn't purchased snow boots for herself when she shopped for the kids. With every step, she regretted that oversight.

Blake had already moved the Malibu to the staircase. He'd brushed off the snow and started the engine to warm the interior. As she climbed inside and fastened her seat belt, she allowed herself to relax, which wasn't her usual state of mind at the start of a project. Being with Blake was good for her in so many ways. She could hardly believe it when she asked, "What should we do next?"

With his cheeks made ruddy from exposure, his blue eyes blazed. Snowflakes dusted the top of his cap. "Taggart wants us to meet him at a pancake house near his motel."

"Why didn't he stay here?"

"Bad weather. From the pancake house, he'll take care of our transportation problem."

Though she didn't like giving up the reins of control, she was relieved. Again. Getting to Denver and showing her scars to the prosecutor while being pursued by murderers and thugs was certainly a problem. But not her problem.

The nightmare investigation was almost over. From now on, all she had to do was show up and tell the truth. She had no reason to be on edge. And yet, when her super-encrypted cell phone buzzed in the pocket of her puffy jacket, her heartbeat accelerated. She was startled. An actual phone call. How odd! Spike usually sent text messages. It took her a while to dig out the phone and answer a number she didn't recognize.

"Who's this?" she demanded.

"Don't hang up. It's Caspar Khaled."

She stared through the windshield, then to the right and left as if she could see the bulky owner of the Magic Lamp standing on the street in his guayabera shirt with the white embroidery. The Malibu bumped over a curb as Blake drove onto the nearly vacant street outside their motel.

"How did you get this number?" she asked.

"Your buddy, Taggart. He has a leak."

"This must be a joke." Khaled ranked high among Hugh's friends. They worked together to defraud the IRS and the feds. She couldn't trust him. "I don't believe you."

"Listen, Jordan, I'm a businessman. At my casino, I sometimes skirt the law to save a buck, but I always play fair and give good odds."

"Why are you helping me?"

"Karma," he said. "I'm not a murderer. Not like Hugh."

She hated that he was making sense. "Go on."

"You're driving into a trap."

He disconnected the call and left her holding the cell phone. Could she believe him? The voice on her cell phone had sounded like Khaled and the karma comment was something he might say. If she trusted the caller, she and Blake needed to switch to her earlier plan, escaping by themselves and not looking back. Since they didn't know who among SSA Taggart's team had betrayed them, any contact was dangerous.

Or she might be overreacting. If the call was a ruse, she ought to ignore it and take her chances by joining the feds for pancakes and coffee.

An important decision loomed over her.

Against the pale sky, she saw the garish neon sign for Pancake Pete's. On the other side of the intersection, the headlights of two black SUVs glared at their spunky little Malibu. Those were the sort of heavy-duty vehicles Hugh preferred.

She turned to Blake. "We've got a change in plans."

Chapter Twenty

At her direction, Blake swerved wildly across the intersection and made a left turn, heading west. The rear tires of the Malibu sedan—not the world's best vehicle for maneuvering in snow—fishtailed on the frozen road as they drove past Pancake Pete's. In the parking lot, he saw the Land Rover that Taggart had been using and Chester's Silverado—a four-wheel drive vehicle he wished he was driving right now.

"Taggart has a leak," Jordan said as she twisted around in her seat to peer through the rear window. "Those two SUVs are following us. We almost drove into a trap."

"Who were you talking to?"

"Khaled." Before he could unleash a torrent of disbelief, she continued. "I don't think he's a good guy. You know that. But somebody believes in Khaled enough to give him my secret cell phone number. I'll send a text to Spike."

He didn't trust Khaled of the Magic Lamp as far as he could throw him, which wasn't far, given that the man had to weigh close to four hundred pounds. Still, Blake couldn't deny the presence of two SUVs with tinted windows that trailed their perky little Malibu. "What should we do next?"

"Do you remember the plan we made before we decided to meet with Taggart?"

Blake still had the map of obscure mountain roads in his head and was fully capable of engineering their escape from Ice Mountain. They made a good team—Jordan and him. She plotted the strategy and he handled the action. He pressed down on the accelerator and raised their speed to a level that wasn't remotely legal within city limits, especially not during a blizzard. "Hang on tight."

She made a nervous chirping noise, like the sound a chipmunk makes when it sights the approach of a predator. "Please don't kill us."

"It's okay. I'm good at this."

On the outskirts of town, there was almost zero traffic at a few minutes after seven o'clock on a weekday after a blizzard. If there hadn't been several inches of new snow clogging the road, he would have been speeding like a bullet. A heavy-duty truck with a snowplow attached to the front gave him an idea. He angled the Malibu around until he was directly behind the plow, riding on the newly cleared pavement.

Catching his breath, he glanced over at Jordan, who held her cell phone in a death grip and stared through the windshield with wild eyes. In a tiny voice, she said, "Are we still alive?"

"We're going back to Pancake Pete's."

"I don't think so. Taggart has a traitor on his team. We're better off on our own."

"Not to join up with the FBI." He reached down and jingled the key chain in the ignition. Chester had a full set of keys for his house and for his other vehicles. "We're going to steal Chester's Silverado."

"Why?"

"This little Malibu isn't going to make it on the back roads. We need four-wheel drive. And a big V-8 engine." He offered no space for discussion. "I'll pull up next to the truck, and you jump in."

"You want me to run across an icy parking lot? In my sneakers?"

"It'd be better if you could fly, but I'll settle for running."

When he swung away from the path behind the snow-plow, the Malibu was slowed by the accumulated snow on the road, and Blake knew he'd made the right decision. On the vacant roads, he skidded and twisted, barely maintaining control while he evaded the pursuing SUVs. In the center of a four-way stop intersection, he cranked the steering wheel and spun the Malibu in a three-sixty.

Jordan screamed as though she was in the front car of a roller coaster.

"I got this," he said.

"You don't." Another scream. "Let me out."

"Can't do that."

"Why not?"

Gunfire echoed through the snowy winter air.

"There's your reason," he said. Using every ounce of horsepower in the Malibu, he drove toward Pancake Pete's. While entering the parking lot, he had to slam on the brake and skidded sideways which he thought was an extremely cool move. Jordan shrieked again.

They were at the truck. He swung the car in a one-eighty so that her door was directly opposite the door to the passenger side of the truck. All she had to do was stagger a few steps and climb up into the cab.

He grabbed his satchel from the back seat, flung open his car door and ducked behind it while he returned fire. This wasn't the best place to make a final stand. He dashed around the rear of the Malibu, whipped open Jordan's door and ran to the opposite side of the truck to unlock the doors. As quickly as possible, he darted to the bed of the truck, crouched down and started shooting, drawing the gunfire from their pursuers. Out of bullets, he took another semiautomatic gun from his satchel and again returned fire. He distracted their attention. This was the moment for Jordan to make her move.

"Now," he yelled to her. "Get in the truck."

She screamed back at him. "I'm trying."

Help came from an unexpected direction. Blake saw Taggart and two other agents burst through the restaurant's glass doors. They moved in tactical formation, firing at the SUVs. The driver of one of the black vehicles with tinted windows gunned his engine and drove away.

"I'm in," Jordan yelled.

Blake vaulted into the driver's seat and fired up the engine. The muscular V-8 gave a deep, ferocious roar. Oh yeah, this was the vehicle he needed. "Jordan, are you okay?"

"Not shot. Not bleeding. Just go."

He threw the truck into Reverse and drove from the parking lot onto the road headed west. The studded tires gripped the pavement under the accumulated snow. Not exactly a smooth ride, but the truck handled the weather. Blake checked the rearview mirrors. "Nobody's following us."

"That was amazing." He heard the tremble in her voice. "Please, let's never do it again."

"You're shivering. Are you cold?"

"My sneakers are soaked through, and my feet feel like two ice cubes."

"Fasten your seat belt. I'm going to race up these steep curves into Ice Mountain." He relished the challenge. "And I'm fairly sure nobody has cleared the snow."

He dodged around a station wagon at a stoplight, muttering an apology under his breath that the other driver would never hear. Blake wouldn't have a chance to explain that he might appear to be a careless driver, but he was actually well trained in vehicular maneuvers and had been responsible for driving top-level diplomats through Beirut, Damascus, Abu Dhabi and Moscow.

He had a feeling that Jordan wouldn't be impressed with his explanation, either. She seemed to avoid looking through the windows by focusing intently on her cell phone. When her gaze flickered toward him, he asked, "You're okay, right?"

"It's better if I don't watch. Then I can't see that Volkswagen you're about to run into. Or those three guys on the curb. Or the bus. Oh, Blake, watch out for the bus."

"Might be useful if you kept an eye out for the SUVs."

"I've seen enough." She squeezed her eyes shut, then opened them. "I've seen too much. Behind the steering wheel in the SUV, I recognized Ray Gruber."

JORDAN STUDIED THE screen of her cell phone as though the mirrored surface was a crystal ball capable of predicting the future. Though she knew Gruber wasn't the person who slashed her wrists, he still scared her. He and Hugh's other security guards represented a mindless evil, dedicated to fulfilling her ex-husband's orders without question or pause.

"Gruber the Gorilla," Blake said.

"That's right." She looked up in time to see Blake hit the brake, swivel and turn into the skid. Her scream died before she had a chance to make a sound. An avid expression of delight crinkled the corners of his eyes. Though she found it hard to believe, he appeared to be enjoying himself.

Slouched in her seat, she stamped her feet on the floorboards to get the circulation going. The heater in the truck was turned on but would take a while to get going. She didn't expect a luxury ride, and she certainly wasn't going to complain. How could she do anything but appreciate

Blake's ability to adapt quickly to a change in circumstance? He'd been prepared.

"Where did you get the weapons?" she asked.

"I told you about the gun safe at my cabin. With mobs of thugs coming at us, it seemed wise to have some firepower."

"Absolutely. And where did you learn those really annoying skills in evasive driving techniques? Is that a marine thing?"

"It's a guy thing."

He merged onto the highway. When she dared to peek over the dashboard, she saw a long stretch of road with no other cars. He was driving fast, probably too fast, but she wouldn't complain. The farther they got from Gruber and the gang, the better. After a half hour, the heater in the truck was beginning to have an effect. Though still cold, her toes didn't feel frostbitten.

Comfortable enough to sit up, she glanced over at him. "Did I thank you for saving me?"

"I think you did. Right after you accused me of trying to kill you."

Her phone rang. Again, she didn't recognize the number. "Who's this?"

"Your favorite computer geek." Spike cackled. "And you're so very welcome."

He spoke with an unidentifiable, oddly flowery accent that could have been French or Swahili. Long ago, she'd given up trying to figure out where he was from or where he was going. She put the call on speakerphone. "What am I supposed to be thanking you for?"

"Caspar Khaled. I daresay we misjudged the fellow. When you confronted him in Vegas, what was your impression of him?"

"I thought he was going to eat me."

"Hah!" In the background, she heard the tappity-tap

of computer keys. She wasn't sure Spike was human. He could just as easily have been a robot. "Khaled is working with the feds. If he'd captured you, he would have protected you from your ex-husband."

"I'm confused." When had Khaled joined the good guys? How could Taggart have a traitor in his midst? More important, who was it? "Which agent turned against us?"

"Not sure. Steer clear of them, all of them."

"Even SSA Taggart?" She looked toward Blake, who was listening while he drove the curving mountain roads with only one hand on the wheel. "Can we trust him?"

"Not to put too fine a point on your plans, my dear Jordan, but trust is not an issue. You have only one job. One project. One plan."

She nodded. "Go to Denver and meet with the federal prosecutor, Orville Peterson."

"Correct," Spike said. "Tell me where you are right now."

Blake spoke up. "We're about a mile from my cabin, which means we're three miles from the old road that runs along the north ridge of Ice Mountain."

She groaned. They'd driven that way before. It was a trail that hugged the side of a cliff on one side and had a sheer drop of hundreds of feet on the other. "Is there another route?"

"You had better find one," Spike said. "If you follow the ridge, you'll run smack-dab into one of those SUVs."

"How do you know that?" Blake asked.

"I hacked their GPS systems," Spike said. "And don't even think of going backwards. The second SUV is following you. And they're getting closer."

Her computer geek was odd but really good at what he did. "Suggestions?" she asked.

"Circle the lake. There's another route on the far side

of Chipmunk Creek. It will take you miles in the wrong direction, but I don't see another way."

"Thanks for the help," Blake said. "Keep us posted on the whereabouts of the bad guys."

She disconnected the call with Spike. As soon as she'd heard that they needed a new route, her brain started ticking. "I have a plan."

"Why am I not surprised?"

"This might not be brilliant, but it's better than driving aimlessly around the lake, hoping we won't run into Gruber and the boys." She leaned forward and peered through the upper portion of the windshield. "Colorado weather is incredible. The blizzard is over. And the sun is trying to break through."

"I've seen days when the temperature changed forty degrees in one afternoon."

"We should take advantage."

He gave her a curious look. "Okay."

"We fly."

As far as she knew, there was still a chopper at Chester's house. She knew how to fly a helicopter and so did Blake.

She'd come up with this plan just in time. When they drove past his cabin without stopping, she caught a glimpse of the SUV following them. Blake guided the truck off the two-lane road onto the narrow path that led down to the lake. Apparently, he had a plan of his own. "Where are we going?"

"Before we fly, we swim. Not literally, but we can elude the guys behind us by using Chester's little red motorboat. It's still tied at the pier."

Not a choice she would have made, but it was a good plan. When he parked the truck, she had to force herself to leave the warm cab of the truck. The accumulated snow on the ground rose higher than her ankles. *So cold.* She staggered through it, lurching toward the short, wooden pier. Blake came up behind her and pressed the keys into her palm.

"It's the metallic red one."

"Of course it is."

In his left hand, he held a short semiautomatic. With his right, he pulled her close and kissed her hard. Then he raised the barrel of his weapon and aimed at the SUV that came to a stop behind the truck.

She tiptoed along the pier as fast as she could without slipping. If she could make it to the boat without falling, she was halfway there. If not…there were worse ways to die than drowning in ice-cold water.

Chapter Twenty-One

After the IED explosion that seriously damaged his career in the marines, Blake hadn't expected to ever find himself in a combat situation again. Firefights and shoot-outs weren't a regular part of most people's lives. But right now, his training and experience as a sharpshooter came in handy, and he was armed with a semiautomatic Remington, an outstanding weapon with an excellent hunting scope.

Three men emerged from the SUV with guns drawn. Gruber joined them. From where they stood on the snow-covered hill above the truck, they might be able to see Jordan creeping along the icy pier but wouldn't be able to get a good shot at her. Blake fired a warning into the air, and the security men scattered.

Hiding behind the SUV, Gruber yelled, "Nobody has to get hurt."

"Correct," Blake responded. "You're free to go."

"Give up, Mr. Marine. You're outgunned and outmanned."

"That's Captain Marine to you."

In the exchange of gunfire, Blake disabled one man and scared the others. He avoided kill shots. No reason these fools had to die for their employer. Blake's purpose was to hold them off, to keep them away from the pier until he and Jordan could make their escape.

Glancing over his shoulder, he saw her in the cockpit of the little red boat. Though the boat was still moored to the dock, she engaged the starter. The engine sputtered once, twice and then it died. *Come on, baby, let's go.* Chester was the kind of guy who kept his equipment in peak condition. The damn boat would start. It had to start.

Though Gruber kept himself shielded, his men took risks. Blake nailed one of them in the thigh—not a lethal wound but enough to make him fall.

From the pier, he heard the reassuring hum of the motor. After another few shots, he retreated down the slope through the snow. Dodging through the trees, he paused every few steps, braced his rifle, peered into the scope and fired.

"Hurry," Jordan yelled.

"Take cover. Get down."

The snow on the wooden pier had already started to melt, but the surface remained slippery. It took forever for him to reach the boat, untie the hitch and climb into the back. He faced the hill where the SUV and truck were parked. The shots he fired as Jordan pulled away kept Gruber and his men at bay.

With Jordan at the wheel, the little red motorboat sliced across the smooth, tranquil water. The blizzard wind from last night had calmed, and the clouds in the eastern sky had begun to fade. Blue skies gave him fresh hope. He slipped into the seat beside her. "Do you want me to drive?"

"It's all yours, Captain." She shivered and leaned away from the edge of the boat where droplets of spray stabbed into them like icy pinpricks. "I've never been so cold."

A surge of adrenaline had caused his heart to race and his breathing to accelerate. Under his parka, he was actually sweating. But he knew that as soon as the rush played out, he'd be hit by the cold. "Tonight, we'll stay in a hotel, maybe soak in a hot tub."

"Heavenly." She wrapped her arms around her middle. "When we get into the chopper, I'm taking my frozen sneakers off."

"Almost there."

"Already?"

"That's Chester's place over there. I'm sure because not many people have a helicopter in the front yard." Lucky for them, the chopper had been swept clean of snow and deiced. The pilot must have already been out this morning. "It'll take Gruber and his pals a half hour or more to maneuver their SUV out of the snowbank where they're parked and get over here. But we should still hurry. I don't trust the weather."

"Or the FBI," she said.

He guided Chester's boat to the pier, secured it and took her hand to help her come ashore. "It just occurred to me that I never asked if you could handle a motorboat."

"I learned in high school in Boston. And don't forget, I can also fly a chopper. Emily taught me the basics."

She latched onto his arm as they walked up the wooden pier to the shore, and he liked feeling that he was her protector. "I'll go up the hill to the cabin and find the pilot. No reason for you to make that hike. Wait for me by the bird."

Before he moved away from her, she caught hold of his arm and pulled him back toward her. On the other side of the lake, he'd given her a kiss for luck. Now it was her turn. Her lips were soft. In spite of what she'd said about being cold, her body radiated heat. Though tempted to stay right there and do much more than kiss, he stepped back and pivoted. "I'll get the pilot."

Over his shoulder, he saw her take her phone from her pocket and answer the buzz of an incoming call. Halfway up the hill to Chester's cabin—which was ten years older than his with twice the square footage—he heard her calling to him. He turned and saw her frantically waving her arms.

"What's wrong?" he shouted.

"Don't go into the cabin."

That didn't make any sense. "Why not?"

"This is Spike. He says it's booby-trapped."

Spike had been a reliable source of information who hadn't steered them wrong. But if the cabin was rigged with a bomb, where was the pilot? Blake noted several sets of footprints in the snow between the cabin and the helipad. What the hell was going on?

The air surrounding him felt heavy and intense as though dark foreboding had swallowed the blue-sky hope. The concussive force of the explosion hit him before he heard the earsplitting blast and was knocked onto his back. Desperately, he tried to get up but couldn't move. Fierce orange flames and trails of black smoke leaped high into the air. He saw more than snow, sky and trees. Transported back in time to a different explosion. His vision filled with images of the men, his friends, who nearly died beside him on a lonely road in the Middle East. He saw their bodies, torn and bleeding.

His eyes closed. Remembered pain held him in a steel grip.

In the analytical part of his brain, he recognized the symptoms. Seeing people who weren't there. Feeling sensory images that obscured reality. He couldn't move. His limbs were frozen. He was experiencing a flashback but couldn't stop it from happening.

STUNNED, JORDAN GAPED at the burning cabin. The front door had been incinerated and the roof caved in. The logs were charred. The deck, destroyed. She didn't think Blake had been close enough to be injured by flying debris, but he wasn't moving. If he'd been hurt, it was her fault, just like Abigail.

She struggled up the snow-covered hill toward him, fighting her way through the freezing snow. The cell phone in her hand rang again, and she held it to her ear.

"Jordan," Spike said. "Are you all right?"

"It's Blake. He's not moving."

"You've got to get him out of there. It's up to you."

"What about the pilot?" she asked. "What if he was inside the cabin?"

"He's the traitor."

The enormity of what he'd said hit her like an avalanche. The pilot had taken the twins to the safe house. She'd had a call from Chester yesterday to let her know they were all right, but the pilot knew their location. "Did he set the bomb?"

"Likely," Spike said. "Later, you can investigate. Right now, help Blake and get the hell out of there."

"I owe you, Spike."

"Correct." He ended the call.

She staggered the last few steps and sprawled in the snow beside Blake. He had turned on his side with his shoulders hunched and his face covered with one hand. The heat from the explosion reached across the grounds and touched her. She welcomed the warmth and despised the destruction.

Reaching out, she touched his back. "Blake, are you okay?"

Lightning fast, he flipped onto his knees and lunged at her. His right hand shot toward her, and he grasped her throat in a stranglehold. The pupils of his eyes were so dilated that she could barely see the blue of his irises. Though looking directly at her, he wasn't seeing her. The explosion had triggered his trauma.

"Blake." She choked out his name. "It's me, Jordan."

He blinked and pulled his hand away from her. "What have I done?"

"We've got to get away from here before Gruber catches up." She rose to her feet and pulled him with her. "Come with me. We're going to the helicopter."

"The pilot. He wasn't in the house, was he?"

"He's the traitor. We have to let Taggart know."

He straightened his spine. Though she couldn't see any sign of injury on him, he moved with a severe limp and held his left arm at a strange angle. His body seemed to be reliving the wounds he received when the IED exploded, similar to phantom limb syndrome where the patient feels pain in an arm or leg that has been amputated.

Though he leaned on her for support, she didn't have the strength to carry him. Blake was twice her size. When he paused to catch his breath, she urged him forward. For a moment she considered taking his rifle, but it was too much to carry. "We're almost there."

"Go without me. You need to get into Denver."

"Don't be a jerk."

"What?"

"I'm not leaving you behind." In spite of his trauma, she roared. Now wasn't the time for nobility. They needed to survive. "You give me hope. You're my reason to keep going."

"Me and the twins?"

"Yes." She dragged him the last few steps to the helicopter.

"Marry me, Jordan."

That declaration would have meant a lot more if he hadn't been half-unconscious. She forced him into the chopper where he crumpled into a heap behind the pilot's seat. The controls for this bird were a lot more complicated than Emily's smaller sightseeing helicopter, but Jordan thought she could handle it. There was no other choice.

Behind her shoulder, she heard a sound and turned. A man separated from the shadows at the rear of the fuselage. Her ex-husband came at her.

She dodged his grasp. "I should have taken the rifle."

"Shoulda, coulda, woulda." His trademark white smile glistened—a horrible contrast to the flames of the explosion that she could see through the open side door of the chopper. "There are so damn many things you should have done differently."

"Starting with our marriage."

"I'd have to agree," he said. "But let me remind you how happy you were when the twins were born. They're good boys. Handsome and smart. When I run for office, it'll look good to have them standing beside me. My poor, motherless children."

"You'll never get away with this. The fire department will respond."

"Gruber will be here before anybody else. We'll drive away. It's over. My problem will be eliminated." He reached into this pocket and pulled out his distinctive knife. "I should have killed you the first time I had the chance."

She drew her titanium baton. With a flick of her wrist, it opened to the full twenty-six inches. The cramped space in the chopper worked to her advantage. She was smaller with more room to move. Hugh was clumsy, had always been clumsy.

"One question," she said. "Did you kill Abigail?"

"Nosy bitch." He made a wide sweep with his blade. "I mentioned to her hubby that she was a problem, and good old Stanley arranged the car accident. He'd been planning her death for months."

"Do all of your friends kill their wives?"

"Only the first wife."

She whipped her baton and hit his upper arm. He made

a grab for her weapon but missed. She positioned herself again. "Ouch, that's going to leave a bruise. Maybe you ought to call for backup. Where's the pilot?"

"He became a problem—wanted too much money for the payoff. I assume he died in the explosion."

"You're a ruthless son of a bitch."

"That might be the sweetest thing you've ever said to me."

He charged. Her only escape was to hit the floor in the chopper and roll, but there wasn't room. She was in trouble.

From behind the seats, Blake staggered to his feet and unzipped his parka. "It's over, Hugh."

He barked a laugh. "You can barely stand up. She's a bigger threat than you are."

"But I have a gun."

When he reached for his side holster and pulled out his Glock, Jordan almost cheered. He was her man—always prepared.

"Drop the knife," he said.

As soon as Hugh disarmed himself, Jordan grabbed that important piece of evidence. The murder weapon. She chuckled. "You know what they say. Never bring a knife to a gunfight."

"He's not that stupid," Blake said. "I'm sure he's got other hidden weapons, but we don't have time to mess around with this criminal. You have a choice, Hugh. You can jump out the side door or I can shoot you and push your lifeless body to the ground. Either way, Jordan and I are taking off in twelve seconds."

Hugh jumped.

"Why twelve?" she asked.

"Sounded good." He took the pilot's seat and handed her the Glock. "If Hugh comes at us, shoot him."

"Why didn't you pull the trigger?"

"That's Taggart's job. I'm out of the lethal force business."

In slightly more than twelve seconds, they took off. Above the cloud cover, the skies were blue and the sun was shining.

She spoke into the headset. "Do you remember proposing to me?"

"I love you, Jordan."

"My answer is yes." She'd have to talk to the twins but was sure they'd approve. "And I love you back."

Finally, the nightmare was over. She looked forward to planning the wedding. Even more than that, she was ready to live happily ever after.

SIX MONTHS LATER, Jordan made the final arrangement for a small ceremony in the landscaped backyard of the house she and Blake had purchased in Richmond, Virginia, which was not far from where Blake had taken a job at the Pentagon. Grudgingly, he'd discovered that he liked working at a higher level, determining policy while always looking out for the men and women who served in the Corps.

Hugh and his minions, including Stanley Preston, who was involved in the murder of his wife, Abigail, were awaiting trial. The final evidence against Hugh came when the medical examiner found the "lost" DNA results for Bianca's unborn babies. A match for Hugh, the DNA was a solid motive for murder.

Jordan returned to the living room through the French doors and stood for a moment, enjoying the presence of family, old friends and acquaintances. Emily Finnegan from Vegas hadn't hooked up with Harvey from Henderson but fixed him up with a friend of hers. Bianca's sister had gone back to school. The nurse who had helped Jordan escape from the Gateway Institute met up with Spike, a classy-looking Englishman, who sat at the upright piano and played "Bohemian Rhapsody" while the twins sang along with wildly inaccurate lyrics. They were coached by her mom, in from Boston, and Chester, who made a great couple.

Though all these friendships fulfilled her, there was still something missing from Jordan's life. She didn't know exactly what it was until she answered a phone call from Hornsby. Her former mentor had an assignment for her that involved a serial killer in the wilderness country of Utah.

She made her decision in less than five seconds. "I'm on it."

As she ended the call, she looked up and saw Blake, resplendent in his dress blues, descending the staircase. His trimmed blond hair had picked up a few strands of silver, which made it shine. And his fierce blue eyes made tender contact with hers.

Now, her life was perfect.

* * * * *

CAVANAUGH JUSTICE: UP CLOSE AND DEADLY

MARIE FERRARELLA

To
Autumn Ferrarella
Welcome to the world, Little One!
All my love,
G-Mama

Prologue

The tightness in his stomach slammed into him when his second call in as many days to his twin sister went to voice mail. The tightness in his stomach coupled with the overall dark feeling that descended.

Something was definitely wrong.

Deputy Sheriff Cody Cassidy could feel it. Feel it all the way down his spine.

There were some who believed the myth of mental empathy between twins was just that. A myth. Well, they were welcome to their beliefs, Cody thought, but that didn't change anything that he knew in his heart to be true. He and his twin sister, Carrie, had always had this unspoken mental empathy between them.

It wasn't as if they lived in each other's pocket. Since she had moved away, sometimes weeks would go by before they talked—but they *always* talked sooner or later. Usually sooner than later.

However it had been almost two months now. Almost two months and *nothing.* Not a word, not an email or a postcard, or even a simple text message in response from Carrie.

Nothing.

He could have put up with that if it wasn't for the uneasy feeling undulating through him that something was off, something was wrong. And that uneasy feeling was growing stronger with each passing day.

Granted, he would be the first to admit that he hadn't taken Carrie's move out to Aurora, California, nine months ago all that well. But he *had* kept his misgivings to himself. Out loud he had told his twin to follow her dreams and that, no matter what happened, he would always be there for her.

At the very least, he had expected Carrie to keep in touch.

After all, Carrie had always been the sensible one, the one who had laid out her entire life for herself from the time she had been a very little girl. He had been the wild teen, drinking and carousing with his friends from early on, incurring her sad disapproval.

No one had been more surprised—and pleased— than Carrie when he had actually graduated college and gone on to become a sheriff's deputy—like their father before him—in the little town of Kiowa, New Mexico, where he and Carrie had grown up. He, Carrie had told him proudly on the day he graduated, had finally gotten his act together. That was also the day she'd told him that she felt it was finally safe for her to leave town, to explore her own options to see what life had to offer her.

Once, she had felt that she'd had everything mapped out, but now, she'd confessed, she was not so sure. Maybe there were other directions for her to go in, other choices for her to make. Maybe her earlier choices had been too rigid for her.

Cody had told her that he felt she could be anything she wanted to be, to reach for the sky. The world was at her feet and completely wide open.

Maybe that was it, Cody reasoned, staring at the phone on his desk. Maybe she was just too busy sampling life to be bothered to pick up the phone.

Or call him back.

She had always been the responsible one. When their mother had had cancer, Carrie was the one who had dutifully come home after school every day to take care of Alice Cassidy, never complaining that she was being deprived of doing what all her friends were doing: having a good time. Instead, she'd claimed that when her mother had finally gotten well, that was truly the greatest day of her life. Cody knew that Carrie had really meant it.

His sister's selfless behavior had been enough for Cody to straighten up and fly right, he reflected ruefully. Carrie had *always* been everyone's shining example. Her positive outlook had been enough to get their father to view life in a brighter light and pull himself out of his own depression.

Carrie had always had the power to heighten everyone's outlook.

And now, Cody thought with a sigh, he couldn't get her to pick up the phone—or return a phone call.

Dropping the old-fashioned receiver into its cradle, he terminated the call that never had a chance to get started.

"Problem?" Sheriff Matt Holden asked, genuinely interested as he passed by Cody's desk.

Cody raised his wide shoulders and then let them drop again in an almost helpless gesture. "It's probably nothing."

"But?" Holden asked, studying the young man's chiseled, clean-shaven face.

"I can't reach my sister."

The sheriff was aware of the kind of bond that existed between the twins. He had known them since their early childhood.

He raised a graying eyebrow. "How long has it been?"

"Two months."

The sheriff frowned. "That doesn't sound like Carrie. Why don't you take some time off and take a trip to her new home? See if you can find out what's going on?" his father's long-time friend suggested. "There might be a new beau in the picture." As the father of four daughters of varying ages, Holden knew what that could be like. "It's been a while since you took some time off," he reminded Cody. "And there's really nothing happening here that requires your attention."

Cody nodded as his eyes met Holden's dark brown ones. "Thanks, Sheriff. I think I just might do that."

He would have thought that just the idea of going out to California to see Carrie would make him feel better.

But it didn't.

The knot in his stomach refused to lessen or go away.

Chapter One

"Up and at 'em, Sky," Detective Skylar Cavanaugh's partner, Detective Beaumont Rio, announced as he walked into the Homicide Division's squad room at a fast clip. It was barely eight o'clock in the morning.

Bleary-eyed, Skylar looked over at the much-too-bright-sounding man she had been partnered with ever since she had been awarded her detective shield less than a year ago.

"Not until my coffee has had a chance to kick in and work its magic," she told Rio wearily. Served her right for staying out late last night and catching that movie, she silently lectured herself.

Holding the steaming mug of black coffee between her hands, Skylar took a long sip, relishing the way it coursed almost seductively through her veins.

Recently married, Rio's newly acquired wider waistline bore testimony to how well he was being fed since he had exchanged vows with Marsha, his wife of the last three months. But right now, he didn't appear to be thinking about the satisfying breakfast he had consumed less than an hour ago. It was obvious that Rio was eager to get at it.

"It" being the latest case.

Ever since his marriage, Skylar's partner had been almost myopically focused on working his way up the ladder. He was attempting to do something noteworthy to catch the Chief of Detectives' eye.

"No time for that, Sky," Rio told her, shifting from foot to foot. "Morrow called in that they found a floater just outside the city limits."

By "Morrow," Skylar knew he was probably referring to Sergeant Jeff Morrow. Part of the Homicide Division for more years than anyone could actually remember, the sergeant was like the proverbial bloodhound when it came to finding bodies.

"A floater," she repeated after taking one last sip of her coffee and setting the mug aside. "Homicide or accidental?" she asked as she opened the first drawer on the left and took out her handgun. Very carefully, Skylar tucked the weapon into her shoulder holster.

"I actually asked him that," Rio answered, pleased with himself for anticipating his partner's question. "Morrow said it was too soon to tell. There didn't seem to be any telltale signs of a homicide or any outward signs of a struggle having taken place," he said, echoing the sergeant's words. "Could just be a simple suicide."

Skylar looked at him, thinking of the last parent she had had to break the news to about the woman's son's overdose. It had taken her more than a couple of hours to calm the woman down. Sitting there and holding Helen Jason's hand had been a truly heartbreaking experience as far as she was concerned.

Skylar's expression and tone hardened ever so slightly. "There is no such thing as a 'simple' suicide, Rio. Every suicide has serious repercussions for someone other than the person who died."

"Sorry, I didn't mean to minimize the end effect," her partner apologized. The way he survived personally, she knew, was to divorce himself from the act.

"I know you didn't," Skylar admitted. She shouldn't have raised her voice like that. "I'm being too touchy," she acknowledged. Taking a breath, Skylar said, "If it does turn out to be suicide, I'm anticipating having to break the awful news to some heartbroken family member."

"That's part of the job," Rio returned matter-of-factly.

"It is," Skylar agreed, "but it still rips my heart out."

"I know, I know." Rio's voice softened. "You do realize that you're way too sensitive for this kind of job, right?" he asked as they went to the elevator.

She looked at him, aware of the fact that a lot of the people who worked within the Homicide Division had self-made walls built up around them. It was a matter of survival. But those were the people who came across as too cold.

"Someone has to be," she told her partner. "Otherwise, we just become robots, working one case after another and going through the motions of being human."

Rio nodded. "I guess that's what makes us such a good team. Between the two of us, we wind up covering both ends of the spectrum."

Skylar absently shrugged her shoulders, wondering if maybe it was time for her to think about switching divisions. But if she did that, who would be left to feel empathy for the victim as well as for the victim's family?

Detective Beaumont Rio was a good guy, but she knew he just wasn't capable of that.

"You want to drive, or should I?" Skylar asked as they got off the elevator.

"Well, since you put it that way—me," he informed her with a big smile. "I'd like to drive."

Since she was still waiting for the coffee to kick in, Skylar decided it wasn't such a bad idea to let Rio get them to the lake. She had a tendency to drive too fast when she was agitated, and she knew it.

So did Rio.

"Be my guest," Skylar told him, waving a hand toward his aged beige vehicle. While it was reliable, it looked utterly uninspiring. The car was parked in its customary spot and she wondered how long that would remain to be the case.

Since his marriage, a lot of things had changed in Rio's world. To be honest, she was surprised he was still driving the same lackluster car. She had seen him wistfully eyeing brand-new, far more colorful vehicles, and couldn't help musing that that was going to be the next thing to change in her partner's life.

Keep your mind on your work, Sky, she told herself.

At bottom, that was all that really mattered. The work, not Rio's quest for a flashy vehicle.

Getting in on the passenger side, Skylar strapped in.

"Did the sergeant give you any details about the floater?" she asked, since Rio was the one who'd caught the case. "Age, time of death, things like that?"

The vehicle came to life. Pulling out, Rio shook his head. "Other than the fact that a fisherman reeled her in and was totally freaked out by the event, no. I took the liberty of calling in the medical examiner and the crime scene investigation unit," he added, glancing at Skylar a bit nervously.

She saw no reason for the display of nerves on Rio's part. Something was up. "Are you waiting for me to bite your head off?" she asked.

"Well, I thought you might feel I was going over your head and usurping your position," he told her.

That had never come up before. For the first time, she found herself wondering if all was going well in Rio's marriage. At times, he had seemed rather preoccupied.

"Look, I know I'm related to more of the police

personnel than you are..." she began, only to have him laugh.

"More?" he echoed incredulously. "I'm not related to any of them. You, on the other hand—"

She didn't let him finish, especially since she knew what was coming. There were a great many Cavanaughs in different positions on the police force and, for some, she knew that could be a very intimidating fact. However, she had never thought Rio had fallen into that category. At least, he hadn't before he'd married.

"But what matters here," Skylar continued forcefully, "is that we're both homicide detectives with decent track records and good instincts. There's no reason for you to feel insecure."

"I'm not feeling insecure," Rio answered defensively.

"Good." Skylar nodded. "I'm glad to hear that, even though it was starting to sound that way. You shouldn't feel vulnerable," she reiterated, emphasizing, "especially since you did everything right." She was referring to his calling the CSI unit as well as the medical examiner to come on the scene.

"Sorry, Sky." Rio flushed. He was obviously uncomfortable with what he was about to confess. "Marsha and I had an argument this morning."

She knew what that meant. That was Rio's way of saying that his new wife was berating him. That sort of thing had started about a month ago. Skylar felt that Rio worked hard and he deserved a little peace and quiet, not a belittling or condescending attitude sent his way. That just wasn't right.

"If you need to talk," she told Rio, trying not to sound as if she was attempting to pry, "you know where to find me."

Rio had managed to arouse her curiosity, but she refrained from sounding as if there was any pressure in her voice.

Nonetheless, Skylar saw her partner's hands tighten on the steering wheel. For a moment, Rio seemed to be engaged in an internal argument with himself.

And then he finally said, "Marsha thinks that I should be higher up in my career by now than I am," he told her.

Her partner appeared embarrassed by what he was sharing with her.

She felt for Rio. She was also annoyed with her partner's wife for making him feel as if he was somehow failing her. If someone told her that it was none of her business, she would have countered with the fact that she felt her partner's mental well-being *was* her business.

Holding her tongue in check, Skylar merely reminded Rio, "Well, you are on the right path and, remember, slow and steady does eventually win the race."

"Apparently, not fast enough for Marsha," Rio muttered under his breath.

Skylar felt the same sort of protective feeling she

experienced when it came to a member of her family dealing with some sort of slight. "Does Marsha have any idea just how good you are at your job?"

Rio stared straight ahead, deliberately avoiding her eyes. "Marsha doesn't think that accolades are very bankable."

That had to really sting. This was a side of her partner's new wife she hadn't been aware of until just now. A side she didn't much care for. But to be totally fair to the woman, maybe things were tighter monetarily than she was aware of.

Skylar told herself not to throw stones until she had more information, but it definitely wasn't easy to keep from speaking what was on her mind.

"Then you'll just have to show her otherwise," Skylar finally told him. She thought of something she had heard her grandfather say to one of her cousins. "You haven't been married all that long and there are always some rough spots to be experienced in the beginning," she told her partner. "My grandfather Seamus is fond of saying that the first hundred years are the hardest. After that," she concluded with a lop-sided smile, "it's all a breeze."

"A hundred years, huh?" Rio asked, taking the news harder than she thought he would. That caused her some serious concern.

Skylar nodded, flashing an even brighter smile at her partner. "That's what the man said."

"Well, between you and me," Rio confided far

more seriously than she was happy about, "I don't think I'm going to make it."

"Aw, have a little faith in yourself, Rio. I know I do. Marsha just wants you to be the best that you can be," Skylar assured him, secretly hoping that she was right.

Judging by the expression on his face, Skylar decided that her partner was going to grasp that excuse she had just given him and hold on to it for dear life. She certainly couldn't blame him for that.

She was strongly tempted to talk to Marsha to make the woman see how her demeaning treatment was affecting Rio—even though she knew that she shouldn't be budding into her partner's life.

As they drew closer to the lake, Skylar saw the cluster of cars parked near the perimeter of the lake closest to their side.

Time to focus on the business at hand, Skylar told herself.

"Looks like the gang's all here," she commented.

Rio pulled their vehicle as close as possible to the crime scene unit's van without risking driving into the lake.

"Looks like we're the last ones to arrive at the scene," Rio noted. "We should have gotten an earlier start."

"Looks like," she agreed. Skylar looked around as they got out of the vehicle. There seemed to be officers everywhere. "Don't worry, I'll let Uncle Sean know that you get full credit."

"Uncle Sean" referred to the man who was the head of the Crime Scene Investigation Unit and the third of the older Cavanaugh brothers who had risen to a high-ranking position within the police force. There had been another older Cavanaugh brother, Mike, who, unlike all the other Cavanaughs of varying ages, hadn't been well regarded and had died while on duty.

Skylar had her suspicions about how the less-than-sterling officer had met his end within the ranks. Part of the known story was that, aside from his recognized two offspring, Patrick and Patience, he had fathered a set of triplets with a woman no one in the family had even known existed.

On her deathbed, she had told her children about who their father had been, as well as who they were related to.

Incensed that their mother had been so badly treated and that their existence had been virtually hidden, the triplets—Kyle, Greer and Ethan O'Brien—had descended on the Cavanaughs for a reckoning.

However, all had turned out well and shortly after the confrontation, all three had been taken into the fold and gone on to be part of the police force as well.

No matter what the difficulty turned out to be, Skylar reflected, things could always be worked out. The only thing that couldn't be smoothed over, she thought as she got her bearings, was death.

Along with Rio, she made her way over to the

body of the extremely pale young woman who had been brought out of the lake.

The medical examiner, Marvin Edwards, began to cover the body with a sheet, then struggled to his feet.

"Definitely a younger man's game," Edwards muttered under his breath to no one in particular. His knees were likely bothering him again.

"If you were any younger, Doc, people would be accusing you of stealing your medical degree," Skylar teased with a wink.

With a groan, Edwards turned toward the familiar voice and then smiled. He enjoyed working with the young detective. "You catch this one, Skylar?"

"Rio and I did," she corrected, glancing at her partner. "What can you tell us about the time of death?"

The gray-haired man nodded a greeting at Skylar's partner. "Detective Rio," he acknowledged and then went on to answer Skylar's question. "Liver temperature puts time of death between five and seven hours ago."

That meant she had been asleep when this terrible thing was happening, Skylar realized. "What was the cause of death?" she prompted. "Was it deliberate, an accident, or—"

"Sky, I'm good, but I'm not that good," Edwards told her. "I need to perform an autopsy before I can answer that."

"Said he modestly," Skylar kidded. "Can you let

me know as soon as you do determine the cause of death?" she asked.

"You'll be my first call," the ME promised. "Luckily, I don't have anything else on tap."

Edwards stood back and quietly sighed as his assistant, Walter, lifted the dead body and placed it on the gurney that would in turn be loaded into the ME's van.

"Time to get to work," he told Skylar as he went around to the front of the van and climbed into the driver's seat.

Chapter Two

As he got off the freeway and drove through the more urban area, Cody had to admit that he could easily see the allure of Aurora. It appeared to be, by all definitions, a very clean city, which he found rather amazing since it had been over fifty years that the one-time little town had incorporated. At last count, Aurora now had a great many more citizens within its borders.

According to what he had just read before beginning this odyssey, Aurora had all the advantages of a large city plus the heartwarming appeal of a small town, the kind where, at one point, everyone knew everyone else.

That truly wasn't the case anymore. Everyone *didn't* know everyone else, his sister had told him. But somehow, it still felt like a small town.

Cody felt part of the reason for that was strong infrastructure and maintenance. Any necessary repairs, be it to the buildings, the roads, or even trimming the trees, were immediately addressed and taken care of. The end result: everything looked neat and clean and completely up-to-date. Cody's own hometown, Kiowa, New Mexico, which at this point was a great deal smaller and older than Aurora, had the same kind of charm and efficiency.

Driving down the winding street on his way to Carrie's "apartment home"—a term he found amusingly quaint—Cody began to entertain the idea that if he couldn't get her to come back home with him, he might consider the idea of moving out here. After all, there was really not all that much keeping him in Kiowa now. His mother's cancer had resurfaced and she had died suddenly. Disheartened over his loss, his father had died shortly thereafter.

Lost in thought, Cody had driven right by Carrie's residential development. Realizing that he had passed it, he made a U-turn at the end of the long, winding block. He then circled back and pulled up into the cheerful-looking complex. Cody went on to park in one of the spaces labeled Visitor Parking.

The apartment home was not what he had come to expect. Bright and sunny-looking, the so-called "building" was only two stories high. The word *homey* instantly sprang to his mind as he looked at the structure.

It had Carrie written all over it, he couldn't help thinking—except, where was she?

Standing in front of her ground-floor apartment, Cody took out his phone and called his sister's number. Nothing rang in response. There wasn't even a message telling him that the call had gone to voice-mail.

There was no response whatsoever.

Had she lost her phone or accidentally dropped it in water and it had gone dead? He recalled that Carrie always worried about short-circuiting her cell phone. She hadn't so far, but there was always a first time.

Well, he had come out all this way. He wasn't about to rent a motel room and sit there, twiddling his thumbs, until he finally got his sister on the phone. He needed to be *doing* something, not just taking up space.

Making up his mind about his next course of action, Cody headed for the rental office. Someone had to be there.

When he reached the front door, he tried it and found that it was unlocked.

The apartment manager, a sweet-faced, well-dressed older woman, looked up the moment she heard the door opening. Putting on a bright, warm smile, she looked over at him.

"Hello, may I help you with something?" she asked. "Are you interested in finding a new apartment home?"

Cody wasted no time. "Actually, I'm trying to locate my sister, Carrie Cassidy. She moved here nine months ago and she hasn't been answering her phone for a couple of months now. As far as I know, she still lives here, and I was hoping you could let me into her apartment." He saw the skeptical look in the woman's eyes and took out his wallet to prove that he was related to Carrie. His deputy badge was immediately visible.

But the badge wasn't the first thing that the woman behind the desk saw. She was looking at the picture on his driver's license and Carrie's photo beside it.

"I *thought* you looked familiar," she cried, pleased with herself. "Did anyone ever tell you that you look just like her? I mean with some differences, of course, but you really do look like your sister."

"Yes, ma'am," Cody responded. He didn't bother pointing out that he and Carrie were twins. Instead he said, "If you could unlock her door, I'd really appreciate it." He was hoping to find something in Carrie's apartment that would give him a clue as to his sister's current whereabouts.

The residential manager, Janice Miller, grasped the arms of her chair and pushed herself up to her feet. "Well, seeing as how you are her brother *and* a policeman to boot, I don't see why not."

Cody tried not to allow his impatience to surface, but it wasn't easy. There was a sense of urgency all but vibrating through him and he was having difficulty dealing with it. "Thank you."

"Of course," Mrs. Miller told him.

Stepping back, he gestured for the woman to lead the way, even though, because of the number on the door, he knew exactly where Carrie's apartment was located.

The rental manager paused by the small wooden boxes hanging on the wall. The boxes contained duplicates of the residents' apartment keys. Finding Carrie's key, she picked it up and then led the way out of the office.

"So, what do you think of our little complex?" Mrs. Miller asked cheerfully. "We've just finished renovating it—not that it was falling apart—but I always believe that staying a couple of steps ahead of the game is always better than hurrying to try to fix something that was beginning to fall apart."

She looked over her shoulder to see how the tall, blond-haired young man felt about her philosophy.

"Staying ahead of the game is always best," Cody responded, sensing the woman was looking for that sort of validation.

The bright smile the rental manager flashed confirmed his suspicions.

Carrie's ground-floor apartment wasn't located all that far from the rental office. Taking out the key she had pocketed, Janice Miller unlocked the door, pushed it open and then took a step back from the doorway.

"Ms. Cassidy?" she called out. "I have your brother here to see you."

There was no answer from inside the apartment. "Did your sister know that you were coming to see her?" the rental manager asked, looking at Cody.

The woman obviously didn't have a mind for retaining details, he thought, since he had already told her that he had called Carrie a number of times and hadn't gotten an answer. That was why he had come all the way out here in the first place.

"No, she didn't," Cody answered, keeping things simple.

"Well," she speculated, "she might have gone away on vacation."

Cody had begun making his way around the small, one-bedroom dwelling, looking for some indication of where Carrie could have gone on this so-called vacation. Nothing struck him. Her clothes were still neatly hung in her closet and her suitcase-on-wheels was standing in the corner. If she had gone on vacation, she hadn't taken anything with her.

"She wouldn't have gone away for any extended time without letting me know," he murmured more to himself than to the manager.

Mrs. Miller had a different opinion to offer. "Oh, I don't know. A woman in love can do impetuous things," she told Cody.

That stopped him cold and he turned to look at the woman. "In love?" he repeated. "My sister was in love?"

Since when? The question throbbed in Cody's head.

Janice Miller nodded. She looked very pleased with herself to be able to throw a little light on the situation. "I guess she didn't tell you."

"No," Cody said flatly, stunned at the news and still not altogether sure that it was true. "She didn't."

"Well, I hate to break it to you, but I guess you two aren't as close as you think you are," the rental manager told him.

"No," he quietly agreed for the time being, "I guess we're not. Did you happen to catch a glimpse of my sister's 'friend'?"

The woman looked a little indignant at the suggestion. "I have better things to do than spy on the people who live here," Mrs. Miller informed him. Then, after a moment, she relented. "I did see him leaving with her a few weeks ago. He was tall, muscular. " She smiled at the memory. "Good-looking."

Cody needed more details than that. "Hair?" he asked.

"Yes, he had hair."

Cody caught himself before the sigh could escape his lips. "What color was it?"

"Brown—I think," the woman answered after a beat had gone by. She sounded far from confident about her response.

All right, he thought, he had a color. He needed more. "Light brown? Dark brown? Straight? Curly? Long? Short? Thin? Thick?"

She shook her head, not in response to his question, but to clear up a misconception before she could even attempt to give him an answer. "I'm not sure."

This wasn't getting him anywhere. "Does she have any other friends here?" he asked the rental manager. He knew that Carrie hadn't mentioned any friends the last time they had talked. But then, she hadn't mentioned a boyfriend, either, but there obviously seemed to be one in the picture.

Mrs. Miller lifted her shoulders in a hapless gesture. "Not that I know of," the woman confessed.

Definitely not getting anywhere, he thought. It served no purpose to keep knocking his head against the wall. Cody took a card with his cell phone number on it out of his wallet and handed it to the rental manager.

"If you think of anything—or if my sister suddenly comes back—please give me a call," he requested.

Mrs. Miller took the card in her hand and looked it over. "I certainly will—Cody," she said, emphasizing his name with a smile. "Cody and Carrie." She nodded her head in approval. "That's cute."

"Our parents thought so," he told her.

During what had turned out to be his last conversation with his sister, Carrie had mentioned that she was in the process of looking for a new, more satisfying job. Since she had never gotten back to him about that, he felt that he only had one option currently open to him.

He needed to file a missing-persons report. "Could you point me toward your local police station?" he asked as he pocketed his wallet again.

Mrs. Miller suddenly became very somber. "Do you think something happened to your sister?"

she asked. But even as the words came out of her mouth, she seemed to discount them. "Aurora is a very peaceful, law-abiding city."

Lord, I hope nothing's happened to her, Cody thought in response to the woman's question. Out loud, he merely said, "I was always taught to cover all my bases."

Janice Miller nodded her head in agreement. "That makes sense."

She led the way out of Carrie's apartment and subsequently took Cody toward the residential development's entrance. There, she pointed to the cross street that was directly on her left.

"Just go out here and proceed about half a block to the left. The police station is right there, next to city hall. You can't really miss it," she told him, then added, "Unless, of course, you're driving with your eyes shut. In which case, the police will find you and bring you in," she guaranteed with a comical smile. "Good luck."

Standing on the edge of the sidewalk leading out of the development, the rental manager remained there with her arms crossed at her ample chest, watching as he drove away. "Good luck!" she called out again.

He hoped that it was just a matter of luck and nothing more. But that feeling that something was definitely off just continued to hover over him and intensify.

He told himself not to focus on the worst happening. He reasoned that there could be a dozen reasons why Carrie had decided to just disappear this way.

But for the life of him, he couldn't come up with a single one.

Maybe he could have if this wasn't Carrie, but it *was* Carrie, and she had always been responsible to a fault. Even as a very little girl, she wouldn't have ever just taken off. She had always let her parents know where she was. Where *he* was as well.

Carrie had behaved like a little old lady from the very moment she could walk, he recalled. And this was in a little town where the population never went over thousand and where everyone not only knew everyone else, they also knew where everyone else *was*.

With all his heart, he wished he had said something to Carrie, had told her not to go. But he hadn't thought it was his place to stand in her way, especially since he had been such a typical wild child in his teen years, or at least, Kiowa's definition of a wild child at the time.

At the very least, he should have come out here with Carrie. But at the time, he was finally making something of himself, finally focusing on working hard and creating a career, one that he realized he had always wanted.

Turning into the police parking lot, he looked around for guest parking. Finding it, he parked his old car and got out, taking in the general area.

There were about twelve, fifteen, steps leading up to an official-looking building that was nestled next to a shorter structure. The latter was labeled City Hall.

Considering what they were supposed to be, the buildings both appeared rather homey-looking. But then, Cody reminded himself, things were not always what they seemed.

And even that went beyond for serial killers like Ted Bundy.

Cody felt his heart skip a beat. Where the hell had that come from, just out of the blue like that? he silently asked himself. Its origin completely eluded him.

No, it didn't, he thought the next moment. He was allowing his imagination to run away with him. Cody silently upbraided himself.

The simplest explanation was always the most applicable one, his father had always maintained. And Elliot Cassidy had had a great deal more experience on the job when it came to dealing with so called "bad guys" than Cody had when his father had finally retired his badge.

Standing in front of the police station entrance, Cody counted to ten, took a deep breath and told himself this was all going to turn out for the best. Only then did he pull open the glass door and walk in.

Cody just wished he could actually get himself to believe that.

Chapter Three

Preoccupied with the result of the autopsy she had just been privy to, Skylar was in the lobby, walking toward the elevator. Belatedly, she did a double-take after she was well past the front desk.

She could have sworn that the blond-haired man talking to Sergeant Elroy Phelps, the officer who usually worked the front desk, looked a great deal like the woman who had been fished out of the lake yesterday.

Except that he wasn't nearly as pale, Skylar observed. But pale or not, the man did appear to be rather distressed.

Curiosity had always been second nature for Skylar. It was actually the reason why she had initially become interested in what was referred to as the "family business" in the first place.

Unable to help herself, she drew closer to the front desk, trying to find out what the man was doing there. She probably would have just been on her way back to Homicide if the distraught-looking man in the worn, tan, fringed jacket hadn't reminded her of the woman who had just been autopsied.

"I need to file a missing-persons report," he was saying to the desk sergeant. "Could you tell me where I need to go or who I should speak to about that?"

That was all Skylar needed to hear. A couple of minutes ago, she'd been bracing herself to conduct a massive search to try to find the dead woman's name as well as attempting to locate some possible member of the deceased woman's family. Now it appeared that she would be spared having to go through all that.

But the man standing in front of the desk sergeant, asking to file a missing-persons report, would not be spared, in any sense of the word.

"I'll take it from here, Sergeant," Skylar told Phelps.

The sergeant instantly brightened. "Thanks. I'd appreciate that, Detective."

The man requesting to file a missing-persons report turned to look at the woman who had just spoken. She had to be part of the police force, he decided. It struck Cody that they had more police officers in Aurora than there were actual residents in all of Kiowa. Maybe he was worrying for no reason.

"If you don't mind my asking, what is your relationship to the person you want to file that report about?" Skylar asked.

By way of an answer, Cody took out his ID and held it up for the woman as he replied, "She's my sister. I'm Deputy Cody Cassidy with the Kiowa Sheriff's Office. Carrie moved here nine months ago. We're ordinarily very close," he went on to explain, "but I haven't heard from her in two months. My calls to her cell phone keep going to voice mail— except for the last call I made."

"Oh? What happened to that one?" Skylar asked, even though she had a suspicion she knew the answer to that.

"That one didn't even ring," Cody answered. He took a breath before continuing. He wasn't normally the type who shared things, but this was Carrie he was talking about. He knew that this edgy feeling he was experiencing wasn't about to go away until he found her. "She's a very dependable person and I'm worried that she's not calling me back because something might have happened to her."

Something had, Skylar thought, but for now, she kept that to herself in case the young woman the medical examiner had just performed his autopsy on did not turn out to be the deputy's sister.

"So, can you tell me where I can file that missing-persons report?" Cody asked when the woman he was talking to refrained from making any comment.

There were times when she hated her job, Skylar thought.

"Follow me, please, Deputy," she said, leading the way to the elevator.

She pressed the down button. When it arrived a moment later, Skylar walked in and waited until the deputy followed her. Once he was inside the elevator car, she pushed the button for the basement.

Cody looked at her curiously. "Your Missing Persons office is located in the basement?" he questioned.

With all her heart, she wished she could say yes, but she couldn't.

"Not exactly," she replied.

The same bad feeling, the one that had been his ever-present companion since he had come out here, looking for Carrie, reared its head and intensified.

And kept intensifying.

He found that he was having trouble breathing.

Cody glanced at the woman. "What's going on, Detective?" he asked. Belatedly, he recalled, "You never gave me your last name."

"It's Cavanaugh. Skylar Cavanaugh," she told him.

She was killing time and she knew it. Killing time so that she didn't have to say those dreadful words that could very well divorce the deputy from any source of hope. *I think we found your sister floating in the lake.*

For now, she kept that to herself.

"But you can call me Sky, if it makes you feel more comfortable," she told him.

Just then, the elevator reached its destination and the door opened. The path was well lit, but it still felt as if there was a lingering darkness about the area.

A darkness that underscored and pervaded the bad feeling Cody was so acutely aware of.

He got the sense that the detective was stalling— and that made him nervous. "What aren't you telling me, Detective?" he asked her.

Skylar knew that she couldn't continue to beat around the bush this way. It wasn't fair to the deputy. Her eyes met his and she felt her heart begin to ache. "I'm afraid we found a body." She took a breath, bracing herself. "I need you to make an identification, Deputy," she told him quietly.

He didn't ask her any questions regarding why he was making this identification. Instead, he stoically followed the detective down the hallway to a room where he instinctively assumed autopsies were performed.

Pausing in front of the door, Skylar put her hand on the doorknob and then turned toward him and asked, "Are you ready?"

Am I ready?

Was anyone ever ready to have their whole life ripped apart and forever changed? he wondered.

His mouth was dry and his throat felt as if it was closing up on him, but standing out here wasn't going to change the ultimate outcome of what he was about to see.

Cody squared his shoulders then, nodding toward the door, said, "Open it."

Skylar had gone through the identification process a number of times before and it never got any easier.

Moving like someone trapped in a bad dream, she opened the door for the deputy and led the way in.

"We might have the victim's next of kin, Doc," she informed Edwards as she entered.

"Brother," Cody corrected, staring straight ahead at the form under the white sheet. "I'm her brother."

Skylar nodded. "My mistake. Her brother," she clarified respectfully for both the medical examiner and the deputy's benefit. "Doc, if you could please pull back the sheet so that Deputy Cassidy can make the proper identification," she requested.

"Of course," the older man replied in a subdued voice. He very carefully lifted the sheet away from the young woman's face.

Skylar was aware that the young man standing beside her instantly recognized the woman on the gurney. He stiffened as if every single bone in his body had suddenly gone rigid.

Cody stared at the lifeless body of his sister. For one awful moment, he felt as if his heart had completely stopped beating—and then suddenly launched into double time.

He hadn't expected this, not in any manner, shape or form. Even as he'd gotten off the elevator and begun walking toward the morgue, he had been hoping against hope that there had been some sort of a mistake made, that the person on the autopsy table would not turn out to be Carrie. Never mind that the dead woman was someone else's sister, or daughter, or significant other. Right now, he just selfishly wanted it *not* to be his sister.

But it was.

It was Carrie.

Taking in the wet hair, the pallor of her face, he felt tears stinging the corners of his eyes.

For the first time in his life, Cody was glad that his mother was no longer alive. This sort of thing would have surely killed her.

"Can I get you something to drink?"

The voice asking the question came to him from a distance, registering belatedly.

He forced himself to take a breath. "What you can get me," Cody told the detective with some difficulty, "is the name of the person who did this to my sister."

Every word felt as if it was sticking to his lips, to the roof of his mouth.

She knew that this was going to be difficult for him to hear, but he needed to know. "Right now, it looks as if your sister died by suicide," she told him.

The medical examiner moved forward and covered the dead woman's face. Skylar gently took the deputy's arm and tried to lead the victim's brother away.

Cody pulled his arm from her, the look on his face suddenly coming alive. His expression was animated.

"That's impossible," he almost shouted. "Carrie wouldn't do that. She was always the responsible one, the one everyone always turned to for guidance whenever something went wrong. Even me," he added quietly.

"The autopsy showed that she had a large amount of fentanyl in her system," Skylar told him. She knew that this was difficult for him to hear, but he had to be told so that he could make peace with what had happened.

Cody balked. "That's not possible. She didn't believe in taking any drugs. My sister didn't even drink alcohol. When I was a teenager, she used to give me a hard time because I would go out drinking with my friends. She was the reason why I finally stopped drinking," he told the detective. Cody shook his head in adamant censure. "There has to be some mistake."

She pressed her lips together. There was more, and she dreaded telling him, but it needed to come out. "The autopsy showed that there was something else as well," Skylar told him.

Cody could feel himself growing almost icy cold. "What is it?"

"Your sister was pregnant when she died."

Stunned, Cody refused to believe what the detective was telling him. "Carrie wouldn't have killed herself and she definitely wouldn't have killed her baby. One of her dearest dreams was to one day become a mother."

"Maybe it happened sooner than she'd planned and things just got out of hand," Skylar suggested, "and she couldn't handle it."

He shook his head. "Even if the pregnancy happened unexpectedly, she wouldn't have done *any-thing* to terminate it, that just wasn't who she was," he told the detective.

"Was there anyone in the picture?" Skylar asked the deputy. "Someone who could give you some insight into your sister's last days?"

Last days.

That sounded so painfully final, he thought. But then, that was what it was, wasn't it?

Final.

Carrie might be gone, but he was not about to buy into the scenario surrounding that event. His sister had *not* killed herself.

Cody tried to think, but it wasn't easy. All his thoughts felt completely jumbled up in his head as he struggled to make sense out of what he had just been told.

And then he grasped onto a thought. "The rental manager at the apartment complex where Carrie lived told me that my sister had a boyfriend."

"So you didn't know that she had a boyfriend until that point?" Skylar asked.

He let out a breath that fairly vibrated with the frustration he was experiencing. "No, I didn't."

Skylar nodded as she took in the information. "Well, first thing I need to do is to put a name to this so-called 'boyfriend.' If nothing else, at this point, the man is *definitely* a person of interest."

"We," Cody corrected. When the detective looked

at him quizzically, he clarified. "The first thing *we* need to do is put a name to this 'boyfriend.'"

"No offense intended, Deputy, but I am already part of a very sharp investigative team," she told him, "and we'll be looking into this. It's our job."

Cody did not find that reassuring. "I either come with you, Detective," he told her, "or I'm going to investigate this on my own." The words rang with finality. "And before you tell me I can't, I am part of law enforcement, same as you, and she is—*was*— my sister. I owe it to her to find out exactly what happened. So, I can either work with you, or on my own. The choice is up to you. And, for the record, there are no other choices on the table in this matter."

Skylar paused for a moment, considering him and pretty much knowing exactly what he had to be feeling. In his place, she would have felt exactly the same way until she was able to unravel everything.

A small smile rose to her lips. "There wouldn't be a Cavanaugh somewhere in your family tree, would there?" she asked.

He stared at her, highly confused. "Excuse me?"

"You're as stubborn as one of my brothers—or one of my cousins, for that matter," Skylar told him.

The deputy shook his head and looked exceedingly sad, in her estimation. "No, no relation. With Carrie gone, there's no one left but me."

Skylar looked up at him, feeling exceptionally distressed for the man.

"I am really terribly sorry for your loss, Deputy,"

she told him. "Those words hardly seem adequate, given what you are going through, but I am sorry about what happened to your sister, no matter how this has to sound."

He knew she was referring to the fact that she thought Carrie could have killed herself. But no matter what, no one would ever be able to convince him that Carrie had taken her own life.

Cody was certain he would have known that she had, *sensed* that she had. No, this had been done *to* her by someone else. Even though the detective felt that Carrie had ended her own life, he was confident that the drugs found in her system had somehow been given to her. Slipped into a drink or into her food.

He knew without a doubt that Carrie would have never taken those drugs willingly.

Cody would have sworn to that.

Chapter Four

"Why don't you come upstairs with me so we can plan your next move?" Skylar suggested. "If you're right and someone did slip that fentanyl into her system—"

"They did," Cody maintained firmly. As far as he was concerned, this was not up for debate.

She wasn't going to argue with him about that, not without proof. "Then this isn't going to be solved in a day or two," Skylar told him, leading the way to the elevator. "If you're really determined to work on your sister's case, do you have somewhere to stay?"

Cody shook his head as he followed the detective onto the elevator. He hadn't thought that far ahead. "I drove straight from Kiowa to my sister's apartment." He could feel his throat closing up again. "I was really hoping to find her there."

Well, that much made sense, she thought. "I know this has to sound indelicate, but do you know if your sister was paid up until the end of the month?" Skylar asked.

He hadn't asked the rental manager, but he was certain that was the case.

"Carrie was always very good about staying on top of her bills," he told her. "Why?"

"You could stay at her place, then," Skylar suggested. "It would give you somewhere to sleep and you could also use your waking hours to go through your sister's things, maybe you could find something with this so-called boyfriend's name on it to steer us in the right direction."

He really couldn't think clearly, he realized. Otherwise, that would have been the first thing to have occurred to him.

"I'll check with the rental manager," he told the detective, then decided to give her her due. "But that's not a bad idea."

Skylar smiled. "I don't have bad ideas," she told him. "Just occasional flashes of brilliance." She saw the dubious expression on his face. "I'm kidding. Sorry, I'm just trying to help you loosen up a little bit. Otherwise, you won't be able to deal with any of this because it'll all be much too oppressive for you."

The elevator came to a stop and he looked at her for a second before getting off. The detective meant well. He should have realized what she was saying. But he was just so anxious to get to the bottom of this, to find the person who was responsible for ending his sister's life, that he was having trouble focusing his thoughts.

He needed to get better control over himself. For Carrie's sake, if not his own.

"Why are we here exactly?" Cody asked Skylar when he realized that, according to the sign on the door, she had brought him up to the homicide squad room.

"Well, for one thing, the squad room might very well be a relaxed atmosphere, thanks to Lieutenant Anderson, but I still can't just take off when I want to. I have to tell the lieutenant that we have a name for the Lady in the Lake—that was the way we were referring to your sister," Skylar explained, suddenly thinking that maybe referring to his sister that way might have been a mistake.

Carrie, among other things had most recently been a substitute English teacher. A romantic at heart, she had always been partial to the Arthurian Legend.

Cody smiled sadly. "She would have liked that," he confided. "She always liked stories tied to King Arthur."

Skylar nodded her head. "Too bad I never got to meet her. I have a feeling we would have gotten along very well."

"Everyone got along with Carrie." And then, abruptly, he realized exactly what he was saying. "Well, almost everyone."

Skylar gave up thinking that this had been a suicide. Cody was too convinced that his sister wouldn't have done that and she tended to believe he was right. His sister had been murdered. The question remained why.

"We'll get him," she promised.

Cody appreciated the detective's reassurance, but there was one thing wrong with her theory.

"By Kiowa's standards, Aurora is a metropolis," he noted. "Finding the person who killed my sister could amount to the proverbial search for the needle in the haystack."

Skylar didn't want him growing despondent. He wouldn't be any use to her that way.

"We have an excellent track record here in Aurora for closing cases. If the guy has a pulse, we'll find him." Indicating her desk, she suggested, "Why don't you sit down and wait here? This shouldn't take too long."

There were framed photographs from one end of the desk to the other. The only other things on it was a laptop and a phone.

"Is this your desk?" he asked.

"It is," she answered.

His eyes swept over the framed photographs. "You do have a lot of photographs on your desk," he commented.

"I have a big family," she told him. Too late, Skylar realized her mistake. Right now, that was like rubbing salt into his wound. She wanted to apologize, but felt that might even make things worse, at least for now. So instead she just focused on the immediate job at hand—notifying Lieutenant Anderson. "I'll be right back," Skylar said as she quickly hurried away.

Left to his own devices and trying very hard not to think about what Carrie had to have gone through in her final hours, Cody studied the various faces that looked up at him from the framed photographs.

If this was her family, they appeared to all be rather good-looking, with similar features. He noticed there was one large group picture of a number of relatives of all ages.

She had an extremely large family, he caught himself thinking just before the wave of sorrow and emptiness swept over him. It made him that much more acutely aware of his loss.

He shook himself free of that sensation. He could grieve later. Right now he had to find that SOB and make him pay for stealing Carrie's life from her.

He didn't know what made him glance up just then, but he saw Skylar approaching him.

When she caught him looking in her direction, she beckoned. It was obvious that she wanted him to follow her to her superior's office.

"Lieutenant Anderson wants to meet you," she explained, then turned on her heel and led the way.

He could see that happening back in Kiowa, but here there just seemed to be too many people in the room for a meet-and-greet situation. And this was just one department. There were a lot of other sections within the Aurora police department.

Kiowa's entire police service consisted of four

people—three deputies and the sheriff. And that was if he didn't count Shirley, the woman who worked the phones.

The lieutenant was on his feet even before Cody had a chance to cross the threshold into the man's office.

Extending his hand, Anderson immediately told the man with Skylar, "I'm sorry to hear about your loss, Deputy. Cavanaugh has pleaded your case and told me your qualifications," he said to the visiting law enforcement officer. "You are more than welcome to temporarily work with my people to find the scum who did this to your sister." It wasn't unusual to accept help from visiting law enforcement personnel.

Looking to Skylar, Anderson nodded at the young woman he had already labeled as a "go-getter" in his mind. "All I ask is that you keep me abreast of your progress." He smiled slightly. "You'll be in good hands with Cavanaugh being your guide, Deputy Cassidy."

"Thank you, sir," Cody said to the lieutenant, adding, "You can call me Cody, Lieutenant."

"All right, Cody," Anderson acknowledged. "Her partner, Detective Rio, will be joining you as well." The lieutenant glanced down at his watch. "Looks to me like he's running a little late—but he will be here," he promised. "Funny thing is that Cavanaugh here is the one who's always on time, if not early. Rio's the one who's mostly late these days. In the world I knew when I was a young guy, women were always the ones who were fashionably late," he re-called with a wistful expression.

And then he looked at Skylar. "I take it that Rio is still adjusting to the life of a newlywed, right, Cavanaugh?"

She thought of her last conversation with her part-ner yesterday morning, before the medical examiner had taken Cody's sister to the morgue.

"So he tells me," she answered her superior. She knew that Anderson loved to gossip. It was harmless gossip for the most part, but she had observed that those exchanges with Rio always seemed to pique the man's interest.

Just then there was a quick knock on the lieuten-ant's door and Rio stuck his head in before Anderson could invite the detective in to join them.

"You're looking for me, sir?" Skylar's partner asked.

"I am," the lieutenant answered. "Turns out that we have a name for that victim who was brought in yesterday."

"Really?" Rio asked, surprised that the case seemed to have progressed to this extent. He and Skylar hadn't had much time to dig into it yet, espe-cially since they had spent most of yesterday tying up loose ends on another case. "Well, that had turned out to be lucky."

"Not for the victim," Skylar said, kicking Rio under the desk to keep him from saying anything further.

Rio's eyes widened as he glared at his partner accusingly. The warning expression in her eyes kept him from saying anything, or yelping in surprise. Skylar indicated the other person in the room with her eyes.

The message was conveyed even before Cody said, "The victim is my sister." He couldn't get himself to use the past tense yet when referring to Carrie. It was still much too painful.

Rio instantly seemed chagrined because of his initial cavalier reference to the deceased. "Hey, I'm really sorry, sir. I meant no disrespect," he apologized in the next beat.

The lieutenant spoke to clear things up. "Deputy Cody Cassidy believes that his sister, Carrie—the young woman discovered yesterday at the lake—was the victim of a homicide. If that turns out to be the case, I need the two of you to find out who's responsible," he told Rio.

Casting a sympathetic glance toward the dead girl's brother, Rio nodded. "We'll do whatever we can, sir," he promised.

"No," Skylar said, speaking up. "We'll *do* it." She emphasized the word. Her look took in her partner as well as the deputy. "We have a damn fine track record when it comes to closing cases. There's no reason to believe that this investigation will go any differently."

The lieutenant nodded. "I agree." Looking at his detectives, he asked, "Does anyone have anything else to add?"

The three other people in the room shook their heads.

Satisfied, Lieutenant Anderson gestured to the door. "Then go off and do me proud," he told his own two people. He went on to add, "If someone did kill your sister—"

"They did," Cody interjected firmly. There was no room for doubt in his tone. He was completely convinced that someone had killed Carrie. What he needed to do was to find out why and who, and he was not about to rest until he had those answers.

"Then Cavanaugh and Rio will find that person or persons," Anderson told Cody with finality. "Be sure to keep me up to date."

"You got it, sir," Skylar promised her superior.

Once all three of them had filed out of the lieutenant's office, Skylar immediately got down to business.

"Why don't we go and talk to that rental manager at your sister's apartment first?" she suggested.

Before Cody could make any sort of a reply— or Rio could ask his partner a question—Rio's cell phone rang. Pulling it out of his pocket, he frowned when he saw the number.

"I'm working right now, Marsha," he began impatiently, about to cut his wife off. And then, right before Skylar's eyes, Rio turned pale. "Where did it happen?" he asked, then queried, "When?"

Skylar recognized the fear in her partner's voice. She held her hand up, halting their progress out the squad room door as she took in the look on Rio's face.

"Where is she?" Rio asked. "All right," he said in a hollow voice. "I'll be right there."

The moment he ended the call, Skylar asked, "What happened?"

"It's Marsha. She was in a car accident," he said, his voice choking. "That was her sister on the phone."

Skylar didn't bother asking how bad the accident was. While she fervently hoped it wasn't serious, what mattered was that it had happened.

"Go," she told him. "Marsha needs to see you and you need to see her."

Rio looked from his partner to the man who had just lost his sister. He was torn between concern and what he felt was his duty. "But—"

"Go," Skylar ordered. "I can handle this end. Give Marsha my love—and call me as soon as you know that she's all right," she told Rio. Then she quickly hugged her partner before he could leave, promising Rio, "She's going to be all right."

The man nodded, clinging to his partner's words. Rather than take the elevator, he dashed over to the stairwell and took the stairs down to the first floor.

Observing it all, Cody looked at the woman beside him. "You want to go back to your lieutenant and ask him to assign someone else to accompany you?"

She looked at him, surprised by the suggestion. "I have someone else," she told him. Her eyes met his. "I have you."

"I meant someone from your squad," Cody clarified.

"I'm not prejudiced," she quipped, her lips curving. "Seems to me that you have more invested in finding the answers than anyone else does. Let's go—" she cast a glance in his direction "—unless you're uncomfortable working with a woman."

He thought of Carrie and, for just a moment, a fond smile bowed his mouth. "I was *born* working with a woman."

He reminded her of her brothers and the way they would have responded. Skylar was glad that the dead woman had had Cody in her life to care about her.

"Then let's go," she encouraged.

Chapter Five

Janice Miller looked up from what she was doing when she heard the office door open. The pasted-on smile turned genuine as soon as she recognized who had just walked in.

"You're back," Mrs. Miller noted, greeting Cody. "Did you find your sister?"

"I did," Cody answered, his voice extremely downbeat.

The rental manager looked at him, clearly confused. Her eyes shifted to the young woman with the deputy. "Is everything all right?"

Skylar answered the question before the woman could prod Cody any further. The faster she was informed of what had happened, the faster they could move this along.

"Ms. Cassidy was the victim of a homicide," she told the rental manager.

A look of disbelief crossed Mrs. Miller's face. Her hands flew up to her mouth as if she was physically trying to suppress the cry that rose to it.

She looked at Cody. "I am so sorry. Your sister was a lovely young girl," she told him, at a loss as to what else to say to the man.

"Was Ms. Cassidy's rent paid up until the end of the month?" Skylar asked, bringing the woman's attention away from Cody.

It took the manager a moment to think. "I believe so, but I would have to check," she told Skylar.

"Please do," Skylar requested.

"And you are?" the woman asked, looking at Skylar. It wasn't that she was looking for some sort of a confrontation, but she did need to know who this woman she was dealing with was, in the scheme of things.

Skylar took out her identification and her badge, holding it up as she answered Mrs. Miller's question. "I'm Detective Skylar Cavanaugh," she told the woman, further explaining, "I am looking into his sister's case for Deputy Cassidy."

"Of course, of course." The woman nodded her head. She hurried back to her computer to look up the current status on Carrie Cassidy's rent payments. Her fingers almost wound up knotting themselves together as she typed quickly, searching for the up-to-date information.

Finding what she was after, she glanced up and announced, "She was paid up to the beginning of next month."

That was what Skylar was hoping to hear. It would make things a lot easier for Cody. "Would it be breaking any rental rules if Deputy Cassidy remained in his sister's apartment until the first of next month?" she asked. That date was almost three weeks away.

The question threw the rental manager. She hadn't been expecting that. She thought for a moment.

"I don't think that would be against any of the rules," Mrs. Miller told the detective, then asked her, "Would this have anything to do with your investigating who killed Ms. Cassidy?"

That was definitely part of it, Skylar thought. But there was more to it than that. However, she felt it was far simpler to merely go along with that excuse rather than to get into any further explanation for now.

"Yes," Skylar answered quickly for Cody.

He didn't want to stand there, answering the woman's questions about Carrie. He had his own questions that needed answering.

"Would you happen to know if my sister was close to anyone in this development? Or was she friendly with any of her neighbors?" he asked.

"Well, this is a very friendly place," the rental manager was quick to tell Cody. Then, in all honesty, she had to add, "But it's also rather a transient place. People here are in the middle of getting their lives set up. By that, I mean saving up to buy what they hope will be their permanent home, or at least close to being their permanent home," the manager explained. "You know, they're on their way from 'here' to 'there.' This just happens to be the stopping-off place in the middle."

Dissatisfied with the way she was conveying her point, Skylar gave it another try. "It's a little like striking up a conversation on the bus. You don't really remember having had it five minutes after you get off." She looked at Cody, feeling for him. "In other words," she concluded, "don't get your hopes up."

Skylar nodded, but she told the rental manager, "We'll still knock on some doors, if you don't mind."

Mrs. Miller gestured around the general area freely, urging, "Please, by all means, be my guest."

"SHE DIDN'T SOUND very encouraging," Cody commented the moment they had walked out of the small rental office.

"Most people don't want to believe that they are anywhere near the presence of evil. It makes them feel vulnerable, as if they're not really safe," Skylar told him. "But at the same time, if we talk to your sister's neighbors, maybe someone observed something that might inadvertently point us in the right direction."

Cody looked at her, a bemused expression on his face as he shook his head.

"What?" she asked, unable to guess what he might be thinking.

"You are the strangest combination of optimism and pessimism I have ever encountered," he replied.

Skylar's eyes crinkled a little as she said, "I've been told that before. Thinking that way actually balances things out for me," she confessed. "That way, I'm not too dour about the crime I'm working, but I can still remain hopeful that I am growing close to the solution. I find that both attitudes are important when I'm working a crime."

He supposed that made sense, Cody thought. But right now, he just wanted to find someone who could tell him if they had seen his sister with the man who had gotten her pregnant.

He couldn't shake the feeling that whoever it was had the answer to what had happened to Carrie.

"How do you want to do this?" he asked Skylar, trying to curb his impatience. "Do you want to split up?"

She wasn't in favor of that. Under the circumstances, she didn't want to let him loose on his own, but she pretended to consider that idea.

"Well, that way we could cover twice as much ground," she agreed. "However, I've always found that two sets of eyes are better than one when looking at evidence."

Cody shifted from foot to foot. "So which is it?" he asked.

Her eyes met his. "I've always worked best with a partner," she told him. Her mind went to Rio. He hadn't called her yet. She really hoped that wasn't a bad sign.

"Well, I don't usually have that luxury," Cody

told her, then admitted, "But then, we don't have that much crime in Kiowa, either." He looked at her. "So you get to choose."

Skylar inclined her head, silently thanking him. "We'll knock on the doors together."

There was no one home in the first three apartments they tried. The fourth and fifth apartment had someone at home, but they looked blankly at the photograph Cody held up for them.

"She kind of looks like you," the sixth woman at home in her apartment commented.

"That's because that's a picture of his twin." Skylar volunteered the information to spare Cody.

"Really? I always wanted to have a twin," the woman said, taking a second look at the image.

Skylar caught herself thinking the woman was not the brightest bulb in the box. She attempted to hurry the conversation along, although she didn't have much hope that it would yield anything.

"So you don't recognize her?" Skylar asked.

The woman shook her head. "I'm afraid not. But if you come in," she said, opening the door farther, "maybe something will come back to me."

By the expression in the woman's eyes, Skylar felt she could just guess what the woman was hoping would "come back" to her.

Skylar took out a card from her wallet and handed it to the woman.

"If anything does 'come back' to you," she said, emphasizing the sentiment, "give me a call. That's my cell phone number and that's my number at the police station."

The woman took the card, tucking it away in her pocket. She seemed rather disappointed to have things end so quickly.

"Maybe you were right," Cody told Skylar as they walked away from this last apartment.

"About…" Skylar prodded.

"About our not splitting up." He went down to the first level. "I got the very distinct impression that the last woman wanted me to 'step into her parlor.'"

Skylar smiled, well aware of the old saying about the fly being invited into the spider's parlor. "I had a pretty strong feeling about the way things might go if you went from door to door on your own," she readily admitted. The man, in her opinion, was much too good-looking for his own good.

THEY WENT ON to knock on another two dozen doors by the time they decided to call it quits for the time being. At that point, they had knocked on a number of apartments on both sides of the residential development, moving farther and farther out as they went.

Most of the people they did find didn't recognize Carrie. Or, if they did, it was only vaguely from passing her by. No one had any information on a possible boyfriend.

Cody was disappointed to say the least.

"That's it?" he asked Skylar.

"Just for now," she answered. "We can pick up

where we left off tomorrow. Listen, why don't we grab some early dinner and then you can use the rest of the evening to go through your sister's things in her apartment? There's a possibility that you could find something helpful right off the bat. You might as well do that, because I'm pretty sure you're not going to get much sleep tonight—if any."

Cody looked at her, mildly surprised at the detective's insight.

Skylar could almost read his thoughts. "This is not my first rodeo, if you'll pardon the expression."

"I will if you will," he told her.

The grin she flashed at him was a broad one. "Consider it done," Skylar said.

Cody caught himself thinking that the detective really had a nice smile. It seemed to brighten the very room around her.

"When it comes to eating, do you have any particular preference in mind?" Skylar asked.

In response, Cody shrugged indifferently. "Just food," he replied.

"That gives me lots of leeway," she said. Then she smiled as a thought came to her. "And I think I have just the place for you."

"Some fast-food place nearby?" he guessed. He'd heard that California had a variety of fast-food places nestled all over. But, quite honestly, he really wasn't very hungry, Cody thought. If anything, he just needed to ingest a little something to keep him going.

"Not exactly."

"I'm not in the mood for a restaurant," he warned her. That was really the last place he wanted to go.

"That's good," Skylar answered, "because I'm not taking you to one."

"So where *are* you taking me?" he asked.

"Malone's," she answered.

That told him less than nothing. He'd never heard of the place. "What's Malone's?"

"Malone's is a bar owned by an ex-cop. He and some of his friends run it. And they serve really good food. I guarantee that going there will make you feel good. I can't explain it any better than that, but the food is excellent and the atmosphere there gives you hope," she told him.

"I wasn't planning on drinking myself into oblivion," Cody told her.

"That wasn't what I was suggesting," she said. "It's almost like a brotherhood at Malone's. They're all mostly cops that stop by there."

"I don't need a brotherhood," he stated.

"Well, we do have questions," she reminded him, "and who knows, they might have the right answers. Stranger things have happened. We don't have to stay very long. Just long enough for you to chew and swallow."

"Can't we just get something to go?" he asked her.

"We could," she allowed, agreeable. "But just do it my way this one time."

He frowned. She was making it sound as if they were going to be involved in some long-term relationship rather than just one that could be over in a matter of days.

He was tempted to ask just how long she expected this investigation to run, but decided he was too drained right now to get into the ramifications of that. So instead, he gave her a time limit.

"Ten minutes."

Because he was still attempting to come to terms with the fact that his sister had been killed, Skylar nodded, amenable to the terms he'd laid out for her.

She thought of the man in the back who prepared most of the food at Malone's. A long-time cop who was a widower, he was now retired. Working at Malone's was his long-term commitment.

"It might take him a little bit of time to get the meal ready," she told Cody, "but I'll do my best to have Dave hurry him along."

"'Him'?" Cody asked as she parked the Crown Victoria police vehicle across the street from Malone's. It was a Monday, but the parking lot was already full.

"Jacob," she told him. "Jacob usually prepares all the meals at Malone's. They'd have to strong-arm him to take a day off," she explained. "They're all good guys here." She sounded as if she was making a promise.

He wasn't looking to form a life-long friendship, or any sort of a friendship at all, he thought. All he wanted was to just grab something simple to fill his empty stomach. His stomach was making itself known right now, reminding him that even if he wasn't hungry, he needed to eat something to give him the energy to put one foot in front of the other.

At least until he could catch the lowlife that had killed his sister.

Besides, he'd discovered that it took less effort to agree with Skylar than it took to argue with her.

Resigned, Cody nodded his head.

Chapter Six

Malone's was fairly crowded, although there were still a few empty tables available in the rear of the bar where they could grab a seat. Cody noticed that several people called out a greeting to Skylar as they walked in.

She returned the greetings warmly.

This was obviously her hangout, Cody realized, though he had no interest in doing that. Still, he didn't want to interfere. He appreciated her efforts to help him find out what had happened to Carrie.

"Look," he told her, putting his hand on her shoulder to stop her, "if you want to stay here, I can grab a cab or an Uber and have it take me back to the police station so I can pick up my car," he offered. He had no intention of getting in her way.

Skylar looked at him in surprise. "You haven't eaten yet," she pointed out. "We're here so that you can get something to eat, remember? Speaking of which, what do you feel like having? A burger or something else?"

He was about to tell her that he was perfectly capable of ordering his own food, but since she probably knew what was good here and what was just passable, Cody decided to leave that choice up to her.

With a shrug, Cody said, "Whatever you pick out will be fine with me."

Skylar nodded good-naturedly. "A male who's not fussy. I've got to say that you're a breath of fresh air, Cody Cassidy," she told the deputy as she glanced toward the bar. "Wait here. I'll be right back."

Cody nodded, not bothering to comment one way or the other. Instead, he look a long look around at his surroundings. As far as bars went, Malone's wasn't all that different from the two bars he frequented back in Kiowa—except for a couple of minor things. Malone's was far better lit than the bars back home, plus there was no smoke lingering in the air. People in Malone's were talking and drinking, and a few of them were eating, but as he looked around the bar again, Cody didn't see a single person in the establishment who was smoking.

Technically, no one was supposed to be smoking back in Kiowa, either, but no one really took that to heart in the small town. Oh, there were a few diehards who did smoke; however, for the most part, the smokers could be found among the old-timers.

He had to admit that the idea of not taking in a lungful of smoke when he ate, especially since he was a nonsmoker, was a rather welcome change of pace from the bars in Kiowa.

Just then, Cody saw Skylar heading toward him. The detective was carrying a tray in her hands. On it were two plates plus a mug of ale and a glass that looked as if it had something in it that was fizzing.

Ginger ale? Cody caught himself wondering.

Rising from his seat, Cody took the tray from Skylar, then looked down at it. He thought she had said something about a burger, but there were no burgers on the tray. Had he misheard her?

She saw the quizzical look on his face. "I got you a hot roast beef sandwich on French bread," she told Cody. "This is actually a little faster to prepare than a hamburger. I also thought you might like to wash it down with a beer."

Setting the tray down, Cody saw that she had gotten a roast beef sandwich for herself as well. But that definitely wasn't a beer next to it.

He slanted a look back at Skylar, his eyes indicating the tall fizzing glass. "Is that what I think it is?"

"Depends on what you think it is," she answered, amusement in her blue eyes.

"Ginger ale." It was more of a question on his part than a statement. For all he knew, it was some fancy California drink.

"Then it is what you think it is," she told him, shifting her plate and the tall glass from the tray to the table. Tucking the tray to the side, she sat. "That roast beef sandwich tastes good even when it's cold, but it's even better if you eat it hot, which I highly recommend."

He obliged and took a bite, aware that Skylar was watching him chew. That made him feel somewhat self-conscious, until the taste had a chance to sink in. She was right, he thought. The sandwich really *was* good.

"Why isn't there some sort of game on in the background?" he asked her. There was a TV set mounted high up on the wall, but it was conspicuously dark.

"I think we're at the end of one season and not quite into another," she told Cody. "Besides, the people who came in are busy catching up with one another. Having a game going on right now would definitely interfere with talking. If nothing else, it would be distracting."

Things were definitely different in Malone's, he mused. "Where I come from, people go into a bar to *get* distracted," Cody told her.

"There are all sorts of ways to get distracted," Skylar assured the deputy. "A lot of times, the people are talking about the cases they're either working or have just solved. As a matter of fact, talking things out and saying them out loud helps the people in here put the pieces together."

Cody felt as if a light just went off in his head. "Is that why you brought me here?"

"I brought you here for the roast beef," she told him innocently, then cheerfully added, "Anything else is just gravy, if you don't mind the comparison."

Cody sincerely doubted that any of the officers or detectives who were here right now could give him any sort of insight into what had happened to his sister. However, being around Skylar and her positive attitude did give him the tiniest sliver of hope.

Still, Cody shrugged at her assessment. If he didn't buy into her words, he wouldn't wind up getting his hopes up. "If you say so."

"Hi, Sky." A tall, broad-shouldered, dark-haired man in jeans and a slightly rumpled, dark blue jacket made his way over and greeted the woman. He was holding a mug of partially completed ale as he quickly assessed the man with her. He nodded toward Cody. "Who's your friend?" he asked, quickly taking measure of the deputy.

"This is Deputy Cody Cassidy from Kiowa, New Mexico," she told her cousin. "Cody, this is Logan Cavanaugh, my uncle Sean's son. Sean heads up the Crime Scene Investigation Unit," she added, thinking it was just a matter of time before Cody met Sean.

Recognition crossed Logan's face. They had never met, but he knew of the deputy. "You're the one who came out here looking to find out what happened to his sister," Logan acknowledged. For the moment, he straddled the third chair at the table his cousin had commandeered. "I'm sorry to hear about your loss, Deputy. We're all keeping our ears open."

Considering that he had only been here for a little more than a day, Cody looked at the other man in complete surprise.

"Sounds like word here gets around really fast," he commented.

Logan ginned disarmingly as he shrugged. "You have no idea, Deputy," he said by way of confirmation. "Do you have anything to go on or any leads?"

"Even less than I thought I did when I got here," Cody confessed. He didn't like spinning his wheels like this, especially since it was all so personal to him.

Logan eyed his cousin. "Is that some sort of code?" he asked her, curious.

Skylar glanced at Cody, leaving the response to him—unless he indicated that he found it less awkward to have her answer her cousin.

In general, Cody was basically a private person. But when everything was said and done, this was not a private matter. Keeping a lid on things was not going to tell him who killed his twin, or why.

Taking a breath, he forged ahead. "Carrie and I were always close, to the point where we could end each other's sentences. We always knew what the other was thinking. But things changed when she came out to Aurora nine months ago. Her calls got less frequent, until they almost stopped coming altogether. And when I called her the last few times, the calls all went to voice mail first. She eventually did return them—until she didn't," he concluded.

"Was her moving to Aurora your sister's first time away from home?" Logan asked.

Cody felt he knew where this was going, but Skylar's cousin was wrong. "Yes, but that shouldn't have made a difference in communication. And if Carrie did meet someone, I would have been the first one she would have called to tell. She didn't."

Logan thought the information over. Coming from what could be thought of as a giant family, he did possess some insight into that situation.

"Maybe she was trying to hang on to her privacy," Logan suggested.

Cody shook his head, rejecting that theory. "Not Carrie."

Logan smiled. "Sisters can be funny that way," he told his cousin's new friend. "They're not always predictable," he all but guaranteed. "Trust me. I've got three of them, not to mention a parcel of female cousins—"

"And none of us have killed him yet," Skylar interjected, "which is pretty amazing all in itself."

Logan rose from the table, taking his all but empty beer mug with him. "And that's my cue to leave," he said with a good-natured nod toward Skylar. "I'll keep my ears open, Deputy. If I hear anything, I'll be sure to let you know," the detective promised. "Until then, I'll see you around."

Curious, Cody looked at the woman who was left at his table after her cousin walked off. "Just what did he mean by that? That he'd see me around?"

"Well," she explained, "we're a very close family. Our paths wind up crossing all the time. Plus, there're also the parties that Uncle Andrew throws practically all the time."

Cody looked at her, lost. "Excuse me, what?" he asked.

To enlighten him, Skylar backed up a few steps. "Uncle Andrew was the former chief of police in Aurora. He had to retire to take care of his five kids when his wife went missing—"

"Did he ever find her?" Cody asked, curious.

"Long story, but yes, he did. Uncle Andrew always had a gift for cooking, and he still likes getting the family together under any pretext he can come up with to cook for them—and the family likes being brought together. And eating, of course," she added with a wide grin.

"What does this have to do with me?" Cody asked.

"Anyone remotely connected to the police department—*any* police department," she stressed, looking at him pointedly, "Uncle Andrew considers them to be part of the family."

As far as Cody saw it, this just struck him as additional obstacles to get in the way of his investigation of his sister's killer and he said as much.

"I just want to find my sister's killer," he told her.

"And we will," Skylar promised with feeling. "This crowd takes things very seriously," she told him. "No matter how much they might seem like they're kidding around, it's just their way of knocking off steam. Every one of them prides himself—or herself—on being not just a decent cop, but a damn good cop."

Skylar had never meant anything more in her life.

He wasn't sure whether or not to believe her. After all, this was her family she was talking about. Would she say anything less than flattering about them? He didn't know her well enough to hazard a guess about that.

In any case, he was way too mentally exhausted and drained to contest what she was saying at the moment.

"Good to know," Cody murmured noncommittally.

As they began to make good their escape, they wound up running into another branch of her family just coming in to grab a quick bite to eat.

After greeting Skylar, they asked to be introduced to her companion. They were all aware that it wasn't often that Skylar came into Malone's with a man who wasn't her partner or someone she *wasn't* related to.

That was when she remembered that she hadn't heard from Rio yet. Catching hold of Brennan, her late uncle Fergus's eldest son, she introduced him to Cody and asked him to handle the rest of the introductions to the deputy.

When Cody looked at her quizzically, she told him, as well as her cousins, "I need to call my partner to see how his wife is doing. I'll be right back," she promised all of them.

The only private place to make the call was the ladies' room.

Going in, she was happy to find herself alone. She knew that wouldn't last. Feeling guilty that she hadn't followed up until now, Skylar called her partner's cell phone.

After five rings, her call went to voice mail. She empathized with Cody, thinking how frustrating it must have been for him to keep calling and winding up being forced to listen to a prerecorded message before leaving a message that wasn't returned.

Skylar decided to try again before going through the routine. So she called again.

And again.

The fourth time around, she finally left a message.

"Rio, it's just me—Skylar," she added in case he didn't recognize her voice. "I hope you're just too busy to answer you phone and that Marsha is all right. Give me a call and let me know—any time. Doesn't matter if it's the middle of the night. *Call me*," she emphasized. "Meanwhile, I'm working with Cody Cassidy and trying to find out just what happened to his sister." She decided to let him know just where the investigation stood at this point. "Right now, it's just frustration all around. No one seems to know anything.

"Again, call me with any news," she requested just before she ended the call. With a deep sigh, she put her cell phone into her pocket.

Walking back into the bar, she half expected to have to go looking for Cody. The deputy struck her as someone who, if he got it into his head, would just take off.

Crossing her fingers, Skylar looked around, then paused by the bar to talk to the owner.

"That guy who came in with me," she said to Nathan. "Do you know if he's still here, or did he take off?"

Looking up from the counter he polished religiously several times an evening, the heavyset man smiled at her in response and then pointed toward the rear of the establishment.

Skylar turned around to see that Cody was talking to several members of her family. Unless she missed her guess, he looked rather comforted by the exchange he was engaged in.

Bless them for coming through, she thought, looking at her family fondly.

Chapter Seven

"Everything okay with your partner's wife?" Duncan asked when he saw Skylar returning to the table that she had just recently vacated. At this point, Duncan and his brothers were sitting around it, talking to Cody.

Cody's back was to her, but he turned to face her and hear Skylar's answer to her cousin's question.

"I don't know," she replied honestly. "He's not picking up his phone."

"You could try calling the hospital and identify yourself, giving them the particulars of the accident," Bryce, another one of her cousins, suggested. "Ask if Rio's wife has been admitted or sent home."

She had already thought of that just now. "I'll do that as soon as I take Cody here back to the police station so he can pick up his car." Skylar looked at the deputy. "Are you ready to go?"

Cody rose to his feet. "Yeah."

"I can take him there, Sky," Duncan volunteered.

She smiled at her cousin. "Thank you, but I always finish what I start. Or have you forgotten that?"

Duncan exchanged looks with a couple of his brothers, rolling his eyes as he put his hand over his heart.

"Heaven forbid," he told her. Duncan's attention turned to Cody. "Nice meeting you, Cody, but very sorry about the circumstances behind your visit to our fair city," he told the deputy.

"Don't worry, we'll get him," Brennan promised, shaking Cody's hand.

We'll get him.

The words echoed in Cody's head. Skylar's cousins made it sound like it was a group project, as if they were all involved in this, Cody couldn't help thinking. Were these people for real?

He believed in being dedicated and doing his job, but as far as he knew, these detectives hadn't been assigned to the case. Why did they make it sound as if they were all involved in finding his sister's killer?

He didn't get it.

On his way out, he stopped at the bar, took out his wallet and said to Dave, "I'd like to settle my tab. Our tab," he corrected himself, glancing at Skylar. Since she had brought him here, he thought it only right that he cover her meal.

Dave waved away Cody's wallet. "It's already been settled," he told.

Cody took that to mean that Skylar had paid the bill. "I can pay my own bills," he told her, annoyed.

"I'm sure you can," she answered. "But don't look at me. I didn't pay the tab. Right, Dave?" she asked the bar's owner.

"Right," the former police officer answered. "And before you ask, the person who did pay your tab wishes to remain anonymous. As a good business-man, I have to respect their wishes." Inclining his head, Dave told the duo, "Have a nice night—and don't forget to come back." His words followed them to the front door.

Cody waited until he had gotten in on the passen-ger side of the detective's car and she had started up the engine before he asked, "Just when did you get a chance to pay the tab?"

"I didn't," she replied, looking at him innocently.

"Okay, then who did?" he asked.

"I guess that's just going to be one of those mys-teries of life that will remain permanently unan-swered," she told him, guiding the vehicle out of the parking lot.

Cody frowned. "You mean to tell me that this is a regular thing?"

"No," she answered, doing a U-turn and pulling onto the road. "It's a once-in-a-while thing," she an-swered, correcting the deputy. "Just accept it as a good deed done by a good person. Most likely, it was someone in my family and they had to pay my bill as well because, otherwise, it would look too suspicious. Consider it as someone saying 'welcome to Aurora.'"

That still didn't sit well with him. He had his pride. "I can pay my own bills."

"So you said. No one said you couldn't," she pointed out. "Just let it go, Cody. Lord knows that you have enough on your mind right now."

That he did, he conceded, struggling to keep the grief from eating him up alive. And then, almost immediately after that thought, he looked at it from Skylar's point of view.

"I'm sorry," he apologized. "I didn't mean to sound as if I was reading you the riot act just now."

Approaching a red light, Skylar glanced in Cody's direction. "Don't worry about it. I know how I'd feel in your place," she told him. "Speaking of which, how are you holding up?"

He was surprised by the question. It was almost too personal, too understanding. "One foot in front of the other," he told her. "Just keeping one foot in front of the other."

Skylar bobbed her head at the admission. "Best way to handle it," she assured him. The next moment, she pulled up into the station parking lot and drove toward where Cody had parked his vehicle.

"Well, there's your car," she said, waving at it. And then she made a quick decision. "Look, why don't I follow you to your sister's apartment?" she suggested.

Did she think that he forgot where the apartment complex was located? Cody frowned. "I know where it is."

"I didn't mean to suggest that you didn't. But a lot of unfamiliar things look and seem different at nighttime than they do in daylight. I just think it might help you if you have someone lead the way to the complex, get you settled in, that sort of thing."

She saw his frown intensifying and knew what that had to mean. "I just think you might feel better that way. And just so you know," she added, "I'm not planning on staying and hovering. I wouldn't want it to be any different than if you were my brother, trying to solve my murder and someone offered you their help," she informed him.

He looked at her, totally surprised by the sentiment she'd just expressed. "You really mean that, don't you?"

"Yes," she answered very simply. "I really do. And I'm not doing this for you. I'm doing this for your sister," she told him, adding with conviction, "She would want me to."

"You never met my sister—did you?" he felt compelled to ask.

"No, I didn't," she answered. "But I have brothers, and we're all close, although I would probably have to put them in an inflexible headlock before they'd publicly admit to that," Skylar told him.

She had pulled up beside his vehicle, waiting for him to tell her whether he was going to take her up on her offer or not.

Cody thought about it for a long moment, then got out of her car. "All right," he told her, opening his car door. "If it makes you happy, you can follow me to Carrie's apartment."

That was undoubtedly a comment on what he took to be her pushiness, Skylar thought. But that was okay. She had meant what she'd said. That she was doing this for his sister—because if something had happened to her, she would want to have someone helping her brothers, as well as her sisters, deal with the situation as well as cope with it.

It was the best way she could attempt to explain the situation—and her reaction to it—to Cody.

There was very little traffic from the police station to the development where Carrie Cassidy had lived the last nine months of her life. Following him, Skylar waited until Cody parked his car in the space assigned to Carrie's apartment.

Once he did, she went on to park the Crown Victoria in guest parking.

Getting out, she locked her car and quickly hurried over to Cody.

He stood there, waiting for her beside his vehicle. "Afraid I'd try to ditch you?" he asked her, curious.

"I just didn't want to keep you waiting."

"Are you always this thoughtful?"

"Pretty much," she answered, humor playing along the corners of her mouth.

The truth of it was, Skylar didn't want him walking into the apartment by himself for the first time at night. She was fairly confident that the loneliness that would register might be too much for him to bear.

She knew she was crediting him with her own thoughts and feelings, but she couldn't really help that.

Cody unlocked the door and Skylar went in first, turning on lights as she made her way through the apartment. Almost all of the lights were on when she was finished.

"Are you afraid of the dark?" he asked her, slightly amused. "Or are you just in league with the electric company?"

"Neither," she answered. "But with the lights on, the apartment just looks warmer and more welcoming."

That struck him as an odd thing to say. And then he realized why she had said that.

"Having the lights on doesn't change anything," Cody told her. His sister was still gone.

"No," Skylar agreed. "But it might make it a little easier to put up with."

He wanted to say that nothing would make it easier to put up with, but he knew that the detective's heart was in the right place, so he didn't want to give her a hard time. In her own way, she was just attempting to make it more bearable for him. "I'll be all right," Cody told her.

She wasn't all that sure that he would be right now. "I can stay with you for a while," she offered.

"There is no need to do that," Cody informed her.

"I know," she replied simply. "Maybe I just want to."

He caught himself wondering if she was afraid that he might do something drastic. "I don't want to keep you up," he told her. "Go home and get some sleep."

"All right," she agreed. The last thing she wanted was to appear to be throwing herself at him, or burrowing her way into his life. "I'll be back first thing tomorrow morning."

"Just what do you consider 'first thing'?" he asked.

"Six a.m. Seven a.m.," she declared. "Whatever you're comfortable with."

What he was comfortable with would be working this case on his own, but Aurora wasn't exactly his home territory, so he wasn't able to dictate terms.

"You pick," she told him.

She stared at him for a long moment. "All right, I'll be back here tomorrow morning at seven," she announced.

He looked at her, surprised. "Seven?" he questioned. "You don't want to sleep in?"

"I never sleep in," she informed him. "For the most part, I've always felt that sleep is a waste of time."

"Carrie would have gotten a real big kick out of you," Cody said with a slight laugh.

"Because she agreed with my philosophy, or because she didn't?" Skylar asked.

A fond look came over his face as he thought

about his twin. "Carrie usually went ninety miles an hour, working really, really hard, so whenever she had a chance to catch up on her sleep, she did."

"She sounds like she was a really great person to know," Skylar told him.

A fond, wistful expression crossed his face. "She was."

Skylar leaned forward and squeezed his hand. "We'll get whoever is responsible for this, Cody. I promise you we will."

He studied her for a very long moment. "You can't make that promise," he asserted. "It's not in your power to make it."

"Oh, yes, I can," she proclaimed.

She was utterly serious, he thought.

Cody wanted to believe her, wanted to believe that she meant this promise that she had just made him, despite the fact that there was no way in the world she could actually keep it.

Cody had no idea what had possessed him, what had made him lean forward, causing his space to invade hers. But one moment he was discounting her words, despite the fact that he felt this overwhelming desperate need to take those words to heart. The next moment, his lips found hers.

He had absolutely no idea how that had happened, or even why. The closest thing he could ascribe it to was that he *needed* to believe her, needed to believe that his sister—the person he had shared every moment with for all these years—couldn't just slip away like that, out of his life, without his at least avenging her.

Cody slipped his arms around Skylar, pulling her to him. Kissing her as if there wasn't going to be a tomorrow. Because if this detective wasn't able to help him solve the mystery of Carrie's death, then there would *be* no tomorrow. Not for him.

Abruptly, Cody pulled away, his lips leaving hers as he dropped his hands to his sides. Clearing his throat, he looked at her as if he hadn't seen her before.

"I'm sorry," he told Skylar uncomfortably.

"No reason to apologize." She smiled at Cody. "Just one soul reaching out to another, looking for some sort of comfort..." Skylar hesitated. "I'll see myself out," she told him as she walked over to the front door. "And I'll be here at seven—unless another time suits you better?" She offered to make the change one last time.

"Seven will be fine," he answered, his eyes meeting hers. Most likely, he wouldn't get any sleep anyway, Cody thought.

"Seven it is," Skylar replied.

She congratulated herself on making it out the garden apartment door without a mishap.

Her legs felt extremely wobbly.

Chapter Eight

By a little past six the next morning, Skylar was not only up and dressed, she had to force herself to wait until it was at least seven thirty.

While she was fairly convinced that Cody had undoubtedly had trouble falling asleep, if he had even managed to drop off at what was probably a really late hour, she didn't want to risk waking him if he *had* accumulated an hour or so of sleep.

To while away the time—and because she believed in being productive—she made herself a quick breakfast to go, packed another one for the deputy, and went on to prepare coffee for both of them. She poured some milk into a separate container, took a few packets of sugar and tossed in a handful of napkins as well.

Once Skylar had everything she thought she might need, she closed the containers and flipped the locks.

She was out the door well before seven, hoping

that Cody hadn't jumped the gun and left before she'd even had a chance to get to his garden apartment.

Settling in behind the wheel of her Crown Victoria, she started up the vehicle. It occurred to her that she was taking an awful lot for granted when it came to Cody Cassidy. After all, how much did she really know about the man? At this point, she was just taking his word for things.

Skylar supposed that she could run a background check on the deputy. But considering the size of the Kiowa police department, she was trusting that the people in Cody's station would volunteer the information she needed without any prejudice.

That might not turn out to be the case.

But then, she came from a family that had taught her to look for the best in people rather than to suspect the worst. So, unless she was shown otherwise, she was going to just assume that Cody was on the straight and narrow.

Besides, she thought with a smile, a man who could make the world go away by kissing her like that definitely couldn't be all that bad.

"Okay, Sky, get your mind back on your work," she lectured herself, pulling into the development where the deputy was currently staying.

She wondered if Cody had gotten any sleep at all. She certainly hoped so. He would have to be clear-headed to attempt to make any sense of the information he was probably going to have to sort through—and that was only if he wound up getting lucky.

Parking proved to be a challenge inasmuch as all the available spaces in guest parking appeared to be taken at first.

There had to have been a great many overnight guests last night, Skylar mused.

She had almost circled the immediate area before she spotted an empty space. Backing up, she reversed toward the spot until she managed to slip into it.

Getting out, she assessed her surroundings. The parking space was some distance away from the garden apartment. But a little exercise, she reasoned, never hurt. She usually ran a couple of miles before breakfast in the morning, but today had been different.

In Cody's place, she would have been anxious to get back to the "hunt." He wasn't going to feel whole again until he found the man who had done this to his sister.

Taking the breakfast she had prepared for them, Skylar walked up to the apartment door. She was about to ring the bell when the door unexpectedly swung open and Cody suddenly exited.

He hadn't anticipated her being right there and they all but collided.

Startled, Skylar took a couple of steps back. Collecting herself, she laughed at his making such an unexpected appearance. "That's some radar you have," she told him.

For a second, the detective had managed to lose him. But then he realized what she was saying. She seemed to think that he'd been anticipating her on his doorstep.

"That's not radar," Cody told her. "I was just getting an early start this morning."

"Without me?" she questioned as she made her way into the apartment.

"I'm a grown man," he stated. "I made it from Kiowa to Aurora. I can certainly handle smaller distances. Besides, the car's old, but it does come with a GPS." He followed her into the small kitchen. She was making herself at home, he noted. "And, when all else fails," Cody went on, "there're always maps to use. I do have one in the car," he told her.

She didn't know if he was being serious, or just humoring her. In either case, she decided to just ignore the incident and especially the sarcasm that came with it. She thought it was safer that way than to risk a flare-up first thing in the morning.

Cody suddenly paused and sniffed the air around Skylar. "You brought coffee," he declared. It was hardly a guess.

"And breakfast," she added. "I thought you might want some. I don't know if you're the type who eats first thing in the morning, but I decided to take a chance and bring you some, just in case."

He watched her unpack. It smelled even more tempting once she took out the individually wrapped packages. He looked over the two bags she had placed on the counter.

"There's no label on the packages," Cody noted.

"That's because I don't have a labeler," she told him.

His forehead wrinkled as he took the information in. "This didn't come from a fast-food place?" he questioned. He'd assumed that she would have just picked up something at a drive-thru before getting here.

"Not unless you consider my kitchen to be a fast-food place," she told him.

She picked up the two bags and placed them on the small kitchen table. She then proceeded to look through the drawers for the utensils and found them on her second try.

Taking out two forks for the breakfast muffins and two spoons for the coffee containers, she set the utensils on the table. Turning, she opened the overhead cabinets. Rummaging through the small spaces, she didn't locate any regular plates.

Instead, there were just paper ones, some large, some small. There were also a couple of plastic plates next to them as well.

"Didn't your sister have any regular plates?" Skylar asked. From what Cody had mentioned, his sister had lived here for around nine months. Not having any plates in that time seemed rather odd to her.

Cody glanced into the cabinet, even though he already knew the answer. "I don't think so," he replied. "Carrie never liked washing dishes." Anticipating her next question, Cody explained, "She kept the knives, forks and spoons because they were a housewarming gift from our father, but I'm fairly sure that she would have rather used plastic utensils."

Cody went on. "Just before she moved out here, I was all set to buy her a set of dinnerware, but she told me to save my money," he recalled. "So I wound up buying her a bunch of sheets and towels instead."

Skylar took all this in, nodding her head. "Your sister was a very unique young woman," she told Cody.

At this point, the detective was just preaching to the choir. "That she was," Cody agreed. There was more than a touch of wistfulness in his voice.

Skylar placed the breakfast sandwiches she had prepared earlier in her apartment onto the paper plates she had taken down from the cabinets, then moved those plates to the table settings, facing one another.

She saw Cody looking skeptically at the offerings.

"No offense, Skylar," he told her, "but I'm not all that hungry."

"Understood," she answered. "But you do need to keep up your strength and consuming this little bit of food will provide at least some of that for you." She saw the stubborn look that entered his eyes. "Let me put it to you this way—if you don't eat, you're not going to go anywhere."

Cody had never liked being ordered around. He dug in his heels. "And who is going to stop me?"

Skylar didn't hesitate for a single moment. "I am."

Which caused Cody to utter the typical challenge. "You and what army?"

Skylar smiled up at him, her eyes meeting his. "Just me."

The woman meant that, he realized. He could practically hear those same words coming from Carrie. The pretty, young detective really did remind him of his sister.

Cody sighed. He was not about to back off from the challenge he had uttered, but for the moment, he decided just to go along with her opposition.

"All right," he conceded, pulling the plate closer to him, "if it makes you happy, I'll eat."

Skylar flashed him a wide, good-natured smile. "It makes me very happy—and deep down, I suspect that consuming the breakfast I made will make you feel very happy, too."

The breakfast she had prepared for each of them was a fried egg, with bacon strips, covered in melted cheese and encased in a toasted muffin. And while the offering wasn't exactly hot, transported the way it had been in a plastic container, it was still somewhat warm, which was all she'd been hoping for.

Watching Cody pick up the muffin and sink his teeth into it, she was more than a little gratified when she saw the startled smile grace his lips.

"So, do you like it?" she asked, rather certain what the deputy's answer was going to be.

"I do," he responded, surprised as he looked at the muffin, egg, cheese and bacon combination. He raised his eyes to hers. "And you made this?"

"Yes. Why does that surprise you?" she asked. "You told me that your sister cooked." Why would he think that she couldn't?

"Yes, but Carrie had to—from a very young age," he told her. "My mother was sick for a number of years, so Carrie just took over all the chores whenever she could. And whenever she couldn't, my father and I would pitch in, although, admittedly, our combined effort didn't match Carrie's."

"In my family, we all took turns doing chores. And I mean *all*—" she emphasized the word "—of us."

"I'm impressed."

And he looked it, too, Skylar thought.

"Nothing to be impressed about. That's just what being part of a family is," Skylar told him, her eyes crinkling just a little as she smiled at him. "You don't have a corner on that particular market."

He looked down at the paper plate before him and was stunned to see that he had managed to finish his breakfast without even realizing it.

Wiping his mouth and fingers with the napkin Skylar had set out, he pronounced, "This was really good."

"I'm glad you approve," she told Cody, tongue-in-cheek. Rising, she picked up the utensils, put them into the sink, then went on to throw out the paper plates. "Well, this certainly made cleanup a lot easier. Maybe your sister was on to something."

He had to admit that he did get a kick out of Skylar's statement. "She did have a way about her," he agreed. Glancing at his watch, he said, "And having breakfast here did eat up a little bit more time."

"Looks like it was a win-win situation," Skylar replied. And then she looked at Cody. "Are you ready to go?"

"More than ready," he told her. "Do you want to use my car—or yours?"

"We'll drive to the police station separately," she said assertively, "so you're not stranded if I get called away. But for the most part we'll use mine. After all, this is official police business and using my vehicle makes it easier to maintain that this is official," she told Cody.

"All right," he agreed as he stepped out of the apartment and looked toward the closest guest parking area. "Where is your car?" he asked.

Skylar pointed off into the distance. Since she had arrived and had parked the Crown Victoria, several spaces, much closer than the one she had used, had opened up.

"It's right there," she told him.

"That's a pretty long walk from the apartment," he commented.

She merely smiled. "Helps me keep my weight

down," she answered. She hadn't mentioned that there hadn't been any opened spaces earlier. He walked with her.

"What weight?" Cody asked seriously.

"See?" she responded cheerfully. "It's working already."

When they reached her vehicle, Skylar paused next to the driver's side and told the deputy, "I'm going to swing by the lieutenant's office to give him an update."

Had he missed something? Cody wondered. "There isn't any update," he noted.

"That, too, is an update in itself," she pointed out. She saw the impatient look creasing the deputy's forehead. "You know as well as I do that these things take time. They only get solved in a set amount of time in the movies and on television programs. Everything else is documented to death," she told him.

Cody blew out a breath. "Yes, I know that," he responded. "But that doesn't make waiting any easier."

Skylar nodded, sympathizing with him completely.

In addition, she had already thought of what their next move was going to be once they left the police station. "Do you know where your sister worked before she left her job?"

"She was a substitute teacher at a local high school," he answered, holding the driver's door for her as she got in.

"Do you know which local high school?" she asked.

"I do. Venado," he recalled.

"Then that'll be our next stop after I talk to the lieutenant," she told him.

"By the way, did you ever wind up reaching your partner?" he queried. "Last night, your call kept going to voice mail."

She was surprised, with all that the deputy had on his mind, that Cody remembered her messages hadn't reached Rio yesterday.

"Yes, I did finally reach him. His wife had to have emergency surgery, but from all indications, she seemed to have come through it well. When I spoke to him, he said she was in a medically induced coma. He promised to keep me informed of her condition."

"When did you speak to him?" he asked.

"A little after one this morning," she answered.

He looked at her in wonder. "You don't seem exhausted. You should be more tired than I am," Cody told her.

Skylar smiled and pulled out her keys. "I didn't tell you, did I?"

She was losing him again. "Tell me what?"

"I run on batteries." She started her engine. "Get your car, Cassidy," she urged.

She didn't have to tell him twice.

Chapter Nine

Within twenty-five minutes, after touching base with Lieutenant Anderson and letting the man know that her partner, Rio, was taking some personal time to be at his wife's hospital bedside, Skylar and Cody were back in her car.

"You said that Carrie previously worked as a substitute teacher before she decided to end her employment. Do you know exactly when she terminated her contract and why?"

He thought for a moment, going back to one of the last conversations he'd had with his sister. He really didn't know why red flags hadn't gone up at the time.

"She said she was looking for a better work environment," he answered. He should have pressed Carrie about that, Cody realized. "That was about a little more than almost two months ago."

"That's just about the time when your sister stopped answering your phone calls," Skylar said. "You didn't think that was odd?"

In hindsight, he did, and he really regretted that he

hadn't acted on that feeling. All he'd had at the time was the reason he had assumed he couldn't reach her. "I just thought she was busy trying to get started in this 'new' career of hers."

That sounded rather suspect to Skylar. "Did she happen to share what this new career was?" she asked.

Cody called himself seven kinds of a fool as he shrugged his shoulders. "She said it was going to be a surprise." The deputy sighed and stared straight ahead. "A surprise," he repeated, mocking himself. "How could I have been such a fool?"

"Because you're not clairvoyant," she told him, trying to get him to lighten up on himself. "Because you wanted to give Carrie her space, like a good brother."

"I wasn't just her brother, I was her *twin*," he decreed, angry with the way he had dropped the ball. "What that means is that I should have *known*, should have *sensed,* that there was something wrong." Upset, Cody took himself to task. "But I didn't."

The traffic light at the intersection turned red and she stopped, glancing at Cody. "I don't profess to begin to understand what that connection between you and your twin was like at bottom. I just have a lot of siblings. What I do know is that you're not going to be able to avenge what happened to Carrie by beating yourself up about it. That kind of attitude won't do you *or* your twin sister any good."

Cody frowned. He didn't like being lectured to,

especially when he couldn't really argue with what she was saying.

Staring straight ahead, he all but grudgingly growled at her. "You're right."

"Why do I get the feeling that you just put a curse on me?" Skylar asked, trying her best to improve the mood just the least tiny bit.

"If I was going to put a curse on anyone," Cody responded, his voice sounding dejected, "it would be on me." What kind of a law enforcement officer did that make him? Cody upbraided himself.

"That would just be a huge waste of time," she replied in all seriousness. "Let's just focus on getting all the information we can so that we can bring whoever did this to justice. That means putting all the pieces together, no matter how fragmented they seem to be right now," she pointed out. Pausing at another red light, she looked at Cody, her eyes all but penetrating into him. "All right?" she asked.

He blew out a breath, trying to separate himself from the hopeless feeling that was suddenly threatening to swallow him whole.

"All right." He all but bit off the words. Then, after a moment's pause, Cody apologized. "I'm sorry. I'm usually a hell of a lot better at my job than this."

"I'm sure you are. This isn't exactly a standard situation for you. You're allowed to be a little rattled. Or a lot rattled," she amended, thinking the situation over and feeling for the man. "Since this involves your sister, it makes a huge difference."

It took Skylar a second to realize that they had arrived at their destination. She pulled into the lot in front of the entrance to the high school, though it took her a little time to find a parking space that didn't have a name posted in front of it.

As he got out, Cody looked in awe at all the cars that were parked in the lot. "Just how many teachers are there working here?"

She really had no idea, Skylar realized. "The usual number, I suppose. Why?" she asked as she led the way to the concrete stairs and then climbed them.

Cody glanced over his shoulder and assessed the vehicles. "Just seems like an awful lot of cars to me."

She knew what he had to be thinking. "Those cars don't belong to the teachers," Skylar told him. "They belong to the students." She knew that from experience. Some things didn't change. "The teachers park their vehicles in the parking lot located on the other side of the school."

Cody was surprised by what the detective said. He looked around the lot again. "Their parents must really be doing well," he marveled.

"To a degree, yes," Skylar agreed. "But I think that you'd be surprised to learn that a lot of the students who go here have after-school jobs and are putting that money toward paying off their cars. The kids today," she told him, "aren't all that different from a generation or two ago. That's not to say that they're all saints, either. They're just the usual mixture of good and bad."

Skylar led the way toward the outdoor stairway, which in turn brought them to the wide, squat, sprawling school building.

Cody realized that he was just following her blindly. "Do you know where you're going?" he asked, curious.

"Of course I do. The registrar's office," she answered. "I used to go to this school. Things haven't changed all that much in that time."

Cody had just assumed that she and her siblings hadn't attended public school. "You didn't attend private school?" he asked.

She turned to look at him as if the question he had just asked was nothing short of inane.

"You're kidding, right? The Cavanaughs are just about as down to earth as you can get," she told him. "Besides, the public school system in Aurora is exceptionally good. There's absolutely no need for private schools—or tutors," she added in case he wasn't convinced.

Approaching the registrar's office, Skylar politely knocked on the door, then opened it.

Flashing her credentials at the startled-looking assistant principal, who was sitting at the desk facing the door, Skylar said, "Excuse me. I'm Detective Cavanaugh with the APD and this is Deputy Cassidy from Kiowa, New Mexico. We would like to speak to the person in charge."

The woman, Ellen Hanks, nodded at the request. "That would be Principal Brad Larson, but he is out sick. I'm the assistant principal. May I ask what this is all about?"

"One of his former substitute teachers." By the look on the assistant principal's face, it was obvious the woman was waiting for a name. Skylar gave her one. "Carrie Cassidy."

There was no other way to say this, Skylar thought, but to say it outright. Avoiding Cody's eyes, she told the woman, "Ms. Cassidy was found floating in the lake several days ago."

Ellen Hanks immediately looked horror-stricken. "Are you sure it was Carrie?" she asked Skylar.

But it was Cody who answered. "We're sure," he said grimly.

The assistant principal took a closer look at the young man standing before her. "Are you by any chance related to Carrie?"

"Yes, I am," he admitted. "She was my sister."

The woman stood and circled her desk, coming out in front of it as if that made her sentiment somehow clearer.

"I am very sorry to hear that. Your sister only worked here for a short while, but everyone liked her. She was a very sweet, outgoing young woman. The students all responded to her," she informed them, predominantly Cody.

Skylar nodded. "Was she friends with anyone in particular? Someone we could talk to? We're trying to find out if she was seeing someone."

"You could talk to Nancy Nelson," the assistant

principal recommended. "She and your sister used to have lunch together on Fridays. Like I said, Carrie got along with everyone, but she seemed closer to Nancy Nelson than to anyone else."

"Is Nancy Nelson here?" Cody asked, trying to move this along.

"Actually, she called in sick today—and yesterday, too, now that I think of it," the woman added.

"Do you have an address where we could reach this woman?" Skylar asked.

Ellen Hanks looked rather uncertain about the question. "We don't generally release addresses. This is highly unusual," the woman told them.

"So is murder," Skylar answered darkly.

"Murder?" the assistant echoed, clearly startled. "You think that Carrie Cassidy was murdered?"

"According to our medical examiner, that is a very real possibility," Skylar answered.

Ellen Hanks moved to sit in her desk chair, faced her computer and typed in the teacher's name. "As far as I know, this is Nancy Nelson's current address. I know she was looking for a bigger place to stay, but I don't think that she found it yet. She certainly didn't update her address for our records."

Writing the address down, the woman handed it to the detective.

Skylar looked the address over. The location wasn't far from where they currently were. "Thank you for this," she said, holding up the address the woman had handed her. "Was there anyone else Carrie Cassidy was close to here?" Skylar asked.

"Like I told you, Carrie got along with everyone," the assistant principal said. "Students and staff," she affirmed. "But I would say that Nancy is your best bet."

About to leave, Skylar looked down at the address again. Something else occurred to her. "Would you happen to know if Carrie was seeing anyone?"

Ellen Hanks looked torn, not to mention a little uncertain about releasing the information. "That would be prying," she answered.

"I'd see it as taking an active interest in the teaching staff," Skylar replied, putting a different spin on it.

"Well, now that you mention it, she did have a different glow about her just before she handed in her notice, but I really can't tell you any more than that with any sort of certainty," the woman confessed.

Skylar nodded. It had been a long shot, but she felt she had to try. "Well, thank you for Ms. Nelson's address," she told the woman.

"Don't mention it." The assistant principal's lips lifted in a quick, spasmodic smile. "Good luck," she called after the departing duo.

"If we don't get anywhere with this Nancy Nelson," Skylar told Cody as she drove toward the address that Ellen Hanks had given them, "we'll come back and see if we can interview the other teachers as well as the substitute teachers and question them. Someone has to know something about your sister's life."

"I was closer to her than anyone," Cody reminded her. "If she didn't tell me anything…" His voice trailed off.

She knew where he was going with this and she had an answer. "Sometimes it's easier to talk to a stranger than it is to talk to family or even close friends."

He glared at her as if she had sprouted another head.

"Trust me. If something was going on in her life and she just wanted to unload, a stranger is easier to talk to than someone who might be close to your sister," she told Cody.

He shook his head. He had always kept his own counsel rather than share things. "You women are a very confusing sex," he muttered.

She laughed. "Funny, that's what I always say about men," she joked. "I guess that's what keeps things interesting between the sexes."

Cody sighed, shaking his head. "If you say so."

CARRIE'S FRIEND NANCY NELSON lived in the city next to Aurora, but it didn't take very long to get there. What did take long was getting her to answer the door.

It took three tries ringing the woman's doorbell before Nancy Nelson finally came to the front door. She appeared utterly miserable, like someone who was in the middle of nursing either the flu or an incredibly bad cold.

Watery eyes stared blankly at the people on her doorstep. The teacher wouldn't have opened the door at all if Skylar hadn't held up her badge and identification for review.

"Is something wrong, Detective Cavanaugh?" the teacher asked, punctuating her question with a deep cough that all but vibrated throughout her chest.

"We're really sorry to bother you, Ms. Nelson, but we need to ask you a few questions about Carrie Cassidy," Skylar told her.

Watery eyes flicked from the detective to the good-looking man standing next to her. A man who looked a great deal like her friend.

Nancy sneezed before taking a step back, out of the doorway.

"Sure. I don't know if I'll be much help since I haven't seen her for a couple of weeks. We were supposed to get together last week, but Carrie was a no-show." There was curiosity in her eyes. "Is something wrong?" the woman asked, punctuating her question with another sneeze.

Rather than answer, Cody suggested, "Why don't we go inside?"

Carrie's friend didn't like the sound of that, but she led the way into the apartment.

Two deep coughs resonated, marking Nancy's path back into her apartment.

Chapter Ten

Looking at the two people through progressively more watery eyes, Nancy gestured toward the sofa in the small living room. "Why don't you sit down?" the woman suggested as she struggled to suppress yet another sneeze.

"I think that you need to sit down more than we do," Cody observed, having her walk in front of them.

Taking in a shaky breath, Nancy nodded wearily. "No argument. This cold is really wearing me out." She made her way over to the sofa and lowered herself onto it on shaky legs. "But you have me worried. Did something happen to Carrie?"

"What makes you ask that?" Cody asked. He couldn't help wondering if this woman had had something to do with his twin's demise.

Nancy shrugged helplessly. "Carrie was always very good about answering her phone, or at least returning her calls. But this time, even though I left her a message and asked why she hadn't turned up for lunch the way we'd arranged, I haven't heard word one from her. I thought maybe she was embarrassed because she was having a little trouble finding another job or..." Her voice trailed off like someone who suddenly felt as if she had said too much.

But Skylar wasn't about to let the matter drop. "Or?" she asked, trying to encourage Carrie's friend to continue. "Or what?"

Nancy sighed. She had started this, she might as well follow it to the end. "I thought she might be arguing with her boyfriend. The last time I talked to her, they'd had a few flare-ups," the young woman confided, lowering her voice even though there was no one around to overhear the exchange except for the three of them.

Cody immediately pounced on the information. "Did you ever meet him?"

"Once," Nancy admitted, then thought about her answer. "He came to pick her up at school about two months ago."

"Do you remember what his name was, or anything about what he looked like?" Skylar asked. She was trying to put together some sort of a picture of the man as well as to get a handle on the sort of relationship they shared.

Nancy nodded. The gesture seemed to hurt her head. "She introduced him as Brent Masterson and at the time I remember thinking that he seemed exceedingly charismatic—not to mention really, really handsome. I do remember that Carrie fell for him right from the beginning," the teacher admitted. "Hard."

About to say something further, the woman had to pause to blow her nose and then dab at her eyes, which had become watery again.

"Would you happen to know what he does for a living?" Skylar asked Carrie's friend conversationally, trying not to sound as if she were pressing her for more information.

Nancy shook her head. "Carrie never actually told me what he did, but I got the impression that it had something to do with the school. Maybe he was some sort of independent contractor," the teacher guessed with a shrug. "I really don't know that much about the man for sure," she told the two people in her living room. And then she added, with a pleased, triumphant smile, "I did sneak a picture of the two of them together."

Cody immediately became alert, exchanging looks with Skylar. "Do you happen to have that picture where you could get your hands on it?" the deputy asked.

The teacher thought for a minute, then nodded. "Give me a minute," Nancy told him. She rose with effort and made her way over to her closet. Her shoulder bag was hanging on a hook.

She fetched it and brought it back over to the sofa. Sitting, she opened the bag and took out her cell phone. Concentrating, the woman proceeded to flip through the photographs that were on it.

"There," she declared elatedly, holding up her phone for them to see. "It's a little blurry," she admitted, explaining the reason why. "I had to do it on the sly. Brent didn't like having his picture taken," she told the pair on her sofa. "Although I don't see why. He's the best-looking man I've seen in a long time—present company excluded, of course." The teacher smiled, looking at her friend's brother.

Red flags had immediately gone up in Skylar's head. She could only see two reasons for Carrie's significant other not liking having photographs taken of himself. He was either exceedingly shy—which hardly seemed likely to her way of thinking—or he was exceptionally leery of leaving behind a trail that would aid people in identifying him.

"I'd really appreciate getting a copy of that," she told the woman. "Let me give you my cell phone number and, if it's not too much trouble, you can send that photo to my phone. That's the only photograph you have, right?" she asked as an afterthought.

Nancy's laugh was half-hearted. "I'm lucky to have gotten that one," she told Skylar. "I don't mind telling you that when I was taking it, my heart almost stopped. Brent turned his head at the very last moment and almost caught me at it. That's why the photo is as blurry as it is," she explained. "He really didn't like having his picture taken."

"You did good." Skylar praised the woman. She recited her cell number to Nancy and then waited for the successful transfer.

Her phone dinged, alerting her of the transfer, and she looked at the screen. "Not bad," Skylar commented, pleased. She held up her phone for Cody's benefit. "I think we've got enough for Valri to work with," she told him. Closing her phone, she tucked it into her back pocket and looked at the woman they had been talking to. "You've been a great help, Ms. Nelson." She rose to her feet.

Cody immediately stood as well.

"I think we should let you rest," she told Nancy, who chose that moment to sneeze again. "Bless you," Skylar said. Walking to the front door, she turned to look at the teacher. "If we have any other questions, we'll be in touch."

"Will you let me know how this winds up going?" Nancy asked, then added, "I really hope that Brent isn't responsible for anything that happened to her. He seemed like a really nice guy and, in my opinion, Carrie was crazy about him, at least in the beginning."

Cody focused on her words. "Oh?"

"Well, I wasn't there for the end of it," Nancy explained, "so I have no way of knowing if things went sour."

Skylar took the woman's words into account. "Hopefully, you're right. Thank you for your time," she said by way of parting.

Once she and Cody were outside, she glanced in his direction. He hadn't said anything except for goodbye. Curious as to how he felt about what he had just heard, she decided to prod him a little.

"Well, what do you think?" Skylar asked Carrie's twin.

"I think," the deputy began slowly, "that this Brent uses his looks to worm his way into women's confidence, then goes from there."

Cody appeared rather angry to her. She paused next to the Crown Victoria's driver's-side door, studying the deputy's expression.

"There's something more, isn't there?" she guessed.

His expression darkened. "I'm not used to Carrie being so naive," he confessed. "She was always a great deal more savvy about things than this picture her friend painted."

"Maybe your sister was just lonely," Skylar suggested. "Loneliness makes people do things they normally wouldn't have ever dreamed of doing."

"If she was lonely, she could have called me," Cody complained.

She knew that it was Cody's sense of helplessness talking. Skylar unlocked her vehicle. "Sometimes a big brother—or twin brother—just isn't enough," she pointed out.

She could see how the interview with Carrie's friend had really disturbed him. She only knew one way around that for now. "Okay, let's get this photograph and the sparse information we did manage to collect over to Valri," she encouraged. "Maybe she can come up with something more concrete for us to work with. Fingers crossed," she added, holding both of her hands up in the air and crossing her fingers.

He looked at her hands. "You're not planning on driving that way, are you?" Cody asked.

Amusement curved her lips as she asked the deputy, "Where's your spirit of adventure?"

"I left it back in Kiowa," he told Skylar.

She looked at him and saw the distress in the deputy's eyes.

No, he hadn't, she couldn't help thinking. The only way Cody Cassidy was going to be able to deal with this situation was if, somehow, they were able to find the person who'd cost his sister her life.

"I'll help you find it," she promised. She was referring to his sense of humor, which had eluded him.

SKYLAR DROVE TO the police station. She was figuratively keeping her fingers crossed that Valri wasn't incredibly swamped, that she could find the time to help them locate Masterson—if that was indeed the man's name.

It took Valri Cavanaugh Brody several minutes before she even raised her eyes to see which of the APD detectives had walked in and was standing near her desk, waiting to get her attention.

When she did glance up, she didn't seem surprised to see Skylar and the New Mexican deputy. A soft look rose to her eyes.

"And here I thought that you'd forgotten all about me," Valri marveled.

"Oh, that would never happen, Valri," Skylar told the computer expert in all seriousness.

A weary expression slipped over Valri's face. "That's what I was afraid of," she murmured under her breath. "Talk faster, Skylar. I'm about two days behind in my work and I'm sinking fast."

If that was actually true, Skylar thought, Valri would never bring herself to admit it. She prided herself on staying on top of things, not sinking beneath them.

"I have great faith in you, Valri," Skylar said, "and I need you to locate this man for me." The detective held up her phone, displaying the photograph Carrie's friend had provided for them.

Valri looked at the photo, then raised her eyes toward Skylar and the deputy. "And who is this?"

"Brent Masterson. Could just be an innocent man caught up in something that at the very least is shaping up to be a melodrama," Skylar answered. "Or he could be a murderer."

Valri frowned. "That's pretty widespread." Her glance swept over Skylar. "Which way are you leaning?"

"I honestly don't know," Skylar admitted. "But I need to."

Valri nodded, then looked at the man standing beside Skylar. "And this is...?"

Cody leaned forward, shaking the hand of the

woman that everyone thought of as a computer wizard. "I'm Deputy Cody Cassidy. Carrie Cassidy's brother."

Valri nodded, looking genuinely saddened. "I am very sorry for your loss, Deputy." Those words always sounded so hollow to her, even though she sincerely meant them. Her thoughts turned so something far more useful. "You wouldn't have a copy of this man's fingerprints, would you?"

Cody shook his head. "No, just his name, which may or may not be his real identity," he told her quite honestly.

"Give it to me," Valri prompted. "I'll see what I can come up with."

He wasn't holding out much hope, but he was aware that miracles had been performed with much less to go on, and at this point, Cody felt that he was way overdue for a miracle. If nothing else, he owed it to his sister.

"Any shred of information or evidence will be greatly appreciated," he told her.

Valri inclined her head. "Duly noted," she acknowledged.

At her urging, they left the department's tech wizard to her work and walked out of the computer lab.

"All right, now what?" Cody asked as he made his way over to the elevator with Skylar.

"Now we go get something to eat—" she stared at him "—and don't give me that garbage about you not being hungry. Unless you're a robot, you're hungry," she told Cody sharply. "And after I'm satisfied that I got you to eat some decent food, I need to stop at the hospital. I want to get an update on Rio's wife."

The latter struck him as being rather odd. "Couldn't that be done with a phone call?" Cody asked.

"It could," she agreed, then told him, "But that's not how I do things."

Cody turned the information over in his head. "So I take it that you're a believer in 'trust no one'?"

"No," she said, denying his flippant assumption. "I'm a believer in seeing things with my own eyes. I don't want to bombard Rio with a bunch of questions at a time like this. I am, however, a firm believer in that old saying 'trust but verify.'"

He thought about that for a second, then said, "Fair enough."

Since he wasn't giving her a hard time about it, she felt she needed to sweeten the pot just a little. "I'll drop you off before I swing by the hospital," Skylar promised.

"No need. I can come with you," he told her. "After all, you spent all this time accompanying me while I tried to locate the answers I needed, the least I can do is return the favor. As a matter of fact—" he thought the situation over "—we can go to the hospital before you take me back to my car."

"You skipped a step," Skylar told him.

Getting into the vehicle, he looked at her, puzzled. "Excuse me?"

"You jumped right over the part where you're going to be getting dinner," she pointed out.

"No, I didn't," he contradicted. "I'm not hungry."

"We've already gone around that part. It didn't hold any water the first time and it's not holding any now," Skylar told him. "As a matter of fact, you can pick whatever restaurant—or fast-food place—you want to go to, but you *are* going to go to one," she informed him firmly.

"You know, you really should have some kids so you have someone to order around. Little people who are bound to obey you—until they get older—like five," Cody commented.

"Okay, I'll keep that in mind," she replied. "But for now, you still have to have some sort of dinner."

"You're not going to stop until I do, are you?" he asked her.

She smiled at him in obvious satisfaction. "Now you're getting it," she told him. "Just pick a place."

He sighed. "You can pick the place."

Skylar shook her head as they exited the parking lot. "That's not the point. You have to choose."

"Fine," he snapped. "I'll pick."

The man sounded far from happy. Even so, she flashed a grin at him. "Atta boy. I knew you would come around."

He decided that it was safer not to make a comment on that.

Chapter Eleven

Ultimately, Skylar brought Cody to her favorite restaurant, Mangia! Very simply translated, the single word meant "eat." It was a homey-looking little
Italian restaurant that boasted more than reasonable
prices. The atmosphere was extremely welcoming.
And as far as the food went, it was very, very good.

The latter piece of information turned out to be
Skylar's way of selling the restaurant to the deputy.
He still looked rather reluctant about the whole idea
of eating anything at all, but in the end, the deputy
from New Mexico finally surrendered and gave in.

The owner, Antonio Gaspare, had a habit of welcoming each and every customer who crossed his
threshold. The warmth that was displayed was something not lost on Cody.

Standing behind another pair of customers, Cody
looked at the woman who had brought him there and
asked, "Is this a slow night?"

Skylar looked at him, wondering if the deputy had
suddenly lost his ability to see for some reason. She

gestured around the restaurant. "Does it *look* like a slow night?" she asked him in disbelief. A number of customers were lining up behind them.

Cody could easily see that it wasn't. "I suppose not," he told her. "But then why is the owner—"

"Mr. Gaspare," she prompted. The man's name was written beneath the restaurant's name.

"Why is Mr. Gaspare going out of his way greeting everyone like this?" He would have assumed that the man would have been better off being at the reservation desk.

Skylar smiled fondly, looking at the owner. "I guess he's just a very friendly man. And he learned a long time ago that if he treated everyone like family, they'll come back—as long as the food is good and the prices are reasonable," she added, knowing that was always the bottom line.

The next moment, the smiling older man had made his way over to Skylar and her friend. Embracing Skylar, the restaurant owner declared, "Ah, Detective Sky, so nice to see you again. You honor us with your presence," Mr. Gaspare enthused. Stepping back, he enveloped her hand in both of his. And then the restaurant owner turned toward Cody. "And who is this?"

The way he asked, it sounded as if he was genuinely interested in the man who had accompanied the detective into his restaurant.

Skylar happily answered his question. "This is

Deputy Cassidy. We're working on a case together," she told the restaurant owner evasively.

Antonio Gaspare nodded as he told the young man with Skylar, "You could not have chosen a better, smarter person to work with." He smiled broadly at the young woman. "Detective Sky is a very hard worker and she is very dedicated. I know this for a fact," he told Cody, winking at him. "Come," he urged the duo, "my best table has just opened up."

"Mr. Gaspare," Skylar said with a laugh. "You and I both know that *all* your tables are your best table," she told the restaurant owner.

Genuinely amused, the older man chuckled. "This is why you are always such a welcome sight here, Detective Sky."

With that, the older man guided them to a newly cleared table conveniently located off to the side of the restaurant, creating a feeling of isolation while still being very accessible.

"How is this?" Mr. Gaspare asked as he gestured at the table.

"It's perfect," she responded, then looked at Cody, waiting for him to express his approval. "How about you?" she queried when he said nothing.

Cody nodded, saying, "It'll do," with little to no enthusiasm.

"Coming from the deputy, that's a very heady compliment, Mr. Gaspare," she told the man she had known for years.

The owner held Skylar's chair out for her, then

tucked it in as she sat. Handing them each a menu, he promised to send one of his sons over to take their orders when they had made their choices.

Looking on, Cody marveled, "This really is a family business."

She didn't quite understand. "Why would I make that up?"

He sighed, shaking his head. "I don't know."

The deputy really wasn't talking about family business. At least, not *this* family. Taking a guess as to what was really on his mind, Skylar reached across the table and put her hand on top of Cody's, giving it a light squeeze. When he looked at her, she decided that a little positive reinforcement might be what was needed.

"We *will* find whoever's responsible for what happened to Carrie. All of it," she attested. When she saw him quizzically raise an eyebrow, she filled him in on the information that she had left out. "For both her death and the death of the baby she was carrying." She saw Cody stiffening.

The next moment, Skylar found herself very grateful not to be on the receiving end of the dark look that had just crossed Cody's face.

Time to change the subject while she still could, Skylar thought.

"Now you need to put all that on hold for the time being so that you—so that we—" she amended, "can eat something." She knew what had to be going

through the deputy's head and quickly continued before Cody could say anything.

"I have known Mr. Gaspare for most of my life,"
she told Cody. "I am not about to insult the man
and walk away before we order dinner, so look at
the menu and pick something. Whatever you pick,
I promise will not wind up disappointing you in the
slightest."

Cody frowned slightly. For a moment, she thought
that the deputy was just going to get up and leave.

But then he actually appeared to check over the
menu and make a choice, picking out the item that
he was the most familiar with.

"I'm ready," Cody informed her in a crisp voice.

Skylar had thought that she was going to have to
do more arm twisting, but happily, that didn't turn
out to be necessary.

When the owner's youngest son, Marco, returned,
ready to take their orders, Skylar exchanged a few
pleasantries with him first. Then, pausing, she
looked at Cody. She didn't want to take a chance on
him changing his mind.

"Go ahead," she urged the deputy.

He ordered a serving of Veal Parmesan, skipping
any side dish. When she raised a quizzical eyebrow,
he told her with finality, "You wanted me to order
something. This is the 'something.'"

"Fair enough," she said. "Make that two orders
of Veal Parmesan," she told Marco, surrendering
her menu to him.

Marco took Cody's menu as well. He seemed surprised that she didn't order a side dish, either.

"The mashed potatoes are extra special tonight," Marco told Skylar. "My aunt Rosa stopped in for a few hours and my father talked her into whipping up a giant bunch. Everyone loves Aunt Rosa's mashed potatoes. She swears she adds a 'secret' ingredient," the server confided. "You really don't want to miss out on that."

"Okay, you talked me into it, Marco," she told the owner's son.

For his part, Marco looked toward Cody, paused just for a moment and then nodded his head, accepting the man's order the way it stood.

"Coming right up," he promised, withdrawing from the table.

"You're in for a treat," she told Cody the moment that the server was gone.

"I've already gotten my treat," Cody said. "You backed off."

Her eyes met his. "My pleasure," she told him.

Cody had no idea if she was being genuine or sarcastic, but he suspected that it was probably the latter.

He had to admit that he wasn't exactly long on patience right now. "So, what's on the agenda?" he asked after a couple of minutes.

"We eat, we leave, you get some sleep and we start fresh in the morning. With any luck, we'll get something to go on from Valri. In the meantime," she said as she watched their server return carrying a tray with two plates, "you enjoy the best Veal Parmesan west of New York City—or possibly Rome," she amended.

Distributing the two plates, Marco smiled. "I'll tell my father what you said. He will be pleased."

"Shouldn't you taste it before you say that?" Cody asked as their server retreated.

"I don't have to. I eat here whenever I can, and I have *never* been disappointed," Skylar confided. "But you judge for yourself," she urged the deputy, confident that unless he was being perverse, he would agree with her.

Cody took a bite, then told her, "Not half bad."

She almost laughed out loud, telling him, "You do have a way of understating things. Are your taste buds officially dead, or are you just being stubborn?"

He frowned, then took another bite. "All right," he grudgingly admitted. "You're right. It is good."

Skylar got a kick out of the way he all but had to choke out the words. "Now, don't you feel better?" she asked with a wide, amused grin.

"It's going to take a lot more than just good food to do that."

"Understood," she granted. "But at the same time, it is a small first step."

Less than thirty minutes later, as she watched Cody consume the very last little bit of his dinner, Skylar waited for him to retire his fork before asking, "Would you like to have anything else?"

His eyes met hers, seemingly speaking volumes. "Nothing that can be served on a platter."

If this were another time and possibly another place, Skylar would have said that his response practically sounded like a proposition. In all honesty, she found herself almost wishing that it was.

But under the circumstances, she knew that he didn't mean it that way. Cody might not have even been aware of the way his words had come across. With all her heart, she caught herself wishing she had met him before the light had gone out of his eyes.

She had learned a long time ago that wishing didn't make it so. An entirely different set of circumstances would have had to come into being for that to have happened. Right now, the best she could do was to help Cody find who had done this to his sister—and why.

"All right, then," she told him briskly, "I'll let Marco know that we're finished eating. He'll write up the bill for dinner and then we can be on our way."

"I'll pay for dinner," Cody informed her. It seemed only right, he thought, since he hadn't paid for anything yet and she had.

She appreciate his offer, but right now, the cost of dinner was far down on her list of things to take care of. "We'll talk about it later," she told him, then added for his edification, "I have a running tab here."

"I don't care if the tab you have is flying," Cody told her. "I intend to pay for my dinner—and yours," he added.

"Thank you. That's very generous of you," Skylar replied.

Her tone of voice gave Cody the distinct impression that she was just humoring him, but he wasn't about to argue with her or carry on any sort of dispute about this matter in public. One way or the other, the Kiowa deputy decided, he was going to make sure that Skylar accepted the money for this.

Shifting in her seat, Skylar raised her hand, catching Marco's attention. The owner's youngest son made his way over to their table within a few moments.

"Anything else I can get you?" he asked as he looked from Skylar to Cody.

"Just the check, thanks," Cody answered the server.

"I'm afraid I can't do that," Marco replied, still smiling.

"Why is that?" Cody asked. Anticipating the answer, he informed the young man in no uncertain terms, "This is *not* going to go on the detective's tab."

"No, sir, it isn't," Marco readily confirmed. "My father expressed a wish to pay for your meals." Before Cody could argue the point, Marco explained, "It's my father's way of saying welcome."

As far as Cody was concerned, that was not acceptable. "I can pay for my meal—and I can pay for hers," he stated flatly.

"No one is arguing that, Deputy. But paying for

people's meals on occasion," Marco continued, still smiling, "gives my father a great deal of pleasure."

Skylar placed her hand on Cody's shoulder to get his attention. "You want my advice?" she asked.

"No," Cody answered decisively.

She pretended the deputy hadn't said anything. Instead, she simply told him, "Don't argue with Mr. Gaspare's son. Just smile and tell him thank you."

Turning toward Marco, she repeated the response. "Tell your dad thank-you. Time permitting," she added, "we'll be back soon." Turning to Cody, she asked, "Ready to go? Or do you want to argue some more?"

Cody's eyes never left her face. "Do I have a choice?"

The smile rose to her eyes as she answered, "You always have a choice."

Cody's eyebrows drew together. They had different views when it came to that. The man he had been before coming out here seemed a million miles away.

But he hadn't lost his manners.

"Tell your father thank-you from me," he said to Marco. "The meal was delicious."

Marco looked very pleased. "Thank you. I will be sure to pass that along to him." The owner's youngest son inclined his head at the deputy and then at Skylar. "Until the next time," he told them.

"Until the next time," Skylar echoed, then looked at Cody. "Shall we?" she asked, nodding toward the door.

Cody made no answer, he just gestured for her to begin walking.

She had almost pushed the door open and walked out when her cell phone began to ring.

She and Cody exchanged looks as she retrieved it from her pocket.

Chapter Twelve

Skylar glanced down at the caller ID number that popped up on her cell phone screen and then looked at the time.

"What's wrong?" Cody asked. After everything he had been through, he immediately assumed the worst.

"I don't know yet," she answered. "Maybe nothing." Or, at least, she fervently hoped it wasn't anything serious.

From his vantage, Cody had already seen who the caller was.

"Do you usually get calls from the computer lab at this hour?" Cody asked her.

"Sometimes," Skylar answered evasively, then pressed the button on her phone, taking the call. "This is Skylar," she announced.

"Hi. I just wanted you to know that I think we might have a handle on who Carrie Cassidy's significant other was. And," she continued, "it appears that the man has a very interesting sideline."

"Well, give," Skylar urged, becoming animated. "Who is it and what is his sideline?" she asked. She could feel Cody's eyes on her, waiting for an answer.

But Valri wasn't about to tell her just yet. "I'll let you know when I can confirm the information."

"C'mon, how about a hint?" Skylar requested, doing her best to get her cousin to come around. Her curiosity was getting the better of her. She was not ready to give up just yet.

"You know better than that, Skylar," Valri admonished her. "Right now, my husband and child have Missing posters plastered all over town with my picture on them. I've got to go home to show them that I'm still alive."

She had heard that song and dance more than once from many members of her family about their particular situations. She knew for a fact that it was incredibly easy to get caught up in the work and forget about everything else.

Skylar wanted Valri to know that she appreciated all the work that her cousin had already put in on the case.

"I do appreciate the update from you. Now go home, kiss that husband of yours and hug that adorable little baby," she advised. "We'll see you tomorrow morning," Skylar promised just before she terminated the conversation.

"So what did she find?" Cody asked the second that he saw Skylar end the call.

"I really don't know," she admitted.

That made no sense to him. "What? Then what was all that about?" he asked, waving a hand at the cell phone.

"Valri just wanted us to know that she was still investigating the evidence and she felt that she was on the trail of something," Skylar said emphatically.

Cody was still waiting for details. When there weren't any forthcoming, the deputy pressed on. "Well, what is that 'something'?"

"Valri didn't want to say anything until she was absolutely sure of the facts," Skylar told him.

"And when will that be?" Cody asked, irritated at the way this investigation was just creeping along and seemed to be going around in circles.

She couldn't blame him for being frustrated. Cody wanted answers. She knew how that was.

"I promise that you'll know as soon as I do," Skylar told him, then felt compelled to explain. "Valri is extremely cautious and thorough. She doesn't like releasing information until she is very sure about it."

"So this is all on hold?" he asked, frustrated about the lack of progress.

"No, it's not on hold, but sometimes Valri has to take a step back in order to recharge and approach the situation with fresh eyes. Just so you know—" she continued "—this is not the first time that she has done this kind of thing."

"And she didn't give you any sort of a clue as to who she suspects and the kinds of things that she believes this person has been up to?" Cody challenged impatiently.

Was this so-called lab wizard attempting to create some sort of a melodrama for reasons he couldn't begin to fathom?

Seeing his growing agitation, Skylar did her best to calm the deputy, using an incredibly soothing, easygoing voice. "She felt she was getting close and, when she is sure of the truth of her information, Valri will let us know."

Eager to get at the heart of the matter, he asked, "Could I talk to her? I can get that information for her." In his mind, Cody was already interrogating whomever the lab tech suspected. "I just need a name."

He didn't see the problem with that, did he? She supposed that, in this case, it was a matter of not being able to see the forest for the trees.

"That is exactly why she's not about to give you a name. Valri is afraid that you're desperate to bring this person, who might or might not have killed your sister, down any way that you can." Skylar told him what she was certain that he already knew. "We have to go about building this case slowly and carefully so that when we do bring charges against the person Valri suspects, those charges are going to stick.

"For now," she advised, "I'll take you to get your car and then you're going to get some actual rest. You need to be clearheaded, Cody. I promise," Skylar went on, finally walking up to her Crown Victoria, "that Valri is very good at what she does. If anyone can deliver and do what amounts to the impossible, Valri can."

She hit Unlock on the vehicle's key fob and all four of the locks popped up, standing at attention like tiny trained soldiers.

Skylar got in on the driver's side and, starting up her vehicle, pulled out of the restaurant's parking lot as soon as the deputy settled in the passenger seat. Once she was on the road, she glanced in Cody's direction and asked, "Was I right about the restaurant?"

They had already gone through this, Cody thought. With a shrug, he answered, saying, "You were."

"I am also right about this," she informed him. "We get your car, you go back to your sister's place and catch a few winks. First thing tomorrow morning, we go by the computer lab and find out just how much progress Valri has made with the evidence she's uncovered."

This latest turn in the case—the killer's possible identity—had left Cody feeling really wired.

"I'm not going to be able to get any sleep," he told Skylar, then added for her information, "I can go for a couple of days without any sleep."

"Well, I can't," she freely countered. "And since I'm the lead on this case, I vote we go to bed." He looked at her in surprise and she immediately realized how that had to have sounded to him. "*Separately*," Skylar emphasized.

Cody sighed, resigning himself to the situation.

A few hours shouldn't make that much of a difference, the deputy silently argued. Besides, he couldn't just waltz off on his own, no matter how much he might want to. If he did, he had no doubt that he could very well get kicked off the case altogether. Being in on this investigation meant far too much to him to risk that happening.

"Judging by the sound of that sigh, you've decided to agree with me," Skylar guessed, barely suppressing a grin.

"Do I have a choice?" Cody asked, less than pleased about the situation.

She didn't bother to beat around the bush. "Nope."

"Then I agree."

Skylar flashed a smile in his direction. "Glad we're on the same page. And, you never know, sometimes a fresh perspective in the morning puts things in a whole new, different light," she told him.

SKYLAR DROPPED CODY off by his car at the police station shortly thereafter.

Glancing up into his rearview mirror, Cody noticed that after he'd gotten into his vehicle and set off, the detective began to follow him. He put up with it for a few minutes, but he pulled over about a block later.

"Why are you following me?" he asked as soon as she came up next to him. "I already told you I'm going to Carrie's place. Don't you trust me?"

"Not really," Skylar told him honestly. "This way, if I follow you, I'm sure you're going where you're supposed to be."

"Are you planning on sitting outside the door all night?" he challenged. This woman was unbelievable, he thought.

"No," she answered. "Because if I can't trust you to stay put once you've gone inside, then there's no real point in our working together, is there?"

Cody frowned. In an odd way, he had to agree with her. "So you're putting me on my honor, is that it?"

Skylar nodded. "That is exactly it," she replied.

His eyes narrowed just a little bit. "Did anyone ever tell you that you're one really annoying woman?" he asked.

"Actually, yes," she replied. "My brothers have. A lot more than you." She gestured toward the road. "So, ready to get back to driving to the apartment?"

Cody mumbled something in response, but she felt that it might be better not to ask him to repeat what he had just said.

True to her word, Skylar did follow him back to his late sister's development, then watched as he parked his vehicle and went inside Carrie's apartment.

Rather than drive away, Skylar waited for a few more minutes, then decided to finally leave.

She sincerely hoped that Cody was a man of his word, but she wasn't about to become his babysitter. That definitely wasn't a way to build a working relationship, even a temporary one, she told herself.

Tired, she drove home a few minutes later instead of going to the hospital the way she had initially planned. But once she walked inside the house, she called to check in with Rio about his wife's condition.

The phone rang four times and, from experience, she knew it was about to go to voice mail when she heard Rio's phone being answered.

Even his hello sounded a great deal more upbeat than the last time she had spoken with him.

"Hi, it's Sky. I'm calling you, Rio, to find out how everything's going. How's Marsha doing?"

Her partner sounded really happy to hear from her. "She's groggy, but she's conscious and she's doing better by the hour. Her surgeon is really happy with the result from the surgery."

She could hear the smile in Rio's voice and was greatly relieved. "So, are you home?" she asked.

"Not yet. Doctor said I could spend one more night here. It makes Marsha feel better," he explained.

In his place, she would have done the same thing, she thought. "Marsha's lucky to have you," she said. "Well, give me a call if you need anything."

"Thanks, Sky. Oh, by the way..." Caught up in his own drama, he had almost forgotten. "How's the search for the deputy's sister's killer going?"

"Valri thinks she might have found the identity of

Carrie's boyfriend—and possibly the father of her baby. We need to find his DNA so we can see if we can make a match."

Taking off like that made him feel that he had dropped the ball. "I'm sorry to have left you in a lurch," Rio apologized.

"Don't mention it. You've got enough on your mind right now," she told her partner. "Give Marsha my best."

"I will, Sky," he told her warmly.

"Uh-huh. Just don't get so caught up in taking care of Marsha that you forget to eat, Rio," she told him.

"You know, you really do need some kids to hover over," he told her.

"There's no shortage on that front," she told him. "I have a whole bunch of nieces and nephews to choose from. Don't forget to give me a call if you need something," she reminded him, then terminated her call.

The thought of having children to take care of lingered on Skylar's mind as she got ready for bed. She had never really actually longed for children, but she had never really discounted the idea, either. For the most part, she liked children and she got along really well with the small people in the family.

However, she wasn't about to run off and have any at this moment. As her mother used to say, *What will be will be.*

Right now—as before—the most important thing

on her mind was finding Carrie's killer. She felt that would go a long way to at least partially erase the sadness in Cody's eyes, and that was really important to her. Bringing people like Carrie's killer to justice, to make them pay for their terrible crime, was what she'd been created to do. Anything after that, she thought, came in a distant second.

THE FOLLOWING MORNING, Skylar woke even earlier than she normally did. Getting out of bed, she took a quick shower, leaving it to the cold water to help wake her up and bring her around.

Moving swiftly now, she dressed and, after making and drinking an extra-large mug of coffee, Skylar was behind the wheel of her car.

As she drove to the development where she had left Cody, she mentally crossed her fingers that she would still find his car parked in the space that had been assigned to his sister's apartment.

Because if it wasn't, she didn't have the vaguest idea where to find him. For a moment, she regretted not planting a tracker in his car.

So, when she pulled into the development and caught sight of his car, Skylar breathed a very loud sigh of relief. Cody had kept his word and stayed put, the way she had asked him to.

That was a huge step in the right direction, she thought to herself. Being able to trust him and take him at his word meant more to her than she had believed it would.

Parking in the first space in guest parking that presented itself, Skylar made her way quickly to his door and knocked.

Her knuckles had barely made contact before the door swung open. She found herself looking up at a bleary-eyed deputy whose hair was tousled, looking as if it was going in all different directions at the same time.

"No offense," she told him, "but you look like an unmade bed. Are you all right?" she asked, slightly concerned.

"For a man who got about ninety minutes' worth of sleep—broken up—I'm doing great," he told her, stifling a rather large yawn.

Cody attempted to focus on his wrist to be able to make out his watch. It took a couple of blinks before he was successful. "Is it tomorrow already?"

That was all she needed to hear to make up her mind.

"C'mon, we're going to get you some coffee, and something to eat for both of us," she told him. Skylar left no room for an argument.

He was in no frame of mind to be ordered around, but she did have a valid point.

"Okay."

That was the sum total of his response.

Skylar thought of it as a victory, even though she refrained from saying as much.

Chapter Thirteen

"So, what's the good news, Valri?" Skylar asked the computer wizard as she and Cody walked into the lab.

She placed a large container of coffee on Valri's desk as well as a breakfast croissant, the kind that she knew that her cousin favored.

Valri looked up. The first things that caught her attention were the coffee and the warm croissant.

The computer tech noted with a smile, "I see you've come bearing gifts."

"Just our way of saying thank-you for your efforts trying to find my sister's killer," Cody told the woman.

Valri nodded, her smile broadening. "I see Detective Cavanaugh has introduced you to the time-honored habit of bribery." Momentarily, the computer expert shifted her eyes to Skylar, then she told the deputy, "That didn't take you long."

Valri paused to take a healthy sip from the takeout coffee cup Skylar had brought in, her second one of the morning. "Not bad," she commented, nodding her head at the coffee in her hand.

Unable to contain herself, Skylar finally had to ask, "So, has your hunch paid off yet?" she asked.

Valri looked from one person to the other, not for dramatic purposes, but to prepare them. "Not a hunch, just evidence. From what I've pieced together, your sister and the man she was seeing were very closemouthed about their relationship—but for apparently very different reasons."

Cody looked at the lab tech. "Different reasons?" he questioned. He wasn't sure what she meant, but he gamely went along with it. "What were they?"

Eyeing the deputy, Valri felt her way around her words very carefully. "Apparently, the whole thing about being in a relationship was very new to your sister and she wanted to savor everything within the situation. Her love interest, however, had a far more common reason to keep his relationship with your sister a secret. He was seeing other women. A lot of other women," Valri pronounced.

Skylar saw Cody fist his hands, the only outward sign as to how the information affected him.

"Supposedly, strictly on a friendly basis," Valri continued, "but I have this gut feeling about that."

"And what is it that your gut is telling you?" Cody asked.

"That this guy's 'friendships' went a little deeper than what might have first been observed," Valri told the deputy.

"How deep?" Cody asked in a voice that was far from friendly.

"Not sure yet," Valri answered honestly. "That is one of the things that I need to have to investigated." The computer expert looked at her cousin and Cody. "I figure that's where the two of you can come in—as long as you promise to play by the rules." The latter statement was aimed at Cody.

"What kinds of rules?" Cody asked.

"The kinds of rules that say you can't maim, strangle or kill a person you're in the process of investigating," she said, trying to lighten the situation, but still very serious about the message she was sending to the deputy.

"He'll behave," Skylar promised her cousin. "Right?" she asked, pinning the deputy with a penetrating look.

"Right." There was absolutely no emotion in the single word he had uttered.

To Skylar, that was a dead giveaway. "Cody, I know how you feel—" She got no further.

Cody cut her off. He didn't want to have to listen to empty platitudes that just fell flat, in his opinion.

"You can't possibly know how I feel—" he began but got nowhere.

"I wouldn't take any bets on that," Skylar interrupted. "You don't have an exclusive stranglehold on pain," she informed him sharply. "Now, we're going to conduct a clean, swift investigation and, when we're done with it, the result we come up with will be beyond reproach. Right?" she pressed, her eyes all but filleting him.

Looking far from happy about it, Cody grudgingly admitted, "Right."

Skylar turned back to her cousin. "Thank you for all your help, Valri. By the way, did your little girl know who you were when you showed up last night?" she asked.

A wide smile blossomed on her lips as Valri nodded. "Yes, she did. Seems it wasn't all that late in 'little girl time.' Alex, bless him, was keeping her up for me—not that that was actually a problem. That little girl has her daddy completely wrapped around her little finger," Valri said with a laugh. She promptly took out her cell phone to show off the most recent photograph she had taken of her young daughter.

Skylar looked at the photo more closely. "She just keeps getting prettier and prettier all the time. Theresa is a real little beauty," she told her cousin.

Valri's expression softened as she looked at her daughter's picture again. There was no missing the pride in her voice.

"That she is," the computer expert agreed. "I just wish I could find a way to split myself in half so I could spend time at home and still do my work here." Everyone knew how really important her work was to Valri and how much they all depended on her.

Skylar laughed at her cousin's comment. "If you ever figure out how to do that, promise me that I'll be the first one you tell."

"You've got a deal," Valri answered, adding, "I'll get back to you two the second I get any more information about this guy."

Skylar realized that she had almost walked out of the lab without asking an all-important question. "Well, you could verify the guy's name."

Valri looked surprised and then embarrassed. Apparently talk about her daughter had caused her to slip up. "The guy's name really is Brent Masterson. Word has it that Masterson is currently working as a supplier at the local high schools," she added as an afterthought.

"And what exactly does this Masterson guy supply?" Cody asked. There was no missing the fact that Cody had decided that he didn't care for Masterson.

"Whatever is needed, from what I hear," Valri said. "Currently, he's associated with the local school district. By the way, looking at a clearer picture of the man, he is extremely good-looking. I gather that the guy has half a dozen groupies following him around. Apparently, everyone seems to like him— or is hoping that some of that charm rubs off on them," she said.

"Where can we find him?" Cody asked.

"Well, like I said, he operates out of the school district—but he doesn't stay put for long, so at this point, your guess is as good as mine," Valri said. "He's no longer at the address he listed on his driver's license. The guys moves around, apparently."

Taking in this information, Skylar nodded. "We'll let you know what we find out," she told her cousin.

"Please do," Valri encouraged.

"So, WHAT DO you think?" Skylar asked the deputy the moment that they walked out of the computer lab.

Cody sighed in a genuine display of emotions. "I think that I wish my sister wasn't so closemouthed about the guy she was seeing."

"What's your best guess as to why she would do that?" Skylar asked. "Be close-lipped," she explained when she realized that she had left the statement just hanging in the air. "Is it that she thought you wouldn't approve of this Masterson in general, or was she silent for a more specific reason?"

"I really don't know," Cody admitted, even though it cost him to do so. "A couple of months ago, I would have said that Carrie and I could read each other's minds. Now—" He lifted his shoulders in a helpless gesture and then let them drop. "It's almost like I never knew her at all," he said sadly.

"You did," she insisted. "This situation is something that is far more specific," she pointed out. "And by that, I mean that when you're in love, all bets are off."

He looked at her with interest. "You're speaking from experience?" he asked.

Skylar smiled. "I have an extremely large family. I speak from keen observation," she answered.

The elevator came to a stop on her floor. Time to get back to work, she thought.

"Let's see how much information we can gather up about the 'charming' Mr. Masterson," she told him.

But the moment they walked into the squad room, one of the detectives, Mike Martinez, hurried over to her as if he was just about to go looking for her. He nodded a quick greeting at Cody, whom he had met briefly, but his attention was focused on Skylar. "Where have you been?"

"At the computer lab," she answered as she glanced at her watch. "And, anyway, it's early. What's up?"

"The lieutenant is looking for you. They found another body in the lake. No ID on her."

She drew in her breath as she glanced at Cody. "Was she pregnant?" She had no idea what had made her ask that, but her instincts told her that this was just too much of a coincidence for it to stop there.

"Too soon to tell," Martinez told her. "The ME had the body brought in the moment the crime scene investigation unit was finished going over the area." The detective watched as Skylar turned on her heel, ready to go back into the hall so that she could try to get the ME to push up his or her schedule.

"Dr. Richter is on duty today," Martinez told her, specifying the name of the medical examiner who was to perform the autopsy. "You know how thorough *and* how slow he is," the detective reminded her.

"I know. That's why I'm going to the morgue to try to urge the man along."

"Lots of luck," Martinez called after her.

Cody matched his pace to hers. "You think that whoever threw that girl into the lake is the same person who killed Carrie, don't you?"

"It's a distinct possibility," she answered. "I don't believe in coincidences. And the lieutenant obviously believes it's the same guy, otherwise he wouldn't be looking to hand the case over to me. I'm nothing special," she told him. "There are a lot of other good detectives in this department who could take the case."

"I wouldn't exactly say that you're nothing special," Cody told her, taking her completely by surprise. "Look at how much effort you've put in to working my sister's case already."

As far as she was concerned, that didn't prove anything. "It's my job," she pointed out. "I wouldn't be earning my pay if I didn't give it my best shot."

"Have it your way," he answered, but it was obvious that he wasn't buying her nonchalant brush-off. Despite the hole he felt in his heart, Cody was exceedingly grateful for the effort the detective was putting into this.

She punched the button for the elevator. "I'm beginning to feel I should have my own express elevator, one that goes straight down to the basement and then back up to my floor, so I wouldn't waste any time." Her mouth curved. "That sort of express elevator would shave off at least five minutes when it comes to the round trip," she quipped, then speculated almost wistfully, "Maybe if I'm extra good for Christmas…"

"You could always try running up and down the stairs. That would keep you in shape—" The words were no sooner out of his mouth than he realized his mistake. "Not that you really need to do anything to maintain a better shape. You're great just the way you are."

The deputy seemed to be tripping over his own tongue, Skylar mused. "Is that a compliment, Deputy?"

Cody thought for a second, then answered, "I guess in a way it is."

Her eyes lit up as she looked at him. "Then I guess, in a way, I'm saying thank you," she told Cody.

His eyebrows drew together. "Is that a joke at my expense?" he asked.

In response, Skylar held up her thumb and forefinger scarcely half an inch apart, showing him how small a joke it was on her part.

The elevator came to a stop, its doors lethargically opening. Skylar instantly made a beeline for the morgue. Cody found that he actually had to hustle just to keep up with her.

"I didn't know you could move this fast," he told her, lengthening his stride.

"I can do almost anything if the incentive is right," Skylar answered. She missed the intrigued smile that rose to his lips.

Reaching the morgue, she pushed open the door that led into the area where the autopsies were performed.

"Nobody's allowed in without a specific invitation," Richter growled, barely looking up. But the moment the medical examiner recognized who had walked in, he uttered a deep, heartfelt groan. He still tried to get rid of the invaders. "I'm working here."

"I know." She looked around, trying to guess which drawer Carrie Cassidy was in. The drawers all looked alike. "Do you think you could work a little faster, Doctor?" she requested of Richter. "I need you to perform a preliminary autopsy on the body that was just fished out of the lake this morning."

The medical examiner's scowl merely intensified. "Despite what you might think, Detective Cavanaugh, the world does *not* revolve around you. Each of these bodies gets my full attention when they're on my table. I am not about to be browbeaten to work faster or to work these autopsies out of order. Do I make myself clear?" he asked.

Skylar held on to her temper, even though more than a few choice words rose to her lips. "You've made a lot of things clear, Doctor Richter. Since you seem to be so swamped, I can get you some help."

A short man, Richter drew himself up to his full height, which barely matched hers. "I do not want any help from you, Cavanaugh," he informed her coolly.

She could see Cody growing more and more annoyed. In an effort to keep things low-key, she placed a hand lightly on Cody's chest while addressing Richter.

"It is obvious that you do need someone's help." Her eyes pinned him in place. "I can call in Kristin Alberghetti. She's off today, but she won't mind coming in and picking up the slack."

The medical examiner's face turned a striking shade of red, but he couldn't oppose the suggestion, not since he had already made a point of the fact that he was swamped. "That's your cousin's wife, isn't it?" Richter asked, looking at Skylar.

"Does that matter to you, Doctor?" she asked innocently. "This place is large enough so that you won't wind up getting in each other's way. I just need a couple of questions answered. After that, you take over and conclude the autopsy yourself, if that is what you choose."

Her eyes met the medical examiner's. "Will that be satisfactory to you, Doctor Richter?"

The medical examiner scowled, but taking her

family connections into account he was in no position to argue with her.

"All right," he told Skylar. "Call in Doctor Alberghetti."

"Thank you," Skylar responded with a smile that looked extremely genuine to any observer who might be passing by at the moment.

Chapter Fourteen

"There's no such thing as being off duty for a Cavanaugh, is there, Sky?" Kristin asked one of the very first women who had befriended her when the medical examiner had initially attended one of Uncle Andrew's gatherings.

Skylar smiled as she looked at Kristin. "What do you think?" she asked.

"I think that you—and I—are going to be working until the day we both keel over…which, I suppose, is not entirely such a bad way to go," the medical examiner commented. "I had planned on doing that myself, actually."

The detective laughed. "I knew we were of like mind."

"Tell me exactly what you're looking for," Kristin asked the other woman.

Before Skylar could say anything to enlighten the medical examiner, Cody spoke up, answering the woman's question. "What we want to know is if this woman was pregnant when they fished her out at the time of her death, just like Carrie was. And if she was pregnant, would you be able to determine who the father was at this early stage, or is it too soon for you to be able to tell?"

The victim certainly didn't look pregnant, but it was possible because, if this was a first-time pregnancy and this was a very early stage, she could very well not be showing yet.

Admittedly, Cody was going with his gut and playing a hunch.

"Well, if you have a sample of the father's DNA that I can match it against, then sure," Kristin answered. "I can tell."

He had no idea who the father of Carrie's baby was—yet. But there had to be a way around that, Cody reasoned. After all, Carrie's friend Nancy had identified Brent Masterson as the boyfriend. "Could you match a sample of it to the DNA of another fetus?"

Kristin gazed at her cousin-in-law, then back at Cody. It was obvious by her expression that the medical examiner wasn't quite clear what the deputy was driving at. "I'm afraid that I'm going to need more than that, Deputy."

Cody hated going over this, but he knew he had to, to get justice for Carrie. And right now, that was the most important thing to him.

"My twin sister was pregnant when she was killed," he reminded Kristin. "I don't know the name of the man who got this latest victim pregnant, but there has to be a way to match the DNA from my sister's baby to the one found in this woman—that is, if it turns out that this young woman *was* pregnant when she died."

Kristin turned the words over in her head, then nodded. "What makes you think that this woman was pregnant?" she asked. She hadn't been able to determine that much yet.

Cody shrugged. "Just a gut feeling," he confessed, expecting the doctor to laugh at him.

Instead, Kristin nodded her head. "Oh, the ever-popular Cavanaugh gut feeling," she murmured. "You've been hanging around Skylar too much," she told him. "It's practically a science with these people." Her eyes swept over first Skylar then Cody. "I take it neither one of you has an ID on who this so-called father is? It would make this a lot easier."

"Not yet," Skylar answered. "But we will." There was no doubting the confidence that resounded in the detective's voice.

Kristin nodded, twice as keen on locating the identifying factors now that she was pregnant herself. "In the meantime, I'll see if we can sort through any matches between the dead women's fetal DNA. With any luck, the two DNA samples found with each fetus might point us in some sort of right direction that we can use."

Skylar spared only a quick glance at the body currently on the autopsy table. Anything longer than that and she knew it would definitely affect her. As it was, the sight filled her with a deep wave of sadness. So much potential, all wasted.

"Well, we'll leave you to your work. Give us a call if you find anything or come to some sort of a conclusion, which we can use," Skylar requested.

"Don't I always?" Kristin asked, humor curving the corners of her mouth.

"Yes, you do, Kristin. Yes, you do," Skylar replied with affection. "That's why we requested you."

"'We,'" Kristin repeated. Her eyes smiled as she turned them toward Cody. "Did you request me, Deputy?" she asked, curiosity sparking her interest despite her feeling that she knew the answer to that question.

"Just following her lead," Cody answered, nodding at Skylar.

She was glad he was finally coming around, but her gut feeling told her that their time was limited. They needed to get going. "We have people to talk to and evidence to follow," the detective insisted.

As Cody prepared to leave, he glanced toward the medical examiner. Nodding his head at the woman, he said, "Good luck."

Kristin nodded. "You, too, Deputy," the woman responded as she got back to performing the autopsy.

"What people were you referring to just now?" Cody asked Skylar the moment they let the door to the morgue close behind them.

"Anyone at the school where your sister worked as a substitute teacher," she reminded Cody. Then she emphasized the fact that Nancy Nelson had mentioned she had seen this alleged boyfriend in Carrie's company before she had left the place. She had gone on to note that he had been exceedingly good-looking.

Cody fought the urge to hurry down the hall. Instead, he held himself in check, Skylar right behind him. "You think this guy she was seeing worked at the school?" he asked, thinking back to what his sister's friend had said.

"I honestly don't know," Skylar admitted. "But we can't totally rule out the possibility." She found herself talking to the back of Cody's head, and lengthened her stride to keep pace. "We have to start somewhere."

"Then let's get started," he told her, still moving fast as he made his way to the elevator.

"Did your sister ever mention any names in passing, anyone she was close to or friendly with?" she asked. They could begin with questioning that person.

He shook his head, pressing for the elevator.

Eternity seemed to pass before it finally arrived. Belatedly remembering his manners, Cody stepped back to allow her to get on first. "Carrie didn't really talk about making any friends at the school. She had mentioned the students she was teaching, how much potential she could see in some of them." He smiled more to himself than at Skylar. She detected a note of wistfulness in his voice. "I felt that Carrie was a born teacher. I never understood why she'd decided to walk away from it to look for another job." He glanced at Skylar, debating if he should say something further. "When I did talk to her, I got the feeling that she was holding something back."

Curiosity immediately crossed her face. "Like what?"

"I don't know. Hence the word *something*," he admitted.

She nodded, making her peace with this non-information Cody had offered. "Okay, back to square one, fingers crossed," she told him as the elevator came to a stop on the first floor. "Let's go."

"To the school where Carrie last substitute taught?" Cody asked.

Skylar nodded and smiled at him. "You're getting good at this."

He ignored the compliment. "So what's the plan?"

"The 'plan' is to talk to every teacher at the school—starting with the ones who have been there the longest—to verify what your sister's friend Nancy told us about Brent Masterson and your sister being together." They made their way out of the precinct and down the stairs into the parking lot. "Any thoughts on that?"

Cody frowned. "Unfortunately, no. Right now, my 'twin' radar is totally failing me."

Skylar sighed as they continued walking toward her vehicle. "That's not the answer I wanted to hear."

He shot her a look, waiting for her to open her

Crown Victoria. Tension felt as if it was making its way through his entire body. "Do you have any idea how it feels on this end?"

Skylar unlocked all the doors on her vehicle and slid in behind the steering wheel. She buckled up, looking in his direction. "Frustrating as hell unless I miss my guess."

He laughed under his breath as they set out. There was not even the barest trace of humor in the sound. "Right on the first try," he told her.

Without even being aware of it, he let his guard down. "God, Skylar, I can't stand the idea of never being able to see her again."

Skylar didn't have to ask who he was talking about. She could feel a weight spreading out like icy fingers in her chest as she put herself in his place. It was an extremely heavy weightiness.

It took no imagination whatsoever to know what Cody had to be going through. Her heart ached for him. She knew what she would be experiencing if this had happened to one of her siblings. Skylar was exceptionally relieved that it hadn't, but at the same time, she felt guilty about that sense of relief.

Going with her gut, Skylar pulled her car over to the side of the road. Turning off her engine, she asked, "Would you like a minute?"

"No," he answered in a deadly quiet voice. "What I would like is to somehow get a lifetime back." He turned to look at Skylar. "Carrie's lifetime."

His dark tone undulated through her. "With all

my heart," she told him, using barely above a whisper, "I really wish that I could give you that." She sighed. "But I can't."

"I know," he replied. He hadn't meant to insinuate that she could.

Skylar shifted in her seat, her eyes all but boring into him. "But what I can give you is my solemn promise that I will get this guy who did this to your sister—and to you—no matter how long it takes."

He looked at her then, her words hitting him dead-center. She wasn't just paying lip service, saying the right things. "You mean that, don't you?"

She raised her chin. "I don't lie," she informed him. "Ask anyone in the homicide squad—or my family," she added. "I occasionally bend the truth a little—harmlessly. But I never lie."

Cody had no idea why he found that to be as extremely comforting as he did, but there was no denying the fact that he did. He also caught himself thinking that Carrie would have liked this woman and he really regretted the fact that his sister would never be able to get that opportunity.

Out loud, Cody heard himself telling her, "I'll hold you to that."

His words seemed to suddenly slither up and down her spine, creating an entirely different image than she would have expected being generated by them.

She felt herself beginning to smile. With effort, she immediately tabled that reaction. Even so, she heard herself telling him, "I'd expect nothing less.

Do you want to get back on the road, or do you need a few more minutes to pull yourself together?"

Somehow, although he wasn't entirely sure just how she had done it, she had managed to leech the overwhelming sadness out of his system. At least for now. And, more importantly, long enough for him to be able to tackle finding this worthless scum who had stolen the very breath from his sister.

"Back on the road," Cody told her. There was no room for doubt.

Skylar smiled at the deputy. "Okay, back on the road it is," she told Cody, pulling away from the side of the road.

The woman had a smile that managed to light up a room, Cody realized. He embraced it and took comfort in the effects that smile generated within him.

"You know, I just had a thought." Skylar spoke up as it occurred to her.

"Just one?" he asked, just the tiniest bit of humor reflected in his expression.

"For now," Skylar answered—and then there was humor reflected in her eyes. "There might be more later."

"All right, what's this 'one thought'?" he asked gamely.

"Maybe the assistant principal we questioned the other day about Carrie not seeing anyone was lying."

"Why would she do that?" he asked. Despite the fact that he was in law enforcement—and had had a sister—he would be the first to admit that the female mind was a complete mystery to him.

Skylar shrugged her shoulders. "Lots of reasons, not the least of which might have been fueled by jealousy. You know… 'What does she have that I don't have?' That sort of thing."

His mind immediately went to one place. "Are you saying that you think a jealous woman killed Carrie?"

"That is one possibility," Skylar admitted. But there were others. "Like I said, there could be a lot of reasons that something took place. My mind is open in that respect. But that doesn't make my promise to you any less vital. I intend to solve this, no matter how long it takes."

Those weren't just empty words, Cody thought. Heaven help him, but he believed her.

Chapter Fifteen

They drove to the high school. Ellen Hanks, the assistant principal, looked surprised to see the law enforcement officers walking into the front office again—and she didn't exactly appear all that pleased about it.

"I'm sorry, is there a question that you forgot to ask the last time you were here?" the woman asked.

Cody began to answer the woman's question but Skylar subtly placed a restraining hand on his forearm. She didn't want to get the woman stirred up from the start.

"Last time we were here, we asked to speak to any of Carrie Cassidy's friends," she explained to the assistant principal. "This time, we'd like to speak to all of your teachers, substitute or permanent," Skylar told the woman in as polite a voice as she could manage.

Visible lines popped up on the woman's forehead, forming deep furrows. "I don't see what could have changed, given that the young woman had already left us and, since she is dead, nothing could have changed in that time frame."

Still playing it safe, Skylar felt that Cody's tone could be somewhat off-putting. "It's a known fact that most teachers tend to be more observant than the average person. Maybe one of your teachers saw something they might not have even realized that they observed. You know, an exchange between Miss Cassidy and a male member of the staff, something like that. It didn't even specifically have to be a teacher," Skylar noted. "It could have been a delivery man or a member of the staff, permanent or otherwise." Skylar's voice trailed off as she watched the older woman's countenance. "Sometimes, the slightest thing could lead to a breakthrough."

She could tell by the expression on the woman's face that she wasn't getting through to Mrs. Hanks.

The next words out of the assistant principal's mouth confirmed it as her frown deepened. "This job keeps me far too busy to have any time for idle gossip—"

Skylar could feel Cody growing impatient. She began to talk faster. "I'm sure it does," the detective said quickly. "If we could speak to the staff here, one at a time, in your conference room or your auditorium…" Skylar's voice trailed off as she looked hopefully at the assistant principal.

Mrs. Hanks sighed as her brow creased. "I suppose something can be arranged," she allowed, looking none too happy about her concession.

"We would *really* appreciate it," Skylar told the older woman with just enough conviction to sell her story. Very casually, she laid her badge and detective ID down on the assistant principal's desk.

Ellen Hanks still didn't look as if she was won over, but she seemed resigned to the situation.

"I'll see what I can do," the assistant principal replied.

"We appreciate your understanding, Mrs. Hanks," Skylar replied. "We'll just hang around the school until you can arrange at least a few meetings today."

The assistant principal's face took on an exasperated expression, but it was obvious there was nothing she could do about the situation. The woman gestured toward the seats that were against the wall.

"Why don't you take a seat?" she invited.

"Not exactly the friendliest invitation I ever received," Cody murmured as he followed Skylar to the freshly varnished seats. "But it's better than nothing."

"My sentiment exactly," Skylar agreed, flashing a smile at the deputy.

Cody waited for Skylar to take a seat, then followed suit himself. Seated, he shifted somewhat so that the assistant principal wasn't tempted to read their lips.

Lowering his voice, he asked Skylar, "How do you do it?"

She wasn't sure what the deputy was actually asking her. "How do I do what?" Skylar asked.

"How do you manage to stay so upbeat?" he queried, expanding on his question.

Skylar caught his meaning and smiled. "That's easy enough to answer. The sum total," she told him.

He was furrowing his brow again. Skylar began to feel this was his go-to expression.

For his part, Cody had no idea what her answer even meant. "Come again?"

"The sum total," she repeated. "In this line of work, there are clearly going to be misses. But there are also hits, and I average more of those than I do misses." She could see that he wasn't following her. She tried again. "The hits represent cases I solved and the people I saved and, in the end, that's all that really counts. That's what I shoot for," she explained. "The big total."

Skylar's eyes strayed toward the assistant principal. Mrs. Hanks was making her way over to them. It was obvious by the way the woman conducted herself that she would have been more than happy to send them on their way—but she couldn't.

"Three of the staff can talk to you at the moment," she informed Skylar and Cody.

"What about the others?" Skylar asked.

"They're busy," Mrs. Hanks answered the question coldly.

Skylar played dumb. "Permanently?" the detective challenged.

"No, not permanently," Mrs. Hanks answered, doing her best to mask her irritation. "Just for now."

"But they do know that we want to speak to them, is that correct?" Skylar asked.

"Yes, they know," Mrs. Hanks replied. She glanced at Cody. Unable to contain herself, she asked, "Are you playing the part of the strong, silent type?" There was more than a touch of sarcasm in her voice.

Skylar raised her eyes toward Cody, the look there clearly asking him to hold his peace. She was extremely relieved when he did.

"Trust me, you don't want him voicing his opinion or putting his thoughts into words at the moment," Skylar warned the assistant principal. "You might get more than you bargained for."

Mrs. Hanks began to respond, but there was something about the dark look on the deputy's face that effectively shut her down. The assistant principal backed off for the time being.

Possibly permanently. Her dark brown eyes darted away from the deputy. "Maybe you're right," she conceded.

"Trust me, I am," Skylar assured the assistant principal, doing her best to maintain a friendly expression on her face. "So, where are we going to go to talk to these staff members?" she asked, thinking it safer to assume nothing, not even the positions they maintained.

As a last resort, Mrs. Hanks proposed, "We could do this some other time, you know."

But they'd finally come this far and Skylar refused to budge. "Now would be better."

It wasn't a friendly suggestion, it was an immovable statement.

Mrs. Hanks sighed, resigned. "Now, it is." The woman beckoned to the law enforcement officers. "Follow me."

They did and found themselves in the principal's very small office. The three staff members—teachers, all of them—were already seated inside the room. However, the principal was nowhere to be seen.

Both Cody and Skylar exchanged looks and then eyed the woman who had brought them into the office.

"Where is the principal?" Cody asked.

"Principal Brad Larson is still out sick," Mrs. Hanks answered.

Skylar addressed the woman. "Nothing serious, I hope."

"That makes two of us," Mrs. Hanks murmured. She glanced at her watch. "You have half an hour before they have their next class. I suggest you get to it," she informed the duo as she waved a hand at the teachers.

Mrs. Hanks gave no indication that she planned to step out to give them their privacy.

Cody was about to make that very suggestion when Skylar spoke up. "We would appreciate some time alone with your staff."

Mrs. Hanks raised her chin. "I intend to stay."

Skylar wasn't having any of it. "Well, unless you're planning on representing these staff members, you can step out," the detective told the assistant principal.

Mrs. Hanks looked far from happy about the suggestion, but she knew she couldn't protest. Looking miffed at being overridden, the woman walked out of the small office.

No one spoke until she was gone. When Skylar glanced in Cody's direction, she noticed that he looked rather impressed as well as almost happy.

Score one for the home team, she thought before she turned to the three teachers. "We assume that you know why you're here," she said, addressing the trio.

Heads bobbed up and down in response.

"This has to do with Carrie Cassidy, doesn't it?" the male member of the group asked. He addressed his question to Cody.

And Cody was the one who answered. "It does. Do any of you know if she was seeing anyone before she left?"

It killed him to be referring to Carrie in such a detached manner, as if he was talking about a victim.

The women both shook their heads, but the male member of the threesome told Cody, "I think she was."

Cody was immediately alert. "Do you know who?"

The teacher shook his head. "Not a clue, but I did

see them leaving the school together once." It was obvious he was attempting to pin down a specific occasion. "I think it was just before she resigned from the school."

Skylar couldn't help wondering if one thing had anything to do with the other. Was Carrie worried that she was going to start to show soon, or was she happy about the event?

Skylar pressed her lips together. She needed to get the simpler things resolved before she tackled the larger ones.

"Was the guy you saw with her a teacher or was he just a regular staff member?" she asked.

The man she was questioning, Joe Warner, shook his head. "To be honest, he was kind of far away and I didn't recognize him," the teacher admitted. "The guy *might* have been a substitute but—" Warner raised his shoulders and then let them drop in a clueless shrug.

It was like doing a two-step, Cody thought, frustrated. So near and yet so far.

It went on like that—back and forth—and in the end, no actual headway was made, no real questions were answered. Joe Warner did, however, promise that if he remembered anything at all, he would call the number on the card Skylar had pressed into the man's hand.

"If you want," Mrs. Hanks told the duo, taking pity on them after having come back into the room, "I will address the other staff members today and you can come in early tomorrow morning, before nine, to ask them your questions. Will that be satisfactory to you?"

Her words were addressed to Skylar, but it was Cody who answered her. "That would be very satisfactory to me," Cody affirmed.

For the first time that day, the woman actually smiled. It wasn't a large smile, but it was still a smile.

"We'll be here at seven thirty," Skylar told the woman. "And thank you for all your help. You might very well be helping us to save other young women from experiencing the same dire fate that Carrie did."

Ellen Hanks almost appeared to be preening. "I'll see you tomorrow morning."

"Count on it," Cody promised.

He led the way out of the office and subsequently, out of the school building.

"This sounds promising," Skylar told him as they walked down the stairway. She turned to look at Cody. "How do you feel about it?"

He made his way into the parking lot. Most of the cars were gone now. "Is this a trick question?" he asked. "What do you mean? How do I feel about what just went down?"

Her brow furrowed just a little. He was one suspicious man, she couldn't help thinking. "This wasn't a trick question," she told Cody, enunciating each word. "Do you think we've gotten through to the woman or do you feel that she's trying to lead us around in circles? Because I, for one, think that she's attempting to be straight with us. She might not have any of the answers that we're trying to unearth, but she could very well lead us to the person who does."

Reaching the Crown Victoria, Cody waited for the detective to unlock the vehicle. He heard himself opening up just a little bit. It wasn't his usual custom.

"I really hope that you're right," Cody told her.

"Well, I can't make any guarantees," she admitted, "but I'm crossing everything I can cross in hopes that I *am* right."

He glanced to his left as she started up her vehicle. The smallest of smiles played on his lips. "As long as you're not crossing your eyes as you're pulling out of this parking lot."

"No," she replied, amused. "No eye crossing. I promise."

Exiting the parking lot, she glanced in his direction and suddenly put a question to him. "Are you hungry?"

He actually hadn't thought about eating. Now that he paused to think about it, Cody nodded in response. "I guess I am at that."

"Do you have anything to eat in your—in Carrie's refrigerator?" Skylar asked, correcting herself.

"No. I haven't had any time to go shopping," he admitted. Food was not his first priority, or even close to it.

Nodding, Skylar suddenly turned her vehicle around, practically doing a U-turn. "I have just the place for you to go."

He shot her down before she could get carried away. "I'm not in the mood for restaurant food."

"That's good, because that's not what you'll be getting," Skylar told him, completely losing him in the process.

Chapter Sixteen

Cody looked around at the neighborhood they were driving through. It was entirely residential rather than an upscale district containing shops and restaurants. The deputy kept his silence for a little over five minutes, at which point he decided that he had been patient long enough.

"Exactly where is it that we're going?" Cody asked. As far as he could tell, they were still in Aurora.

She spared him a glance before saying, "We're going to, quite possibly, have the best meal that you've ever had in your life."

He still didn't see anything that even vaguely looked like a restaurant. "I'm not in the mood for riddles, Cavanaugh."

"And I'm not spinning any," she told him in all seriousness. "I just thought you might enjoy a welcome break. But since you seem to be taking a dim view of all this—" her mouth curved in amusement

"—I'll tell my uncle not to jump out from behind his stove and yell 'surprise.'"

Cody stared at her, more lost than ever thanks to her glib explanation.

"What the hell are you talking about?" he asked.

Skylar backed up a little, telling him, "You might recall my mentioning that my uncle, the former chief of police, had a gift for cooking."

Cody vaguely recalled hearing words to that effect when he'd first met the detective, but seeing his sister's body in autopsy had wound up blocking out everything else.

The deputy shrugged now. "Maybe," he acknowledged.

Since he didn't stop her, Skylar continued with the story. "When his wife went missing and he wasn't able to find her, Uncle Andrew resigned his position and took an early retirement to raise his five children.

"After his kids went on to join the force themselves, he picked up his hobby again. Uncle Andrew found that he drew great comfort from cooking as he became even better at it than he had initially been. It wasn't long before he began finding a host of different occasions to gather the family together so they could enjoy good food and each other's company." Skylar made a right turn then continued on her way. "From there, it was a very small leap to using any pretext for gathering everyone together."

"That's all very entertaining, but what does any of this have to do with me?" Cody asked.

He still didn't get it, Skylar thought. Her uncle felt very close to law enforcement agents. "You are in law enforcement. You're trying to capture a killer, find your sister's murderer—take your pick." Her smile grew wider as she made another right turn. "Uncle Andrew doesn't need much of an excuse."

Cody put his own conclusion from her words. "I don't need pity," he objected.

"Number one, it's not pity—nor charity, if that's your next comment. And believe me, this will definitely be worth your while. The man knows his way around a great meal."

"If you don't mind, I'll just take a rain check," he told her, thinking that would be the end of it.

But he'd thought wrong.

"No need for a rain check," she cheerfully informed him. Skylar gestured to her right. "We're here."

"Here?" Cody questioned. He looked around both sides of the street.

Skylar had pulled up at the curb right next to a driveway. Gesturing to the two-story house in the background, she stated, "Here."

Swinging her legs out of her vehicle, she began to get out. "C'mon, we don't want to keep Uncle Andrew waiting."

To keep him waiting, she would have had to notify the man that they were coming, Cody thought. "So you called him ahead of time?"

"It wouldn't be polite just to show up," she told

the deputy. "Besides, the man has worked—and solved—more cases than we've ever had between us. Who knows, he might have had an experience that can give us insight into your sister's case."

Finished pitching the idea, Skylar looked at him expectantly. "So, how about it? Have I managed to twist your arm?" she asked. Raising her eyes, she saw a shadow approaching through the upper portion of the glass door. "Think fast, because he's heading our way."

Cody was about to say that she was kidding, but then he heard approaching footsteps and knew that she wasn't. Apparently, his time to make good his escape had come and gone.

Cody had no choice but to get out of the Crown Victoria and face the front of the former chief of police's house.

"Smile," Skylar whispered through barely moving lips. "I promise that it'll all be painless," she told him as she got out of the vehicle. "Uncle Andrew!" the woman exclaimed as if the sight of the former chief had come as a complete surprise to her.

Throwing her arms around the man, she hugged him—hard—then began making her introductions. "Uncle Andrew, I'd like to introduce you to Deputy Cody Cassidy. He's from Kiowa, New Mexico."

Andrew extended his hand to Cody, grasping it warmly as he shook it.

"How do you do, Deputy? I've heard a great deal

about you." He smiled as he paused for just a second before adding, "All of it good, I'm happy to say."

Cody was genuinely surprised to find out that the man had heard anything at all about him or why he was here in Aurora. The former chief was undoubtedly just being polite, Cody thought.

Still, the deputy decided to challenge the man's claim. "You couldn't have heard about me, sir."

Cody was about to add that there was actually no reason for the chief *to* have heard about him.

But as Andrew ushered the duo into the house, he told Cody, "I'm the former chief of police, Deputy. I hear everything because everyone keeps me in the loop." His eyes twinkled. "They know if they don't, I won't feed them," he added with a chuckle just before he turned toward Skylar. "Isn't that right, Sky?"

"Absolutely," Skylar agreed. She looked around just as she crossed the threshold into the brightly lit house. "Is Aunt Rose here?"

At that moment, a handsome, vibrant, older woman entered the kitchen from behind the couple. "Of course I'm here, dear. Where else would I be?" she asked.

Coming up behind her husband, Rose slipped her arms around the man and gave him a quick hug, even though she had been in the room with him just a short while ago.

It struck Cody that the two acted more like newlyweds than a couple who had spent more years together than he had lived.

Acknowledging her presence, Cody smiled at the chief's wife. "Hello, Mrs. Cavanaugh, I'm Deputy Cassidy."

The woman nodded. "Yes, I know, dear. Word spreads very quickly around here, faster than you might think," Rose told him. "But my 'source' neglected to tell me how handsome you were, Deputy Cassidy."

"Rose," Andrew said, amused as he called his wife out. "The deputy doesn't know you yet. We don't want him getting the wrong idea about you," he told his wife with a wink. Ever since Rose had managed to turn up and return to him, the woman had embraced life with both arms.

"Sky," the chief continued, "take our guest into the dining area." He gestured toward the area for Cody's benefit. "Make yourself comfortable, Cody— I *can* call you Cody, can't I?" the chief asked.

"You're feeding me, sir. You can call me anything that you want," Cody told the man.

Skylar clearly appeared impressed as she looked at the deputy she had brought to the chief. "I didn't expect that from you."

"And I didn't expect to be invited to the Cavanaugh lair," Cody told her.

"The word *lair* makes me think of people's lives being in danger," Skylar commented on Cody's choice of word. "I'd prefer just calling it the Cavanaugh home," she told him. Skylar saw a strange look cross the deputy's rugged face. "What is it?"

Cody gestured around the wide, open room. "Where I come from, this wouldn't be referred to as a home."

"What would it be referred to?" Skylar asked.

"It's more along the lines of a small palace," Cody answered simply.

"It's hardly that," Skylar protested. "But we do have a very big family. Over the years, Uncle Andrew has added on several wings to accommodate the various members of the family—not to mention the branch of the family that was discovered, thanks to one of my uncles tracking down the uncle who had been switched at birth. He grew up to have several kids of his own before the mix-up even came to light."

"Don't bore him, Sky," Andrew chided as he came out of the kitchen carrying the brisket he had just finished preparing. Rose followed behind him with the mashed potatoes, gravy and breaded green beans, also all freshly prepared.

Cody shook his head. "She's not boring me, sir," he told Andrew. "To a guy who no longer has any remaining members of his family, this is like being offered a huge serving of dessert."

"You definitely need to come to one of Andrew's impromptu gatherings," Rose told the young deputy. Setting her tray down on the table, she sat directly opposite her husband. "Although I have to warn you, when everyone gets going, you can't even hear yourself think. By the time the evening comes to an end, a little solitude is a very welcome thing," she promised their guest. "Andrew, what do you say?" she asked.

"I'm definitely game," he told his wife. "Spread the word. Is next weekend good for you?" he asked, looking at Skylar.

"That all depends on how far we get with our investigation. Right now, we're at step one," she told her uncle with a sigh.

"Sometimes all it takes is one," the chief said, then amended his statement. "Maybe one and a half."

Beginning to feel more comfortable around this family, Cody laughed softly to himself. "I can see where Skylar gets her optimism from."

Exchanging glances with his niece, Andrew winked. "I get it from her."

"Don't let my husband fool you with his protests," Rose advised Cody. "Andrew here influences everyone. His brothers, his children, and a whole slew of nieces and nephews—far too many to keep track of," the chief's wife told Cody.

"When was your sister found?" Andrew asked.

"According to your medical examiner…" Cody began and then realized that he didn't remember the woman's name. "I'm sorry," he apologized, "I'm not much on names."

He had managed to arouse Andrew's pity. "That's all right, son. There're so many of them, at times I find that I need to keep a crib sheet handy just to keep their names straight."

Rose laughed out loud. "Don't let him fool you,

Cody. The man has a mind like a steel trap," Rose told their visitor. "Andrew only pretends not to remember names. He figures that way, whoever he's talking to will not remain as vigilant as he or she might have been at one point." Rose aimed her smile right at Andrew. "Am I right, darling?"

"You are always right, love of my life," he professed innocently.

The conversation over dinner went on like that, continuing a lot longer than Cody had banked on. He also found himself having not just one serving of the brisket, but two.

Stunned, he looked down at his plate. "I had no idea I ate this much," Cody confessed.

"Don't apologize," Andrew told him. "I like seeing a healthy appetite on display. Lets me know I made a meal worth savoring."

"Well, you certainly did that, sir," Cody replied with enthusiasm.

Andrew beamed. "Oh, you are definitely coming to the next family gathering," the chief told Cody. "Now then, tell me about this case you're dealing with," he prompted encouragingly.

Cody sat there quietly for a moment.

Skylar debated leaving the details up to him, then decided to make a judgment call. Her uncle had years of experience under his belt and at this point, they both needed all the help they could get in solving this case. It was the reason she had suggested coming to her uncle's for dinner in the first place. Her intention was to break Cody in slowly when it came to her family.

"Cody came out here because he hadn't heard from his twin sister in two months—with good reason, he discovered," Skylar told the couple at the table.

When Skylar had asked the chief if he'd mind having her and the deputy she was working with drop by, Andrew had placed some calls and had made a point of learning all he could about Cody's back story.

Andrew never liked being caught unprepared.

"Did your sister know anyone in Aurora when she moved out here?" Andrew asked.

"No," Cody answered. "That was the whole point of coming here. Kiowa is a postage-stamp-sized town where everyone knew everyone else. In addition, Carrie was always the one who took care of everyone else. After my mother passed away, Carrie decided it was time that she thought about doing something for herself.

"In order to do that," Cody continued, "she wanted to go somewhere where no one knew who she was. When she read about Aurora in a magazine, she decided that this was the place for her—especially since the weather was so perfect," he added. "We kept in touch, talking every week or so," Cody told the older couple. "In addition, we had that twin-radar thing going." And then his expression grew very serious. "Until we didn't. Whenever I left a message, she didn't call me back. It wasn't like her, and I really couldn't shake the feeling that something was very wrong." He glanced briefly at the chief and his wife. "Sadly," he concluded with a sigh, "I was right."

"Oh, Cody, you have our sincerest condolences," Rose told him.

Cody looked at the chief, then back at the man's wife. "No disrespect, ma'am, but I would rather have your husband's help in finding the person who killed Carrie."

Andrew nodded his head. "You have that, too, son."

Chapter Seventeen

Skylar drove Cody to his sister's apartment.

The trip from her uncle's home to the development where the deputy from New Mexico was temporarily staying was undertaken, for the most part, in silence. She thought it was because Cody was possibly nursing a grudge, or, at the very least, was annoyed at being tricked into attending the small, intimate dinner at her uncle's house.

Consequently, Skylar was in no way prepared to hear the deputy quietly murmur to her, "Thank you."

Blinking, she looked in the deputy's direction, more than a little convinced that she had to be imagining things.

"Did you say something?" she asked, wanting to be certain that she hadn't made a mistake.

Cody took in a breath. She was going to make him stretch this out, he thought. He couldn't really say that he blamed her, given the way he had initially behaved toward her. "I said thank you."

Now he really had her concerned. Skylar watched

Cody a little uncertainly. "For what?" Was he thanking her for the meal he had eaten at her uncle's house, or was he thanking her for something else?

She hadn't a clue.

They were almost at the garden apartment complex. Cody knew he had to get this out before he lost his nerve. Apologies weren't customary for him.

"For giving me some hope for the first time since this horrible ordeal all started." He glanced in her direction then went back to staring out the windshield. "I have to admit that, up until now, this all felt rather hopeless to me, like I—we—weren't making any headway in finding out who killed my sister—and why, if there *was* a why."

Well, that made sense, she thought, happy to have been of some help in bringing Cody back among the living.

"Uncle Andrew is going to spread the word, ask around if anyone has heard anything. Aside from being a great cook—or maybe because of it," she amended, "the man has a great many connections in a lot of places. It may take a while, but if we all put our heads together, we *will* find the killer," she told the deputy with certainty, "especially since I have this gut feeling that this man who killed your sister is also involved in other murders.

"Tomorrow," she continued, "we'll go back to the school the way the assistant principal suggested and see if any of the other teachers have anything to add to the information that we've already managed to gather.

"There was your sister and that other victim who was just fished out of the lake," Skylar recalled, going over the information they had managed to pull together. "Killers usually don't change their MOs, so my guess is that both murders were undoubtedly committed by the same person. If we knock on enough doors and ask enough questions, this may all start to come together for us," she told Cody. "At least," the detective emphasized, "we can hope so." Mentally, she crossed her fingers.

Skylar pulled her vehicle closer to the apartment building. She'd intended to keep her motor running, then decided to turn it off just for a moment. She made no effort to get out of the vehicle.

"I'll be by first thing in the morning," she promised Cody, then speculated, "You're probably going to want to use your own car. We can swing by the precinct at that point so you can pick up your vehicle. That way, we can drive to the high school separately." She glanced at the deputy. "You driving yourself over to the school might make you feel better."

Cody had no idea where she was going with this. "Why would my driving my car make me feel better?"

She thought that was obvious. Maybe not. "The feel of doing something familiar has been known to create a very comforting sensation for a person."

"There is *nothing* comforting about this scenario," Cody informed her.

She supposed that as far as he was concerned, the deputy had a point. Skylar felt rather disappointed that she wasn't able to get through to him.

"Sorry," she apologized. "I was just trying to help."

"I know you were," he told her, feeling somewhat contrite. "I apologize. I have to admit that I haven't been myself since my worst fears came true and Carrie wound up being murdered." Cody blew out a breath. "But I'm working on it. I really am," he said with feeling.

The smile she offered was nothing short of encouraging, as well as blinding.

"I have every faith in you," she told Cody. Her smile widened and spread as she repeated, "*Every* faith."

Skylar had every intention of waiting for Cody to open the door on his side, get out of her vehicle, and then she'd drive away. But she didn't. She didn't have a clue what motivated her to move closer to the deputy, lean in and press her lips against his.

Before she could even begin to dissect her actions, she was already doing it. It was difficult to say which of them was more surprised, Cody or her. All she knew was that the end result felt absolutely exquisite, filling her with a very warm, happy feeling.

When the kiss was finally over, Cody drew back,

staring at Skylar in surprise. And then, clearing his throat, he apologized.

"I'm sorry," he told her. "I didn't mean to take advantage of the moment."

Taken aback, it took her a minute to find her tongue. "You didn't," she finally said, brushing her hand against his cheek and smiling into his eyes. "Why don't we just call it a draw?"

The unexpected smile on his lips went straight to her gut, stealing away her breath. "All right," he agreed. "My sister taught me never to argue with a lady."

Skylar nodded her head. "Your sister was a smart woman," she told him.

Every fiber of her being wanted to kiss him again, but she knew that if she gave in to this overwhelming urge, there was no telling where it might go or, even more importantly, where it would end.

"Well, unless you intend to sack out in my car, I'd suggest you make your way to the apartment. Both of us are going to need to get some sort of rest if we're to make some headway in this case," she told the deputy.

He nodded, finally opening the door on his side. "See you in the morning," he told her. Then, at the very last second, he brushed his lips quickly against hers, before finally slipping out of the Crown Victoria.

He closed the door behind him.

Making his way to the apartment, Cody paused

for the slightest second to look over his shoulder in her direction, then unlocked the garden apartment door and went inside.

He heard Skylar start up her car and pull away. Cody realized he was smiling to himself although, for the life of him, he really couldn't say why.

SKYLAR COULD HARDLY wait for morning to arrive. In the interim, she found herself tossing—turning one way and then another—while sleep continued to elude her. She was convinced that she wasn't going to get any sleep at all and eventually decided to make her peace with it.

Skylar didn't remember falling asleep, but she must have because she suddenly found herself stretching as she opened her eyes. Daylight had begun to creep into her room, blending with and chasing away the shadows.

The first thing she recalled was the sensation that Cody had created within her when he had kissed her last night. She would love to just lay there and savor that feeling, at least for a little while, but there was no time for that. Cody was probably already up, dressed and waiting for her to come by and pick him up.

She definitely didn't want to hear him say something witty about women always being late, especially since she was usually the one who was earlier than anyone else.

Grabbing her clothes, she laid them out on the bed. Showering quickly, Skylar was dressed and ready to go even faster than she usually was. That gave her a little extra time to prepare breakfast for herself and for Cody.

She caught her reflection in the kitchen window and realized she was smiling. Cooking had never held any sort of an attraction for her before, but she thought now that she could easily get used to this if it meant preparing food for Cody.

Get hold of yourself, she warned.

Skylar kept it simple. She made two individual servings of scrambled eggs, toast and bacon. Those she packed separately in plastic containers, then snapped on the lids. She placed the containers into the carryall she had dug up, then made her way to her vehicle.

The whole thing, from start to finish, had taken her less than half an hour.

Skylar drove to the local coffee shop to pick up two steaming takeout cups of coffee, then headed straight for the garden apartment.

Finding a spot to park was a little trickier. It was obvious to her that more people than usual were entertaining overnight guests. Pulling into a spot, she took the carryall and the bag with the coffee with her and made her way to the ground-floor apartment where Cody was staying.

She rang the doorbell. When there was no answer, she rang it a second time. Muttering under her breath, she was about to press it again just as Cody finally opened the door.

His hair appeared to still be wet and he smelled of some sort of muted bodywash that undulated into her senses.

"You're here," Cody declared with a slight note of surprise.

"Certainly looks that way," Skylar responded, amused as she walked in. Turning to face him, she asked, "Did you have trouble sleeping?"

"How did you—" He wasn't able to complete his question.

"I figured it had to be something like that, otherwise you would have already been dressed and standing outside the door, waiting for me to make an appearance."

He shrugged a shoulder as he took the carryall and bag from her. "Yes," he admitted after a moment. "I had some trouble falling asleep."

"Did you manage to get *any* sleep?" she asked, following Cody into the tiny kitchen. She took out a couple of paper plates, put them on the table, then placed the utensils next to them.

"A little. Enough," he added before she could make a comment about that. He drew in a deep breath as he opened the carryall and took out the plastic containers with the breakfasts she had made. "Smells good," he told her.

"Well, it's not anything like what my uncle is capable of creating," Skylar admitted, "but I promise you won't choke on it."

He laughed to himself. "Good to know," Cody

said. "Right now, what I'm really looking forward to is having some coffee."

Skylar gestured toward the containers on the table. "Have at it," she told him, gesturing at both the containers and the takeout coffee cups she had brought. "If it turns out that you don't like what I made, you don't have to feel obligated to eat it. We can stop by a takeout place. I promise that my feelings won't be hurt."

She was surprised that he didn't answer her. Instead, she watched Cody wolf down his portion and wound up smiling. "Either you were *really* hungry, or what I prepared for you wasn't half bad," she said, silently congratulating herself. "You can take your time, by the way. The school doesn't open for another half hour. I just thought that you'd want to be able to eat at a leisurely pace."

"I appreciate that. For some reason, after eating at your uncle's house, instead of getting so full I could barely walk, I just managed to whet my appetite for more food. This was a whole new experience for me," he confided.

"I'm glad I could broaden your horizons," she told him.

Admittedly, part of her had expected to find him less than happy about the questioning they were about to conduct today.

"Are you up for this?" she asked Cody.

"It's something I would have never wanted to face up to," he admitted, thinking that these questions had to do with his sister's murder. "But since I need to, I'm glad that I'll be doing it with you."

She looked at him, mystified by what he had just shared with her.

"Did I miss something here?" she asked. "When we first started out looking into your sister's death and trying to reconstruct what went on, you gave me the impression that you had this huge chip on your shoulder. You actively seemed to resent having me conducting this investigation."

"I did," he admitted. "But I was wrong. You've managed to approach this from a calmer direction. I'm too close to this, and that caused me to lose my perspective. If not for you, I would have."

That couldn't have been easy for him, she thought. But she knew that saying as much would only succeed in embarrassing him. Moreover, it might even cause a schism between them.

"Thank you," she told Cody as she picked up their plates and put them into the trash. She glanced at her watch. It was close to the time that the school opened its doors. "Shall we go?" she asked.

He rose from the table. "Sounds good to me," Cody told her.

"Ready to swing by the police station and pick up your car?" she asked, reminding him that they had agreed to do that first.

"Why don't we just go straight to the school?" he countered. "I don't see any reason for both of us to drive over separately. We can just drive there together. Since our destination is the same, it'll cut down on air pollution," he said with a smile.

Surprised, Skylar nodded. "Let's go," she urged, leading the way to the front door.

"Right behind you," Cody told her, picking up his pace.

Chapter Eighteen

"I have what I believe is some good news for you," Ellen Hanks announced the moment that Cody and Skylar walked into the registrar's office.

Skylar felt her breath catch in her throat, but she told herself not to get too excited. This could all very well just be a red herring.

However, on the other hand, there could very well be something to this.

"We're listening," Skylar responded, waiting to see what the assistant principal had to say.

"Audrey McMillan just returned from taking some personal time," the woman volunteered. "The first thing she asked me when she signed in this morning was if I had heard from your sister. According to Audrey," Ellen continued with what was beginning to sound like a familiar story to Cody, "she had placed a number of calls to Carrie, but your sister never answered any of them." Ellen paused for a moment. The look on her face told them that this had been a very hard morning for her and it was only seven thirty-five. "When I told her that Carrie drowned, she turned very pale and became almost speechless. If anyone knew who your sister was seeing, my guess is that it might actually be Audrey," she told Cody.

Another name, the deputy thought. "And this woman is here now?" he asked, as he looked around the area.

The assistant principal nodded. "I have her waiting for both of you in my office." Ellen gestured for them to follow her.

The moment they walked into the assistant principal's office, the young woman was instantly on her feet. One look at the woman's face, it was clearly evident that she had been crying.

Audrey McMillan brushed the back of her hand against her tearstained face, attempting to dry it.

"You're her brother, aren't you?" Carrie's friend asked. Before he was able to answer her, Audrey told him, "I can see the resemblance. Is she really..." Audrey almost choked on the words. "Really gone?"

It was as if giving voice to the situation made it seem all too real to Audrey. Fresh tears sprang to her eyes.

"I'm afraid she is." Skylar avoided looking at Cody. "We were hoping you could tell us who she was seeing."

Audrey's eyes dropped and she became slightly evasive. "What makes you think she was seeing someone?"

Skylar could see that Cody was growing extremely irritated. She felt herself becoming increasingly protective of the man. This had to feel like a never-ending nightmare for Cody. She was honest with Carrie's friend—and hoped that Audrey would be honest with her.

"She was pregnant when she drowned," the detective told the teacher.

Audrey suddenly became horror-stricken. Her hands flew up to her mouth to keep the distressed cry from emerging.

It did anyway.

"She didn't tell you?" Cody asked his twin's friend.

Like a robot, Audrey moved her head from side to side in adamant denial. "No—" her voice barely sounded like a whisper "—she didn't. Carrie was very closemouthed that way." Audrey stared incredulously at Cody. "Were they sure that Carrie was pregnant?"

"They were sure," Cody confirmed. "There was an autopsy done," he told the stricken young woman. "Once again, do you have any idea who she might have been seeing?" Cody asked Audrey.

Carrie's friend didn't answer immediately. She stopped to think. "There was only one person she ever mentioned to me," she told Cody. "He's an exceptionally outgoing guy and, just between us, I didn't believe that he was seeing Carrie. At least, not exclusively."

"Would anyone else know if this guy was seeing

someone else?" Cody asked. He thought of Nancy Nelson, the teacher who had first told him about Carrie seeing someone. All of this had a very common theme to it. What was Carrie's boyfriend hiding, other than the obvious?

"I was closer to her than anyone," Audrey maintained. "Like I said, Carrie was very tight-lipped when it came to her love life. I certainly didn't know that she was pregnant," the young woman protested. She looked from Cody to the woman with him. "Carrie loved kids. If she was pregnant, I really don't think she would have been able to contain herself. Are you *sure* that she was pregnant?" Audrey asked, still not convinced that was the actual case.

"I'm sure," Cody answered, his tone dark.

Audrey was just beginning to absorb the information, both that Carrie was dead and that she had been pregnant at the time. Her so-called close friend was desperately attempting to make her peace with the information.

"She never told me," Audrey murmured, completely stunned.

"She didn't tell me, either," Cody replied, surprising the woman. "And I used to call her every week or week and a half ever since she moved out here. We shared absolutely everything," he maintained. Then sighed. "Until we didn't."

"I'm sorry for your loss." Belatedly the woman realized that she hadn't extended her condolences to

Carrie's twin. She was feeling devastated, but what he had to be enduring had to be a great deal worse.

Cody blew out a breath, doing his best to make peace with the numbness that was traveling inside him. Feeling he needed to say something—*anything*—Cody told her, "Right back at you."

"Do you have a name to give us?" Skylar asked, trying her best to move this along. Maybe Audrey actually did know who this unknown boyfriend was and, for some reason, was trying to shield the person's identity.

"Well, like I said, there was someone she was friendly with, but I didn't think it was anything really serious," Audrey told them. "As a matter of fact, now that I think about it, the guy was kind of a flirt. Good-looking," she quickly emphasized, "but I didn't think there was actually anything really serious going on between them. I think she would have told me if there was. We were friends."

Skylar rolled the words over in her head. "When Carrie didn't let on that there was anything serious going on between them, did you believe that?"

Audrey thought about it and appeared to be on the verge of saying yes, then suddenly denied it. "I really don't know," she admitted. "I'm having a lot of trouble making peace with the fact that Carrie's gone," she confessed.

Clutching her hands together, squeezing and unsqueezing them, she looked from Carrie's brother to the woman who was questioning her. "I thought that

Brent was seeing someone else. Like I told you, the man was a flirt," Audrey emphasized.

"Brent?" Cody questioned, repeating the name that Audrey had just used. He wanted to verify that the man was using the same name.

She nodded. "Brent Masterson," Audrey said.

They were finally getting somewhere, Skylar thought, relieved. She could see by Cody's expression that he was feeling the same way.

"Does this Brent Masterson work here at the school?" she asked.

"Not exactly," Audrey told her.

"What do you mean by 'not exactly'?" Cody asked. He felt it was difficult pinning the information down.

"He's a supplier," Audrey told the two people sitting directly opposite her at the table.

"What sort of a 'supplier'?" Cody asked.

"He brings foodstuffs to the school," Audrey told him. And then her voice lowered. "I also heard that sometimes he helps women place their unwanted babies."

Skylar's radar instantly went into high gear. "What did you just say?"

Audrey began at the beginning. "Word has it that Brent would talk women into letting him find a loving home for their children."

"Sounds like the man's a saint," Skylar commented sarcastically.

She looked directly at Audrey. "Tell me, what do

you think of this Brent Masterson?" she asked. Pinning the woman with a piercing look, she added, "Honestly."

Audrey thought her answer over for a moment. "I think he has a silver tongue and I got the impression that a lot of the women he interacted with fell for him."

"Does that include you, as well?" Skylar asked.

The teacher shrugged carelessly. "In the beginning, yes. But he lost interest in me."

That didn't make any sense to Cody. In his opinion, Audrey was an exceedingly attractive young woman. He told her as much in a very matter-of-fact sort of way, then added, "May I ask why?"

She was about to tell the deputy that the answer was too personal. Then, because of her allegiance to Carrie, Audrey changed her mind. "Because I wouldn't sleep with him. He didn't get nasty about it," she told Cody quickly. "There was no name calling or anything like that. He just said that he didn't think we were really all that compatible."

"Would you happen to have his address or his phone number?" Cody asked.

"No, but I'm sure that the principal probably does," Audrey told her friend's brother. "After all, he needs to be able to get in touch with Brent to place his weekly orders."

"When was the last time you saw this Brent?" Skylar asked.

Audrey didn't have to think about her answer. She knew.

"Not for over a week. I was away on leave," Audrey reminded the duo. "And it was just after Carrie made her decision to leave the school."

Skylar exchanged looks with Cody. The timeline that Audrey cited was within the timeframe they were looking at, she thought. "If we need to get in touch with you, do you have a number where *you* can be reached?"

The young woman rattled off a phone number. "If you find out who did this to Carrie, would you let me know?"

"You'll be one of the first to know," Skylar told the young woman.

With that, Cody and she went to talk to the principal.

"I can't believe that that woman could be so naive," Cody said.

"Maybe it's not so much about being naive as it is just not wanting to believe the worst in people," Skylar suggested.

"If you say so. But if you ask me, that teacher, Audrey, was damn lucky to escape with her life intact," Cody said. "I don't think that this Masterson is as blameless as she seems to think he was."

Skylar tended to agree with him.

Brad Larson was at the end of his long, lackluster career. When they walked into his office, they found the principal to be in less than a good mood.

Barely glancing at the pair, he waved a disinterested hand at them.

"Unless this is something involving earthshaking importance, I don't have any time to discuss it at the moment," the principal told them. "I've got to locate a food server by tomorrow. The guy who used to make the school's deliveries just up and quit on me and the place he works for doesn't have anyone to cover for him immediately."

"Are you talking about Brent Masterson?" Cody asked.

The principal looked up sharply at the woman and man who had just barged into his office. "You know him?" he asked Cody, about to begin shooting questions at him.

"No, but we're trying to locate him," Skylar told him. When Larson looked at her curiously, she felt that it would save some time if she produced her identification and shield, along with a quick explanation.

Looking over the two identifications, he handed them back. "Why are you looking for him?" the principal asked.

"We thought he might have been the last person to have seen Carrie Cassidy," Skylar explained.

"My sister," Cody put in.

The principal looked up again as if he hadn't really taken close notice of Cody previously.

He did now. "You know, now that you mention it, you do look like her," Larson said.

He had been hearing that all of his life, Cody thought. It struck him with a pang that that would no longer be the case.

"If you talk to your sister, ask her if she would reconsider her decision about leaving the school," the principal told Cody. "She was an extremely good teacher. I hated losing her, especially out of the blue like that."

"I'm afraid talking to her isn't possible," Cody told the principal.

"May I ask why?" He looked from Cody to Skylar.

"I'm afraid Ms. Cassidy drowned." Skylar spoke up, wanting to spare Cody the ordeal of having to go into any details.

The principal looked stunned. After a moment, he found his voice. "I'm very sorry to hear that. Is there anything I can do?"

Skylar immediately spoke up. "You can tell us how much you know about Brent Masterson."

The principal paled as his eyes darted back and forth. "You think that he had something to do with it?"

"We'd like to talk to him in order to rule him out," Skylar said matter-of-factly.

"I don't know how much I can really help," the principal said. "I do know the man was like catnip when it came to the ladies. I can give you his employer's address. I can tell you that Masterson was a really hard worker who had his finger in a lot of pies. But on the other hand, he hadn't been with his company all that long. He hired on about six, seven months ago," Larson recalled.

Turning on his computer, he looked through several listings before he located what he was looking for. Finding it, he printed up the information, then held it out. "Which of you wants this?" he asked.

"We'll share," Skylar informed him before Cody could say anything.

"So he's gone for good?" the principal asked.

"That is what we're trying to find out," Skylar told him.

"Well, if I hear anything on my end," Larson told them, "I'll be sure to let you know. To be honest," he told them, dropping his voice, "there was something about Masterson that just didn't seem to add up."

"What do you mean?" Cody asked.

"He was too friendly too quickly," he told the two people in his office. "You know the type. But then, my wife says I'm just too suspicious."

Skylar glanced in Cody's direction. "Maybe Carrie would have been better off if she had some of that suspicion inside her, too," Skylar said to the woman's brother.

There was no doubt about that. "Maybe," Cody allowed.

Chapter Nineteen

Their next stop was Brent Masterson's former—or present—employer, depending on how Skylar and Cody viewed the situation.

They pulled up in front of a two-story building. The office they were looking for was located on the second floor.

Land of Plenty had been in business for the last eighteen years, delivering food to the local schools, both elementary and secondary.

Cody was the first one to enter the manager's office. The nameplate on the desk proclaimed her to be Alicia Wells. The woman's eyes swept over the duo walking into her office.

"May I help you?" she asked coldly.

"Yes, you may," Cody answered. "I'm Deputy Cody Cassidy and this is Detective Skylar Cavanaugh of the Aurora Police Department. Could you tell us if Brent Masterson works for your company?" Cody asked.

"'Works for' is a matter of opinion," the woman

told the two people facing her desk. Alicia Wells had been the manager of Land of Plenty since its inception. She appeared far from pleased with being faced with these questions. "Why do you ask?"

"Well, we'd like to find out how someone who is employed by your company managed to get involved with helping unmarried young women find homes for their babies, instead having the young women in question talk to their physicians and make their decisions that way," Cody said.

It didn't sound to him as if the two things went hand in hand in any manner.

The manager shook her head. "It was news to us when we first found out about what Brent was doing," the woman admitted. Her voice grew colder. "That isn't what we do here," Alicia Wells insisted. "When I confronted Brent about his 'extracurricular' activity, he said he was just trying to help the young women who came to him. It seems that his name got around for being able to 'help' these troubled young women. But he did promise, once confronted, that it would never happen again."

Mrs. Wells paused, trying to remember details. "That was more than a couple of weeks ago," the woman told them. "We haven't heard from Brent since." She looked from Cody to Skylar. "I'm of the opinion that he quit, but nothing was submitted in writing." Steely brown eyes swept over the deputy and the detective. "Do either one of you have any idea where Brent might have gone?"

"We were going to ask you if you knew," Cody told the woman. This wasn't easy for him to give the manager of the company a reason why he was asking, but he knew he had to explain their presence here. "We think that my sister was last seen in Masterson's company."

The manager looked genuinely distressed by the information. "I'm very sorry to hear that," she told Cody. Her look encompassed both of them. "And you haven't learned anything from the police department?" Mrs. Wells asked.

"We've already told you that we *are* the police," Skylar stressed, informing the woman. Thinking that the woman didn't believe them, Skylar produced her ID and badge and held it up for the manager's benefit. "I'm a detective with the Aurora police department and this is Deputy Cody Cassidy with the sheriff's department from New Mexico."

"When his sister didn't respond to his numerous phone messages, he came out here, looking for her. Aurora was her last known location," Skylar explained.

Having Skylar inform the company's manager why they were here, Cody nodded in the woman's direction. "Your turn."

It was obvious by the expression on her face that the deputy had lost her. "My turn what?" Mrs. Wells asked.

"From what we can tell, you were Brent Masterson's last known employer," Cody told the woman.

"Do you have Masterson's address or his phone number or email address?" Cody asked. In his opinion, it stood to reason that, as his employer, Alicia Wells had to have at least one of those things available to her, if not all of them.

Still seated her desk, Mrs. Wells looked up Brent Masterson's personnel file on her computer, then turned the monitor around so that the two people who were asking her these questions were able to see the answers.

"Yes, I do, but I've never had any occasion to use this information until just this week," she admitted. "When I finally did place the call to him, Brent didn't pick up. He's still not picking up," she confided, none too happy about the admission. "I just tried his number again a few minutes before you walked in." She shook her head. "Still nothing. What I *do* know is that up until this last point, Brent got along with everyone, male *or* female. Especially female," she stressed, pausing as a somewhat wide smile crossed her face.

"What can you tell us about Brent Masterson?" Skylar asked the woman. "Other than the fact that he 'got along with everyone'?" the detective repeated.

Mrs. Wells shrugged, at a loss as to how to answer that question. "That's about it—except that he was a hard worker and never gave me a moment's trouble," she told them.

The woman looked from one law enforcement agent to the other. She appeared to be slightly chagrined as she apologized. "Sorry I can't be of any more help."

Cody looked at the woman, wondering just how sorry Alicia Wells actually was about the matter. She didn't appear all that remorseful, just rather annoyed at the inconvenience. "If Masterson does turn up here, can you give us a call?"

Taking out a piece of paper, the deputy quickly wrote down his cell number as well as Skylar's number below it.

"The top number's mine, the bottom one belongs to Detective Cavanaugh," he explained, nodding at Skylar.

"If Masterson does turn up and I call you, what is it that you intend to do with him?" Mrs. Wells asked.

It might have been his imagination, but the manager sounded rather protective of the man. Cody couldn't help wondering if there was something to that.

He answered the woman as honestly as he could. "I just want to talk to him about my sister, see if he has any information as to what happened to her, who she might have been seeing," Cody said. He wondered if the answer coincided with the one he had gotten from Carrie's friend.

Mrs. Wells raised her head, her tone just the tiniest bit defensive. "She wasn't seeing Brent, if that's what you've heard," the manager said, her eyes meeting the deputy's.

That had come right out of the blue, Skylar

thought. "Why would we have heard that?" she asked, the look in her eyes challenging the manager.

"Masterson got around," Mrs. Wells told them. "There was nothing 'exclusive' about him, trust me." She glanced at the phone number the deputy had written down for her. "But I will call you if he turns up on my doorstep, looking to get his job back."

Skylar's antennae immediately went up. "Do you think that he might do that?" she asked.

Alicia Wells laughed softly under her breath, although there wasn't a trace of humor in the sound. "I've learned never to be surprised by anything."

Folding the paper that Cody had handed her, she slipped it into her pocket, once again promising him, "I will call you if he gets in contact with me."

Cody felt drained as well as rather disappointed as they walked out of the building. "Back to square one," he murmured under his breath.

"At least we've confirmed where he was employed," Skylar said.

"The operative word being *was*," Cody pointed out.

"What do you think his placing those unwanted babies is all about?" Skylar asked.

"I'm more curious as to where they came from," Cody told her.

"I think you're a little old to be wondering where babies come from, Cody," Skylar said.

•

"Want to hear my theory about where those babies came from?"

"Go right ahead, tell me your theory," she encouraged.

"I think this Masterson guy gets women pregnant, then talks them into surrendering the babies, promising to find them all good homes."

Skylar frowned, getting a really bad feeling about this. "Okay, what's in it for him?" she asked.

"Money," he answered simply. "A lot of people are desperate for children. Especially people who might not qualify through the regular channels," he pointed out. "So they resort to less than acceptable channels.

"I have a feeling that this 'irresistible' Brent guy provides his own inventory. He wines and dines these young women, gets them pregnant and then provides them with a solution to their 'problem' that winds up lining his pockets."

It made sense, Skylar thought, but it also made her ill.

"You're making me want to strangle him," Skylar told Cody between clenched teeth.

She noticed that Cody was clenching his hands at his sides.

"Get in line," he told her. He couldn't help thinking about how his poor sister had been used. "If I ever get my hands on this scum…" Cody allowed his voice to trail off.

"You'll blow the case," Skylar told him pointedly,

coming to a natural conclusion. "We'll have to proceed slowly with this," she said. "Agreed?"

Cody frowned at what he was proposing. "I had no idea that you were such a killjoy, Cavanaugh," he told Skylar as he got into the Crown Victoria.

Her eyes met his. "You would be surprised how many things you don't know about me."

A slight, ironic smile curved his lips. "Then educate me," Cody told her, placing the invitation before her.

Skylar smiled at him. She was not about to get into that at this point. "All in good time, Cody. All in good time. Right now, we need to gather together all the names of the young women that this supposed Good Samaritan tried to help out."

"Think we can?" Cody asked. "Maybe this socalled Good Samaritan wanted to keep his good deeds a secret in order to protect himself," the deputy suggested.

"This was a school and Masterson got around. People liked to gossip," she reminded Cody. "And women can be jealous creatures if the occasion calls for it."

"Isn't that rather a broad generalization?" he asked.

"I learned a long time ago that the reason generalizations usually ring so true is that they have such an element of truth about them," Skylar told the deputy.

Cody shook his head, genuine sadness in his eyes.

"I really wish that Carrie had told me about this slime bucket she had this affair with."

"Maybe she didn't tell you she was involved with this guy was because she knew what your reaction would be when you found out. It doesn't take much stretch of the imagination to know that you would come riding to the rescue, ready to hang this Brent character from the highest tree."

Stopping at a red light, Skylar looked in his direction. "Am I right?"

"Maybe," he conceded evasively.

"Just maybe?" she asked.

"All right, yes," he answered impatiently, surrendering.

"Since we have the possible father's name let's see if we can match his DNA to the fetus Kristin found your sister carrying when she did the autopsy. If we turn out to be right, it'll reinforce our theory," she told Cody.

She placed her hand on Cody's arm and could all but feel the tension radiating there. "I know this part is extremely hard for you to take, but the best thing we can do right now is to avenge Carrie and prove that Masterson got her pregnant in order to sell her baby."

"Then why did he drug her and drown her?" Cody asked.

"You know your sister better than I do. What reason would you come up with?" she asked.

He thought for a moment, and then it came to

him. "Because Carrie turned him down when he suggested giving her baby away—especially if the bottom line was watching that baby being sold," Cody told Skylar.

The detective nodded her head as she smiled at Cody. "Give that man a cigar," she declared.

"I'd rather you looked the other way when I find Masterson," Cody told her.

"Sorry, no can do," Skylar told him. "No matter how much I sympathize with you, I want to send Masterson to prison for what he did to your sister, not to mention most likely a number of other young women. The one thing I don't want to do is to have to send *you* to prison," she told Cody. "Now, lock up your temper and help me out here. If you wind up being sent to prison because you avenged her death, Carrie would never forgive either one of us. Understood?"

He sighed. "Understood. But when we finally find this guy, I want five minutes alone with him. Just five minutes," Cody stressed.

Skylar looked at him pointedly. "No," she said firmly. "It doesn't take five minutes to kill a man."

That made him laugh. "Remind me to keep my distance from you," he told her.

"Consider yourself reminded. Losing you would be a great loss to New Mexico and to justice in general," she pointed out. "Understood?"

"Understood," he acknowledged.

"I think we've put in a full day," Skylar told him.

"If you're up to it, we can swing by this creep's place to see if we find him in, or at least find something in his place that might implicate him in this 'babies for sale' venture."

"Oh, I'm up to it," he assured her. "Definitely up to it."

"Then let's go," Skylar told him.

Chapter Twenty

Brent Masterson lived in an apartment complex that surrounded a very fashionable courtyard. Parking close by the actual building, Skylar and Cody got out of the vehicle and looked around the area.

"How does a guy who sells foodstuffs to the local schools in the area afford a place like this?" Skylar asked, shaking her head. "The rent on this place has to amount to one hell of a pretty penny."

"My guess is that he's supplementing his income by placing—or selling—these babies," Cody said.

The words were no sooner out of his mouth than Skylar saw his anger taking hold of Cody again. Attempting to distract him, Skylar nodded toward Masterson's apartment. "Has he answered his phone yet?"

Pressing the phone number on the sheet Masterson's former employer had given them from the man's personnel file, Cody shook his head. "Not yet."

He had already tried to call the phone number twice.

"Then let's go bang on the man's door," Skylar suggested as their next move.

Cody liked the fact that the detective didn't just sit back and wait for things to evolve. "It can't hurt," he agreed.

Approaching Masterson's apartment, they knocked a number of times, but the man didn't answer his door despite how much they knocked.

"I guess we could talk to the landlord and get him to open the door," Cody commented.

"Not without a search warrant," Skylar said. "And to get one of those, we'd need probable cause. Which means bringing the case to a sympathetic judge and getting him or her to rule on it."

"Maybe," Cody said.

He got her attention. Skylar gave him a quizzical look. "What do you mean 'maybe'?" she asked.

"Why don't you see if there's another way into his apartment?" he suggested.

She had already thoroughly examined the door, searching for an opening. "There isn't."

"Humor me," Cody told her as he gestured down the hallway.

He was up to something, Skylar thought. "Just what is it that you have in mind?"

Cody cocked his head as if he were listening to something. "Do you hear that?" he asked her.

She hadn't, but Skylar decided to play along. "Hear what?"

"I can swear I just heard someone calling for help," he told her.

That was the excuse he would use for breaking in, she realized.

"Now that you mention it, I think I *did* hear someone calling for help." Skylar had no sooner admitted that than she found herself watching the New Mexican deputy using his "gifts" to pick the lock on the door.

"Where did you pick up that little habit?" she asked.

Cody looked at her over his shoulder. "You have no idea how many people in Kiowa manage to lock themselves out of their houses and their cars in the course of a year."

Done, he turned the doorknob, pushed it and wound up opening the door.

Observing him as he stepped through the door, Skylar announced, "Brent Masterson, this is the police. We're coming in."

Cautiously making her way in behind Cody, her weapon drawn, Skylar looked around. But to her disappointment, it didn't look like there appeared to be anyone in the apartment.

"Where is this guy?" she asked, voicing her frustration as she scanned the two-bedroom apartment.

"Why don't we go see the landlord?" Cody suggested. "Maybe Masterson gave notice and took off after that second body turned up in the lake."

"You mean when it looked like his perfect gig was unraveling right before his eyes?" she asked.

"Yeah, that," Cody agreed.

"Maybe we can conduct a manhunt for this guy," Skylar suggested. "I can have some of the people on the police force pass around Masterson's photograph as a person of interest, have them try to find out if anyone had seen him. Who knows, we might actually get lucky," she speculated.

Cody appeared to have his doubts about that actually happening. "Aurora isn't exactly a small town."

"True, but the Aurora PD isn't exactly understaffed. If Masterson is anywhere in the city, we'll find him. I can get my relatives to fan out, start knocking on doors and showing that creep's photograph around." Skylar smiled at him, happily informing Cody that, "We are a force to be reckoned with around here."

His eyes met hers. "I'm beginning to see that," Cody agreed.

They went down to the ground floor to talk to the landlord.

James Holder didn't appear overly pleased to have his dinner interrupted. Holder's "What can I do for you?" sounded weary and far from happy.

There was a bulletin board mounted on the wall behind him with all sorts of requests and lists of things from the tenants to address.

Cody took the lead. "Sorry to bother you, Mr. Holder, but we're looking for Brent Masterson."

Holder smirked. "Good luck with that," the landlord told him cryptically.

"I take it from your tone that you don't know where Masterson is," Skylar said as she showed the man her badge and identification.

Holder looked both items over carefully before returning them to Skylar. "Not a clue. Not since his check bounced when he made his last rent payment," he told the duo on his doorstep. Looking from one to the other, Holder asked them, "Did he stiff you, too?"

"I'm afraid the reason we're looking for him is a little more serious than that," Skylar replied. "We're looking for Masterson in connection to a case we're working on," she explained, thinking that might motivate the landlord to answer their questions and help them locate the man. Secretly, she was beginning to suspect that Masterson had more murders attached to him than just two, but she really couldn't tell for sure.

Interest suddenly flared in the landlord's eyes. "Do you mean some woman finally said no to that leering leech?" he asked them.

Skylar glanced at Cody before asking the landlord, "Could you explain that, please?"

"What's to explain?" Holden mocked. "Masterson thought he was God's gift to women and, apparently, most women seemed to think so, too. But I heard one of the tenants recently tell Masterson to get lost. It seems she was really upset that Masterson had backed her up into a corner and was trying to touch her. I turned up just in time to make him leave."

"Do you think we could talk to this woman?" Cody asked.

"You could," the landlord said. "But she took off about a week ago. Can't exactly say that I blame her," the landlord confided.

"You don't, by any chance, have a forwarding address for this woman?" Skylar questioned. She wanted to talk to the woman as much as Cody did.

"None whatsoever," Holder told her. "She paid off her account and took off. Sorry. Now you know the glamour of the rental game."

Skylar's gut feeling suddenly kicked in, front and center. Taking out her cell phone, she quickly went through the photographs until she found one of the second woman discovered floating in the lake.

"This wouldn't be the woman you said took off, would it?" she asked the landlord, holding up her cell phone for his benefit.

Holder squinted slightly at the photograph, then drew the cell phone closer to him for a better look. After a moment, he suddenly cried out, "Yes," surprise all but echoed in his voice. "That's Abigail Juarez." He looked up from the photo, then at the two people standing in his apartment. "She looks kind of pale," he commented, concerned.

"That's because she's kind of dead," Skylar answered.

The man's eyes widened in utter shock. "She's dead?" he queried as he raised his eyes to look from Skylar to Cody. "What happened to her?"

Looking to spare Cody from having to repeat the story, which was also his sister's story, she simply told the landlord, "She was discovered floating in the lake."

Holden stared at the victim's picture. "That poor kid," he sympathized. "Who was the one who—"

"We're not sure yet," Cody answered, anticipating the landlord's question. "But the ME said she was pregnant at the time of her death. Pregnant, and the medical examiner found fentanyl in her system. It was injected into her arm."

The landlord continued looking at the woman's photograph. "Oh, wow."

"That's the word for it," Skylar agreed. "*Wow.* Do you know where we could find her next of kin?" she asked. To her knowledge, no one had notified the woman's family about what had happened to her.

"She didn't have any, at least not out here. If you find out who did this to her, let me know," Holder requested. "She was a good kid and this shouldn't have happened to her."

It struck Cody that the man sounded really sincere.

"And if this Masterson guy winds up turning up, you call us," Skylar instructed.

"Do you really think he was the one behind this?" the landlord asked, nodding at the cell phone, his meaning clear.

"At this point, nothing is certain. We just have a lot of puzzle pieces spread out all over the floor," she told him, "and we're trying to put them together to form a visible whole." And then she nodded behind Holder, toward his kitchen. "I hate to tell you this, but your dinner's getting cold."

Holder looked over his shoulder. "I've kind of lost my appetite," he confessed.

They left the landlord with a business card, promising to be in touch if there was anything further to tell the man. Holder said the same to them.

"I had no idea that there were so many dead ends in the world," Cody confessed as they walked back to the Crown Victoria.

She found that she agreed with the deputy, but she took a healthier point of view of the situation. "Eventually, they have to lead somewhere," Skylar insisted as she got into her vehicle and buckled up.

"Why?" Cody challenged as Skylar started up the vehicle.

"Because they just do," she insisted. "This creep is preying on lonely young women, lavishing attention on them and then, when he gets them pregnant, he talks them into giving up their babies—barring that, he steals the babies from them.

"I believe in justice and, somehow, this has to be set right. Otherwise, I've just been spinning my wheels and I'm wasting my time. I refuse to believe that," she told him adamantly.

"Well, I wish I had your faith," Cody said.

She smiled at him, then pressed her thumb against

his shoulder. "There, I'm sharing my faith with you," she told him.

Cody laughed, shaking his head. "You are one very unusual woman, Skylar Cavanaugh. If that's all it took…"

"You just have to believe," she told him, "and it'll all work out in the end. Otherwise, what is it that we're doing here?"

"I'd love to be able to agree with you," he sighed, "but…"

"No one is stopping you," she declared. "C'mon, dinner's on me."

"Are you taking me to your uncle's house?" he guessed.

"No, I think you need some alone time," she told him. "We can grab some takeout and take it over to my place, or to your sister's former apartment. That way, you don't have to talk if you don't want to, but you won't be alone, either."

"What makes you think that I don't want to be alone?" he asked her.

She smiled at him. "That would be because of my 'coply' instincts."

"Your what?" he questioned.

"My 'coply' instincts," she repeated. "All the best cops have them."

"That's a new one on me," Cody told her. "But I do have to admit that you have a way of making me smile."

Her eyes met his as her lips spread in a wide

smile. "Good," she told him. "Now, what are you in the mood for?" she asked him.

You.

The answer just jumped into his head. The next moment, Cody backtracked. "I don't think that's a safe question to answer right now. I'll have whatever you feel like having."

Her eyes met his and then held for a very long moment. In what seemed like an incredibly short amount of time, she felt exceedingly close to him. But she had the feeling that saying so would completely destroy their working relationship.

Deciding to play it safe, Skylar answered, "How does pepperoni pizza sound to you?"

"Filling," he responded.

She nodded. "Filling it is. Next question…" she began.

He wasn't about to get sucked into this or have a long discussion. "Just use your judgment."

"All right, I will. As long as you remember that this was your idea," she told him.

He sighed. "*What* was my idea?"

"Where we're eating," she told him.

"Where are we eating?"

One step forward, two steps back, Skylar thought, resigned. "Your place or mine. Pick one," she reminded him. "The choice is yours. I figured you would welcome having some say-so in the matter."

"All right," he agreed. "Since we're using your car, after we pick up the pizza, drop me off at my sister's place," he told her. "It'll cut down on travel for you."

"Don't worry about me," Skylar said.

"Still, I'd feel better not putting you out," Cody told her.

She supposed that made sense to her. "You got it."

Chapter Twenty-One

He had to stop allowing that soft smile of hers to keep getting to him, Cody thought. He could feel it weaving its way into his system.

He blamed it on his being tired as well as over-wrought and, yes, even slightly hungry, he admitted.

Cody focused on the warm smell of pizza that seemed to fill every square inch of the inside of the vehicle they were in. It succeeded in further whetting his appetite.

When Skylar pulled her Crown Victoria into the guest parking area in front of his sister's apartment, Cody was the first one out of the vehicle. He took the oversize pizza box out with him. For a moment, Skylar watched the deputy make his way to the ground-floor garden apartment door. Skylar was quick to follow, catching up to Cody just as he unlocked it.

"Maybe we should have gotten two large pizzas," Skylar commented with an amused smile. She nodded at the pizza. "You look as if you could chew right through that box."

Cody glanced in her direction and his eyes lingered on the detective just a few seconds too long. No matter what, it felt as if he couldn't seem to outrun his feelings.

Opening the door, Cody carried in the pizza and placed the closed box in the center of the table.

"I guess I didn't realize just how hungry I was," he told her by way of an excuse. It wasn't quite the truth, but he decided that it would do for now.

"We can always order a second pizza to be delivered if this doesn't succeed in filling your empty stomach," she told him.

Cody laughed dryly. "I'm not a bottomless pit," the deputy told her.

A smile played on her lips as her eyes swept over him. She hadn't been trying to insult him. Quite the contrary.

It was clearly obvious by the expression on her face that Skylar liked what she saw. A lot.

"Not with that trim waistline and those abs of yours," she told him.

His eyes met hers, and once again, lingered appreciatively. "Are you objectifying me, Detective?" Cody asked. For once, there was more than a touch of humor playing on his lips.

"No, not objectifying," Skylar corrected. "I'm just admiring the view," she told him innocently. With that, she opened up the cabinet, then took down two paper plates and proceeded to place them on the table.

For his part, Cody distributed a couple of napkins beside the plates, then raised his eyes to hers. "What would you like to drink? There's one old can of beer in the refrigerator and what looks like a more recent can of soda," he told her. "Both unopened."

Skylar glanced over Cody's shoulder, taking in the near empty shelves inside the refrigerator. "Looks like your sister swore off alcohol and artificial sweetener when she realized that she was pregnant."

Cody couldn't help thinking about the way Carrie looked when her body had been discovered. "That means that she wasn't all that far along before she found out about her condition." He sighed, his frustration surfacing again. "Why didn't she tell me, Skylar?" he asked, turning to look at the detective. "We always talked about everything. *Everything*. I would have never believed that she would keep something like that from me."

Skylar thought she had one explanation for what had happened. "Maybe she kept it from you because your sister was afraid of what you would think of her."

"I wasn't judgmental, if that's what you mean," Cody protested. "Carrie was always the one who toed the line, not me."

"Maybe she was afraid that your opinion of her would change once you knew about her...shall I say 'transgression'?" Skylar specified.

"It wouldn't have," Cody objected with a deep sigh as he shook his head. "I thought she knew better than that. But I guess she didn't, and now she'll never know."

Skylar stopped eating as she looked at him. "Oh, she'll know," Skylar guaranteed with feeling. "She'll know," she repeated, momentarily glancing upward.

"You believe in that stuff?" Cody sounded more than a little skeptical about faith and what it entailed.

She could tell from the tone of his voice that somewhere along the line, Cody had lost his faith. The man no longer believed, she thought. For all the world, he sounded like someone who had definitely lost his way.

Her heart ached for him.

"With all my heart and soul," she told him, referring to her thought on the matter. "C'mon, Cody. You *have* to believe. If not for yourself," she continued, "do it for Carrie." And then she paused before continuing. "And for you. It would have meant a great deal to her. And, in case you missed this fact, *you* meant a great deal to her."

"How would you even know that?" Cody challenged. "You didn't know my sister."

"No, not personally," Skylar admitted, taking out a slice of pizza and putting it on his plate. She pushed the plate in his direction. "But I have managed to put together the details that you told me about her. And, moreover, I put together certain things I read on her social media page. I couldn't sleep," she explained.

Cody stopped eating and stared at her in stunned surprise. "Carrie had a social media page?"

This was all news to him. He hadn't thought that Carrie was the type to preserve things on her social media page—or even *have* a social media page. It didn't seem like her.

Amused by the stunned look on Cody's face, Skylar's eyes smiled at him. The man could be a complete innocent at times.

"You know, for a really smart guy, you can be such a babe in the woods about some things," she told him.

Cody pushed aside his plate as if he hadn't just been making short work of the slice he had been eating. Like a man on a mission, he rose from the table and immediately hurried off to grab his laptop.

Within seconds, he brought it back to the table. The laptop was over eight years old and took a while to warm up when he turned it on.

When it finally come on, he looked over to Skylar.

He was versed in certain aspects when it came to working the computer, but far from all of them. "What do I—"

Skylar guessed what he was about to ask her. She sincerely doubted that the deputy had ever set up a password for any of the programs on the laptop, which meant that he wasn't able to sign in.

"May I?" she asked, drawing the laptop over so that it could face her.

"Be my guest," Cody told her, gesturing at the laptop.

The moment she got his permission, Skylar began

typing. "I'll sign you in," she volunteered just before she glanced in his direction. Belatedly, a thought occurred to her. "I take it that you don't have a social media account?"

Cody frowned as he shook his head. He didn't like being so predictable, but that was really a minor point right now. "I don't have time for that sort of foolishness."

Skylar shrugged. "I'm sure that you have a different way to amuse yourself," the detective suggested, turning slightly so that her eyes could meet his.

Standing behind her, he turned her chair just enough so that their eyes could hold for a moment. "Yeah," he said, answering her question. "I amuse myself by catching the bad guys."

She considered his answer as she nodded her head. "In the sum total of things, I'd say that your way is the better way to go, hands down," she told him as she turned back to the task at hand.

Cody watched her fingers fly over the keyboard. "You have an account," he noted in surprise as she signed in to her social media page.

"Mostly to catch up with old friends. But if this thing disappeared tomorrow—" she nodded at the page she was typing on "—I can't say that I'd miss it."

Finished typing, she pushed his laptop back a little, allowing him a better view of the page she had pulled up and had belonged to his sister.

There wasn't that much on it, but it was enough,

she thought. "Carrie was proud of you. Proud of the kind of work you did as a deputy."

He grew quiet for a moment as he not only read what his sister had placed on the page, but eyed the handful of photographs that were on it. "I never knew that this even existed," he confided.

"Well, now you do. And this will stay up for-ever—unless you take it down," Skylar pointed out.

He grew serious, scanning the pages. "Did she mention that guy, the one who got her pregnant?"

She shook her head. "If he was on here, he found a way to remove his image before you could open the page."

Cody looked through the photographs that re-mained posted. Some he had never seen before. He realized that this was a way to allow him to keep his twin alive. "I never hung on to photographs," he con-fessed. "I suppose I just always thought that Carrie would be around forever."

"A lot of us make that mistake," she agreed. "I can print those photographs for you, you know, mount them in an old-fashioned photograph book."

He frowned a little at the suggestion and the image it suggested. "You must think I'm some sort of an old-fashioned throwback," he told her, feeling as if he were completely out of sync with the rest of the world as well as out of step.

Skylar shook her head, dismissing the image he had summoned. "There's nothing wrong with being unique," Skylar told him.

"Yeah, but there's something wrong with being a dinosaur," he corrected.

The hopeless note in his voice hurt Skylar's heart.

Rising, she turned toward him and lightly ran her fingertips along his face, her fingers memorizing his features. "You're not a dinosaur," she insisted with feeling. "You're a really vibrant man with his own unique likes and dislikes."

There was compassion in her eyes.

"I think you're giving me way too much credit," he told Skylar.

"And I don't think you give yourself enough credit. You came all the way out here to find out what happened to your sister and you didn't just go off the deep end. You're making it your mission to bring this guy to justice.

"Now, we haven't managed to track down this scum yet," Skylar continued, "but I guarantee that we will and you bringing attention to what he's been doing is the reason why—as well as the reason why he won't be getting more women pregnant—or stealing and selling their babies," she said vehemently.

He was overwhelmed by the intense feelings that were flowing all through him. Cody laughed softly. "You have a way of saying things…" he told her.

"No," she said matter-of-factly, "I have a way of *seeing* things."

Unable to distance himself from her, Cody framed her face with his hands. Fighting the very strong urge to kiss her.

"I won't argue with you," he told her.

"Good, because by now you have to realize that arguing with me is pretty useless," Skylar responded.

"I've picked up on that," he murmured. There was more than a trace of humor in his voice. And then, as he drew closer to her, Cody lowered his lips to hers.

The intimate contact created all sorts of heat within him. Heat as well as desire. He tugged her closer still—and then, realizing what he was doing and the way he could feel her heart pounding in response, Cody forced himself to pull back.

"I didn't mean to take advantage of you like that," he apologized, searching her face to see how much damage he had done as he began to draw away.

Skylar caught hold of his shirt, holding him in place.

"You didn't," Skylar told him. "Trust me, if you were taking advantage of me, I would be sure to let you know."

Unconvinced—maybe she was just being nice— Cody searched her face. "Are you sure?" he asked uncertainly.

The last thing in the world he wanted was to have her think that he was coming across like Brent Masterson. Cody was still convinced that Masterson had taken advantage of Carrie, and who knew how many other women, in his desire to procreate and then sell those same children to couples desperate for a family. He had managed to satisfy himself, then appeared to ride to the rescue to help distraught, young, pregnant women, and wound up earning money on the side.

"Oh, I am very, very sure," she told him as she threw her arms around his neck.

Finding himself in this vulnerable state with his defenses all but completely evaporated, it was all Cody needed to hear.

When he kissed her again, there were layers of passion surfacing within him, moving in all different directions and weaving through Cody's body.

The more he kissed her, the more he *wanted* to kiss her and the higher the flame burning within him rose.

He knew in his heart where this was going to end, although he told himself that it was going to end differently, told himself that he could control what he was feeling and his reaction to it.

For the first time in far longer than he could remember, he felt something—*really* felt something.

Skylar Cavanaugh made him feel like a flesh-and-blood man rather than someone who was just going through the motions.

This wasn't the time or the place for him to feel this way, Cody told himself, yet there it was, reminding him that he was once capable of caring about a person, like a man cared about a woman, rather than a law enforcement officer who cared about the people whose safety he was entrusted with caring for.

Cody had forgotten what that felt like.

And he had to admit, it felt extremely heartening and invigorating.

Chapter Twenty-Two

If he continued this way, he wouldn't have the strength or the wherewithal to pull away from Skylar, no matter how good his intentions might be.

"Maybe you should go home," Cody suggested quietly.

Skylar said nothing for a moment, then finally asked Cody, "Do you want me to go?"

He paused for a long minute and then said, "I think you should."

"I didn't ask you if you *thought* I should go," Skylar pointed out, "I asked if you *wanted* me to go."

He had to tell her the truth, even though he knew that it would work against him, and what he felt meant his doing the right thing. "No. Oh God, no," he told her with feeling.

"That's all I wanted to hear," Skylar told him, taking Cody's hand in hers. "Come with me," she urged softly. With that, she began to lead the deputy toward his sister's bedroom.

She could see the doubt and uncertainty rising

in the deputy's eyes. The corners of her lips curved slightly. "I promise to be gentle," she whispered.

That was when Cody began to laugh, really laugh.

It was a truly heartwarming sound, but making Cody laugh hadn't been her main intention. "I didn't mean to tickle your funny bone to that degree."

"Oh, Sky," Cody told her, genuinely amused, "you really are something else."

That was practically the nicest thing he had said to her. "Keep talking," she encouraged.

Unable to help himself, Cody began weaving a network of warm, increasingly more passionate kisses along the side of her neck and throat. "I'm not much of a talker," he admitted.

"Then you go right ahead and do whatever you do best," she told the deputy, feeling herself responding and reacting to Cody. "Don't let me stop you."

The feel of his warm breath filtering along the length of her skin created gooseflesh all along her body. It made her desire grow proportionately until she could all but feel her blood heating.

Her breath caught in her throat as she sealed her mouth to his again. A chill went up and down her shoulders and trailed along her spine, causing her yearning for him to steadily increase. Whatever the reason, whatever the cause, Skylar could have sworn she felt electricity shooting off sparks between them.

And then, before she realized what she was doing, she did it.

She was putting her entire heart and soul into kissing Cody.

It was hard to say who was more stunned by the passion that had suddenly materialized, Skylar or Cody.

Or who was more surprised when it happened again.

She hadn't even recovered her breath yet, but there she was, sealing her lips to his a second time, as if to convince herself that the first time had actually happened and that the head-spinning euphoria that took hold of her hadn't been something she had just imagined.

It had to be real, she reasoned, because there it was again, taking her on another erratic-pulse journey, dilating all her blood vessels. It was causing her heart to pound even harder than it had that time she had competed in a 5 K run her first year in college.

Just as she was about to draw back for a second time, she felt Cody's hands on her face, framing it. Holding it as he deepened his kiss and managed to leave his mark indelibly on her soul.

Cody was kissing her as if she was really, really special. And that only made her desperately want to be special—to him.

After a long moment had passed, Cody finally pulled his head back.

Part of him wondered if he had suddenly been catapulted into some sort of an alternate universe. Or maybe he was asleep somewhere and this was all just part of a dream. A very soul-arousing, vivid, wonderful dream.

Struggling to catch his breath, Cody finally gave voice to what he was feeling, "Well, that was certainly a surprise."

"For both of us," Skylar agreed, her voice only a little louder than a whisper.

Taking Cody's hand in hers, she slowly drew him into the bedroom he had pointed out as belonging to his sister.

Once she had crossed the threshold, her legs felt almost shaky beneath her. Lovemaking was nothing new to her, but she honestly had never felt like this before, not even her first time. What was it about this man that spoke to her this way? That made her want him so much?

Yes, he was handsome, there was no arguing with that, but he aroused something within her that went far beyond his good looks.

Get it together, Sky, she silently ordered herself. *If this is meant to be, it will be. If not...well, that was still one hell of a great kiss.*

As if reading her mind, Cody took her back into his arms and started kissing her again, putting his whole heart and soul into that singular, isolated moment.

She felt herself all but melting into his arms, her body pressed against his. She could feel her heart hammering hard beneath her ribs. Sky was surprised that he didn't comment on it, surprised that her heart hadn't just jumped out of her chest.

What was it about this man that spoke to her this way? she silently asked herself again.

"I'm probably going to regret this," Skylar told him in a low, almost melodic voice as she threaded her arms around Cody's neck.

"You don't know that," he told her, closing his arms around her waist and gently drawing her closer to him again.

Yeah, I do.

Skylar thought she had said the words out loud, but maybe she hadn't. Maybe she had just thought them.

But it was too late to find out because his lips were on hers again and there were all sorts of delicious, hot explosions happening inside her at this very moment.

It was too late, much too late, for her to stop herself.

And even if she could, Skylar thought, she wouldn't. Because the truth was, she really didn't want to. At this particular moment, she needed to make love with this man, needed to feel the wild, demanding sensations that she instinctively knew Cody could create within her.

From the moment her lips had touched his, she just *knew* that this was what she had been missing. That somewhere on some lofty plane, it was written that he could satisfy all the needs she was experiencing, all the needs that were throbbing within her.

Her fingers swiftly flew along the front of his shirt, freeing the buttons from their respective holes.

The next moment, she was tugging his sleeves off his muscular arms until he was free and unencumbered by that material.

And as she did that, Cody's fingers drew down the zipper along her back until it reached the end of its journey. Her whole body tingled while the simple shift she had worn today almost sighed as it floated down about her ankles and to the floor.

She stepped from the colorful blue pool her discarded dress formed, abandoning her shoes at the same time. Her breath caught in her throat again as she tugged at the belt at his waist, uncinching it. She felt the hook at her back loosening.

Her bra slipped away from her body just as his trousers did the same from his.

Skylar could feel her skin heating all over again as Cody coaxed her remaining undergarment from her body. Breathing hard, she did the same with his, her fingers gliding possessively along his skin.

And then there were no barriers, no material obstacles left to get in between them.

There was nothing but naked desire to cloak them.

Eager for the final breathtaking fulfillment, Skylar totally expected Cody to take her right then and there. Instead, he took his time, moving slowly.

Making love to her by increments.

Cody pressed a kiss to her shoulders, to her arms, as well as to the sensitive area of her throat before he systematically moved on to other parts of her body.

Skylar struggled to do the same with him, but it was extremely difficult for her to focus when her head was spinning wildly, like some sort of runaway top.

Heaven help her, but he made her feel utterly beautiful.

And cherished.

And oh so wanted.

She might have been the one to begin this, but he was the one responsible for making the delicious sensation continue.

She tried very hard not to get lost in this burning awareness that was all but completely consuming her, but it was definitely not easy.

Skylar was hanging on to reality just by the ends of her fingertips.

What Cody was creating within her felt almost unreal, like a cherished fantasy that had come to life.

This might not have been her first time.

Or her second.

But it was definitely the very first time she had *ever* felt passion flowing through her to this degree.

And that was what she was going to remember when this all just became a faded piece of yesterday.

She had no idea how many women had been part of Cody's life, if it amounted to an entire squadron or just a few. But whatever the number, she was determined that he would remember being with her like this tonight.

She did things with Cody that she hadn't even contemplated doing until this very moment.

For every caress he bestowed on her, she returned one in kind. For every stroke, every touch, every wild, passionate, soul-melting kiss that he pressed along her eager, pulsating body, she did the same with him, summoning just as much fire.

Or doing her very best to try to summon it.

Lost in each other's arms, they had almost made it to the bed. But some things couldn't be restrained.

They wound up making love the first time on the floor at the foot of the bed.

After covering what felt like every single, pulsing, eager inch of her body with a network of hot, passionate kisses, Cody had drawn his throbbing body along hers.

Watching her intently, he entered her, his hands linking hers just as their bodies formed one joined entity.

As Cody slowly began to move his hips, at first slowly, then with increasingly faster urgency, Skylar felt the explosion within her grow with each deliberate thrust.

And when it came, when that final wondrous climax seized them in its grip, Skylar cried out and wrapped her legs around his torso, holding on for dear life.

Ever so slowly, the incredible feeling receded,

leaving her feeling as if she was literally glowing in the aftermath.

But that, too, faded and then reality slowly elbowed its way back in.

Skylar lay there, breathing hard and heavy. And waiting for her pulse to finally begin to level off.

When it did, she expected that now that this exquisite moment was over, Cody was going to say something politely inane, then wait for her to get up, get dressed and leave.

Or maybe he wasn't even going to be polite, just wait for her to leave.

She braced, telling herself that she wouldn't be disappointed, or hurt. After all, she wasn't looking for a commitment, just a momentary diversion, right? If she expected too much, she knew disappointment was only going to be her reward.

Skylar felt Cody stir beside her.

It was starting, she thought. Cody was going to ask her to leave.

To her surprise, he moved over and continued lying next to her on the floor.

He raised himself slightly on his elbow to look at her. "Are you all right?" he asked.

"Yes," she replied cautiously, not knowing what was to come. And then she looked at him. "Why?"

"Well, for a second at the end there, I thought you'd stopped breathing." He wasn't bragging. It was an observation. And then the deputy actually sounded concerned as he asked, "I didn't hurt you, did I?"

This was decidedly a lot more thoughtful than she had thought Cody was going to be.

Swallowing her surprise, she told him, "I'm a great deal heartier than I look."

"Oh, there's no doubt about that," he assured her. "I just wanted to make sure that you were all right."

She realized then that Cody had threaded his arm around her and was now cradling her against him. His heart beat against her chest and she instantly found that incredibly comforting.

"I'm fine," she assured the man who had just managed to totally surprise her.

"Good," he pronounced. Saying that, Cody leaned in closer and pressed a kiss to the top of her head.

He did it as if there was actual affection between them, not just torrid sex that would soon manage to play itself out. Skylar had no idea what to make of that. He was systematically destroying all her preconceived notions about the quiet, morose Deputy Cody Cassidy.

There was a warmth within him that clearly wasn't extinguishing.

This was a whole different person than she had believed him to be.

Chapter Twenty-Three

When Cody finally rose to his feet, he carried Skylar into the bed, where they proceeded to make love all over again. But this time they did it slowly, deliberately, and with what definitely felt like a great deal of mounting affection, as well as passion.

And when the final moments came and then faded away, they were both in a state of incredible exhaustion.

Cody gathered her in his arms and held her close to him, feeling better and more fulfilled than he had in a very long time.

He honestly didn't remember closing his eyes, and he definitely didn't remember falling asleep. But he must have because the very next thing Cody was aware of was hearing a phone ringing in the distance, intruding into his consciousness.

Opening his eyes, the next morning, he looked around, trying to pin down where the ringing was coming from. When he did, he realized that Skylar had picked up her phone and was sitting up, talking to whoever had called her.

Cody was about to ask Skylar who was on the phone when he heard her asking, "Where?" Responding to the tone of her voice, the deputy instantly became alert.

"I'll find Cody and we'll be there as soon as we can," she told the caller just before she terminated the call.

"Well, you found me," the deputy informed her, spreading his arms out as amusement curved his mouth. "Now, what was that all about?" he asked.

She looked far from happy about what she had to tell him. Putting her cell phone back on the nightstand, she ran her hand through her hair, trying to pat it down into place.

She was stalling, he thought. Why?

The next moment, he knew why.

"They found another body in the lake," Skylar told him. "From all the signs, according to the initial findings by the medical examiner, it looked as if the victim had just recently given birth. She also bore all the marks of having been strangled as well as drowned."

Cody shook his head. "Brutal," he declared with feeling.

"Oh, yes," Skylar agreed. "From all indications, that's what it was."

"Did this involve Masterson?" Cody asked, tossing aside the sheet and blanket that had been covering him.

Skylar had already gotten out of the bed and was gathering up her clothes. "That would be my guess," she told him, "although there's no way to be sure. Yet."

He forced himself to look away even though he still continued picturing her being nude. But keeping that image in his mind wasn't going to help him move this case along, Cody silently insisted. Especially when all he wanted to do was to make love with Skylar again.

It had been several hours since their last time.

"Gut feeling?" he suggested, referring to her comment about Masterson.

Skylar nodded. "Gut feeling."

"Tell me, is that some genetic thing that runs in your family, or is it something that you wound up developing gradually?" Cody asked, curious where this "gut feeling" originated.

Sitting on the edge of the bed, Skylar began to dress. She tried not to notice the way Cody was looking at her, but it was completely impossible not to.

"You're staring," she finally told him.

"I know," Cody admitted. "I have such very few pleasures in life."

Finished dressing, Skylar stood as she stepped into her shoes. What Cody had just said had made her smile.

"Well, as long as you put it that way..." Skylar

watched Cody pull up his jeans and tried her best not to let herself get distracted. Vivid images of their earlier activities were still alive and very fresh in her mind.

Skylar pressed her lips together. "Are you ready?" she asked.

"To see another dead woman?" he stated grimly. "No, not really. But hiding our heads in the sand isn't going to bring her back from the dead—or stop the next woman from becoming another victim."

"My thoughts exactly," Skylar agreed.

Leaving the apartment, she led the way to the Crown Victoria that she had left in guest parking. "I swear," she said, unlocking all four of the sedan's doors, "when we find this guy, it's going to be very hard keeping my hands away from his throat and just ending him."

His expression mirrored her thoughts. "You and me both," he told her. "How does a guy like that get around so much?" he asked. "According to our information, until just recently, Masterson was working."

Skylar had her own theory about that. "There're a lot of lonely women out there, women who feel invisible. Masterson ingratiates himself to them, pays attention to them the way that maybe no one else has. He makes them feel pretty, maybe even desirable and loved, at least for a little while, and they become putty in Masterson's hands.

"When they find themselves pregnant, he tells them about a service he knows of that can place those babies with families that will give them the sort of life that these girls can't begin to give them," she concluded.

"If he offers them that sort of solution," Cody posed, "then why does he kill some of them?"

She was attempting to work that out in her head. "Because at the last minute, maybe they change their minds about giving up their babies. They don't realize that the moment they said yes to giving the baby up, the deal has been struck. In all likelihood, Masterson has already collected the money from whoever he sold the baby to, so he can't let these women back out of the deal. His reputation would be shattered."

Skylar saw the way that Cody clenched his jaw. She knew just how he felt. "As much as I'd like to kill this worthless excuse for a human being, we both know that taking the law into our own hands definitely is not the solution."

"Some of us aren't as convinced about that as others," Cody told her.

She glanced at him as she turned the corner, going toward the lake. "You know you don't mean that."

"Oh, I don't know about that," he said. "If someone had terminated this guy, life would have been a lot better for at least three young women, if not more. This guy is not some Good Samaritan who took a wrong turn, he's doing this for the money, no other reason."

Skylar sighed. "You're right. But that still doesn't change things. We swore to uphold the law, not take it into our own hands," she reminded him. "No matter how tempted we might be. Otherwise, this would become vigilante justice."

Reaching the lake, she parked her vehicle and got out, making her way toward the section of the lake where apparently the latest body had been found.

Cody reached the area where the crime scene investigators had parked their vehicle. Passing the van, he looked down at the dead woman on the stretcher. In his judgment, she couldn't have been dead for more than six or eight hours.

That had transpired while he and Skylar had been making love, he thought. That hit him hard. Very hard.

He tried not to dwell on it.

Skylar looked down at the dead woman grimly.

"She doesn't even look like she was twenty years old," he noted somberly.

This particular medical examiner, a man named Peter Chambers who had been at this a number of years, pushed to his feet as he turned around. "That's because she's not. This is Karen Wakefield and she isn't going to get to see her nineteenth birthday." Chambers's face turned a dark shade of red. "This guy's a monster who preys on impressionable young women that fancy themselves as being worldly," he told Skylar and the angry-looking deputy at her side.

Chambers, the father of four daughters, looked at the two law enforcement officers before him. "Do the world a favor," he told Skylar. "Get rid of this vermin when you track him down. Do it before I forget all about my Hippocratic oath."

It was Cody who answered him. "Believe me, there's nothing that I'd like more," Cody told the medical examiner with utter sincerity. "But that would wind up raising a whole host of other problems."

Skylar looked at the deputy, a sense of overwhelming relief washing over her. It sounded to her as if Cody was finally coming around about the matter, at least a little.

She turned to another question plaguing her. "What about the baby and how far she was in her pregnancy?" Skylar asked the ME.

"My best guess is that the killer recently cut the baby out of her, possibly in the last few hours. This character has a string of victims and it looks like he knows his time is all but up."

"I certainly hope so," Skylar said with feeling. She noticed that Cody was taking in the surrounding area, specifically paying close attention to the trees surrounding the lake on their side. Something had caught his attention. "What are you thinking?"

Cody slowly looked around. "What kind of reception does this area get?"

"Fairly decent, from what I hear," Chambers answered. "Two of my daughters like to come up here with their friends. I'm told that they record these gatherings of theirs for 'posterity.' I've already told them that they have to stop doing that for the time being. They're not happy about it, but they'll listen," he said. Looking at Cody, the medical examiner asked, "Why would you ask that?"

"Because I'm wondering if we might be able to capture activities on camera," Cody answered the doctor. He looked at Skylar. "What do you think?"

She turned the idea over in her head, surveying the trees. She took them in from a completely different vantage point.

"I don't see why not." Skylar speculated, "We would have to get some battery-powered, motion-sensitive cameras and mount them in several different places, all out of view. But I can't see why that couldn't be done."

Skylar thought of Valri. "I'm sure that my cousin could rig up something for us." As she spoke, her face lit up. It was definitely an idea. "I'll talk to her as soon as we get back and tell her about your idea."

"It's not 'my' idea," Cody pointed out. "I wouldn't have thought of it if the medical examiner hadn't started talking about his daughters."

Cody didn't want to take credit for coming up with any solutions, he just wanted this whole ugly situation to go away as quickly as possible.

"WHAT ARE YOU going to do when I go on vacation?" Valri asked as she watched her cousin and Cody walk in. They hadn't even asked a question yet, but she had anticipated that they would.

"Who are you kidding, Valri? You don't go on vacation," Skylar told her. "For all we know, you spend your nights just haunting these halls. At least, there are times when it certainly feels that way."

Valri raised her eyes off her screen. "Okay, what do I need to do to make you go away this time?" the computer tech asked.

Skylar immediately spoke up. "We're going to need your strongest, newest cameras."

Well, that had certainly been unexpected, Valri thought. "I know this is a silly question to ask, but what do you need them for?"

"We want to hang them up inside the ring of trees around the lake. It would be to alert the Homicide Division that another homicide was taking place," Cody told the technician. "At least three bodies have turned up around Lake Aurora in the last couple of days. This guy had upped his game and since it seems to be taking place in the same area, motion-sensitive cameras might wind up catching him in the act," he told her. "My question is, do you have anything that's strong enough and sensitive enough to be able to do this?" Cody asked.

"This way, we can set up the cameras and bring this guy down before he kills someone else," Skylar said, adding her enthusiasm to the idea of catching the guy on video.

Valri smiled. "I just got in some brand-new equipment. I can have a couple of my best techs mount the cameras in the area. With any luck, we'll be able to get this guy before he does any more damage."

"Do you have any way we can monitor the cameras on an ongoing basis?" Cody asked.

Valri looked at the deputy. "I'll pretend you didn't just ask that, Cody."

"Not everyone knows as much about cameras and computers as you do," Skylar pointed out to her cousin. "As a matter of fact, I'm fairly certain that *no one* knows as much about any of this tech stuff as you do."

And then Skylar raised her eyes, directing her gaze toward Cody. "Sorry, I didn't mean to insult you," she apologized.

After the night they had spent together, he was fairly certain that nothing she could say or do would actually wind up insulting him. "You didn't," he told her. Cody shifted his attention to Valri, getting back to the business at hand. "How fast can your people put up those cameras?"

"Fast," Valri answered. "But you don't really expect this maniac to kill again so soon, do you?" she asked.

"We really don't know what to expect," Skylar answered honestly. "We just want to be prepared for any contingencies. That, and to have a monitor that is prepped and ready to pick up any photos in the immediate area. Is that doable?"

"We'll get on this right away," Valri promised, sounding angrier than Skylar could ever remember hearing her. The anger was directed at Masterson. "This maniac deserves to be put down like the mad dog that he is," the tech wizard declared. Taking a breath to calm down, she told the law enforcement officers, "I'll be in touch with you both as soon as everything is ready to go."

"And just when will that be?" Cody asked.

"Pushy, isn't he?" Valri asked her cousin, indicating Cody with her eyes.

Skylar laughed in response. "You have *no* idea," she told Valri, then said, "Be sure to give us a call the minute the equipment is all set up and ready to be used."

With that, she and Cody crossed their fingers and walked out of the computer lab.

Chapter Twenty-Four

Hoping to follow up on various clues they had managed to come across in an attempt to locate Masterson before he killed again, Skylar and Cody spoke to all the women they could find who had had any dealings with the man who had cost some of the women their babies.

They had been at this for over three weeks now and had made very little headway.

"How can one man be in so many places at once and still remain invisible?" Skylar marveled, disgusted. She felt exhausted and somewhat shell-shocked at the same time as she lay in Cody's arms one night.

Having been placed in the position of either renewing Carrie's lease or moving out, Cody had set out to find another place to stay for the duration until he was able to bring this killer to justice.

It was Skylar who had suggested that Cody remain at her place for the amount of time it would take to locate the killer. Her reasoning was how much longer could it take with so many more detectives on the job now than there had been initially? She had made a whole slew of copies of the photograph that she had managed to lift from the one rather blurry copy that had been cleared up of Masterson.

Consequently, Cody and she had been putting in one fifteen-hour-day after another, all to very little avail. A few times, they had almost managed to catch Masterson, but each and every time, the baby trafficker managed to get away, frustrating all their efforts.

"Obviously, Masterson has been at this for a while now. Probably longer than we initially thought and, rather than be satisfied with all the money he has managed to amass, he's getting greedier."

She ran her fingers slowly along Cody's chest, arousing both of them to a degree, despite the fact that they were both rather tired.

"Masterson—or whatever his real name is— upped the ante, trying to get even more money together before he calls it a day. Not that he ever would," she told Cody. "People like Masterson are insatiably greedy." Resting her head against his chest, she raised it to look at Cody. "But eventually, he *will* make a mistake and this reign of terror of his will finally be over. I just really hope that it will be sooner than later."

Cody's eyes met hers. "And just what will we do until then?" he asked her "innocently."

He was doing it again, she thought. He was looking into her soul with those big green eyes of his and unraveling her. "Oh, I think I might have an idea or three about that," she answered.

"Do I get a vote in this?" Cody asked.

"Be my guest. Vote away," she urged, slipping her arms around his neck as she pressed her lips against his.

Cody could feel his blood heating a little more with each and every kiss.

"That," he told her, doing his best to catch his breath. "I definitely vote for that," Cody said like a man who knew he had lost the confrontation and didn't really care that he had.

"Good call," Skylar agreed, her eyes smiling at him as she curled up even further into his arms.

SKYLAR WASN'T QUITE sure what woke her up. If it was something in her dream, she had no memory of it when she opened her eyes.

Moreover, when she opened her eyes, she saw that the spot beside her was empty.

Concerned, she got out of bed and threw on her bathrobe. Tying the sash at her waist, Skylar went looking for Cody.

She found him sitting in the kitchen at the table, nursing a cup of black coffee. It didn't appear to be his first one of the morning.

It was still dark outside, she noted.

Skylar quietly walked into the room rather than

call out his name because she didn't want to startle Cody.

"Everything all right?" she asked him quietly.

He turned to look at her. "I couldn't sleep," he told her by way of an explanation.

"So you decided to have some coffee in order to put you to sleep?" Skylar quipped with a soft laugh. "I'm not sure you're exactly clear on the concept of what coffee is supposed to do." Moving toward the coffee maker on the counter, she asked, "Did you leave any for me?"

Cody shook his head. "I didn't mean to wake you, Sky."

"You didn't." She filled a coffee cup with what was left in the pot, then poured in some cream, turning the liquid into a very light shade of chocolate. "My dream did. Although, now that I'm awake, I can't tell you what it was about," she confessed, returning to the table.

"You're lucky. I can tell you what all my dreams were about," he told her soberly.

She didn't have to guess. Of late, whenever he was having a bad dream, she was aware of it. She could hear him moaning in his sleep. She never bothered waking him, she just went on holding him until the moaning ceased.

Right now, she covered his hand with her own. "We'll find him," she promised Cody not for the first time—or the second or third. "I can feel it."

He looked at her, a trace of wonder in his expression. "How do you do it?" Cody asked.

"'It'?" Skylar questioned, not really sure what he was asking.

"How do you manage to stay so upbeat?"

"Positive thoughts," she attested. Finishing the little bit that was in her cup, she rose. "I'm going to make us some breakfast and then get ready. One of my brothers managed to find some witnesses for us to talk to," she told him.

This was all news to him, Cody thought. "When?"

"He texted me about it last night. We're going to be talking to them—separately—first thing this morning. There are two of them, both women. He might be able to find more."

"Why didn't you tell me when you got the call?" he asked.

"Simple. I wanted you to get some sleep." Opening the refrigerator, she began taking out the necessary ingredients for a typical breakfast. "If I had told you when he called me, you would have wanted to go and get started on the interviews right away. This way, you got a little bit of rest," she told him. "In my opinion," she said fondly, "you earned it."

"You're looking out for me," Cody commented.

"Someone has to," she told him, then ruffled his hair affectionately. "Go, get ready. Breakfast will be ready and on the table by the time you're finished dressing."

Cody pushed up from the table and kissed her before he went upstairs to take his shower. His manner silently told Skylar that he wasn't taking any of this for granted.

His hair was still wet when he returned to the kitchen and sat opposite her at the table.

"You got ready really quick," Skylar noted, impressed.

"I could smell the bacon frying all the way upstairs. Fastest way known to man to convince said man to come to the table," Cody told her, amused.

"And here I thought the draw was my sexy clothing," she said, pretending to pout.

Cody nodded, displaying a wicked grin. "There's that, too," he agreed. "Except in your case."

Skylar had just started to get up. That stopped her. "Oh?"

"Yes, in your case, no clothing does a far better job in luring me than sexy clothing does," he told her.

She pressed her lips together. "I'll have to remember that."

"Don't worry," Cody assured her, his voice filled with promise. "I will be sure to remind you."

That same warm shiver she was becoming increasingly familiar with slithered up and down her spine quickly. Skylar more than fondly welcomed it.

"Give me ten minutes in the shower," she requested.

"Ten minutes for a shower." Cody shook his head in absolute wonder. "You have to be the fastest woman I've ever known when it comes to getting ready," he told her. "Go, get ready—" he waved her off "—I'll take care of the dishes." He saw the laughter in her eyes. "What?"

"Oh, nothing. It's just that you're coming along very nicely," she said with a laugh.

Cody thought of the way they had made love last night. There was no real way to quite put it into words, but there was something about her that was making him feel as if he was finally turning into a real human being.

It felt good, he thought.

"Yeah," Cody said, smiling at her. "Right back at you."

KATIE LOPEZ WAS the second person they'd talked to this morning. She was a young woman of about nineteen, possibly twenty, although that was probably a stretch. She was looking at them with the saddest eyes that Cody could remember ever having seen.

After he and Skylar had introduced themselves to the young woman, she told them a story that was becoming all too familiar. Certainly one that they had heard over and over again.

Masterson had befriended her, she told the duo, making her feel as if she wasn't some impossibly ugly duckling, but a desirable young woman. She admitted to fairly glowing in the his presence, ready to do anything for the handsome, rugged man paying such undivided attention to her, making her feel as if she was the very center of his universe.

That was why, when he'd made love to her, Katie hadn't paid any attention to using any method of birth control and why, when she'd gotten pregnant, he had talked her into giving up the child she hadn't been prepared—or wanted—to raise.

Until she'd suddenly felt that she changed her mind.

But he had a way with words, a way with making her do what he wanted her to do, without using a single ounce of persuasion.

"Brent said it was perfectly normal to feel the way I did." The laugh that escaped Katie's lips had an exceedingly bitter sound to it.

She continued talking. "The baby was part of me and I was just feeling her absence. He said I'd 'get over it.' He told me I just needed a break from everything—including him. So he left," she concluded.

Katie searched their faces, trying to make them see what she was feeling. "That was almost a month ago," she sighed. "I'm not feeling any better. If anything," the young woman admitted, looking from Cody to Skylar sitting next to one another in her tiny rented, furnished apartment, "I'm feeling worse."

Katie looked down at her stomach, which she still cupped protectively even though there was nothing there any longer. "It's like a huge chunk of me is missing."

There were tears in the young woman's eyes, falling freely right now. "I know this is foolish and I should have gotten over this by now, but I just can't seem to get past it.

"He said he loved me," Katie cried. "He *acted* like he loved me," she insisted. "How could he just walk away from me like that?"

"Sometimes people are just this huge lump of self-absorbed scum," Cody told the young woman. "They're just focused exclusively on what they want and, when they get that—whatever 'that' is—they just move on."

Cody looked at the unhappy young woman. "I promise you that it has *nothing* to do with you," he assured her. "It's just their own lack of character."

"Take it from me, you're a lot better off without him," Skylar stated.

"But my baby," Katie lamented. "I should have never given up my baby."

"He puts them up for adoption, doesn't he?" Cody asked.

Katie nodded her head. "That's what he said, but I don't know who he gave her to. I have no documents. He told me he would take care of everything—but he didn't," Katie moaned.

Skylar frowned, trying to connect the dots. "You didn't marry him, did you?"

"No," Katie answered sadly, like not marrying him was her biggest regret.

"We're going to do our best to track your baby down for you," Cody promised.

Stricken, Katie nodded, beginning to weep uncontrollably.

It took them a while of talking and consoling before they were able to leave Katie on her own and walk out of the woman's tiny apartment. They sat on a bench to go through the details of the interview. For what seemed like hours, they analyzed Katie's words and demeanor.

"At least Masterson left her alive," Cody commented.

"Ordinarily, I'd agree with you, but she looks as if she's really having trouble coping with this whole situation. A lot of new mothers experience postpartum depression. Sometimes it's just a mild case. Other times, the experience can be overwhelming. This woman doesn't even have a baby to show for it, which makes it exceedingly difficult for the new mother. I think Katie falls into that category. Maybe we can have her doctor recommend someone she can talk to and focus on getting better."

Skylar heard her cell phone ring. She sighed. After this last interview, she didn't feel up to dealing with another bereft young mother. They seemed to be coming out of the woodwork.

But the voice on the other end belonged to Valri.

"Take a look at your monitor," the computer expert advised her. "Looks like Mr. Romance is at it again," she told Skylar.

"You're kidding," Skylar cried.

Out of the corner of her eye, Skylar saw Cody looking quizzically at her.

"Not something I'd kid about, Sky," Valri said grimly.

"Call whichever one of my brothers is on duty, give him the coordinates at the lake and tell him that he needs to grab one of my other brothers and get there as soon as humanly possible. It's an emergency," she insisted. "Cody and I are on our way," she promised. "And thank you!" she added enthusiastically.

"I live to serve," Valri told Skylar. "I'm hanging up now." But she hadn't needed to say that. Valri found herself talking to a dial tone. Skylar had disconnected her cell phone. She and Cody were already on their way to the lake.

Chapter Twenty-Five

Skylar fairly flew to the lake where the collection of cameras had been suspended, capturing different views of the area. She hadn't turned on her siren because she hadn't wanted to alert Masterson that they were on their way and scare the man away.

Because this had become a complete group effort, Skylar and Cody had several detectives staked out along the perimeter to prevent anything from going wrong.

Their main intent was to catch Masterson in the act: stealing a baby from yet another gullible young woman who had surrendered her free will to Masterson. The police detectives positioned through the area had absolutely no intention of allowing the situation to escalate and certainly no intention of letting it become dangerous.

Leaving her vehicle parked at a distance from the lake, Skylar and Cody made their way quickly toward the sound of a sobbing young woman.

"This does not sound good," Skylar whispered to Cody.

"I came here with you because I thought you wanted to talk," the crying young woman—Katie Lopez—told Masterson. Katie sounded absolutely pathetic as she sobbed. "I was hoping I could change your mind about keeping my baby. I know I said I couldn't take care of her and wanted to give her up, but I've changed my mind," Katie insisted. "Once I saw her, she just burrowed her way right into my heart. I don't want you giving her to those people who said they could take care of her." Katie wiped the tears from her eyes.

The exchange was definitely getting to Cody. The deputy was reliving what his sister had to have gone through before she'd been murdered. Skylar totally sympathized, but she really hoped that Cody could hold on to his temper before it got the better of him.

"Oh, Katie, that's what you say now," Masterson was saying. "But if you actually cared about that tiny baby, you'd see that this is the best thing you could do for her. She deserves parents who can give her the kind of life she needs, not a parent who selfishly makes decisions based on what *she* wants."

Masterson's tone had turned ugly. Skylar fought the urge to punch the man out. He might be good-looking and silver-tongued, but he had a black, empty soul.

The girl's heartbroken sobbing mingled with the sound of the baby that she was holding in her arms.

Infuriated, Skylar looked at Cody. She could guess what he had to be going through. "Enough is enough," she whispered to the deputy. "Let's go." Beckoning him forward, she walked out into the area that surrounded the lake. The lake that had already seen at least three young women meet their demise there.

Surprised at hearing the unfamiliar voices, Masterson looked at the approaching couple. "Can I help you?" he asked with just a trace of annoyance evident in his voice as he directed his question toward Skylar. It was obvious that Masterson felt he had always had better luck with women than with men. "This *is* a private conversation," he informed Skylar.

Skylar had no desire to play this game with Masterson. "No, it's not. This young woman doesn't want to give up her baby—and no matter what you're thinking, you have no right to take this baby from her."

"You're wrong." Masterson all but spat the words, losing his patience. "I'm the baby's father."

"Being the baby's father doesn't automatically give you the right to sell that baby—or any child— to the highest bidder," Cody snapped angrily.

Feeling cornered, Masterson's face darkened. "You don't know what you're talking about."

"Oh, but I do," Cody informed the man coldly. "And a veritable *ton* of DNA found in at least three crime scenes can be used against you. I suggest that you spare yourself—and this young woman—a lot of agony, and just confess what you've done."

"I have no idea what you're talking about," Masterson snapped.

"Oh, but you do. You know exactly what we're talking about. Are you going to end this saga by coming off like a liar and a coward in this girl's eyes?" Cody asked.

Horrified, Katie instantly came to Masterson's defense. "You can't talk to him like that!" she cried.

Disgusted by the lack of backbone she had just witnessed, Skylar shook her head. "Oh, there are none so blind as those who refuse to see," she murmured under her breath.

"Open your eyes, Katie. Your so-called lover currently makes a living by impregnating young women who fall all over themselves to get his attention, then he sells those babies to couples who are desperate to adopt and who, for one reason or another, aren't able to meet the agencies' requirements."

The look on Masterson's face indicated that he felt they were much too close to the truth for his liking. Desperate, Masterson turned on the charm that had stood him in such good stead all this time.

"Look, can't we come to some sort of an agreement?" Masterson asked. Putting his hand into his pocket, he pulled out a wad of bills and waved it in front of Cody.

"Put that away before I stuff it down your throat," Cody growled angrily.

"A simple no would have done," Masterson informed him haughtily.

"You don't strike me as someone who would take no for an answer," Cody told the man.

"You're right," Masterson agreed. "I'm going to need to work on that."

"Prison would be a great place to work on that," Cody pointed out. His eyes narrowed as he ordered, "Turn around." With that, the deputy produced a pair of handcuffs and snapped them on the indignant Masterson's wrists.

Suddenly infuriated, Masterson tried—unsuccessfully—to pull away. "Is this really necessary?"

"I'm sure all the young women you killed asked that very same question," Cody told him, disgust vibrating in his voice.

"Look, maybe you and I can come to some sort of an understanding," Masterson suggested again, giving bribery one last attempt.

"Not in this lifetime," Cody informed him coldly. By that time, several detectives had surrounded them, joining their circle, which continued to grow.

Then, before either he or Skylar, or any of the others realized what was happening, Cody heard a rustling noise and felt himself being shoved aside.

It was then that he saw the raised arm. Before he or Skylar could stop it, a syringe was being plunged into the side of Masterson's neck. Caught by surprise, Masterson screamed.

"Not another move," Skylar warned. Closest to the perpetrator, Skylar grabbed the woman's wrist, knocking the now empty syringe out of her hand and sending it flying to the ground.

"He doesn't deserve to live!" the young woman who had just materialized on the scene cried. "He tried to do the same thing to me. He tried to use that kind of syringe on me because I wouldn't give up my baby. I saw him fill it with fentanyl, but I managed to knock it away and escape."

Cody knelt beside the body, but he couldn't rouse Masterson, or find the man's pulse. The fentanyl had done its job.

"He's dead," Cody finally pronounced.

The woman looked down at the dead man's body. She appeared beyond pleased. "I'm glad he's dead. He won't be able to get another young woman to do those terrible things he ordered, or to give up her baby," the young woman, Jean, declared, sobbing.

"She has a point," Cody said as Skylar's brothers, their guns drawn, gathered around the body on the ground. They were leaving nothing to chance.

"While I can't come right out and condone what this woman just did, I can totally understand why she did it. Carrie's avenged," he said, letting out a long, relieved breath. "And there's no telling how many people the woman's impetuous act just saved from having their life completely ruined."

Skylar sighed and then nodded. "I'm just glad that this whole thing is finally behind us," she commented.

Cody was more concerned with something else. "What are they going to do to her?" he asked, nodding at Jean.

"Most likely, considering what she has gone through," Skylar speculated, "she'll be placed under psychiatric care until she's deemed well enough to be able to stand trial."

Cody rolled that over in his head. "She's going to need decent representation. Maybe I can get up a collection for her." Cody debated. He sounded more than willing to do just that.

Watching Masterson's body being loaded into an ambulance, Skylar put her hand on Cody's arm. "No need to take up a collection," she told him. "I have a cousin who can defend her."

Cody laughed dryly. "Why doesn't that surprise me? You Cavanaughs seem to have people around to use for a variety of different occasions."

Skylar smiled at him. "We like being prepared for all sorts of things," she told Cody.

The deputy looked rather impressed by her statement. "Good philosophy to have," Cody said.

"Hey," Skylar's brother Finley called out, joining the duo and slinging one arm around each of their shoulders, just as another one of Skylar's brothers, Murdoch, came up behind them. "I just heard the good news. That you two managed to solve this case. Congratulations!" he declared. "You've just given Uncle Andrew his next excuse to host another family gathering. Nothing makes him happier than celebrating a killer being stopped in his tracks." Murdoch looked closely at Cody. "Speaking of which, you don't look very happy about this. Something wrong?" Murdoch asked.

"Well, I'm glad the guy's killing spree is over, but I would have rather had him stand trial and be sent to prison to serve time for doing away with so many young women—not to mention stealing and selling those babies he's responsible for creating."

"None of that would have come to light if it hadn't been for your sister's death," Skylar pointed out.

Cody frowned and shook his head, apparently not taking any of that to heart.

Skylar wasn't about to let him dwell on the down side.

"Just look at the positive side," Skylar stressed. "There might be a lot more dead women around in the future if it hadn't been for your sister bringing all this to light. You have to be able to find that to be comforting—at least to some degree."

"Oh, I do. I do," Cody told her, although there was no conviction in his voice.

Skylar's eyes swept over him as they walked back to her Crown Victoria. "You'll forgive me but, to me, you don't exactly look like a man who's been comforted," she told Cody.

"Well, that's because I just realized that this chapter is finally over. Not only that, but there's nothing really left for me back in Kiowa." Getting in the vehicle, he settled into the passenger seat. He had been dreading thinking about this point. "My parents are gone, my sister's gone—I'm having her cremated so I can have her ashes scattered here. And after working in Aurora, that little town in New Mexico seems much too tame to me."

Cody considered the situation he was faced with. It wasn't his habit to ask questions like this, but he felt as if he didn't have a choice. Not if he wanted to be around Skylar. He was at the point where he wanted to see where this relationship between them could go.

"Are there any job openings in Aurora?" he asked, doing his best to sound nonchalant.

Skylar felt her heart leap up and practically lodge in her chest.

Her eyes swept over his face. "There are *always* job openings in Aurora—if you're talking about law enforcement."

"I am," Cody confirmed, humor playing along the corners of his mouth.

She was hoping that was what he had meant. "I can fast-track your application to the police department if you like. I might not have mentioned it," she teased him, "but I know several people in a position of authority that you might like meeting and who might be able to hook you up to the department of your choice."

A grin played on his lips. "I vaguely remember you mentioning something to that effect," he told her. "I'd appreciate any recommendation you might be able to give me."

Her eyes gleamed. "Consider yourself recommended," she told him. "In addition, my uncle Brian, the Chief of Ds, has taken a special interest in you ever since you turned up on his radar."

"How far does his radar extend?" Cody asked.

She read between the lines. "Far," she assured him. "And in case you're wondering—the man does not see through walls."

"I wasn't worried about that," Cody told her.

Just then, Fin hurried over to Skylar's car and knocked on the door before she could head for the main road. She stopped driving and looked at her brother quizzically. "Anything wrong?" Skylar asked.

"On the contrary. Uncle Shane just called this in," Fin said, mentioning the head of the CSI department, "and word just reached Uncle Andrew." He looked beyond Skylar at Cody. "He'd like you to be the guest of honor at the family gathering he's planning on holding this weekend. You are going to be staying until then, aren't you?" Fin asked.

Cody exchanged glances with Skylar. "I plan to be staying a lot longer than that."

The latter nodded his approval. "Good. To put it in my uncle's words, 'Aurora could use a good man like you,'" Finley said. "And so could my sister," he added with a wide grin.

"I'll have to ask her myself," Cody said just as Skylar pulled away from the site.

Skylar was quiet for as long as she could be, then finally had to ask. "Are you? Going to ask me?" she completed.

"If *you* have to ask me that," Cody told her, "then you're not nearly as good a detective as I thought you were."

Her eyes caught his. "Oh, I am," she told him with conviction. "I am. Tell you what. Why don't we go to my place and talk about this?" she told him.

"Perfect ending to a perfect day," Cody declared.

Her eyes teased him. "Not yet," she said, referring to the idea about it being the perfect ending to a perfect day. "But it will be," she promised.

Anticipating what was to come, Cody's face lit up. "Drive faster, Detective. Drive faster," Cody urged.

Skylar spared him an amused glance. "Remember, anything good is worth waiting for."

"Amen to that, Sky. Amen to that."

She merely smiled in agreement—and pressed down on the gas, anticipating the night that lay ahead of them.

* * * * *

COMING SOON!

We really hope you enjoyed reading this book.
If you're looking for more romance, be sure to
head to the shops when new books are
available on

Thursday 13th October

To see which titles are coming soon, please visit

millsandboon.co.uk/nextmonth

LET'S TALK
Romance

For exclusive extracts, competitions
and special offers, find us online:

f facebook.com/millsandboon

🐦 @MillsandBoon

📷 @MillsandBoonUK

Get in touch on 01413 063232

For all the latest titles coming soon, visit
millsandboon.co.uk/nextmonth

JOIN US ON SOCIAL MEDIA!

Stay up to date with our latest releases, author news and gossip, special offers and discounts, and all the behind-the-scenes action from Mills & Boon...

 @millsandboon

 @millsandboonuk

 facebook.com/millsandboon

 @millsandboonuk

It might just be true love...

GET YOUR ROMANCE FIX!

Get the latest romance news, exclusive author interviews, story extracts and much more!

MILLS & BOON
MODERN
Power and Passion

Prepare to be swept off your feet by sophisticated, sexy and seductive heroes, in some of the world's most glamourous and romantic locations, where power and passion collide.